Knot Their Burden

Melissa Huxley

Copyright © 2023 by Melissa Huxley

All rights reserved.

No part of this publication may be reproduced, distributed, or transmitted in any form or by any means, including photocopying, recording, or other electronic or mechanical methods, without the prior written permission of the publisher, except as permitted by U.S. copyright law. For permission requests, contact melissahuxleyinfo@gmail.com.

The story, all names, characters, and incidents portrayed in this production are fictitious. No identification with actual persons (living or deceased), places, buildings, and products is intended or should be inferred.

Book Cover by Melissa Huxley

Editing by Erin Newman

Hello there!

Thank you for reading *Knot their Burden*. This book is written in British English which is a weird language at times - but if you feel like you've found an error please drop me a message at melissahuxleyinfo@gmail.com I would greatly appreciate it!

For a full list of trigger and content warnings check my website melissahuxley.com

CHAPTER ONE
Sage

This paperwork is never ending, and it's only going to get worse. I closed another file, leaning over to put it away in the industrial grey filing cabinet. Turning back to my desk, I stretched my neck, groaning when it gave a satisfying pop. In the three years since I'd started working at Norden, never once had my workload died down. I was far too familiar with long days, harsh deadlines and extended periods of time at a desk. It didn't bother me, in fact I loved it...most of the time.

Norden was a huge conglomerate with its fingers in many pies. Working deep in the accounting division, I spent my days filling out spreadsheets and writing up financial reports. Numbers made sense to me, there was always a definitive answer, and I loved rooting said answer out. I kept my head down after joining the company fresh from graduating, shooting up the ranks to project manager after just a year and being given my own office. Granted, it was a tiny room in the corner of an overcrowded floor, but still, it was my own.

A knock on my door frame diverted my attention from the new spreadsheet I had just opened.

"I've got another file for you, Sage." Alex, a fellow accountant, stood in my doorway, brandishing a folder. I groaned at the sight of the manila menace.

"Another one? I haven't had a moment to rest today," I grumbled.

"I just had three more sent to my desk, but they're tiny jobs so they won't take you long, thank God. You made yourself far too useful, so all the tough jobs get sent your way now," he laughed. Alex was a sweet guy, a beta like me, with blonde hair he kept gelled back, so he almost looked like a Ken Doll with a boyish smile. He didn't irritate me like some of my other colleagues did, but I wasn't overly fond of him, either.

"Let me guess, Cora assigned said folder to me?" I raised my eyebrows in question.

"Well, I doubt she assigned it, but she did find joy in telling me this folder was for you."

Cora—a pretty platinum blonde with a chip on her shoulder—had been a small thorn in my side for a while. While I technically outranked her, the assistant loved finding ways to antagonise me. It was common knowledge that she had sucked off a manager several months back for a few more 'responsibilities' to lord over everyone else. Cora was the kind of woman who would take any opportunity to assert her dominance or let others know she was the top dog. Frankly, it was exhausting, and I wanted nothing to do with it.

"She really doesn't like me, does she?"

"You're just too pretty." Alex grinned, his eyes crinkling as I rolled mine.

It wasn't my mediocre appearance angering Cora, it was more the fact that she was pissed at the world she wasn't born an omega. She thought the life of a lowly beta wasn't good enough for her and she wanted to be spoiled, given riches and pretty clothes, like omegas. To compensate she tried to make herself overly important and attractive, like if an alpha had a tumble with her then she was instantly so much better than the rest of us, but I didn't want to say that out loud and risk her wrath, as she could be petty and vindictive.

"I'm sure that's it." I laughed sarcastically, reaching my hand out for the file. "Give me that, surely you have your own job to get back to?" I wasn't comfortable with the compliments, and Alex could be a little over friendly. He was like a puppy who needed a good scolding to stop humping your leg, harmless, but you didn't want to encourage the behaviour either, so I wasn't overly engaging with him.

Alex passed me the folder, huffing. His scent wafted into my office with the movement. Toner, like the kind you would use in a printer. It wasn't repulsive, but it wasn't pleasant either.

"Thanks for reminding me. I was hoping to avoid work. That's what normal people do," he chuckled, throwing his head back while he lingered in my doorway.

"Go!" I exclaimed in an exasperated tone, keeping a small smile on my face so I didn't come across as bitchy. He threw his hands up, walking away with a wave.

Turning back to my desk I opened a new spreadsheet on my laptop and looked in the file Alex had handed me. Receipts. At least a hundred of them, all needing logging and categorising. Groaning at the sight, I immediately dove in as there was no point delaying the task. Work had been piling up lately, and even with my love of numbers it was starting to cause a strain. It didn't help that I now appeared to be the go-to for the more time consuming jobs because I hardly ever complained—but that meant others on my level often passed work along to me. The crick in my neck was screaming and I wanted nothing more than to get through this day and relax in the bath with a glass of wine.

With a sigh I closed my laptop, I needed something sugary to make the gargantuan pile of work a little easier to manage. The sad homemade veggie sandwich in my bag wasn't going to cut it. Throwing my honey blonde waves into a low bun to keep it out of the way, I pushed myself away from the desk and got up with a stretch. I grabbed my wallet and left, ensuring to lock the office behind me: I had too many confidential files in there to leave it open for anyone.

I made my way down the corridor, nodding at folks as they passed me on the way to the elevator. The Norden offices were large, taking up several floors of a skyscraper in the middle of the city. Thankfully, I was the only one on the elevator, so I didn't have to make small talk during the ride to the cafeteria. The moment the doors pinged, and I stepped off the elevator, a scent washed over me, making me stiffen as I was momentarily paralyzed.

Alpha. A dark, smoky cherry aroma assaulted my senses, making my insides hum. I ignored it, forcing my muscles to move, making a beeline for the food.

I did my best to avoid alphas. They weren't bad per say, they were just very... alpha. I had seen and even met a few while working at Norden. They were usually upper management members who were as big as brick shit houses and could make anyone crap their pants with a single long look. They were also apparently quite growly. I'd never seen that myself, and I wasn't unhappy with that. Alphas usually panted over omegas, who were genetically built to be their perfect partners, not betas such as myself and my entire family, save for an uncle I'd never met. I didn't mind that—being an omega was far from my dream—unlike many women who would kill to be an omega, despite the fact that it was rarely safe for them. Men could be omegas, but that was rarer than gold dust. Omegas were spoiled; riches, bags, property, all the material things a woman could want. But omegas had hardly any rights and were usually maternal figures—or at least that was my understanding. Not much was really known about omegas, as they weren't often seen in public, merely property of the pack that claimed them.

Some alphas would get testy if you even looked at them the wrong way, and the last thing I wanted to do was upset an alpha. The consequences would not be good. The smell was overpowering, and as badly as I wanted to escape it and all the potential stress an alpha could cause, part of me wanted to roll around in it. Alphas usually smelt strong, but I had never had the urge to roll around in their smell before.

Grabbing my usual chocolate chip cookie and a soda, I did my best to ignore the thick masculine scent and smiled at the elderly lady behind the checkout as I paid. Goods in hand, I was eager to get back to my little office. Turning to leave, I crashed into someone who felt uncannily like a brick wall. My body pressed up against theirs momentarily and I stumbled back, startled.

"Oh my word, I-I'm sorry," I stammered, righting myself, when the strong smoky, dark cherry smell that had been coating the room hit my nose full force. *Alpha.* Looking up in panic, I had to crane my neck to meet his gaze. Strong jawline, brunette hair neatly styled back, dark eyes, and a muscular chest. The alpha's hands were lightly holding my upper arms, keeping me balanced after crashing into him. My skin burned where he touched, and I internally cursed myself for wearing a short sleeve blouse to work that day. With wide eyes, he looked down at me, slightly startled and confused.

Before I could formulate my next sentence, a deep pulse rippled through my midsection. Now was not the time to be getting cramps. Heart rate pounding, I apologised again, ducking my head and avoiding eye contact. I recognised him—I had seen him before when taking reports to the top floor to leave with Mr Dennings' assistant.

Mr Beckett was an alpha, and close friend to our alpha COO, Max Dennings. An alpha could take offence. Get angry. Demand I be fired. It had happened before. Joe from my division had stood on an alpha's foot once and was immediately dismissed.

"M-Mr Beckett, I am so sorry! I didn't mean to!" I stuttered yet another apology, looking away from his piercing eyes. My face burned with embarrassment as I took a step back, his hands dropping from my arms, making me shiver as they brushed along my skin for a moment. Turning around, I left with another quick apology, making my way hastily back to the elevator, not daring to look back at the powerful alpha I had just run headlong into.

The moment the elevator doors closed behind me, I slumped against the wall and took a deep breath of air untainted by alpha as my heart raced and adrenaline coursed through my veins. Just a whiff of an alpha and I was a mess. What on earth was that? I was acting like a scent drunk bimbo. Looking down, I groaned when I saw I had accidentally clutched so tightly onto my cookie it had crumbled in its clear plastic wrapper.

Just wonderful.

CHAPTER TWO
Sage

There seemed to be no ill consequences from my little stumble into the alpha, and I thanked my lucky stars for that. I spent the rest of the day hiding out in my office, afraid to poke my head out in case Mr Beckett was there, which was a ridiculous notion because he would be relaxing in the fancy offices on the top floor with his friend. No one bothered me, my office was out of the way and people tended to avoid the accounting department. Steadily, as I finished my work for the day, filling out numerous reports; organising and colour-coding the receipts, the cramps got worse, which was baffling because I wasn't due for my period anytime soon.

Finally, after several hours it was time to pack up and go home. Cramps and hunger gnawed at me as I'd had only eaten a cookie all day, having decided against leaving the office and potentially embarrassing myself again. When it finally hit five, hurriedly shoving everything into my bag, I left the office, waving at the security team at the front door.

I was lucky there was a spare seat on the train, so I sat, thankful because my feet ached. Closing my eyes I tipped my head back, breathing a deep sigh of relief. A few passersby gave me odd looks, eyebrows raised, I frowned, then realised that I probably still smelt like alpha. I cringed. I had pretty much crashed into Mr Beckett and plastered the front of my body to his, so that rich, smoky-sweet scent clung to my clothing—why hadn't I noticed that in my office? Do they think I'm an alpha whore? The not so polite term was given to a beta woman who slept with alphas and were often looked down on by other betas. It wasn't uncommon for a beta and an alpha to have an entanglement, but beta men often looked down on women who did so, usually out of jealousy. They didn't have the strength or raw attraction most alphas possessed, and they despised that.

I did my best to make myself small, curling in on myself and avoiding eye contact with anyone else. Praying for the journey to pass quickly, I cursed the fact that I had forgotten to put any perfume in my handbag that morning, otherwise I would have spritzed myself.

The moment I got back to my little apartment I hung my bag up and threw my keys onto the coffee table. Padding over to the bathroom and turning on the faucets, I ran a steaming hot bath with plenty of rose salts and bubbles. Using my cell, I ordered some Chinese takeout to arrive right about when I would finish. Throwing my phone onto the small table I stepped into the tub, hissing at the initial shock of the heat. The warmth helped ease the tension in my muscles, and as they slowly relaxed, I scrubbed my skin with my favourite honey and salt body scrub to remove any trace of his smell off me. Mr Beckett probably wouldn't be at Norden tomorrow, so if I hadn't been reprimanded already, I likely wouldn't be. Once I could no longer smell him on myself, I started to relax, but a deep-down part of me also missed it. There had been something oddly comforting about the smoky sweetness of him.

After my soak I threw on my favourite soft cotton pyjamas, a deep green tank top and short set. Despite the bath my stomach still cramped every now and again, the heat of the water having done nothing to ease them. Rummaging in my cupboard I found some ibuprofen, downing them with a glass of water to ease the pain. The doorbell alerted me to the arrival of my food, and I tipped the driver, wandering to the kitchen to pile a bowl high with noodles. Popping open a bottle of wine, I poured a heavy glass, before crawling into bed to eat. Flicking on the TV, I nestled down into the covers with my food. I had always loved bedding, and my bed was piled high with continental pillows, throws, and comforters. It was my happy place. I hardly ever ate on the couch, because I much preferred the soft comfort of the down duvets and pillows. I had a TV in the room, so what else could I possibly need?

Eventually, wrapped up in my lavender scented sheets I drifted into a fitful sleep, tossing and turning, my dreams plagued with thoughts of walking through a smoky, cherry orchard.

The following morning, my cramps were persistent and painful, despite the two ibuprofen I had taken, and I resorted to sneakily taking a hot water bottle with me to work to help. I had considered calling out sick, but management was being brutal with the upcoming tax audit, and I couldn't really afford to take any time off. Everything felt extra irritating, my usual sleek bun pulled on my scalp so much I took it out, raking my hands through my limper than normal hair and opting to braid it to the side. There were bags under my eyes when I looked in the mirror. My heels pinched, though they had felt fine yesterday, but I wouldn't be able to take them off until I was safe in my office and away from everyone else. I could have worn different shoes, but I was so used to heels that anything else felt wrong to wear to work. With a sigh, I resigned myself to an uncomfortable day and grabbed my laptop and hot water bottle, making my way to work.

After spending the train ride cursing my shoes and struggling to sit in a position that didn't irritate me, I made my way through the glass doors to Norden. The security guard waved me through with a smile, not even bothering to check my credentials anymore as they knew me so well. Xander, an older beta who had been working there several years, inhaled deeply as I passed, giving me a funny look.

"New perfume, Miss Miller? You smell really pretty today," he commented, eyes wide.

I stuttered in surprise. "N-nope, nothing new today, thank you, though!" I moved quickly through the turnstile into the main portion of the building, giving Xander a small smile and wondering why today, of all days, he decided to comment on my scent. I practically charged to my office, desperate to sit down and get comfy. The comment about my scent weirded me out. What on earth was that about? No one ever commented on how I smelt before. It was actually rather rude to comment on anyone's scent, as it could easily be seen as a come on. Males often bragged about their scents, beta or otherwise, but women were usually more reserved.

As soon as I was in my office I threw my keys in the general direction of my desk and discarded my shoes and blazer, leaving me in only my silk camisole and pencil skirt. I looked professional enough, though the exposed arms were a bit much. Only today I just couldn't cope with the feel of the material on my skin, professionalism be damned.

Holding the hot water bottle over my midsection, I sank into my desk chair. It was one of those comfy chairs that more resembled an armchair that I had bought myself to make my office more comfortable. I dug out a few folders to start working on. About a dozen financial reports needed finishing before the end of the week, which was only three days away, and I had several stacks of receipts to approve, along with a few detailed deep dives into specific account spreadsheets. I needed to be focused, head in the game, not daydreaming of sweet bonfires on a dark night or curled up in pain with cramps from hell. If one of the male employees saw me doubled over with cramps they would only judge me, and I had worked too hard to be judged on the fact I was a woman and not on the merit of my work.

Grabbing the first file I could reach, I opened the manila folder, looking for the receipts I needed to log. I easily lost myself in the math, becoming distracted from the irritation of my current situation, focusing on my calculations.

Hours slipped away while I worked, filing report after report.

Lifting my hand to rub my aching temples, I quickly pulled my hand away when my fingertips met my overheated, clammy skin. *Am I coming down with the flu? It feels like I'm getting a nasty fever.*

Eventually the ache was too severe, and work wasn't enough to distract me. When I sat up, dizziness washed over me. Admitting defeat, I grabbed my phone and tapped a few buttons.

"Hey, Alex?" I croaked, my voice rough. "I'm going to send

you a few urgent files. I'll be taking a half day and going home. I must have caught the bug that's going around."

I sent the voice message, and with what little strength I had gathered my things. Dreading putting my four-inch heels back on, I simply sat for a moment with my eyes closed.

"Hey, Sage, I got your message—" Alex opened the door to my office, I peeked open one eye, seeing him still in the doorway.

I just wanted him to go away so I could have some peace and a good nap.

"Yeah, I'm sorry to do this to you. I think I need to get home," I mumbled, rubbing my temples in circular motions, closing my eyes. When he didn't reply, I sat up more and focused on him, groaning at the stiffness in my neck. Alex was staring at me in shock, his hand gripping the door frame so tightly his knuckles were white. "Alex?"

"Omega." His voice was strangled, and he was staring at me without blinking. I sat up straight, eyeing him warily. The rapid change in his demeanour woke me up, my arms breaking out in goosebumps. That word. Omega.

"Are you okay, Alex?"

He inhaled deeply, closing his eyes, seemingly savouring the smell before opening his eyes again, his pupils dilated. The hair on the back of my neck stood up, my whole body tensing with the understanding that something wasn't right.

Alex snapped out of his daze, shook his head, and barged into the room, grabbing me roughly by the arms, and pulling me out of my chair. I yelped in pain, trying to struggle out of his grip, but his hands were vise-like on me. It was so unlike Alex that I couldn't find the words, instead letting out a small squeak of shock. He was close enough that his strong inky scent assaulted my nose. Yesterday it was tolerable, but today it was repulsive.

He leaned in to deeply smell my neck, pulling me into a crushing hug I snapped out of my shock, shoving him with all my minimal strength. It took him by surprise, and he stumbled back a few steps, his hands leaving scratches where I pulled myself out of his grip. Thankfully he was just a regular beta, were he an alpha I wouldn't have been able to move him an inch.

"What the hell are you doing?" I roughly yelled as I stumbled back, tripping over my own feet.

"Omega," he repeated. "Come with me, Sage, please." He took another step toward me and I shrunk back.

This had to be a sick joke.

"No!"

Alex looked surprised at my answer, shaking his head in confusion. "I-uh. Sage, you smell..."

At that moment Cora chose to appear in my doorway. Her platinum hair in a perfect sleek ponytail and makeup that wouldn't be amiss at a Hollywood party adorning her face. She was holding several folders she'd likely planned to dump on me, and she paused to take in the scene before whipping her head around, her ponytail whizzing around with her. The moment she took a deep breath her nose, her eyes narrowed as she looked me over in my bedraggled state. Her face twisted in anger.

"You're one of them!" she accused me with a glare. "I'm getting the alphas! You're going to be in trouble for hiding your status!" She pulled Alex backwards to the door, seemingly unafraid of him as he stared dopey eyed at me.

"Get out!" I yelled, my voice cracking from the stress, not caring if anyone else on the floor heard me. I was tired, in pain and now felt the dirty scent of Alex clinging to my skin. Alex and Cora retreated just to slam the door closed, and I heard the click of the lock. Staggering forward, I tried to pull open the door, shocked to find it didn't budge. They locked me in? In my own office? I hit the door with my fist and shouted at them to open it, but there was no answer.

I proceeded to hit the door several more times until the wave of cramps became too painful, and I hunched over. Placing my back against the door I sank to the floor, trembling. What on earth was happening? What was Cora accusing me of, and why was Alex acting so out of sorts? This whole day needed to end, and tomorrow would hopefully be better. Resting my head on my knees and wrapping my arms around myself, I sobbed lightly, confused at the turn my day had taken.

CHAPTER THREE
Alaric

Max and I had spent all morning working on some new security protocols. He'd asked me for help a few days prior, and I could never say no to Max. He'd been good to my pack and if I could return the favour, even in a small capacity, I felt obligated to. I hadn't been too excited at the idea of another day at the Norden office, but I wanted to catch another glimpse of that little beta who had crashed into me the day before. The urge was irritating. I shouldn't be pining over a beta; it was bad form for an alpha. I had kept my eyes peeled for her, doing my best to subtly glance over any employees I passed, but none of them smelt anything like her. I remembered the scent well because it had clung to me the previous evening. I hated that I kept catching myself looking for her, but the previous night I fell asleep with that mental image of her on her knees running through my mind on repeat.

When I finally made it home Bellamy had given me a once over and grinned at the scent, assuming I had decided to give into my baser instincts and have a tussle with a beta. I had shoved my packmate away with a growl and told him the truth, acting like it was no big deal, but for some reason I still waited as long as possible to wash her scent from my body.

Thankfully, my morning had passed quickly, Max and I were just finishing lunch and were sitting down to hammer out the finer details of the next few weeks. We had ordered our food from a local deli—delicious subs with artisanal coffee—which was better than anything we could have gotten in the cafeteria at Norden.

"The coffee okay for you, Ric?" Max asked as he took a sip of his own, grimacing. "It all tastes like rocket fuel to me."

"That's because you have the pallet of a toddler." I smiled fondly at him. "I like it. Bellamy would be able to tell you if it was actually good coffee. As long as it's dark and bitter I'm happy."

"You? Happy? That'll be the day!" Max laughed around a mouthful of his bacon and brie sub. "How's Bellamy doing?" he asked, his face turning serious.

I glared at Max, but there was no real fire behind it. "Bellamy's good, still mother hen-ing us at every opportunity, much to our annoyance, but he's probably going to open a new coffee shop soon so that'll distract him." I mixed a single brown sugar into my coffee with a wooden stirrer.

"He needs an omega to look after so he stops mothering the rest of you," Max proclaimed. "But considering how hard they are to come by, a puppy may be a better bet."

I snorted. "I'll never be approved for an omega—you know that. Not with my family history. You're pretty much the poster boy for a good little alpha, and you only got approval to court omegas two years ago. Where is your omega?"

"Your time will come." Max shrugged. "As will ours.

Finding a partner isn't something you can really rush." He put his sandwich down, wiping his hands on a napkin. "So, what I'm saying is…I think a golden retriever, or a lab would be your best bet for Bellamy to baby. He can even dress it up and feed it a special diet seeing as he likes to cook so much."

I laughed. Bellamy was the caring type, and I could see him getting a hat or jacket for a pet dog. "Don't say this in front of him, you'll give him ideas."

"Or you could always try dating a beta, if you really think you'll never be allowed an omega."

"I couldn't go for that," I declared. "Nor would Everett. He has this picture perfect idea of what a pack should be because he comes from a near perfect family himself. If we bring a female beta into the pack it'll be a stark reminder that we'll never have kids."

"How dare Everett have an idea of how he wants his life to look like!" Max chuckled, leaning back in his chair with a groan. "I am so full. I guess now we've eaten, we should get back to work. Have you got that thumb drive?"

"I have, in fact—"

A loud bang, and several raised voices drew our attention to the closed office door.

"Is something happening?" I asked with a scowl. We had a lot to do, and I didn't want any petty distractions.

"Maybe, it could just be someone being a little loud. I'll check."

Max had just thrown his napkin down when a blonde beta woman dressed immaculately strode in without bothering to knock. She smelled slightly metallic and was out of breath as she stood in the doorway. She looked between Max and I, as I glared, unhappy at the intrusion and she just looked at us with a smug grin. "Who are you?" Max growled.

The beta stood up straighter, the scent of her fear permeating the room.

"Apologies, Mr Dennings. I'm an assistant on floor eight. We have a problem. It appears one of the accountants, Sage Miller, has been lying about her classification. She's an omega, not the beta she claimed to be when she started working here. She's tricked everyone, and now it's causing a problem with other employees who can smell her damn perfume. It's stinking up the whole office."

Max was already out of his chair, anger at the beta's intrusion forgotten at the mere mention of an omega. "Are you sure? Where is she now?" he asked, his voice was laced with concern and confusion. Omegas were rare. What were the chances there was an unchaperoned one here at Norden?

"She's in her office. She was claiming she felt unwell, she was about to go home, but I couldn't let her just walk through the office disturbing everyone with her stink." The beta looked at the ground, not daring to make eye contact with us. We exchanged glances, and without another word, headed towards the door, leaving the blonde to trail behind us.

"How the hell would an omega end up an employee here?" I asked as we practically jogged down the corridor, ignoring the curious looks from those we passed.

"They wouldn't," Max told me simply. "You know what chaos an unclaimed omega can cause. We could never allow one to work here. She would cause riots anytime an alpha was near her."

Just a whiff of an unclaimed omega could send an alpha into a frenzy. Omegas were loved in our society, but they were often raised out of sight or in Havens, from the time they presented at puberty until they attached themselves to a pack for their own safety.

It wasn't hard to spot where the Norden omega was. A crowd had congregated on the eighth-floor, all looking and pointing toward a closed office door, talking amongst themselves. All the scents mingled together making the air thick and unpleasant.

"Everyone! Out!" Max thundered, his voice laced with an alpha command, leaving no room for disagreement, I was one of the few unaffected as an alpha myself. Everyone scattered, returning to their offices other than a select few.

Striding towards the door, we were hit with the smell: honey—sweet and potent. It enlivened every nerve ending in my body, and my cock stiffened. Every animal instinct of mine was demanding I find the source and claim it. The honey beta.

Max was clearly struggling with the scent as well, his posture was stiff and rigid. He was a highly controlled alpha under most circumstances but even the strongest of us would struggle when faced with the scent of an omega perfuming like crazy unless they were mated themselves, which neither of us were, and this scent seemed particularly strong so the female in question clearly wasn't mated herself.

"Definitely omega," Max muttered, looking over at the office door. "The scent of fear is bloody strong as well. I don't like it."

"I met a beta here yesterday, I would swear she smelt just like this, only less potent and more beta. Tiny blonde woman."

"The one who ran into you?"

"Yeah, her."

Max went to open the door and tried the handle, but it didn't budge. "Did she lock herself in?" he asked the blonde assistant who had run after us and was lingering a few feet behind.

"No, we locked her in once we realised what she was. We

didn't want her causing any problems or upsetting any of you." Cora frowned. By 'you' she meant alphas. The metallic smelling assistant smiled proudly, I growled in response.

"You locked a scared and unwell omega up?" Max asked, a bite to his voice.

The woman's eyes went wide. "S–she was already causing problems, sending males crazy with her messed up scent, I–we had to."

"Leave," I growled. I didn't want to hear any more. Locking the woman in her office seemed like overkill. Though a lot about omegas was mysterious, what was well known was that they had fragile natures and needed protection. She could be hurt in there. I was a bastard, but not totally heartless as to leave her there.

Max leaned up to the door and spoke while taking shallow breaths to avoid inhaling too much of the omega's scent.

"Hello? Sage, isn't it? It's Max Dennings here. Are you okay?" He kept his tone gentle and soothing, like he was speaking to a scared child.

"I–I think I have the flu. I don't feel very well," a small, shaking voice replied, panting for breath. She didn't sound fully there, like she was drifting on the precipice of sleep, but even so her terror was evident in every word.

Max gave me a confused look before mouthing "The flu?" He had no idea what was happening, but the smell of the omega was clearly wrong: it was burnt with fear and it held the tiniest hint of bile, of sickness.

"Sage, do you know what's happening?" he asked.

"No. I want to go home," she whimpered, breaking into sobs. "They locked me in here."

"Max," I spoke softly, so the omega didn't hear. "How could she not know what's happening?"

Max shrugged before leaning against the door again. "Sage, what are you feeling?"

"I'm really hot...and, and my stomach keeps cramping. I'm also lightheaded. It's the flu, it's got to be. Alex, he tried to...he tried to grab me."

She sounded so quiet and broken. We could hear her shuffle, moving ever so slightly and letting out another whimper of pain.

Standing up and walking back to me, Max leaned in and whispered, "She could be late presenting."

"Can that even happen?" As far as I knew their status was known from before they hit puberty. I had never heard of a beta suddenly becoming an omega, though I would be the first to admit I knew next to nothing about the ways of omegas.

"It's rare, but it happens. She seems confused."

"What's the procedure here? She's definitely the beta from yesterday, but she wasn't anywhere near this potent."

"We'll call the proper authorities. She'll need to be escorted to a Haven. I don't like the smell of her fear." Max grimaced, rubbing his chest like he was trying to ease the pain it was causing him. Every inch of our alpha nature drove us to protect omegas, and my own chest was tight with the knowledge that a nearby omega needed care.

"I've never actually smelled an omega before, have you?" I asked.

"Briefly. When we were courting that omega several months back, we got far enough in the process for a face-to-face meeting. It was nowhere near this strong though. Fuck me." He looked around at all the folks nearby with distaste. Groups of people congregated in the corridors and bullpen, watching. I didn't like all the attention either, the omega—Sage—was going through enough without being treated as a circus exhibit.

"Why is her fear painful?" I asked.

"It's a defence mechanism to stop alphas from going mad with lust while around a perfuming omega."

Omega Haven services were called by one of the secretaries while we stood guard outside.

A short alpha who I had never met came round the corner, a grin on his face. "Max, is it true?"

"Yes, we've called the Omega Haven services," Max confirmed, before turning to me. "Ric, this is Connor, he works in our legal department."

"Can I see her?" Connor asked, his face lit up with hope.

"No," Max growled, at the same time I did.

"You can't keep me from her, she's unhappy!" Connor snarled, launching forward as if he could reach the omega by going through the two of us. I stood in his way, holding him back as Max grabbed him by the scruff of his neck, throwing him away from us both.

"Connor! You're scent drunk, get the fuck out of here before we make you!" Max growled back, his face pissed. Connor was challenging him, even if he didn't realise it.

The snarling alpha seemed hellbent on getting through us. "He's never like this," Max muttered under his breath.

"Her perfume could send any of them into a rutting frenzy," I agreed, turning to two of the security guards. "Get him out of here!" Between the two beta guards and Max they managed to strong arm Connor off the floor.

This wasn't good. Any alpha in sniffing distance would be wanting to check out Sage. She smelled phenomenal but I was clear-headed enough to understand she needed help, while other alphas may not be.

Walking back to the door, Max and I listened to Sage's even, albeit shallow, breathing.

"Do you think she's passed out?" Max asked.

"Her body must be going through a lot if she's changing designations right now." I shrugged, trying to hide my uncertainty.

Max knocked on the door. "Sage? Can you talk to me, let me know you're okay?"

There was no answer. She wasn't responding at all, and while her breathing was still audible it was far too shallow for my liking.

"We have to make sure she's okay, if she's passed out or a danger to herself..." I frowned.

"We could break down the door and check on her, but I don't know how I'll react to the scent."

"We have to make sure she's okay—but you're ahead of yourself, buddy—the blonde has the key if she's the one who locked her in there." I grimaced.

"Oh yeah." Max looked sheepish, scanning the crowd until he saw the blonde in a corner, his face hardening. "The key!" His voice left no room for debate.

She ran forward and handed him the key without a word.

"You do it, Alaric. I'll wait back here. You've got way more restraint than I have."

I looked between the door and Max. I probably did have better control out of the two of us, but still, I wasn't a saint. We were both so far out of our depth, but we couldn't just leave her.

"Okay, give me the key."

Max handed it to me and backed up.

Knocking on the door softly, I leaned in to listen for an answer. "Sage, are you okay?" No reply. "I'm coming in, okay?"

I knew she was unlikely to answer, but I didn't want to startle her.

The moment I opened the door I was assaulted with the thick, honey scent. Taking shallow breaths, I cursed my inevitable hard on and stepped inside.

Slumped on the floor in the corner was the woman who ran into me yesterday. Her hair was plastered to her face, and she looked feverish, her face and neck bright red and glistening with sweat. Striding over to her, I knelt, cupping the back of her neck, trying to get her to look at me.

"Sage? Are you okay?"

Her only answer was a low whine that tugged at my heart. She was clearly in pain. Her skin burned my hand, but I didn't want to pull it away. Despite my efforts her head remained tilted back, eyes closed. She mumbled something unintelligible.

"Sage." I gently shook her. One of her eyes cracked open and she regarded me, like she couldn't fully make me out.

Her chest rose and fell as she took in a deep shuddering breath. The moment my scent registered, her eyes shot fully open, her nostrils flared, and she stared at me with blown pupils before flinging herself into my arms with a long, low whine.

I instinctively wrapped my arms around her tiny form as she buried her nose in my neck. For someone so small she launched herself at me with impressive strength.

"Hey, hey, hey," I soothed as she whimpered and tried to fuse her body to mine, seeking my comfort. "You're okay. It'll be okay."

I pacified her by running my hand over her hair. I was hard as granite from being in her proximity, but I did my best to keep her away from my crotch while she inhaled my smell.

Sage's body went lax as I was trying to figure out what to

do, her hands still gripping my shirt as she passed out. I shook my head, willing my boner down, which was futile. This hard on isn't going to die for days. I stroked the omega's hair as she snored lightly in my lap, hoping help wouldn't be too long, because she smelt too damn good to resist for long.

CHAPTER FOUR
Sage

I slowly woke to the feel of unfamiliar sheets. The bed was comfy and soft on my skin, with clean crisp white pillows that I nestled into. It smelt wrong; in fact it didn't really smell of anything at all, not the usual scent of my laundry soap or room spray I occasionally used.

At home I'd spray the bedding down with a lavender mist to help relax at the end of a long day, but that was noticeably absent.

I ignored the painful cramping in my midsection, I sat up and looked around groggily. The room looked a lot like a hospital, with clean white walls and linoleum flooring. The blood pressure cuff attached to my arm, constricting painfully, so I weakly pulled that off when it finished, and tossed it to the side of the bed.

Did I have something nastier than the flu? Was that why I was in some weird medical room? I didn't remember getting there, only that I'd been feeling terrible. Taking stock of my body I felt sore, and exhausted, but no longer as sick and woozy as I had been last time I was awake... When even was that?

"Hello?" I called out, voice croaking painfully. Running a hand through my hair, I racked my brain for memories of the last few hours. Where am I? How did I end up here? Where even is here?

The last thing I remembered was being in the office, Alex acting weird, and Cora angrily locking me in. Mr Dennings, the COO, had spoken to me through the door. Surely I'd imagined that? Why would he be talking with a lowly accountant? He never came to the accountancy department.

Swinging my legs over the side of the bed, I noted I was still wearing the pencil skirt and camisole. My hair had fallen from its braid and was now a tangled mess, and still slightly damp from all my sweat.

My shoes were nowhere in sight, which was fine because I wasn't in any condition for heels right now. I eased down from the tall bed. The moment my toes touched the cold linoleum, the door opened, and a short woman with a chin length bob of bright red hair walked in, dressed professionally in black slacks and a matching black jumper.

"Oh dear, you shouldn't be up!" She hurried forward, pushing me, with surprising force for one so small, back into the bed.

"Where am I?" I asked.

"You're at the Mencaster Haven. Don't you remember being brought in? You were pretty out of it."

"Haven? Why on earth am I here?" I tried to finger comb my hair with a frown. I felt off, like I was hypersensitive to everything around me.

"Oh my, you really are out of it, dear. Well, my name is Claire. I'm a Keeper here, and you're an omega. You started presenting at work earlier today. Did you not realise what was happening with your own body? We were called to get you and help you assimilate." Her voice was sickly sweet, in a condescending way that didn't sit right with me.

"That's not possible. I'm a beta," I said quietly, lightly brushing my hand over the skirt to try and reduce the wrinkles from sleeping.

"Late presentation is rare, but it happens. You're just a late bloomer, but how lucky for you! All your fortunes are about to change! It's very, very rare—but here you are! You know omegas outnumber alphas fifty to one!"

I shook my head. I didn't feel lucky. Could I really be an omega? The very idea sounded impossible. Omegas were hidden from a lot of the world. They were isolated, solitary, on their own in the world other than their packs. They couldn't hold jobs, or own property without an alpha to "protect" them.

"I don't want to be an omega... I want to leave." My voice wavered as I went to move away from the bed, but Claire stopped me.

"Dearie, you can't. There's no denying you're an omega now. You practically sent an entire office floor into a rut with your scent. It's not safe for you out there, not until you've found a pack, at the very least!"

I started to hyperventilate.

"That's impossible, I can't be an omega," I insisted.

"Your parents are betas, aren't they? That is unusual, but you must have alpha or omega somewhere in your family tree. This has only happened a handful of times in the last century, you're special! It'll get you plenty of attention from your packs!" Claire reached out to me, trying to gently push me back towards the bed.

"I don't want a pack! I want to go home, back to my job, my life!" I batted away Claire's arms as she tried to keep me in place once again and started pacing the floor, trying to figure out the next move. "Surely I can be put on suppressants or something?" I could just go back to my calm and quiet life and I wouldn't bother anyone. Claire nodded. "We gave you a suppressant shot when you arrived here. We didn't want you going into a heat before you acclimated and understood your position. It'll stop some of the pain, but you'll still get the odd cramp. They're good, the suppressants, but they're not that good. You still smell distinctly omega, and if we let you leave there's nothing stopping the first alpha who comes across you from kidnapping you and claiming their right to indulge in their baser instincts. We will keep you safe, Sage."

My stomach sank more and more with every word. Claire was right. If I really was an omega, which I didn't entirely believe yet, then I wouldn't be safe out in the world. How could I be an omega? I was a beta raised by betas.

"This is a good thing, though." Claire smiled. "Omegas are treasured! You won't want for anything. There's already several packs that have indicated an interest in meeting you. You'll be spoiled, have several men to look after you, and all your financial needs will be met."

"But I won't have anything of my own. I can't go back to my apartment?" I pleaded

"Your apartment will be left untouched until you pick a pack. We shall give your keys to your pack and I'm sure the alphas will escort you back to collect anything you want, even though they'll surely shower you with much nicer things. Until then we have everything you could possibly need here while all the packs visit and court you!"

I stopped my pacing. "Court me?"

Claire rolled her eyes in a manner that felt slightly patronising. "Oh my, I forget you're totally new to this. How about we get you some food and check you over to make sure you're okay? While you eat, I'll talk you through what happens here."

What other choice did I really have?

Claire picked up the monitor and reapplied the cuff when I sat down dejectedly, also attaching the same oxygen monitor onto the end of my ring finger. "I've been working here for a few years and seen several omegas find happiness with their packs. Do you have any allergies that you know of? We're still waiting for your medical records to arrive."

"No, I'm not allergic to anything." Unless you counted bullshit.

"Good, and do you like chicken? I think tonight the chef is making chicken and broccoli."

I nodded as neither of those items were particularly offensive.

"You look to be in good health," Claire continued. "We want to monitor you for a while because you were in distress when you got here. I'll go grab you a tray of food, but you must stay put and rest!"

"Am I safe here?" I asked, hating that my voice sounded small and tired.

"Of course, we have plenty of guards outside the omega rooms, they're well trained at dealing with omegas and their scents—also it's highly unlikely they'll ever be within sniffing distance of you. You're actually our only omega at the moment, so you're well protected." Claire turned with a smile, promising to be right back.

Once Claire was out of the room, I sighed and laid back on the pillows. I couldn't escape with guards at my door, and even if I did, my life as I knew it was over. A future being mated to a pack wasn't appealing. But given the situation it was best to go along with everything and at least see what the options were. My experience was limited to say the least, so the idea of pleasing several alphas made a pit grow in my stomach. Surely there was no way I would be enough to please them? I had also lived alone for my entire adult life, so living with several large hulking males wasn't exactly appealing.

Claire returned carrying a tray with a bottle of water, two apples, and a plate of chicken, broccoli and green beans. Placing the tray in front of me, Claire smiled. "Eat up. I don't know when you last managed to eat."

"It's been a while I think." I grabbed a forkful of chicken. It was slightly plainer than what I was used to, but I dove in, the appearance of food reminding me just how hungry I actually was. As I dug in Claire sat in a chair next to the bed and chatted away.

"So, I guess I'd better explain what Omega Havens do, how we operate and such. You've likely never really looked into or found out what a Haven is! First and foremost, our job is to protect omegas and match them safely to a pack. The omega ultimately gets to choose the pack they are tied to."

"Wait, I get to choose? It's not decided for me?" I asked, swallowing a mouthful of chicken.

"Of course not! We help guide the decision, but an omega has all the power here. Several packs will want to meet you, and all packs have been vetted beforehand to weed out any of ill repute. If they like you, they can put in a bid, which is just an official way of saying they're interested and would like you as part of their pack. The omega can take their time to look into the alphas who are interested in her. A Haven may only step in on occasion if it's in the best interest of the omega."

"How long do I have to do this?"

"As long as you need, usually, but we would encourage you to find matches sooner rather than later, since you're already a lot older than most omegas when they are matched. We don't know how long we can suppress your heat for, and going through a heat alone is really quite painful, and we don't want our omegas to suffer. The courting process is all completely safe as well. Your room actually has a window that you can talk to alphas through. That way you can meet, chat and get to know one another but they can't smell you, or get to you in case their alpha instincts take over. Later on in the process you can exchange articles of clothing to scent each other out in a safe environment."

I chewed thoughtfully on my chicken. "So I'll be protected? They can't, like, take me?"

"Oh no! Not at all, you're completely safe. Actually, once you've eaten, I can take you into your room. This is just a medical room we kept you in while you recovered. How do you feel now that you've eaten?"

"Not bad actually, in fact, I feel normal, besides being a little woozy still. The cramps are nearly gone."

"That'll be the suppressants doing their job," Claire said. "Now, I think it best we get you settled in a proper bed."

I followed Claire out of the room, my bare feet smacking against the ice cold linoleum floor.

My room was large, and beautiful. I turned on my heels to take it all in. One of the walls was made entirely of some sort of heavy-duty glass and on the other side was a small room with a few armchairs.

"That looks like a viewing room at a zoo," I commented with a frown.

Claire tilted her head before answering. "It is, in many ways—but it's the best way for you to get to know the packs that come to meet you. The door to that room will always be open for packs to come meet you, only one at a time though. They'll visit regularly, but they'll usually respect you if you're asleep."

Speaking of sleep, a super-sized bed was piled high with crisp white bedding and throw pillows in various shades of white, matching the overall sterile feel of the room. There was a bookcase with a few books piled on it for reading, and there was even a tablet computer next to my bed.

My eyebrows raised at the clawfoot tub on a raised platform on the other side of the room. It wasn't something I had expected.

Claire laughed at my look. "Oh, most omegas love a good soak, so we tend to include a tub in all their rooms. There's a bucket of spa products over there as well."

"The alphas can come in whenever they want? What about when I want to bathe?"

Claire laughed, waving her hand in a dismissive gesture, but she wouldn't meet my eyes. "Most omegas aren't modest. There's nothing wrong with potential alphas seeing what you bring to the table."

I bristled. "And the guards?"

"Oh, they won't come in."

No way in hell was I going to get even slightly naked when any old alpha could walk right in at any moment.

"Anyway, I'll leave you to settle in. Your food will get delivered regularly by one of our staff, but the priority now will be focusing on the alphas. You won't be able to leave this room, hence why it's well equipped with everything you could need, especially when there can be alphas in the building, it's just for your own safety. Usually, omegas would dorm together before they reach the age to find a pack, but you're more than ready! You can communicate with me using the intercom on the wall, but I'll be fairly hands off from here on. The first pack will probably be popping in at some point in the next few hours—we've had a lot of interest in you so we want you to hit the ground running!" Claire didn't even give me a chance to reply before she walked out of the room with a happy little wave and a goodbye.

Turning and looking around the room, I padded over to the wardrobe located on the far side of the room. It was filled to the brim with some of the comfiest looking pyjamas and lounge sets I had ever seen. A camera blinked in the top corner of the room, the small white dome obvious. I recoiled, noticing it for the first time. Who was watching behind that camera? They clearly didn't care about modesty here, and I didn't want to put on a show, so I was stuck in my pencil skirt and camisole for now. Was there even somewhere to pee? I located a tiny toilet room connected to my room that was so impossibly small I couldn't even sit on the toilet without my knees poking out of the doorway.

Padding over to the bookcase I picked up the Omega Haven manual from the miniscule selection and made my way over to the bed to sit down, flicking through it. It detailed the ins and outs of how the Havens were run, but for such an important topic, it was hardly thicker than a pamphlet.

With nothing else to do, I read.

Omega's will experience many changes as they transition to their new life, both physical and mental. Decades ago, alpha and omegas often paired up, but as the omega population declined, packs became the norm. While omegas often resided with their families until they came of age and found alphas, when the population declined further and instances of kidnapping and brutality became commonplace, the Havens were established to protect the omegas and ensure the longevity of their species.

For a brief moment, I was thankful that I was in a Haven instead of just out in the world, vulnerable and alone.

The relief didn't last, though.

Things felt off: Claire's too sweet smile, the almost sterile nature of the room, the fact they expected me to expose myself to any alpha that appeared. It made my skin crawl. Several lines in the book were redacted in what appeared to be black marker. What were those marks covering? It also appeared that a few pages had been ripped out of the book. The book made a big deal of how for every fifty alphas there was only one omega, and how packs were vital for procreation, but there were no details on how that happened, which was one of my burning questions that would have to remain unanswered.

CHAPTER FIVE

Alaric

I had found myself thinking about the omega on my way home that day. I hadn't told the pack yet of what had unfolded at Norden, but I would as soon as we gathered to eat. The woman had looked in a bad way when the Haven employees had removed her from the office: drenched in sweat and whimpering in pain while unconscious. It had taken all of my strength to let her go. I'd wanted to rip her away from the employees and drag her back to my home where I could protect her. Once the Haven employees had removed her from the office, Max and I had backed off. Her scent had called to me in a way I had never experienced. Every fibre of my being wanted to go to her, to hold her, to comfort her. I needed to make her suffering stop.

Maybe if things were different, I could have stayed with her, but the black mark on the family name meant I would never be allowed near an omega, at least not in an official capacity. I didn't want to tell my pack I was open to looking for an omega when it was highly likely we would be rejected because of my past.

My phone had pinged with a message from our pack leader when I'd sat down in the car.

> CALLAN:
>
> Will you be home soon? I've just had a call
> I need to discuss with everyone at once.
> Pack meeting.

I frowned, but replied I was on my way and threw the phone on the passenger seat.

Everett was already in the kitchen when I got home, thumbing through takeout leaflets. "Pizza tonight? I told Ma that we woul—" He abruptly stopped speaking as my scent hit him. His nostrils flared as he inhaled deeply. "Holy fuck, you smell good. Who the hell have you been up to?"

"I'll explain later. It's been a long fucking day." I had stayed at Norden for over four hours after the situation with the omega while waiting for the Haven employees to turn up and finishing our jobs for the day.

"Well, everyone's home for food tonight," Everett said. "Callan wants an official pack meeting."

"I got a message from him about that. Why on earth is he calling a meeting? You think the Dillan property fell through?" Usually we just hung out naturally or talked via the group chat. Callan rarely called proper meetings.

"No clue." Everett shrugged. "He'll be here soon though. So what pizza do you want?"

"The usual."

Everett nodded. He had the entire pack's order memorised at this point.

The pizza arrived while I took a shower to wash the scent of omega off. I lamented the loss of the sweet honey notes. I would have kept the shirt on, but I didn't want to distract my packmates, especially if Callan needed to discuss something important with us—and I knew I was smelling mighty distracting. Callan and Bellamy appeared as Everett laid out the food, gathering round the kitchen island to dive in. They had been out on a job all day, and probably hadn't had much time to eat.

"So wanna tell us why you decided to summon us all so formally?" Everett shoved half a slice of pizza in his mouth.

Callan. Our head alpha was a fair man, with dirty blonde hair that fell around his ears in a messy way that contradicted the slacks and shirt he was wearing. "I got an invite today. For us to court an omega."

My packmates stilled, staring at Callan with varying disbelieving looks.

"Wait." Everett frowned. "I thought that beta bitch at Fort Alexandria had it out for us, and she was our only chance?"

One of the employees at the Fort Alexandria Haven hated us, mainly because Callan turned her down several years ago and her ego never recovered. She'd made it her mission to bar us from all the omegas at her facility since.

"Also, invited? Usually alphas go to them, don't they?" Everett crossed his arms. "What's wrong with her for us to be invited?"

"All of us?" I frowned, ignoring his question.

"All of us, Ric," Callan confirmed. "They named all of us."

"Why? There's no way I could ever be approved after my uncle..."

Callan shrugged. "I don't know, honestly. The omega isn't in Fort Alexandria or Clearmont, she's in Mencaster. She's also in her mid-twenties. Late presenting. The Haven is keen to get her placed and decided to reach out to packs they deemed suitable. Since business boomed last year, we've become quite eligible it seems."

"Do you want to go for it?" I asked, brow furrowed. "I thought we'd decided not to take an omega."

"We didn't want to deal with the rat race of thirty alphas mooning over one spoiled princess, and there were the...other complications."

I didn't say what I wanted to. My criminally abusive family meant we shouldn't be allowed in the same zip code as an omega, let alone the same building.

"Is anyone going to tell us what's wrong with her so that we've been invited?" Everett asked. "Also, what does late presenting mean? She just wasn't ready to be placed until now?"

"It seems this omega was living as a beta until she presented recently," Callan informed them.

The pieces clicked, and I cursed, everyone turning to look at me.

"Something wrong, Ric?" Callan asked.

"I know who the omega is. Her name is Sage. She works at Norden, or at least I suppose she used to." I ran my hand through my hair, trying to find the right words. "I was in a meeting this morning when someone burst in saying an omega was causing a fuss. Turns out the poor girl had presented at work and a beta went for her. Max and I found her locked in her office, terrified. He spoke to her through the door, and she clearly had no idea what was happening to her."

"Was that who I could smell on you when you got home?" Everett asked, his pizza forgotten.

"Yeah. The Haven was called, but her scent flooded the whole floor. Her panic and terror were fucking painful. I hated it." I rubbed my chest at the mere memory of her fear.

"Did you see her?" Callan asked, the cool alpha's gaze firm. Both Bellamy and Everett could tell his curiosity was piqued now that he knew one of us had interacted, however briefly, with the omega.

"I did. I actually met her the day before, but she didn't smell at all like an omega then, she had that acidic smell betas have as well as honey—the honey smell was dialled up to a thousand today. She crashed into me, literally, in the cafeteria while I was grabbing water. Probably five foot one, a tiny thing. Stunning face, blonde wavy hair that almost reaches her ass," I recalled. "And uh, today we got close. I was the one who checked on her in her office."

Bellamy gave a low whistle. "Sounds like you liked the look of her."

"She was fucking stunning. I thought about going there, maybe getting her number, and you know how I am with beta women." I chuckled ruefully.

Everett suddenly got up and dashed out of the room, leaving everyone confused. Ev was the kind to go bounding around like a toddler with endless energy, but we usually knew why—even if the reason was something small like he remembered he had a cupcake.

"What's his issue?" Bellamy asked, laughing.

"I wish I knew," Callan sighed.

It only took a moment for Everett to return however, holding an item of fabric up in his hands triumphantly. "I knew you wouldn't have put this in the wash."

I recognised the shirt I had been wearing that day.

"Anyone want to smell the omega in question? Alaric's shirt is dripping in it. Just ignore the sweaty Ric mixed with it." He lifted the shirt to his nose and sniffed. "I knew you smelled far too good when you got home today."

"Give it here." Callan held out his hand and took the shirt carefully, pausing to take a deep inhale. He passed the shirt to Bellamy before speaking. "I won't lie, that smells…"

"Fucking amazing?" Bellamy commented, looking at the fabric in awe.

"I've got a boner just from second-hand scent." Everett buried his nose in the shirt. "How the fuck did you survive being close to her, Alaric?"

"Not all of us are as weak willed as you," I informed him with a grin, and Everett feigned shock letting out a dramatic gasp and putting one hand on his chest.

"You want to meet her, don't you?" Bellamy asked Callan. If he said no, then we wouldn't be seeing her. I had decided long ago to place my trust in him.

"I think I am inclined to do so, especially if Ric met and liked her. Her scent alone is pretty seductive. We've grown as a pack and built in strength, I can't help but wonder if now is the right time to add an omega into the mix."

"You know I'm down," Everett grinned. "I want something like my mom and dads have. Hell, I'd mate her based on scent alone."

Bellamy nodded.

"It's a good time for us, as you've said." They all focused on me, the only one who hadn't voiced an agreement. "Do we think this is the right thing? I would like to see her again. I think we need to be prepared though. She's been through an ordeal and it's probably going to take her time to settle into her new reality. She could cause problems down the road." No matter how good she smelled, I would always protect the pack first. "I don't want this to end in disappointment…"

"We can go slow. Remember she gets to choose if she sees us, and how long she sees us, at least I think that's the case,"

Bellamy said. "I'm sure the Haven has been preparing her thoroughly for what's to come."

"I guess we're doing this. We'll go tomorrow," Callan said.

"Tomorrow?"

"They wasted no time in throwing her to the wolves." Callan grimaced. "She started meeting with packs as soon as she arrived."

I frowned. "She was sick, Callan. She couldn't form a sentence and it felt like she was running a fever. She was in so much pain. How can they have her meeting packs right now?"

"I don't know, but I guess we will find out."

CHAPTER SIX
Sage

"Hello," a deep voice called out.

I jumped, looking up from the manual. Several tall, handsome men stood on the other side of the window wall. I didn't need to smell them to know these were alphas, their sheer size and dominating stance showed them for who they were.

"Oh, hello!" I mumbled. Putting the book down, I faced the men, all of whom were eyeing me up, gazes running over my body. Was my bedraggled appearance off putting? My clothes were dirty and wrinkled, my hair was tangled, and I probably had undereye circles, too. Self-consciously I crossed my arms, but they didn't seem to notice my discomfort.

The first pack were kind enough, they asked me some generic questions about my hobbies and skills, if I wanted children and such. They stayed until their phones pinged with a message telling them it was time to leave.

Exhaustion weighing heavily on me, I slumped on the bed

the moment they left. Despite my racing mind I started to drift into an uneasy sleep.

The next pack was far from impressive. I had managed to get all of ten minutes rest before they entered the room. Three alphas sat in the armchairs and stared at me, they didn't say anything, simply gawking. Groaning internally, I accepted that I probably wasn't going to sleep for a few hours.

We spent an awkward hour hardly speaking to one another, the alphas seeming content to stare at me instead of attempting any real communication. I settled in a chair and tried to engage with them, without much luck.

When they finally left, I sighed in relief. This was never going to feel normal. I took the time to grab one of the bottles of water on my bedside table and chugged half of it while flicking through the rest of the books. At least the first pack I had met were chatty.

It could be a lot worse.

I was pulled out of my nap by the sound of the intercom buzzing and Claire's voice filtering through the room.

"Wake up sleepy head! You've got some VIP alphas coming in to see you in a moment!" Her voice crackled through the speaker.

Sitting up, I fiddled with my hair, undoing my braid and running my fingers through it to detangle it. Before I could even contemplate brushing my teeth, several alphas stalked into the viewing room. They smiled at me, the same as the packs before, but this smile seemed far more...predatory. It put me on edge immediately, instinct making the hair rise on the back of my neck.

They didn't greet me, instead just standing there in a line, looking over me. I was regretting the choice to remove my hoodie to take a nap.

"Uh, hello," I greeted them, voice trembling. "I'm Sage. You are?"

"Lex, and the rest of my pack, Mitch, Dean, and Peter."

"Nice to meet you. What do you guys do for work?"

"We work in...entertainment."

"Oh, that sounds interesting!" I answered lightly, for lack of anything else to say.

"You would certainly be some fun entertainment." Lex grinned.

My skin crawled at the comment. The insinuation of what sort of entertainment I would be was making me uneasy.

"What are you guys looking for?" I asked, but Mitch scoffed.

"An omega, simple enough."

"Surely you want more than just that?" I asked, confused. I get that we're rare, but there was more to omegas than biology? I didn't want to condemn myself to a life with a pack who saw just my designation.

"Yeah, it's nice to ensure you're attracted to each other, but all omegas are attracted to alphas. It's biology. You can't help but get wet for an alpha. We just like to look at an omega before we put a bid in, to ensure it isn't defective."

My stomach turned at those words, and I schooled my features to stop my disdain showing. Defective? These morons were clearly defective ones. I thought omegas were supposed to be respected?

Was I merely an appliance to them? As much a blender as an omega? Useful, but only if working to its full potential, or I'd be thrown on the scrap heap.

I wish I could throw these fuckers on the scrap heap.

I didn't like the way they were staring at me like I was something to eat. Raw hunger and lust filled their gazes and I got the distinct impression they weren't listening to a thing I was saying. I was prey to them, nothing more.

"You are really pretty, small, but pretty," one of them commented.

"Thank you?" My reply was more of a question than actual acceptance of their comment. I wasn't small, I was the average height. Alphas were just super tall. They're so creepy. Can these ones please hurry up and leave?

"Do you think she would be too small, Lex? We want to be able to breed her, not break her." Mitch never looked away from me when he asked, his hands shoved into his jean pockets as he stood tall—was he trying to look intimidating?

I sputtered in shock at the question. Clearly he has zero filter or decorum.

"Of course not. She's an omega. She's built to take multiple alphas," he stated, resting his elbows on his knees as he continued to stare. I suppressed a shudder, would this glass actually protect me if they decided to do something untoward? "I bet it would be a tight fit to knot her. Imagine it."

They spoke so plainly and frankly about things that should be private, I wasn't used to anyone discussing me in this manner—as if I were a possession. It didn't sit right with me. It made me want to go home all the more where I could be left alone and sleep in my own bed. My skin was crawling just being near these guys, and I wanted out. Only I was in a room, unable to leave.

After a few minutes of silence where they continued to stare at me, discussing amongst themselves, one of them got a text.

"Looks like our time is up for today. We'll be back tomorrow. Hopefully in time for you to have a bath." Lex leered. "That would certainly be some good entertainment."

His friends all agreed, eyes lighting up in excitement at the prospect.

I recoiled. That would not be happening. They filed out, all of them leering at me as they left, muttering promises to see me tomorrow.

I sat curled up on an armchair near the glass. Today hadn't been terrible, but it hadn't been good. I had been kept busy talking to various packs; some were at least polite, but the thought of Pack Bove, Lex's pack, still made my stomach turn. Still no matter what I did I wasn't able to settle in the room. Despite the luxury it felt wrong. I was dirty and wanted to get clean, but there was no way in hell I was going to have a bath when anyone could walk in.

I padded over to the intercom, pressing the button to speak.

"Could I have privacy to bathe, please?"

"Omegas don't do that, and you're an omega now."

That was helpful.

I hadn't seen another Keeper since Claire had escorted me into the room. I had been here for a whole day and the only other people I saw were alphas through the thick glass.

Claire had offered to call my family, to let them know I was safe, but there wasn't a need. I hadn't been close to my parents in years. They were too involved in their own lives, and they had been that way since I was young. It was why I'd been so independent. They wouldn't even notice I was missing for months. I also suspected that they would suddenly be more interested in me if they realised I was an omega because they could gain status and wealth from my new position...and I didn't want the pain of dealing with that.

At least Lex's pack hadn't visited again. Claire had texted me an excited message full of exclamation points letting me know that the Bove pack—Lex's creep show of a pack—liked me and would be returning.

CHAPTER SEVEN
Callan

The next day Everett was practically vibrating with excitement as we pulled into the parking lot of the Haven. We were all on edge, anticipating the next few hours. I'd been assured over the phone that if we arrived at ten in the morning, we would have some time with the omega without any other packs in the building.

Though I would never admit it, I had even tried to improve my appearance by brushing back my mane of hair. The others didn't dare comment on fear of death, though I could see Bellamy was desperate to crack a joke at my expense, shooting me sly, knowing looks.

We were greeted at the door by a slimy looking beta whose scent of egg made my stomach turn. Still, we were polite, after all the Haven could bar us for any number of little reasons. Their society took the protection of omegas seriously, as they should. The only way alphas could even have children was with an omega, and now alphas outnumbered omegas fifty to one.

We knew some of the process, but we were far from experts. If today went well, we would have to do some serious research. I hated that this visit was sprung on us with so little warning, but we couldn't turn it down, either.

We were shown to the meeting room door by a small, unpleasant looking woman by the name of Keeper Claire who told us about the omega as we made our way through multiple corridors on the way.

"Now you gentlemen must respect the rules of the house, but I must warn you this omega is a little... difficult."

"Difficult?" I asked with a frown.

"She's not used to the process, so she's a little belligerent. Because of this it's perfectly okay to be...firmer with her. You don't need to indulge her as much," she explained, looking back at us with a sickly sweet smile on her face.

"When you say a firm—" Bellamy started to speak, a confused look on his face.

"She only presented yesterday. Are you sure she's ready for this?" Alaric butted in, cutting Bellamy off. He was tense next to me. Something wasn't right here. Ric gave me a confused look, shaking his head as if to tell me don't discuss it here, wait until no one else is in earshot. The Keeper didn't feel completely trustworthy—I had never heard someone speak of an omega this way, but I was raised by betas and hadn't been part of this world.

"Oh, she's more than ready!" Claire waved off our concerns. "We want her to settle quickly. It's why we're willing to give alphas extra time with her. She's a lovely omega, just a little unrefined. She hasn't even bothered to bathe yet, but she'll learn her place quickly."

"She's healthy as well after yesterday, correct? We heard about how she presented, and that it was stressful for her." I left out the information that it was Alaric who was with her yesterday. I didn't want to draw attention to him, but I was concerned given what Ric had told us about her state.

"Of course! You shouldn't have any concerns in that regard. She'll be more than able to complete all the duties of an omega once chosen, and she'll entertain you while you're here."

I shared another confused look with Alaric. I'd wanted to know about the health of the omega for her own wellbeing, not because I wanted her to pander to us. I didn't have that much of an alpha ego.

Bellamy voiced what we were probably all thinking. "Entertain us? Aren't we meant to be the ones convincing her?"

"Yes," Claire admitted, swiping her keycard to open yet another locked door. "But as I've said, Miss Miller isn't a normal omega—you're on far more even footing with her. She won't be making any demands of you."

What on earth had I gotten my pack involved in?

We filed in, and immediately caught sight of Sage. She was curled up in a ball on the bed, snoring lightly. We exchanged a glance. The last thing we wanted to do was disturb her. Why hadn't the Keepers stopped us if Sage needed sleep? Her golden waves spilled out, and her face was pressed rather adorably into the pillow she clutched.

Alaric made a noise of discontent. "She's still in the clothes she was wearing at the office. She must be fucking exhausted. She shouldn't be seeing packs so soon."

"She must have been too tired to bathe yet. The Keepers should have helped her and held off on meeting packs," I commented. "She is a beauty, that's for sure, even in this state. I can see why you liked her."

The rest of the pack nodded and mumbled their agreement.

Everett smiled. "Imagine waking up to that each day. She's so soft and cuddly looking compared to us bastards." He groaned in happiness, like he was looking at a new video game or a pizza.

Alaric was opening his mouth to speak when a small sound escaped the omega, interrupting whatever he'd wanted to say. She turned over before sitting up, looking sleepy and rumpled.

Sage stilled as her eyes met mine. "Why didn't you wake me?"

"We only just got here, and it didn't feel right disturbing you."

Sage gave a playful little snort. "The whole point of this is to be meeting you guys, not snoozing through the meetings, or so I've been told." The last part sounded sarcastic. What was she being told? She brought her knees up and hugged them.

Her eyes landed on Alaric, and I could practically see the gears turning in her head.

"Oh! I crashed into you the other day, Mr Beckett. I'm sorry again about that, by the way." She stumbled over her words.

"No worries, call me Alaric. Or Ric, if you prefer."

"Were you there yesterday, when I..." She trailed off.

"I was the one who was with you when the Haven staff picked you up."

"That explains it. I thought the scent was familiar." She nodded. "Thank you."

"There's no need to thank me," Alaric spoke gruffly.

"So, what are your names?" She smiled slightly as she

climbed out of bed to move closer to us. "No wait, let me guess. You look like a Callum!" she declared with a small grin, pointing at me.

I broke into a rare smile. "Close, I'm Callan Rivers, head of Pack Rivers."

Sage bounced in place before calming herself, covering her mouth with her hand. "Sorry, this whole situation is insane. I've gotta do something to have a little fun in this place."

I shook my head with a rueful smile, pleasure bursting beneath my skin. What wasn't there to like about her? We couldn't even smell her yet thanks to the partitioning glass but we already knew her scent was honey.

"Don't apologise, Honey. I dread to think of the names you would give these grumpy bastards." I jerked a thumb in the direction of my packmates.

Sage laughed and took a moment to look over them. "It's nice to meet you. I suppose you should tell me a bit about yourselves? I'm not really sure how this process goes. So far I've had one pack who seemed okay, and one who just wanted to gawk at me... That was interesting."

"That doesn't sound too good, apologies if some of us seem to be ill mannered. We can at least attempt to make conversation." Bellamy pointed to each of us in turn. "You know Callan and Alaric, but this is Everett, and I'm Bellamy."

"Nice to meet you. So what do you do? I know what Mr Beckett... Alaric does. Do the rest of you work in a similar field?"

"We own a trading company, but we branch off and do a lot more than that, cyber security, real estate," I told her.

"That sounds both interesting and dangerous."

"It's not that dangerous really. We're usually locked in offices most of the day."

"Well that sounds significantly more boring!"

"But safe," I assured her. "What about you? You were at Norden in accounting, correct?"

Her eyebrows raised and she gave me a piercing look. "I was head of one of the accountancy divisions."

"That's impressive," I acknowledged. She preened at the compliment, a bright grin lighting up her face.

"I know Alaric was working on some things at Norden. You know you could have got a much better deal." She scrunched her nose as she spoke.

"They're good friends." Bellamy grinned. "We have to be nice to them."

"That's good, though Mr Denning's employees can be a little underhanded and grabby," she admitted.

The idea of anyone being grabby with her made a growl bubble up from Alaric, and I agreed with the sentiment, but managed to remain quiet. Sage shuffled back a bit, mumbling an apology, and the sight of her looking down and backing away twinged in my gut.

I swung, clipping Alaric round the back of the head, irrationally angry at the sight of Sage shrinking away from us. She should be coming toward us.

"Be polite, you idiot." I turned to Sage, who looked startled that one pack member had hit another. "I apologise for him. He's been all wound up over work the last few weeks. I promise he's usually not such a surly ass...well he is, but usually he's a more tolerable surly ass."

She gave me a small smile, and I glowed with pleasure at being able to make her feel more at ease.

"You seem a lot more...relaxed than the other packs I've met. Friendlier with each other."

"That's a good thing, isn't it?" Did she want a pack that was on more professional terms with one another?

"It is. This whole situation is so bizarre, I apologise if I'm making a mess of things. I seem to be saying all the wrong things of late." She shook her head and ran her hand through her hair, lips tugging down in worry.

"It's an adjustment." I rushed to reassure her. "Remember most omegas have years to prepare and understand what life will hold for them—and you're not messing anything up, I promise."

Sage snorted. "I spent the last eight years of mine studying and climbing a career ladder that I can't even work in anymore thanks to this. Anyway," she stated as she paced around the bed, looking over the room, "this is reality now. I'd better adapt."

She ran her hands over her arms, trying to warm herself up. Her nipples were poking through the thin fabric of her camisole, and I diverted my eyes, nudging Ev to bring out her gift.

Everett held up the package we'd bought for her. "We picked this up for you on the way here."

"Oh, thank you. I didn't know gifts were really a thing. I thought all that stuff came later, I think you'll have to give it to the staff, I can't…" She gestured to the glass.

I tapped a section of the wall. "There's a secure hatch here so you can receive pack gifts. I'll pop it through." I took the parcel off Everett, who was so confident in his gift for Sage that he was bouncing in place.

Sage wandered over to the hatch when it beeped, and once our side was securely locked, hers opened, revealing the package. She picked it up carefully, giving it a little squish, and looking shyly at us. "Can I open it now?"

We all nodded, eager to see if she liked it.

"Of course you can."

Sage padded over to the bed and laid the parcel down to open. Her luminous expression when her hands traced over the soft fleece was exactly the reaction we'd been hoping for. Sage tugged the dark green fabric, her face lighting up even more when she realised it was a giant hoodie that was big enough to envelop her entire body.

"Thank you! I've been wanting one of these for ages. I'd been planning to reward myself with one after the audit was over, but then...well."

"I wish we could take credit for it." Bellamy laughed. "Ev spoke to his mom last night and she said you could probably use some more comfort and nesting things, that the Haven probably wouldn't provide enough to keep you happy. She's been in love with those things for years and insisted it was the best thing for a fellow omega going through this process."

"Your mom?" Sage perked up and pulled the hoodie over her head before coming back up to the glass.

Everett nodded "My ma went through all this about thirty years ago now. She's our source on what things you would like."

Sage laughed. "Well that's handy, because I'm not even sure what I like anymore! Thank you, and please thank her for me. This is so thoughtful." The hoodie dwarfed her, falling past her knees, the hood drowning her face. A genuine grin was visible just below where the hood ended.

Ric tried to keep his preening to a minimum, but I could tell he was pleased. We all were. We'd pleased our—an—omega.

"Surely you've been receiving gifts since you woke up?" I inquired. "Most omegas are buried in them."

Sage huffed. "I've only met two packs before you and

neither brought me anything. It would be hard to top this, though." She twirled, revealing a little more of her happiness, and sparking a laugh through my pack.

A pang rippled through my chest. She was so happy over a hoodie. Most omegas would probably have demanded a display of wealth, something to prove that we were capable of providing, but Sage was perfectly content with such a simple gift. She was sweet and open with her thoughts. Everything they had been told about the omegas had made them seem far more self-centred, at least in this phase of their lives.

"Well, I'm glad you like it." Everett beamed.

"Are you kidding? I love this, I mean...I'm like stupidly excited right now!" She padded over to the bed grabbing a blanket for her legs, wrapping herself up on the armchair near the glass.

"You're probably nesting."

"What is that? I mean, I know that's meant to happen with heats, I read something about that, but there wasn't much detail."

"Most omegas tend to find themselves with a serious love of bedding, pillows, anything soft and comfy. My mother drowned our home in blankets and throw pillows growing up."

"Oh, that makes sense! I did have a pretty amazing bed setup before all this. I like my creature comforts."

I held my tongue at the thought of her bed—her actual bed and not the temporary one we had just seen her in—or maybe even my bed. We had only just met, but I knew exactly what she smelt like and it was making my instincts run wild.

Everett didn't hold back though. "Your bed was pretty nice, you say?"

Sage groaned, tilting her head back slightly. "Yes, it was. I got these really nice sheets when I was just a baby accountant getting started. They cost like three hundred dollars but it was totally worth it! I saved for months and never regretted it. This is nice and all," she waved to the bed in the corner of the room, "but it's just not mine. Oh, look at me rambling about bedding. Sorry, I'll be boring you." Her words were rushed, and she had totally missed the dirty meaning behind his words.

"It sounds like a lovely bed. You know why it was probably extra lovely?" He wiggled his eyebrows with a smirk.

Sage covered her face with her hands and groaned, his meaning now obvious to her. "You," she pointed at Everett, "are an insufferable flirt, aren't you?"

Everett looked so startled at her calling him out that I couldn't help but laugh, and my laughter triggered the others.

"You've got him pegged," Bellamy nodded at her. "He's an idiot, but he's our idiot."

My phone buzzed in my pocket, and I reluctantly checked it, knowing it was probably the Keepers telling us our time was up. We had only just scratched the surface, and I wasn't ready to leave yet.

"There's another pack waiting to meet you."

Sage deflated at my words. I would take that as a good sign, and hope that she would want us to return.

"Will you come back?" She gently touched the glass. It twisted my heart to see her looking at me with so much uncertainty in her eyes. I wanted to pick her up and cradle her, to comfort her as best I could. I spared a glance at my pack mates and judging from their expressions, they felt the same.

"Of course," I replied. "We'll be back as soon as we're able."

Her uncertainty vanished, replaced by elation—a reward that nearly sent me to my knees.

My pack didn't speak a word as we left the Haven, waiting until we got back into our SUV.

Everett was the first to break the silence. "Please tell me we're registering interest with her."

"Of course we are." Bellamy's tone made it clear he was in. "Callan? Alaric?"

Alaric nodded from the passenger seat. "She looks a hell of a lot better than she did yesterday."

"She still doesn't look fully well, but I'll call in the morning and register our interest," I agreed. "She seems like a nice girl—sweet—like maybe she could work with us."

"Fucking beautiful, that's what she is," Everett said. "I thought omegas were meant to be stuck up princesses. She didn't ask once what we could give her, fucking hell, she was shocked we'd even thought of the hoodie."

"You forget she's only just become an omega." I pulled out of the parking lot to begin the drive home. "She's not used to being treated this way. We need to get to know her better though. We can't let our dicks control our choices here."

Everett leaned toward me through the seats. "Have we even got the space ready for an omega? She'll need her own room."

"We can have the south suite redone for her. That'll be easy," Bellamy said, brushing Everett's concern away. "But there's going to be at least fifty packs interested in her. Even if we register interest, our chances of getting picked are extremely slim. She'll be drowning in knot heads wanting her attention."

Everett pouted. "She did ask us if we were coming back though, remember?"

Bellamy groaned, "Yes, I remember, and fuck if it didn't

sing to every one of my instincts. My nose is saying she's pretty perfect, okay? Even Alaric would like having her around I bet."

Alaric growled. Who knew what was going on in his head. I knew that he did like her, it was easy enough to tell, but beyond that he hadn't yet said.

"That sweet face, those eyes. Man, I want to get lost in them." Everett sighed dramatically, leaning back. "I'm really glad she liked the fleece."

"Yeah, what was with that?" Bellamy asked. "She seemed so startled that someone would give her a gift?"

"She said no one had brought her anything yet," I reminded him.

"Isn't it standard to take a small gift when meeting a potential mate?" Bellamy asked.

I nodded. "It definitely is."

"Are you fucking kidding me? Why would the Haven allow alphas to behave so poorly with her?" Bellamy snarled.

"I don't know, but something seems off about this sanctuary. From the way they contacted me to the set up of the room, to the way they didn't even give her a few days to recover before thrusting her into pack meetings. It's not right. I get they want her future settled but there's no shortage of packs seeking omegas at any of the other havens?"

"Well, we can offer her a much better home," Everett said happily.

"She needs to choose us, and I doubt she's really ready to pick or choose anyone yet," I grimaced.

Something didn't feel right, but I wasn't sure who I could go to in order to express these concerns. The Haven ran these situations, but it was the Haven that didn't seem to be treating her well.

"Did they bring up fees at all on the phone?" Alaric asked.

"They said if we register interest we'll need to pay. They also spoke a lot about financial donations, how the most generous and helpful packs always get well looked after, basically insinuating they get more time with the omega."

"That seems a touch immoral," Alaric commented. "We'll have to pay the fees no matter what though. What is it now? $500,000?"

"Nope, $750,000. Competition is higher now and they want to ensure the pack's applying are financially able to take care of the omegas."

"We knew it would be a steep price, and a few years ago we couldn't have done it, but today it's hardly a dent in our collective wallet."

"She's worth it," Everett spoke quietly, and everyone in the car grunted in agreement.

We went our separate ways for work and when we convened that night around the dinner table with our buckets of fried chicken, the conversation about Sage resumed.

"Am I insane to think we actually have a chance with Sage?" Everett asked around a mouthful of chicken.

"She did seem really happy to see us, but I don't want to get my hopes up," Bellamy said.

"Should we start making preparations? Just in case?" Everett's voice was full of hope despite what Bellamy had just said.

"Maybe not just yet," I cautioned. "She could easily take months to decide. As she said today, it's a big decision."

The rooms we could use for her were totally untouched. We'd planned to turn the space into a larger gym and a den prior to finding out about Sage.

"How do we guide her to choose us?" Everett asked.

Bellamy mused, "I thought you were meant to woo omegas with shiny gems and all things designer. Sage…"

"Is the opposite," I finished for him.

After we finished eating dinner that night Alaric and I cleared the table while the rest of the pack did their own thing, Bellamy rushing to place a supply order and Everett to do… whatever it was that Everett did.

"How are you feeling about this, Ric?" I asked, scraping chicken bones into the bin.

Alaric took the dish off me, placing it gently in the dishwasher rack. His face was twisted in a frown, his brow furrowed. "I don't want to hope," he admitted, "if by some insane twist of fate we end up with an omega, how can we ensure she's protected? Our family…"

"You haven't spoken to them in years. They won't know. You're no longer associated with the Morel family in any way. There isn't a single black mark on the Rivers' name."

"I know that, but I'm concerned. What if she came here, just to be ripped away from us? I could survive that, but could Bell and Ev? They're far more fragile."

"You're kidding yourself, Ric. You've had heart eyes for the girl since you first crashed into her four days ago." I put down the glass I was rinsing, giving Alaric an intense, all-seeing stare. "I know you've still got that shirt drenched in her scent under your pillow."

"Cal–"

"There's nothing to be ashamed of. You can want this. I know you thought it would never be possible for you, but this is good for us. Even if she doesn't pick us."

Alaric sighed. Did he really think he could hide that he still had that shirt? I was chilled, but I was observant, and the sweet honey had subtly followed him for the last few days. "What if this is our only chance?"

"Then we need to be honest with her and let her see the good in everyone here. Including you."

"She may run screaming. My family history isn't exactly ideal."

"You're not your family. Besides, she seems strong," I said. "Let's see how this plays out."

CHAPTER EIGHT
Bellamy

We made our way to the Haven early the next morning. I had already been up for hours sorting out a café delivery, but judging by the sleepy state of Everett, he had just crawled out of bed.

Callan led the way, as always. Everett and I were all smiles and Alaric was stoic as ever.

When we entered the room, Sage was crouching by the small bookcase, browsing through the few books she had. Several gift bags were dotted around the room, and there was a definite increase in throw pillows on her bed. Other packs must have gotten wise and done a little gifting. Even though I wanted us to be the only one giving her gifts, if they made her happy that was all that mattered.

Upon hearing us enter her head whipped up, a smile breaking out over her face. She was bundled up in the fleece we had given her, and it gave me a rush of satisfaction to see her enjoying it. We had provided her that comfort.

"Hi!" she chirped with a smile. "You came back!"

I was the one who replied, "Of course we came back. How have things been for you?

"Oh you know, same four walls for me." She laughed lightly.

The guys all settled into various armchairs opposite her, and it felt almost normal were it not for the three inches of glass between us. "So we didn't really get to talk much before the Keepers decided it was time for your next visitors."

Sage snorted lightly. "I would have much preferred if you guys stayed, the ones after you were buttheads."

"Well, it's your choice who visits, and you control how long they stay. We thought you had set the time limit and that's why the Keepers made us leave," Callan told her, frowning.

Wasn't she made aware of how this all worked? Callan hid it well, but I could see the tension in his shoulders. He was uncomfortable.

Sage tilted her head, confused. "The Keepers told me they were in charge of all that stuff."

Callan raised an eyebrow, shooting Everett a look that clearly said 'We're asking your mother about this later' because that didn't sound right at all. Everett looked just as confused. We could have asked the Keeper, but something about the officials here was off.

Everett's ma was always visiting Havens and working with omegas or guiding them. She often told Ev about the pretty omegas she was working with and how she wished they could meet.

"Things may have changed. We've never really been to a Haven before either so we aren't the most knowledgeable in this area. We know snippets thanks to Ev, but not much," I told her.

"Fair enough. I suppose we should discuss the really important stuff," Sage grinned. Callan tensed. We'd thought Sage was different. Was she wanting to discuss claiming, finances, gifting, and all that stuff already? Was that a good sign, or a sign she was just as focused on what she could receive? Most omegas were thorough in their acquisitions. This was one of the few times in an omegas life they could gain things for themselves.

Sage's face scrunched up. "Tacos or pizza?" she asked, her tone dead serious. "There is a right and a wrong answer, I love my food and my sweet peach tea!"

I laughed at Callans startled face. None of us had expected that.

"That's the important question?" I asked.

"What other questions are there?" Sage asked, face adorably indignant.

"Your financial situation? Housing? Bonding?" Alaric asked with a growl, it didn't deter Sage though, she sat up straighter, frown on her face.

"My financial situation?" she asked.

"How much a pack will bestow on you," Callan clarified.

"Okay, you guys are going to have to explain that one, because it sounds like you're offering to basically buy me, which is creepy. Several packs have been telling me how much money they can give me, but my financial situation is just fine, I'll have you know. I own my apartment and I have a fair amount of savings."

Callan held up his hands in a surrendering gesture. "Apologies, it's just customary for a pack to gift their omega money and other items when joining a pack. Courting gifts."

Sage snorted. "I don't need your money."

"Sage," I said softly, "you do know that omegas are only allowed a bank account if it's attached to their pack name, right? I know it's not ideal... but you do need our money, or money from whatever pack you join."

She ran her hand through her hair, sighing. She looked weary, and I didn't like that one bit. "Omegas aren't allowed anything of their own it seems. I'm not trying to be difficult, I'm sorry. All of the alphas coming to see me have money, but I'm just interested in other things."

I didn't want her to be upset, so I latched back onto her original question. "About your important question: in our house pizza reigns supreme."

Her mood lifted instantly, her whole countenance brightening.

"Okay, there is an equally important follow up question in that case. Does pineapple belong on a pizza?" she asked, cocking her head and smiling. Such simple facial expressions could have brought us to our knees, she was stunning and didn't even realise it. There was a chorus of "no!" from all but Alaric and she frowned.

"Well, that's the wrong answer. Can't you guys appreciate some salty sweets?" She pouted.

"These idiots have no taste, don't worry." Alaric gave her a wry smile.

"Ah! So Mr Grumpy likes pineapple. That's fine, he and I can share all the pineapple pizza while you idiots have... I'm going to take a guess and say something meaty?"

I choked on thin air, trying to catch my breath. "Meaty?"

"Yeah, like a meat feast." She shrugged. "Was I wrong?"

"Ignore him," Everett laughed, "his mind was in the gutter. Meat feast sounds like an omega's favourite pastime." He immediately cursed lightly to himself, too quiet for Sage to hear, but loud enough for me to catch it. Everett had a big heart and he was terrified of messing this up for us.

Instead of righteous indignation, Sage lent forward her body wracking with laughter. "Oh my god! That's so true isn't it! Oh my, meat feast! May as well call it a sausage party." She wiped her eyes. "I'm a chicken or ham and pineapple girl myself, I guess I'm letting the side down, an omega who doesn't want a sausage party!"

"You're new to it, you'll adjust." Everett smirked.

"I suppose I'll have to. So what does a normal evening look like for you guys? That's been one of my favourite questions to ask. I forgot to ask you because I got distracted by Mr Beckett and then our time was up!"

"Well, we always eat together in the evenings, even if we're working on our computers," Everett said. "Usually we order takeout or Bellamy cooks, or brings food home from one of his cafes."

"You have cafes?" She focused on me, and I was relieved that she seemed genuinely interested instead of just asking out of politeness.

"I do, it's a pet project of mine. I like coffee. Do you?"

"I don't drink it often but I'll get an iced coffee delivered on the weekend mornings when I'm working on my laptop in bed."

"What do you drink?"

"Iced white mocha with hazelnut syrup and a sweet vanilla cream."

I couldn't stop my grimace of displeasure at that. "That's sugar, not coffee."

Sage grinned. "But it's delicious sugar!"

The others chuckled at my horrified face.

"Does anyone else cook?" Sage asked, diverting the subject from coffee. "Or is that something you want your eventual omega to do?"

Callan laughed. "Not really, we order a fair amount of food because we're rubbish at cooking. Everett once set our kitchen on fire trying to make toast."

"Cheese toast. And in my defence I didn't know that you could only put bread in the toaster, I thought cheese would be fine!" Everett protested.

"Oh dear," Sage giggled.

"Do you cook?" Callan asked once their laughter had died down.

"Not really. I can when I need to, but I'm a fan of ordering out. According to the book I read most omegas take cooking classes from a young age, but that just wasn't my sort of thing and as a beta, it wasn't expected of me so much." She looked self-conscious, as if the reminder that she wasn't the perfect omega stung.

"Nothing wrong with that," I assured her.

"What will you guys be doing for the rest of the day?" Sage asked with a head tilt.

"I've got a few meetings," I admitted. "I need to pick a new supplier so they're all wooing me with chocolate samples."

"Must be nice," Sage huffed.

"It's fairly fun, even if Ev steals most of the samples!" I nudged him playfully.

"I would ask how you were going to spend your day, but as you are sort of stuck here I'll ask how you spent your evenings when you were still a beta?"

"I'm a homebody. I'm usually crocheting, watching a show in bed or reading. Nothing too exciting."

"Sounds peaceful." I could easily imagine her doing all of those things in our home. We could create little nooks for her to read, maybe create a nice built-in one to hold and organise all of the yarn we could buy her.

"I guess it is." Her gaze turned inward and she smiled softly to herself.

"Isn't crochet complex?" Everett asked. "I don't know how people find that relaxing."

"It's all down to numbers," Sage explained. "That's why I like it. Number of stitches, number of rows, rotations and such. I like numbers, they make sense."

"Do you have supplies here to crochet?" Callan asked.

"Uh, I don't at the moment. They never offered anything like that."

I watched as she looked around the room, wilting slightly. Taking the opportunity to look her over without making her feel uncomfortable, it was obvious she wasn't exactly thriving. The transition must be proving hard for her. Her face was looking hollow after only three days, and the bags under her eyes meant she wasn't sleeping nearly enough.

"Could we bring you some?" Callan offered.

"You don't have to do that," Sage insisted. "I have more supplies than I know what to do with at home, I can wait until the Keepers get my things."

"But," I interjected, "we want to bring you gifts you'll enjoy. If you want books, crochet supplies, or anything else you can tell us. It'll help pass the time."

Sage chewed her lip, and I wanted to pull it into my own mouth and soothe it with my own. "You would really do that? I don't want to put you out."

"Sage, it would honestly be no bother."

She considered for a moment, chewing on her lip.

"Maybe some books? There's a new book out in one of my favourite series and I never got my pre-order because of all this." She tucked deeper into her hoodie.

"What's it called?" Alaric asked, pulling out his phone.

Sage dithered for a second, but relented when he gave her a stern look. She told him the title and the author's name. "Done. We'll bring it with us tomorrow," he confirmed.

Her face brightened "You'll be back tomorrow?"

"Of course we will be, Pretty Girl." Everett gave her an easy grin and I knew it was a cover for his nerves. "If it's okay with you?"

"It's more than okay with me." Sage grinned.

CHAPTER NINE
Sage

That night I curled up in bed hugging the hoodie Pack Rivers had given me. It was too warm to wear it to sleep, but I wanted it close. Something about it just felt so right. Laying back on the pillows, I grabbed one of the bodice ripper romance books that had been on my sparse bookshelf and settled down to read. I loved a good romance, but I could quickly tell these books weren't for me. They were all about omegas being good little girls and doing as they are told because they should be naturally submissive to their alphas, and that's apparently how an omega shows love.

I was actively resisting the urge to throw the book across the room when my door opened, and in strode Claire, a grin on her face and a tray of food in her hands.

"How are you doing? I've got some good news!" she spoke in a chirpy voice as she placed the food tray at the end of the bed. I frowned at the plate. One tiny chicken breast with no seasoning in sight and a few pieces of broccoli and carrots. The portion was tiny, like you would give a child.

"Good news?" I asked, looking from the pathetic excuse of a meal to Claire, who was rubbing her hands in glee.

"Yes, Pack Bove have officially indicated their interest in you. You must have charmed them—well done!"

Pack Bove? That was the pack that had talked down to me, accusing me of being defective.

"Oh, uh…" I didn't know how to reply, grabbing the food and taking a small bite.

"They're a very good pack for you. I think you would suit them well. A few more meetings and you could even go home with them for a trial courting!"

The flavourless food turned sour in my mouth at the thought of going home with those pigs. "They… uh, they weren't very nice," I admitted. My understanding was that omegas were highly sought after, so surely I would have more packs registering interest soon?

Claire frowned. "Oh dear, maybe you accidentally mistook something. You aren't used to being around alphas, remember, you won't be used to how they operate. Rest assured, Pack Bove is a very good option for you. Just…may I be honest with you, Sage?"

I suspected the honesty wasn't going to be a good thing, but still I nodded. "Sure."

"I, and a few other Keepers agree, that you shouldn't really be talking about your job. It's offending the alphas. It insinuates they aren't enough for you. Now I know it's what you're used to, but you're an omega now and you need to start behaving like an omega. The last thing I want is for you to be matched with an inappropriate pack because of something small like this."

"Why would I match with an inappropriate pack?"

"Suppressants will only last so long and eventually you will need a pack to survive. If you've scared off all the good packs by behaving like a beta you may be left with very few options, and between you and I, inappropriate packs can lead to terrible situations. Omegas have been abused in those situations—we don't want that for you."

I certainly didn't want that, but I couldn't shake the feeling that Pack Bove wasn't a good pack either. They had been the rudest of all those I had seen over the last two days. Would alphas really be so offended by me talking about my work?

"What else can I talk about, though?" I asked. "My work is my life."

"Hobbies, the family you want, etc. Those sorts of things will make a pack far happier."

"I'll...I'll try. Can I possibly get some more food?"

"Lovely. I'll bring some fruit, but we can't give you more than that, these portions are for your own good. No one wants a chubby omega!" Claire laughed, turning and waltzing out of the room before I could call after her.

My sleep schedule was fucked. There was no natural light in my room and as a result I didn't get any sunlight to tell me when I should be sleeping. I had a clock, but the visits had set me off kilter.

After tossing and turning I had just managed to fall into a fitful sleep when the sound of the door crashing open made me jump up, blearily looking around. Someone had entered the viewing room, and as they entered all the lights had turned on. Not to full brightness thankfully, but enough for it to startle me awake and hurt my eyes. Sitting up, I rubbed my eyes, looking around to check the time, and groaning when I saw that it was five in the morning.

Through the viewing glass stood Pack Bove. Lex standing at the front, a leering grin on his face.

"Hello, omega." Nothing about his greeting or expression was friendly.

"It's early." I frowned. I was trying my best not to be rude, but I was sleep deprived and disoriented.

"We wanted to see you, and we haven't gone to sleep yet." Lex shrugged.

"We got you something!" Dean, I think it was, stated, slurring his words.

"Have you been drinking?" I asked. It was pretty obvious they had been. They all looked a little unsteady on their feet, other than Lex.

"Nothing wrong with a few drinks. You'll learn soon enough that alphas like a few drinks in the evening," Mitch said, lounging on one of the armchairs, kicking his feet up like he owned the place. "Your gift is in the hatch." He nodded in that direction while Lex came and joined him in sitting. His gaze was downright predatory.

Cautiously, I slid out of bed. I didn't miss their sneer at seeing I was still in my skirt and camisole.

"We thought you could do with something else to wear." One of the others, Peter, chuckled.

Dread crept up my spine. I wasn't happy about my lack of clean clothing either, but I didn't dare bathe with the revolving door of alphas giving me zero privacy. Keeping my eyes on the pack, I made my way over to the hatch, pulling out the fancy looking black box. Mumbling a thank you to be polite I opened it and stilled when I saw the contents.

I was by no means a prude, and I liked dressing up and feeling pretty in fancy things, but the scraps of fabric in the box I was holding could only be described as tacky: a bright red, almost latex-looking lingerie set that was so small it likely wouldn't even cover my nipples.

"Uh...I..." I didn't know what to say, I just looked in the box, my brain working a mile a minute. What could I say? No thank you? That would only piss them off.

"Put it on," Mitch told me. "We want to see."

"I'm sorry, I—I'm not comfortable doing that." I shook my head, pushing away from the box. Revulsion shook me to my core. I wanted them gone. I wanted to be alone, but I knew being polite was my best move. If I got aggressive or demanding, they would get pissed at me and refuse to leave.

Lex's grin dropped, and fury took its place. "It's an expensive piece," he said, like that would make me immediately put it on. "We want to see it on."

"As I said I'm not comfortable with that." I backed up a few paces, instincts on high alert around an angry alpha.

"Fucking ungrateful omega," Mitch growled. "Put the fucking thing on! You're a mess. You should be thankful we want to see you in it."

"No. I think you should leave." I did my best to keep my voice calm despite how hard my heart was beating against my ribcage.

"No. We paid to see you, and we will fucking see you," Lex snarled and hammered his fist on the glass.

"You've clearly been drinking and this isn't appropriate." I backed up further, putting the bed between myself and the window and setting the box on the end of my bed, not wanting to throw it in front of them. I considered shouting out for the guards but I wasn't sure how these temperamental alphas were going to react, or possibly spin this, so I was, once again, the new omega overreacting.

"The bitch isn't going to show us anything, Lex. We need to talk to that Keeper, tell her to keep her in line," one of them grumbled, but I didn't see who.

"We'll be back tomorrow," Lex snapped. "Maybe your attitude will have improved once you've been reprimanded. We are going to talk to the Keepers about your disgusting behaviour!"

Was I going to get into trouble for this? For refusing to parade myself in lingerie for men I didn't like or feel safe around? Frankly, I didn't care, any repercussions would be better than wearing that in front of Pack Bove. I would rather stub my toe every day for the rest of my life than do that.

CHAPTER TEN
Bellamy

All of us had taken time off to visit Sage, and after our second visit we were all buzzing with excitement. We had opted to visit early, it wasn't even eight in the morning, but when Callan had called ahead the Keeper had assured him that Sage was awake and seeing alphas, which I found hard to believe was her choice because she looked exhausted when we'd last seen her.

"Fuck me. When does she sleep?" I had asked with a frown when Callan told us we could go early.

"Does she know she can turn packs away?" Everett asked. "Has she been told that?"

"I don't know," Callan admitted. "Maybe we should reach out to one of the bigger Havens with our concerns about her care?"

"That might cut off our access to Sage," Everett pointed out. "They might start digging into us."

This time we bought some fancy chocolates and a giant

cuddly body pillow. Callan had looked at the pillow mildly horrified when Everett brought it home the previous day, the thing was giant, almost bigger than Everett himself. Between those monstrosities and the entire bag of books Alaric had bought we were coming off a little eager, but I didn't mind laying my cards out for Sage.

"You'd better get used to it," Everett said with a laugh. "Ma insists that if Sage chooses us the whole place will end up filled with soft and squishy things. She also said a heated blanket would be good, at least until she chooses us."

"Only until she chooses?" Callan asked.

"Oh yeah, the pack will ultimately be her favourite heat source, but until she has one, in that room it can apparently be comforting."

I looked between the two of them. "Order one today then, we want her to be as comfy as possible."

"I'll do it." Callan grabbed his phone. "Bellamy, you drive. I'll find one and order it."

Alaric was already leaning on his BMW in the parking lot when we pulled up with a bag of books in hand from his early morning detour to the bookstore.

"Guess who I saw storm out of here just now?" Everything about Ric was tense. "Who?" I asked.

"Lex Bove and his minions, he seemed pretty pissed as well, and possibly drunk."

"The fuck? The drug trafficker Lex Bove?"

"Human trafficker as well from what I've heard," Alaric replied.

"What the hell?" I snapped. "Why would he be anywhere near Sage? How can the Haven allow it?"

"How the fuck did his pack get approval to court an omega?" Callan asked, eyebrows raised. "They'd have seen his records if they'd taken more than a minute to look into that pack."

"I don't know, but something is off," Alaric snarled. "We've been saying it all along. Sage mentioned that some packs were dicks to her, and they weren't immediately shown the door. Let's just go see our girl."

We all raised our eyebrows at Alaric using that term of endearment for the omega but not one of us dared say anything.

Sage was angrily pacing her room when we entered. Her frustration was palpable, and she was hugging herself, eyes snapping toward us when the door swung open.

"Hey, Pretty Girl," Everett spoke softly to announce our presence.

Sage jumped at the sound, her hand coming up to her chest. "Oh! You scared me."

"What's wrong?" Alaric set down his bag of books and moved to stand at the glass.

"Ah, I'm sorry. I just had a real ass in here, I guess I'm still a little off." She laughed shakily, running a hand through her hair, wincing when her fingers got caught in the tangles. She was still wearing the hoodie we had gifted her, and though I would never admit it, her hair was looking a little dirty, the honey blonde ever so slightly darker, like she hadn't even had a chance to wash.

"I'm sorry, what happened?" I asked, keeping my voice soft, not wanting to agitate her. If Lex and his pack had just been here, whatever they'd said or done couldn't have been good.

Sage sighed. "Don't worry, I'll get over it. Hopefully they'll stop visiting at some point because I can't stand the rude ones."

"Rude?" Callan asked.

"They gave me a gift and got angry when I wasn't excited or wanted to try it on." She bit her lip.

"What did they give you?" Alaric asked. His fists clenched at his side, his knuckles turning white. "You don't have to accept anything you don't want to."

"Uhhh... clothing of a revealing nature... Can we just forget about it? How did your lunch go with your friends?" Sage asked, trying to change the subject by turning from Alaric to me.

I was surprised that she remembered the meeting I had mentioned briefly the previous day. That wasn't going to stop me from remembering what she just said about the gift she received. Glancing around her room I could see the bundled up lingerie box thrown in a corner.

They fucking gifted her lingerie and expected her to wear it? What sort of shit show was the Haven running here? I tempered my rage, Sage had just asked me a question and I didn't want her to see my anger.

"It went really well."

"Is this a bad time to say we bought gifts?" Everett held up the pillow he'd selected and motioned for Alaric to pick up the bag he'd been carrying with a bookstore logo on it.

"You remembered?" Sage asked in quiet shock.

Had she thought we'd forget so easily?

"Of course we did. Here." Alaric took the books over to the hatch.

Sage's face grew even more shocked as she looked through the pile, finding not only the book she'd asked for, but several more Ric had picked for her as well.

"Thank you so much! These are lovely." She clutched one of the books to her chest and focused on Alaric. "I'm sorry for being so grumpy, you have been so sweet."

"You're handling this better than any of us would," Callan told her. "No need to apologise to us."

Sage shivered and sniffled as she hugged the book in her arms. "I still haven't really accepted that my future is going to be nothing like the one I had planned. I keep thinking I'll be going home at some point, or back to the office, but I doubt I'll ever be allowed back there."

"What was your plan?" Callan asked.

"I wanted to run a department by the time I turned twenty-six. If I got tired of that I was going to start my own business. At some point I'd have married a nice normal guy and maybe once my business was self-sufficient I'd have a few babies."

"Run a department? What did you do exactly at Norden? You only touched on it last time but what exactly were your duties?"

She frowned. "I've been told I'm not really supposed to talk about my life before anymore, especially my work. The Keepers think it'll make this whole transition easier."

"Nothing wrong with letting us know your job, it says a lot about a person. We knew you were somehow involved with the finances, were you an assistant accountant?" I asked, given her age she couldn't have been long out of university. Sage frowned.

"An assistant? Bellamy, I ran a sub-department and I specialise in forensic accounting. I've seen all the numbers involved in your deal with Norden. Which is how I know you could have negotiated better terms." She glared at me, but there wasn't much heat in it. "I spend most of my days combing through accounts picking up all the little details, I assure you I am a lot more than an assistant."

Crap, had I offended her by misjudging just how impressive she was? I didn't want to put my foot in my mouth and ruin this for my whole pack.

Callan couldn't help but grin at the omega's little glare at me, and I made sure to look thoroughly chastened. She was smart, smarter than she let on.

"Ha! Alaric, you hear that?" Everett nudged him in the ribs. "Sage is exactly what you need. He's been trying to make heads or tails of a company's finances for weeks and is suffering."

"Really, how come?" Sage cocked her head again.

"I can't make the numbers add up," Alaric admitted. "Something isn't right, and I can't figure out what."

"Didn't your accountant find anything wrong?"

"No, which is odd."

"I could double check them," she offered, then looked surprised, like she was remembering she shouldn't be offering. "I mean, I'm sorry. I shouldn't overstep, uh, ignore me."

"Sage, you just finished telling us this is exactly what you specialise in. You're not overstepping when you know I need help. Here." He opened the documents on his tablet and set it into the gift station so she could access it. "Take a look for yourself."

"Really?!" Sage's entire demeanour perked up, her eyes widening and a grin spreading across her face.

Alaric nodded, and she needed no further encouragement, hopping up and practically running to the hatch.

"Most women wouldn't be so happy about being given work." Callan quirked an eyebrow at her.

"I've been bored out of my mind here. Getting to actually work with some numbers is amazing!" She was vibrating with anticipation waiting for the hatch to unseal, and she almost ripped the door off its hinges in her excitement to get the tablet. Padding back to her chair, she swiped on the tablet, grabbing the attached stylus with a small noise of happiness.

She was entirely too cute.

"Oh wow, this is messy," she muttered, scrolling through the spreadsheets.

"Tell me something I don't know." Alaric sat down in the chair nearest to where she was on the other side of the glass. She bit her bottom lip when concentrating, and regularly ran her hand through her hair, lost in her own world.

"Whose company is this?" she asked after a moment, looking up at Alaric. She pulled her lip between her teeth, shrinking back ever so slightly as she spoke like she was... nervous?

"One of ours," Callan explained. "Don't worry if you can't figure it out though."

"Oh, I can figure it out. I think I know why it's not adding up, I just need a bit more time to be sure."

"It only took you twenty minutes?" Callan asked, eyebrows raised in surprise.

"I think some of these transactions aren't completely legit."

"That could just be us?" Callan asked with a frown, "We all use these accounts."

"No, it's not any of you guys," Sage swallowed. "I can clearly see your spending, and which accounts you four use. Including...uh one account called 'EvThePussyDestroyer.'" She blushed. "It's kind of obvious whose account is whose."

"I think I better change my username." Everett grinned sheepishly. I was thankful I didn't decide on a lewd username like Ev, I had been considering one.

"Uh, here." She started tapping away on the screen. "I'm highlighting a few transactions and leaving a few notes—give this to a forensic accountant and they should be able to figure out the situation and give you a full report."

"Our finance guys couldn't make heads or tails of this, claiming it all looked right even though we are missing a lot of money. It's why they pawned this shit off on me," Alaric groused.

"Are you sure your finance guys are loyal? Maybe a third-party accountant would be better." Alaric nodded as Sage padded to the hatch, going to open it but frowned when it wouldn't budge.

"You can keep the tablet if you want, if you want to keep looking."

"That would be great, are you sure you don't mind? Half an hour ago you thought I was a mere assistant and you're gonna let me rummage through your dirty laundry?"

"We've got nothing to hide." I shrugged. "If you can figure it out, we would be daft not to let you."

"You don't have to though," Callan said firmly. "You should be resting, not stressing yourself out."

"The only thing that will stress me out is seeing this puzzle and not being able to solve it," Sage laughed.

"I can access all the documents I need on there via the cloud. Keep it as long as you like. There's even a streaming catalogue you can watch," Alaric said.

"Wait, could I watch streams on this thing?" Sage asked, eyes lighting up.

"Go for it. It's got so much downloaded because it has a spotty internet connection."

"This is amazing, thank you, Alaric."

His name out of her sweet mouth made my packmate puff out his chest ever so slightly in pride, we could see it even though he tried to hide his reaction by quickly shifting in his seat. "Grumpy, you are officially my favourite, you like pineapple on pizza and have provided me with entertainment and books! Pretty brilliant, I must say."

"Seriously?!" Everett exclaimed, glancing between the pair, startled. "Hell must have frozen over," he muttered, leaning back in his chair with a pout.

"Ev's used to being the favourite, pay him no mind." I laughed.

Sage looked tired, the dark circles under her eyes were becoming more pronounced every time we visited. Maybe next time I could bring her some coffee from the shop—she liked the sugary stuff that would rot your teeth, but I couldn't judge her for that. If it made her direct that smile my way, I would give her the most disgusting syrupy coffee I could make.

Sage scrolled through the tablet, her eyes never leaving the screen. "You know I am going to judge you on your TV choices, right?"

Alaric smiled indulgently at her. "Go ahead, Sweet Girl."

She flashed him a smile before turning back to the tablet.

After a moment she looked up sheepishly. "Sorry, I'm being rude, aren't I? I'm paying more attention to the tablet than to you guys."

"You're excited, it's understandable. I would be bored to tears in your situation." Everett replied.

"Oh really?" She put the tablet down on a little table and sat right in front of the glass. "I get the impression that any guy would love to be in my situation, having tons of beautiful ladies vying for your attention?"

Everett pursed his lips. "I suppose. To be fair most omegas love it as well."

"Well, I'm an oddball then, because this is stressful."

"You shouldn't be stressed," Callan spoke.

"My entire life has changed and now I've got a limited amount of time to make a decision that is going to impact the trajectory of my life in a huge way, and I don't even have all the information I need to make that decision."

"Well, when you put it like that," Callan agreed.

"I can help with the information," Alaric said, pointing to the tablet. "I wanted to do my research before we accepted the invite to meet you, so I downloaded a bunch of books about omegas and how this whole process works. They're all under the ebook app. Read as many as you'd like."

"That's so sweet, thank you. Why are you guys so damn nice? I'm waiting for the catch. Is there a corpse in the basement? Foot fetish?" Her eyes narrowed as she glared at us, but there was no real fire in her gaze.

"We have flaws, but you'll have to decide if they're catches," Callan said. "Alaric is an ass who likes control, Everett is an overgrown child who forgets he's in a grown man's body and spends the majority of his time napping and Bellamy can't clean a dish to save his life despite being the cook of the pack."

"I clean occasionally," I groused. "Besides, I shouldn't have to wash dishes and be the cook."

"Anything else I should know?" Sage asked with a smile. "Because none of that sounds that bad. Gambling addictions? Oh! Maybe some skeletons in the closet?"

"It's only the third meeting, Pretty Girl. We can't divulge all our secrets yet." Everett had taken to calling her Pretty Girl I noticed.

"Well, I guess you just have to keep coming back. That is... if you guys want to." She sounded uncertain. How didn't she realise that they were already hooked on her?

"We want to," Callan confirmed. "We would stay longer today but we have a board meeting in a few hours."

"That sounds mind numbingly boring."

"It is, but an unfortunate part of the job."

"I used to have to sit in on some. They felt like a waste of time, and I got so sick of it I hired someone else to go take notes for me." Sage's nose scrunched.

"I need to do that," Callan pondered. "You're smarter than I am."

"Don't you forget it." She laughed, and I was relieved that she seemed so relaxed and at ease with us.

Was that a promising sign?

CHAPTER ELEVEN
Sage

It was past two pm. Pack Rivers was meant to be here at ten. They hadn't shown up. I checked the clock for the dozenth time. Had they decided they didn't want to come? Were they tired of me? Had I come on too strong? The thought made my stomach turn violently.

Claire brought me lunch: steamed veggies and salmon. It looked delicious, but all I wanted to do was drown my feelings in a tub of ice cream.

"Can I possibly get a little more to eat? Maybe a carb? I'm actually quite hungry," I asked when Claire handed me my plate.

"Oh, this is plenty. All omegas meals are planned by a nutritionist. We've gotta keep our omegas healthy and looking their best!" she informed me with a bright smile. I seethed quietly at the woman's words, if I wanted a potato I could have a damn potato. Instead of yelling though, I merely shut up and took the salmon.

"Also, you should really take a bath and get changed soon, you're getting dirty and disgusting. That gift is nice, and I'm sure you like it but it really hides what you've got from the potential packs. A big part of this process is them seeing you, and you don't want to make that difficult for them."

"I'm not a bit of meat on display."

Claire sighed. "In many ways you are, Sage. But the sooner you agree to match with a pack the sooner it'll be over. In fact, one pack has already put a bid on you!"

I sat up straighter. "Which pack?"

"The Bove Pack. They immediately registered interest. It looks like they took a shine to you! They're a good pack, financially stable and powerful. They would be a good choice."

"I think I'll wait to make any decisions. It didn't seem like they were too fond of me when they were here," I replied. I kept quiet about how they had given me the creeps, spoken inappropriately to me, and had gifted me scraps of fabric that could hardly be considered lingerie.

"Of course, I'm sure they'll come see you again tomorrow, but rest assured, they clearly like you— otherwise, why would they register interest?"

After a failed attempt at a nap where I stayed in my pencil skirt and camisole with the fleece hoodie on top, I accepted I was awake for the day. I was refusing to get in the bath without the promise of privacy and Claire wouldn't give me that. Alongside the camera and the viewing window, Claire's gentle encouragement had only further served to put me off that endeavour. I despised feeling like I was under a microscope. I was tired and crabby the next morning when Lex and his pack appeared at my window when I was trying to rest. I pretended to sleep to see if they would leave me in peace, but instead they stayed and spoke amongst themselves.

"What is that ugly thing she's wearing? The least she could do if she's going to be a lazy bitch is wear what we got her."

"We came all the way here to see this princess. The least she can do is wake up."

"Or give us a view worth looking at."

I opened my eyes, rolling over and sitting up. It was a lot less pleasant than waking up to find Alaric and his pack there.

"Hello again," I kept my voice kind and polite, even though I wanted nothing more than to pelt a high heel at their smug face.

"What the fuck are you wearing?" Mitch barked at me.

"It was a gift. It's comfortable and I like it."

"What sort of bitch of an alpha gave you that? Why would they have you covering up? That's not fair, why would they allow that? We should get a chance to see the goods! We fucking got you a gift and you choose not to wear it."

"See the goods? I'm a human being, not a piece of livestock," I snapped, clutching the hoodie to my chest further.

"No, that's exactly what you are. We've paid $750,000 just so we can see you. Why would you behave so poorly? You're so fucking filthy you won't even change. What was the fucking point in getting those fucking cameras if you won't show off?" Mitch snarled.

I blinked. Okay, that was a lot of money. I knew the fees were steep, but not that steep—and what did he mean about the cameras? Was Claire letting alphas watch me through them? The thought made my stomach turn.

"That's a lot, I'll admit, but it still doesn't give you the right to see what I'm not comfortable with." I wouldn't have been so bold were it not for the shatterproof glass between us. Lex stilled, giving me an eerie stare.

"We are the only pack who's registered interest in you. You should be a little more thankful."

"I'd like you to leave now," I whispered loud enough for them to hear.

"Jesus fucking Christ!" Lex snapped, walking right up to the glass and making me jump. "We are the only pack you have to choose from. You're already bought and paid for. Eventually you'll have to accept us. When you do, I'll see to it you're punished for all the bullshit you've been pulling. I think we'd better leave you to think for a while. If you have any sense, you'll have changed your tune when we come back." Lex stormed out of the room, anger radiating off him. His pack all followed, giving me equally pissed off looks.

The moment the door closed behind them I collapsed to my knees, shaking violently despite the thick glass. The sheer strength of the alpha's anger chilled me to the bone. Tears spilled over my face. I already knew I would rather stay in this room for the rest of my life than choose them willingly, but I was starting to worry I wouldn't be given that option.

CHAPTER TWELVE
Alaric

I felt like murdering someone. A pile up of issues had meant we had no choice but to move seeing Sage to much later in the day. She would have been expecting us in the morning. Callan had messaged Keeper Claire, asking her to inform Sage that we were stuck, but we hadn't received an answer.

When we finally arrived at the Haven that evening, all of us in varied forms of hurried messes, we said nothing, heading straight to see Sage.

The security guard waved us in immediately, and we didn't see any staff while entering, but we did see one in Sage's room. A redheaded woman was standing angrily in front of Sage who was hugging herself, tears running down her face. My heart started beating erratically at the sight. My omega was distressed. I wanted to fix it. I needed to fix it.

"I won't do it." Sage sobbed, running a hand across her cheek to wipe away tears, the sound stabbing me, and undoubtedly my packmates, right in the chest. An omega's cry was particularly potent to an alpha, it clawed at their insides, demanding that it be rectified.

"You're an omega. You should listen to them. If they want to watch you bathe, then that's their right. You're making yourself seem like a slob wearing the same clothes you came in and that shapeless disgusting thing."

Callan stilled at those words, making a quick gesture telling us to be quiet as well and listen in. I nodded silently. I wanted to see what Claire was saying. The women hadn't noticed our arrival, and I knew we were likely to find out more by not declaring our presence.

"I hate being watched constantly. I thought those cameras were only for security, but you give the packs access to them? Lex made it clear he could watch me whenever he wanted to. I don't know much, but I know that's against the norm. I read it in the ebooks I was given."

She was being watched? We didn't know much of the process, but we knew that was wrong. There was no way in hell an omega would be okay with being watched day and night by a pack unless it was their pack.

Claire sighed. "He shouldn't have told you that, but yes. Lex and his pack have been very generous to this Haven. We let them see the video feeds so they can get to know you better. You're still so rough around the edges. Now, where on earth did you read about Haven norms? We provided all your reading material."

"It was gifted to me." Sage sniffed.

"You shouldn't have other materials like that," Claire tutted. "I'll be taking that tablet."

"No!"

"Pack Bove are the only pack interested in you. Remember,

you're not exactly a prize here. The least you can do is help yourself settle down!"

"Yes! I get it. I'm rude for not wanting to wear disgusting lingerie because a dickhead of an alpha bestowed it upon me. I need time to make any decisions!" I could hear her voice crack.

"Time isn't a luxury you have."

"You keep saying they're the only ones who bid on me, yet other packs have clearly told me they're interested," Sage sniffled.

"We are here to guide you," Claire insisted. "Pack Bove are good for you. Their gifts are because they find you attractive. Would it really hurt to let them see you try something on?"

Sage scoffed.

"They're one of the better packs, Sage. If you don't behave, you'll end up with a much more brutal and cruel pack. God knows how those packs would treat you. Pack Rivers didn't even bother to turn up to see you today!" Claire snarled and Sage shrunk away from her with a glare. "You're out of options."

"What the fuck is going on here?" My voice was low and powerful, full of the alpha authority I usually contained, and even through the barrier the two women jumped, eyes widening.

"Alpha!" Claire quickly recovered and spoke in her happily fake voice, running a hand over her hair, making sure she looked put together. "Apologies, we are just resolving a few issues. Give us a moment and Sage here will be happy to receive you."

I looked over at Sage. She looked like she'd lost more weight since our last visit and she was trembling, her body still cloaked in the fleece we'd gifted her, her eyes red and puffy. I hated it.

"No," I snapped. "Let her speak. Why is she upset?"

"It's just the way this process goes, Alpha," Claire stuttered.

"Sage," Callan spoke softly, "talk to us. What's going on?"

Tears leaked out of the corner of Sage's eyes. "She...she's been trying to make me take a bath in front of a pack who have been mean. She's given them access to the security cameras. I don't like it."

A chorus of growls from us made her jump, but Callan shook his head. "We're not mad at you," he quickly assured her. "You've got access to a private bathroom, yes?"

"Alpha, this isn't appropriate," Claire spoke in her sickly-sweet voice, looking at Callan with an innocent expression that was clearly bullshit.

"I'm asking the questions," Callan snarled, before turning to Sage and speaking with a softer voice. "Do you?"

"...No." Her voice was so quiet we could barely hear her. "I can only bathe where others can see me. It's all she's allowing me. I can't leave the room."

"The fuck?" Bellamy glared at Claire.

"Has Sage been made aware we registered interest?" Callan asked. Sage's head whipped round to him, the surprise on her face evident. The bitch hadn't told her, and she looked surprised that we would register with her?

"Sage's case is unique. You knew this when we invited you to visit."

"No, it fucking isn't," Everett muttered pulling out his phone. "I've got to make a call. I'll be right back."

CHAPTER THIRTEEN
Everett

Storming out of the Haven, I dialled the familiar contact, pacing around the parking lot. My mother answered on the first ring, her soothing voice happy and warm. "Everett! How can I help you my dear? Oh, your dads just—"

Normally, I would let her chatter on, but this was time sensitive.

"Sorry Ma, it's a little urgent. It's about your experience in the Haven."

"Oh my! Are you actually seeing an omega? I know you discussed maybe doing it, with the gifts and such but—"

"We started seeing an omega, yes." I ignored my mother's excited squeal, "But I think something is wrong, Ma. Were the Keepers able to revoke your privacy, your access to private bathrooms and such?"

"Of course not, why do you ask? Oh, did you get her some comfort items? Your dads got me that giant ratty pillow we keep on the bed, I still have it nearly thirty years later."

"Mom, focus. We gave her the gift you suggested, but more importantly, it seems this Haven put a bath in the omega's room, won't let her out and the door is always open to alphas so she has zero privacy to wash. She's also being spied on from the cameras—apparently they've given access to some packs and they can watch her at all times."

There was a moment of silence while my mother processed that information. "Oh fuck, that isn't right!" Ma's voice was thunderous.

I opened and closed my mouth a few times, trying to find words. I had never, in twenty-four years, heard my mother cuss. She continued, ignoring my stuttering shock.

"Everett, listen to me. Every omega is entitled to her privacy, sleep and solitude. She doesn't even have to receive alphas if she doesn't want to! Omegas are taught this long before they start meetings. Why is she being treated like that? And more importantly why is she putting up with it? Doesn't she know her rights?"

"She was a beta and she presented late. I think she has no clue what her rights are and the Haven seems to be taking advantage of that. She's terrified and doesn't know where she stands."

"Okay, that's unacceptable. Tell me where you are. I'm going to make some calls because no Haven should be allowing that."

I gave my mother all the details, and I could hear her scribbling away as she jotted down the details.

"Leave it with me, I'll ring back soon, Evvy." She hung up before I could even say goodbye. Confident she would have it in hand, I turned back to the Haven. I wanted my eyes back on my omega.

. . .

I strode back into the room where Alaric's fury was palpable, I bet the small omega could feel it through the glass, and even though it wasn't directed at her, it still made her tremble all the same. Alaric looked livid. She took a step back.

"No," he growled, and Sage froze. "I'm not pissed at you, I'm pissed at her." He jerked his head in the direction of Claire who was still smiling overly wide at him.

"Now alpha—"

"Shut the fuck up. I know whatever is going on here is wrong. This is what's going to happen. First, you're going to give Sage some fucking privacy to bathe and get comfortable without you breathing down her neck."

"Second, I'm going to follow you to the control room and ensure every single camera in this room is turned off," Callan thundered next to him. "Don't you dare say anything about security, because clearly, you've not been using the cameras for their intended purpose."

"Alpha, you know I can't allow—"

"If you don't allow this, we will be making several calls. Firstly, to the Clearmont Haven to triple check all your procedures. Do you want that? What do you think will happen if you're found to be abusing an omega?"

"You can't get us shut down. Sage would be left unprotected," Claire threatened, her voice turning to ice.

"She would be transferred to Clearmont, a proper, legitimate sanctuary, and I'm pretty sure you would be prosecuted." Callan shrugged. His intent stare was a stark difference to his relaxed posture.

"We are a proper sanctuary. Don't be insolent!" Claire sniped.

"Then get the fuck out this room and let Sage shower and

rest in peace. When did you last sleep?" Alaric turned to Sage as he asked the last question and she looked deep in thought.

"There's been alphas here all through the night. I'm not allowed to sleep when they're here," she replied in a hushed voice.

Alaric turned to Claire. "You've been purposely depriving an omega of sleep?" His voice was impossibly deep, all his alpha strength behind it.

Submit.

That tone of voice demanded it.

Claire paled. "I guess...I guess we can make this work," she stuttered. "But only because the omega clearly needs rest. I'll escort her to one of the private showers."

I doubt Sage wanted to go anywhere with Claire right now. With the way the Keeper was snarling at people, I wouldn't have been surprised if she shanked Sage on the way to the shower.

"No, we will escort her, we clearly can't trust you."

"No way. Alphas can't step foot past security for the omega's protection."

"I guess it's a good thing another omega will be here in a moment," I said casually from where I was observing in the back of the room. "My mother, Claudia Thorn, is on her way. She'll be twenty minutes. You know you can't stop another omega from entering."

Claire opened and closed her mouth a few times before making an indignant huff and glaring at me. "You just love to cause issues, don't you?"

Before she could even reply, Callan's growl shook the room. Claire jumped in fright as Sage's knees buckled, and she sank to the ground as if some invisible force was shoving her down, glueing her to the ground.

Alaric cursed softly.

Callan was the one who spoke up. "Get the fuck out. Now." He directed his anger at Claire, who fled with wide eyes. After a moment, Callan took a deep breath, ensuring his voice was calmer before he addressed Sage where she still sat on the floor. "Sage, I'm so sorry. I didn't mean to bark."

"It... it's okay," she stuttered, staring at the floor, utterly confused. I doubt she had heard an alpha command before.

"It's not. I needed her gone, but I hate that it hit you as well. Can you get up for us?" Callan spoke softly, soothing her, and she did just that, only making it half-way up before sheer exhaustion took over and she sank to the floor again.

"Someone else is coming?" she asked, unable to keep her voice from wobbling.

"My ma," I confirmed. "I told her what was going on. She's gonna come and make sure you can shower and change in peace because we can't go past the doors."

CHAPTER FOURTEEN
Sage

"I'm sorry you've been treated like this." Alaric knelt so he was eye level with where I was still on the floor.

I could move, but it felt like a monumental task, and I was so exhausted. "Talk me through everything that's happened here."

"I was told this was normal?" I whispered, looking around the room slowly. Nothing had felt right since I presented, but I trusted the Haven because that was where all omegas came from.

"It's not. I researched a lot before we decided to register interest in you, and Ev's mother is an omega, so she told us a little over the years about this process. This isn't how it's meant to be."

"Claire told me no other packs had registered interest in me. I'm confused. You didn't turn up today." I looked to Alaric for answers.

"There were some issues," he explained. "We sent a message

to the Haven to say we would have to come later tonight, but I'm guessing Claire didn't pass it on."

"No, she didn't."

"You seemed surprised when we mentioned that we'd registered interest, though. I thought we'd been clear by now that we liked you. You're stunning, sweet, and kind-natured, how could we not register interest?"

"I was told that Lex was the only one to register interest, that I should just go with his pack despite how they treated me." I shook my head.

"We registered interest straight after our first meeting," Alaric said with a smile. "We knew you were special right away."

"Thank you," I whispered, and turned to Everett. "This seems like a lot just so I can wash and sleep, are you sure your mother is okay coming here?"

"She's more than happy to—in fact I don't think I could stop her even if I wanted to. This place has something wrong with it."

"Why do you think it's like this?"

"If I had to guess I would say money. Sounds like Lex and his pack have been bribing the Haven. You're not as closely monitored as other omegas by the right people. Others are watched from the moment they present by several official bodies to protect them. They ensure only suitable packs meet with the omega when it's their choosing time."

"What does suitable mean in this case?"

"Money, usually," Alaric explained. "They need to know the omegas will be secure outside of the Havens. That's why the fees are steep to join a Haven. The pack must also be in good standing. Usually, if there's a whisper of scandal or inappropriate behaviour a pack wouldn't be considered."

"Lex's didn't exactly act like a pack with a good reputation," I mused.

"They aren't. We were shocked when we saw them here. They shouldn't have let them within a mile of you. They've got the cash, but they can't be trusted with an omega."

"You make me sound like a pet," I grumbled.

"Not at all!" Everett declared loudly.

"Quiet, pup," Alaric grumbled, before turning to look at me. "Sage, it isn't like that at all. I know you're new to this. Having an omega as part of your pack is a privilege, but unfortunately some would abuse that privilege. A pack needs to have decent people who will actually protect their omega, not simply use them. You wouldn't be a pet, in our home you would be our equal, fuck what people in public think."

"Use them?"

"Selfish alphas have used omegas for their own needs and to reproduce. it was a bad situation and omegas not only suffered but their birth rates declined because of their emotional distress. Omegas should be cared for. They're the heart of the pack." Everett snorted. "In my family my mother rules supreme. I don't think my fathers have ever told her no."

"But she can't work, or have her own life outside the pack, can she?"

"Honestly, I don't think she wants to. If she wanted to do a part time job though, the dads would bend over backwards to help her."

"They would actually let her work?"

"Of course, I know most omegas don't but that's because they were raised to be home makers in many ways. My mother busies herself with projects constantly. Once an omega is claimed, they're a lot safer and can live a much more normal life. Ever since my brothers and I reached adulthood she's been making and selling jewellery online to fill her time. They would also help her with the legalities of it all, because technically omegas can't work."

"Claimed? What do you mean by that, once an omega selects a pack?"

"No." Everett scratched the back of his head, not looking me in the eye. "It's something else, I mean—I guess..."

Alaric cut him off, getting straight to the point. "When omegas and alphas have sex they get an overwhelming urge to bite one another. It's a claiming mark and it slightly changes the scent of the omega, linking them permanently to their pack."

Sage stilled. "Oh."

"Yeah." Alaric laughed wryly. "They've really taught you nothing, have they?"

"Within an hour of waking up I was thrown into this room and told to start meeting packs. They didn't really provide me with an education. Biting? That sounds painful."

"Claiming like that only happens after a pack has been connected for a while."

"So can a—" I was cut off when the door into my room opened. A middle-aged woman with a brown, grey-streaked bob stood in the doorway, two large bags in hand. She beamed at the sight of me.

"Oh hello! You must be Sage!"

"Hi Ma." Everett smiled with a cute little wave. "Sage, this is my mother, Claudia."

She bustled into the room, dropping the bags off and pulling out a few items. "I have a few things for you dear, some comfy clothes and a heated blanket. I came as soon as my boy called me and let me know of your situation. I can't believe they're treating you like this. A bath in the middle of your bedroom? Downright creepy! Now, I have some spare clothes, so I think the first order of business is a shower. They have private shower rooms, so let's go get you in one of those."

"Thank you."

"Have you eaten yet?" she asked as I took a deep breath. Something about Claudia and her sweet cinnamon scent was so relaxing. I didn't feel on edge with her like I did with Claire.

"No, they've only been giving me two meals a day."

"Have you requested more food?" Claudia's eyes narrowed.

"I did, but they made it clear I didn't need any." Alaric's responding growl made me jump slightly, reminding her of his presence.

"Ignore the grumpy boy. He's just mad at this whole situation, dear. Well, not feeding you is a load of rubbish. Alaric, be a dear and order some food while I take Sage for a shower."

"Of course, Mrs Thorn," Alaric replied with a nod, pulling his phone out.

Gently cupping my elbow, she guided me out of the room, and through the open doorway, still carrying her huge tote bag in her other hand. The shower room was a regular bathroom, with a shower cubicle inside that was opaque so no one could see inside. "Do you want me to wait in the corridor or in here? I don't know if I should be too far where I can't hear you, given the oddities of this place," Claudia asked.

"You can stay here, thank you. I feel safer with you close by."

I went into the shower cubicle finding it rather well stocked and spacious. I pulled off my clothing in the privacy of the stall, throwing it over the door to Claudia who said she would have them washed.

The shower was bliss. Hot water cascaded down my back,

relaxing my muscles. I scrubbed my skin and hair until I was sparkling clean.

Claudia chatted happily from her perch on the toilet seat while I showered.

"I'm going to make a few calls and see about you being moved to a better facility. I've never seen anything like this."

"How is it normally?" I asked.

"Usually there's more omegas than you know what to do with. I was always surrounded by them during my time at a Haven, and we were never forced to do anything we didn't want to under any circumstances."

I turned the shower off, pulling the towel off the door and wrapping it around myself before exiting the cubicle. "That sounds nice, it's been lonely here. Uh, I don't have clean clothes."

Claudia pushed a tote bag toward me she had brought into the bathroom with her. "Here take any clothing you want. Most of it's really soft and comfortable, I even included some fuzzy socks. I didn't know what they provided you with here."

"Thank you." The sight of the clothing filled me with warmth. Claudia had just breezed into my room and insisted on helping me. I should have been nervous, scared, or worried, but something about this woman was just so peaceful. She was the kind of mother you could imagine baking apple pie every Sunday.

"No need to thank me, dear. You should have been treated better from the start. Now get dressed!" She turned around, giving me some privacy.

I rummaged through the clothing, picking out a man's T-shirt that was far too large for me, but it smelt woodsy and divine. I added a pair of leggings and the softest, fluffiest socks I had ever felt, pulling them on quickly as I hummed in contentment at feeling clean again. After towel drying my hair I threw the towel to the side, putting my damp hair into a messy bun.

"All dressed?" Claudia asked. "Perfect, let's get back to your room, I bet the food will be here!"

The idea of going back to my prison room was far from appealing, but I couldn't deny there was a part of me that wanted to get back to Pack Rivers.

Everett grinned at me when I entered the room, Claudia hot on my heels. "Nice shirt, a little big though. You look a lot better now, no offence."

"It is a little big, but it smells really damn good, and it's comfy." I lifted the neck of the T-shirt to my nose and inhaled, closing my eyes with a little smile.

Once I was in sight of the alphas again, Claudia dipped out of the room saying she was going to hunt down some decent food.

"You look cute," Everett reassured me. "And I apologise for my mother. I may be able to convince her to leave."

Alaric snorted "Fat chance."

"I could at least try!" Everett didn't look that positive in his ability to do so.

I giggled. "No, I like her. She's sweet. It's nice to meet another omega, I've never actually met another."

"Mom will answer any questions you have, and probably tell you a load of things you didn't even realise you needed to ask questions about."

"Are you talking about me?" Claudia asked, striding into the room, two boxes of Chinese takeout and chopsticks in hand. "Here, why don't you sit down and eat while I dry your hair. You'll get sick otherwise. Boys, you can go get more food off Callan, leave me and Sage alone for a bit."

I felt a pull to be near the alphas, but I was more than

happy to be left with Claudia. Taking what ended up being beef chow mein, I sat on the floor so Claudia could take the brush to the mess my hair had become while I ate. She was so gentle, and it felt wonderful.

"So we've made a few calls, unfortunately we can't get you moved to a better Haven yet, for some reason you legally need to be at this Haven for three weeks. But we will be watching over you, from what I've heard they've been treating you appallingly."

"I don't want to see Pack Bove anymore. Can I stop seeing them?"

"Of course, that's your right. May I ask what they did to make you dislike them?" Claudia spoke carefully, but it was obvious she was curious.

I gave her a rundown of our various conversations and gifts.

Claudia hummed, her face set in a frown. "They sound like dicks, but they are certainly not your only choice. I bet at least half the packs you've met have registered interest, if not most of them. I know my boys have."

"Alaric said that. Wouldn't I have been told?"

"You should have been. Were you a regular omega who knew the process and knew your rights, you would have known there was something off about receiving only one bid. Even the worst of omegas get interest from the majority of the packs. Alphas outnumber us so greatly, it's just the way of things. You were different though, you only learnt you were an omega recently?"

"Two weeks ago now, I think. I was doing my normal day job, going about my life when I started getting these nasty stomach cramps, and my scent changed. I presented at work, Haven Services were called and that's how I ended up here."

"What did you do for work?"

"Forensic accounting. I was head of a small department in the larger finance department. I got my masters in accountancy a few years ago. I like numbers, they make sense."

"That's impressive, and you're still young!"

"It doesn't really matter now, does it? My life has completely changed."

Claudia hummed, running the brush through my hair. "It has, but that doesn't mean you can't still use your skills. My boys run a few businesses, I'm sure they can use an accountant."

"Would I be allowed? Lex made it very clear what my job in any pack was."

"Let me guess to just breed with them and be their plaything? Ugh. Men like that disgust me. Maybe ignore absolutely anything that low life has said to you. You have a world of choice. Packs that will treat you like a princess and lay the world at your feet. I adore my guys more than anything. We are really happy, and you can have that too."

"Some packs have been rude, some have actually just stared at me. Callan and the others are the only semi-normal people I've seen, I even helped them with some financial paperwork. Some others were okay, just not... chatty?"

"They are good boys, aren't they? I like you Sage, you seem sweet and down to earth. I have to tell you my boys are the best, and they would treat you with respect. I would be a bad mother if I didn't try and convince you how lovely they are. When Everett admitted they were seeing an omega I was ecstatic!"

"He told you?"

"He wanted advice on what to get you and this whole situation you find yourself in. The prospect of seeing my son settled down is very exciting. I won't lie."

"He got me the hoodie. I didn't take it off until I had that shower, I would put it back on, only it needs to be washed now."

"There's laundry service here, I'll make sure it's cleaned and back to you in twenty-four hours. I'm glad you like it. I have several at home, even though my guys get grumpy when I don't use them as a heat source. Alphas radiate heat, it's amazing! I suppose you've never been up close and personal with an alpha before...unless? You're a stunning girl, and I wouldn't blame you if you took a walk on the wild side and had an alpha romp."

"Oh no, I haven't." I blushed.

Claudia only hummed.

"The extent of my experience is a crappy prom night with a fellow beta, and I don't wish to repeat that!" I explained.

Claudia laughed. "You won't have to worry about that with a pack."

"What's it like, being shared? It seems quite daunting to me, like how would I keep up?"

"The omega gets to set the pace, if you're not ready, then you're not ready. As for keeping up with them, once your first heat hits you'll find you can easily keep up with several males. I've heard of omegas with only two males who were unsatisfied since we crave constant attention and affection. It's just part of our nature. Having so many partners is honestly a comfort, and sexually it's fun. A lot of fun, and if you don't find it fun you can deal with them individually or not at all. The power is with the omega." Claudia pulled out a hairdryer, gently scraping her hand through my hair while she dried it, scratching my scalp in a soothing manner that could have easily put me to sleep.

Twenty minutes later my hair was thoroughly dried and my eyelids kept drifting closed. After being on edge for so many days, now that I felt semi-safe, the exhaustion was hitting me like a truck.

"So, what happens now?" I asked, sitting down on the bed next to Claudia.

"We couldn't get you moved to another Haven, which is odd. We've messaged several important folks about moving you, but everyone seems to believe that this place would never do you wrong. We can get an official transfer in a week or two. I'm pretty sure Harold, one of my guys, has scared the bajeezus out of the staff into treating you better. Ultimately, it's still a case of waiting until you make a decision about a pack. I am going to be visiting a lot though, if that's okay with you? They won't refuse me entry. I'm an omega who knows her rights, and you have the right to omega council because these daft betas don't understand how we work. They wouldn't dare stop me, and I would raise hell if they tried."

"Will I meet new packs, or do I have to decide from my current options?"

"You should be able to meet more packs."

"I'm just not ready to jump into things yet, I mean, Everett's pack is the only decent one I've met, and don't get me wrong, they're really nice but...everything is still so new. I thought when it came time for me to settle down, I would have years to think. How long did it take you to pick?"

"I think I took a month and a half to two months to make my decision. But the decision isn't always final, changes can be made right up until claiming, but it is rare."

"But if I agree to leave here with a pack, aren't I basically saying I'm open for business?"

"Not at all! I know of a few omegas who waited several

weeks after joining a pack to get to know them for sure before deciding to mate with them."

"Yeah, Alaric and Everett explained claiming to me, it sounds painful. Biting hard enough to break skin?"

"Oh no, trust me, one thing every omega agrees on is how damn good a claiming bite feels. Best orgasms ever."

I blushed furiously, looking away.

Claudia just giggled. "Don't worry, I'm used to discussing it."

"Ma?" Everett was in the viewing room, smiling at the sight of his mother and I sitting together. "Do you need anything? Are you still hungry, Sage?"

I shook my head. I'd had so many noodles I felt like I was going to burst. "I'm full, but thank you."

"Ev, baby, could you see about getting Sage a phone? I want her to be able to contact us whenever she wants."

"I'll run to the store." Everett nodded. "Anything else?"

"That's too much, I can't let you guys get me a phone! I already have a phone, and a bank account you can use if we can't find my phone. I can't let you guys pay for everything," I whined, my voice taking on such a childish tone I was almost ashamed of myself.

"It's no bother to us, sweetheart. I'll be back in a moment." He grinned as he walked out, ignoring my spluttering.

With my phone all set up, the newest, top of the range phone no less, Claudia input her number and gave me a hug goodbye.

"I'll be back first thing in the morning. Call me if anything happens, or if you have any questions. The alphas will start visiting again, but I reminded the staff here of the rules. One pack per hour, and none after ten at night and before nine a.m. so you can rest. The cameras have also been disabled, Callan saw to that. Between those hours your doors should be locked, and you'll have total privacy. Why there are no normal dorms here is beyond me."

I was sad to see her leave, but it was getting late, and I would have to see packs in the morning. Clambering into bed, I was lulled to sleep by the woodsy scent of the T-shirt I wore.

CHAPTER FIFTEEN
Sage

The next day Claire didn't speak a word as she dropped off my breakfast, but she did glare daggers at me. I couldn't find it in me to care though. From the sounds of it, Claire had been thoroughly chewed out. Breakfast was eggs, bacon, and toast, much to my joy. It was gone in minutes. Not long after I had finished and placed the empty plate on the side table did the first pack come in. Three brothers, all of them with the same dark curls and blue eyes. They made polite conversation and I jotted down their nice demeanour in the notes app of my new phone.

The second pack of the day was a group of seven. I was startled by the sheer volume of men, but they had a good laugh about it. They had even bought me fresh cookies from a local bakery which I munched on while they discussed films that were coming out that year. They had also heaped on the praise, and I was convinced my blush was now a permanent addition to my face.

Two more packs came through and they made small talk, but none were overly offensive or crass like Lex had been. My thoughts kept drifting back to Pack Rivers, though. They had stood up for me. They were stunningly handsome, kind, and from what I could tell they worked together really well. I wanted to get to know the other packs, but deep down I knew I was favouring them. There was something so damn likeable about men who ensure you get takeout and a hot shower.

While my treatment had improved, I couldn't shake the feeling that something was wrong. Pack Bove showed up despite my refusal to see them. I had been texting Claudia on and off all day, much to Claire's anger. I had no doubt that the redhead would take the phone away if she wasn't terrified of angering Claudia or her alphas.

I didn't know when I had started referring to them as mine, but it just felt right. Lunch time rolled around and Claudia popped by, bringing me a milkshake.

We were sitting in the armchairs, sipping on shakes when I decided to ask what was on her mind. "Claudia?"

"Hmm?"

"When I finally do decide, what usually happens? And how can I be sure that a pack is willing to take things slowly?" I had to find out as much as I could from Claudia, she was the most trustworthy source of information I had.

"If a pack goes expressly against an omega's wishes they can be punished pretty harshly. Other than that, most packs understand that a happy omega makes for a stronger pack. As for choosing, you simply need to tell the Keepers your choice and then the alphas will usually take a day or two to prepare their home before the omega goes with them. Are you asking for any particular reason?"

"Just between us?" I asked. "I appreciate your son is involved in this, I just need the advice of another omega."

"I won't betray your trust, Sage. My bonehead of a child can figure things out for himself." Claudia laughed.

"It's been two days and things don't feel...right here. I'm kinda nervous about the Keepers, their intentions. I keep thinking about doing something...well, choosing a pack, just to be a little safer."

"You've got a pack in mind?! Who?" Claudia asked excitedly "And don't feel bad if it's not my boys, this is about what's best for you, Sage."

"I, uh. I was actually considering accepting Pack River's interest," I spoke in a rush, "They at least treat me like a human being and I am sick of this place, it freaks me out, plus they all seem like good men. Even Grumpy."

"Grumpy?" Claudia was beaming.

"Alaric, I call him Grumpy for obvious reasons," I admitted, my entire face heating as Claudia hooted with laughter.

"Oh my dear, this makes me so happy! Now, listen to me. I know you're scared, but this can be done however you want. They won't rush you into anything. You won't even have to leave the Haven anytime soon if you want. You can go onto solely courting them, so you don't get visits from any other alphas, it's just you and them spending a lot more time together getting to know each other. There are also other options where you can stay at the pack house while courting them if you feel comfortable. You have to stay for a short period of time to give the pack time to get to know you and show you they're a good option, but it isn't long at all. Solely courting here at a Haven has no time limits, you can do it for as long or as little as you want, and you'll always have a pack member with you, at least in the adjoining room. Or possibly even tonight."

"That actually sounds nice." I nodded. "Are you sure they wouldn't mind if I do this?"

"Mind? I think they would love it. If you go for single pack courting, then you'll never be alone, other than when you want privacy or sleep. It helps give you an idea of what pack life with them is like."

"I mean, that does sound kind of nice, but they're all so busy I don't want to pull them from their lives."

"Sage, they've been working for over a decade, they could do with the break."

"Okay. I'll discuss it with the Keepers tonight." I smiled.

Unable to contain herself, Claudia pulled me into a bear hug. Normally, I would have felt awkward, but instead I revelled in the human touch.

"Can I ask you guys something?" I sat on an armchair, legs tucked under me as I picked at the burrito they had bought me.

"Of course you can." Everett grinned. "And before you ask, yes, I am naturally this handsome."

I snorted. "I wasn't asking about that." I laughed, before forcing myself to be serious. "Am I taking you guys away from work? Don't you have more important things to be doing?"

Bellamy frowned. "Why do you ask? We love coming here."

"It's just... y'know, I don't wanna take up your time if you have places you need to be, you've been so wonderful, and helpful..."

"Are you asking us to stop coming?"

"No!" I rushed to say. "I like having you here."

"Then what's this about?"

"Well... Uh." I fidgeted in my seat, moving my legs. The guys looked at each other nervously.

"Speak your mind, Sweet Girl. We won't get angry."

"Well, I was thinking about solo courting." I couldn't meet their eyes. "Would you guys even be able to do that? Claudia said one of you would have to be here at all times, and you've got the merger and I wouldn't want to throw a spanner in the works by demanding your time."

"Wait, are you saying you want to solo court us?" Alaric asked, his voice cool and controlled. Everett and Bellamy were both grinning like loons. "Or another pack?"

I looked up in shock at his words. "Uh... you guys." I blushed, my facing heating, averting my eyes again while Everett made a whooping sound of happiness and Bellamy muttered a curse of happiness under his breath.

Callan scooted his armchair so he was directly in front of me. "Look at me," he instructed softly. I reluctantly met his eyes. "Why do you think we wouldn't want to solo court? We've been here every day. You're wonderful."

"But you're so busy. I don't want to be a distraction."

"Sage, some things are more important than work, and if one of us is here, the rest can be taking care of the business. That's the beauty of the pack: there's always someone to pick up the slack. So, are you really considering solo courting us?"

"I-I mean, only if you want, I don't want to push you into anything," I stammered.

Callan laughed, and my cheeks heated. "Hey," Callan said softly, realising I was embarrassed. "Don't be embarrassed, not at all. We would be honoured to go forward with solo courting."

"You haven't even discussed it amongst each other."

"Oh, we have, Sweet Girl." Bellamy grinned. "Everyone's answer was a resounding yes when we registered interest."

"Yes, interest, but solo courting isn't the normal thing, is it? It means more time away from your pack, your home."

"And we're happy to do it," Callan said. "Have you spoken to the Keepers about it?"

"Not yet, I wanted to talk to you first." I ran my hand through my hair, unable to keep my eyes on his.

Callan shook his head, still smiling.

Everett spoke up, "Well talk to the Keepers, make sure they have everything in place to solo court. We're fucking thrilled! I'll grab a sleeping bag and never leave!"

"We will give her space when she needs it," Callan's voice was firm when he turned to Everett with a glare, before softening when he turned back to me. "Whatever you need, Sage."

"Thank you."

"I think we should be thanking you, not the other way round. We're also well aware this doesn't mean you're coming home with us, and that it's just a step. If you want to call it off at any point, we'll respect that," Callan assured me.

"I'll talk to the Keepers today."

"Perfect. We're grabbing dinner with Claudia and her mates tonight, but one of us can return after, if you want?"

"Yes please."

"We'll see you then, sweetheart."

Every one of them left that room with a shit eating grin on their face.

Once they left, Claire popped into my room. Her face was

painted in an overly fake smile, a plate with a sandwich and potato chips in hand. "You requested to see me, omega?" she asked in a sweet voice, passing me the plate.

I immediately tucked in. "I want to start solo pack courting," I said after a few quick bites.

"Oh, thank god you came to your senses. Lex will be ecstatic." She grinned, this time more genuine.

"Oh no, I want to solo court the Rivers's pack," I clarified, and watched as Claire's face fell.

"The Rivers pack have shown themselves to be unworthy of an omega. I would be doing you a disservice if I allowed you to solo court them."

"It's my choice," I kept my voice firm.

"They've bullied you into this, haven't they? I'll bar them from coming here." Claire nodded, speaking more to herself than to me.

"No! You invited the Rivers pack here, and I've made my decision. If it's not honoured I'll be contacting the Clearmont Haven immediately and refusing to see any other alphas until I am moved. It's Pack Rivers or nothing."

"You can't!"

"I can! I'm an omega, and I get the say here." I had developed a new shiny spine of steel thanks to Claudia.

Claire looked...scared? She fiddled with the cuffs of her shirt, shifting uncomfortably. "Omega, listen to me. It is in everyone's best interest for you to solo court Pack Bove, you'll see. I'll give you the night to think on this." She turned to leave, practically sprinting out the door.

"I don't need time to think about it!" I shouted at her retreating back, irritated. Groaning, I put my sandwich down and indulged in a sulk.

Checking the time on my phone, I was happy to see it had passed ten p.m. Now was officially my alone time, no more packs and some peace. Quickly changing into a pair of sleep shorts, I opted to keep wearing the delicious smelling shirt. Grabbing one of the books Alaric got me, I crawled onto the bed. My guys would probably be there in the morning or tonight possibly, and the thought excited me more than I thought it would.

Snuggling down into the sheets, I opened the book. I stilled when I heard my door open. What on earth did Claire want so late at night? Did that woman never go home? I was just getting comfortable! A figure much larger than Claire stood in my doorway with a grin on his face and no glass between us to protect me

Lex.

"Omega," he grizzled.

"You shouldn't be here." I shuffled off the bed, putting it between us, my heart thundering with anxiety. "You're not allowed to be in here."

Panic rose fast. Every one of my instincts were screaming at me to run.

"Come here," he commanded, that familiar alpha tone to his voice, but instead of responding as my body had done with Callan, I cringed back.

"No. Leave," I said, my voice small.

Lex strode toward me, trying to back me into a corner. I bolted to the side, towards the door, making it only two strides before I was grabbed around the waist and hauled towards the nearest wall. The impact winded me. Lex's scent—rotten nature, like rancid vegetables— made me want to vomit.

"How dare you disobey me?!" he thundered, his face inches from mine. One of his hands snaked up to my neck, holding me in place. "I will admit, you smell fucking good." He shoved his nose into my neck and inhaled deeply, the hand around my throat tightening to the point I couldn't speak.

I furiously hit his arm with my fists, but he didn't budge. I struggled even harder when he reached to palm my breast.

"Why won't you fucking behave!?" he growled. "Omegas are meant to submit!"

He was an alpha, I wasn't meant to fight him. His hand had loosened as he yelled at me, just enough for me to gather some saliva and aim it right in his face. It hit under his eye. Lex stilled, a deadly look in his eyes. His hand connected with the side of my face, sending me sprawling. My head swam from the pain and I crawled away, only to have my ankle grabbed, Lex dragging me back toward him, pinning me under him.

One hand was over my mouth, the other arm snaked down at my flimsy sleep shorts. I scratched at him, drawing blood with my nails. It only angered him further. Pressing his body down on mine I could feel his erection and the sensation made me sick to my stomach. My head swam as I tried to figure out how to break free.

"Fine. If you won't behave and submit, I'll just have to make you."

CHAPTER SIXTEEN
Everett

After a quick dinner with my family at our local pizza joint, we decided to buy an extra pizza and drop it at the Haven for Sage, Ma was convinced they weren't feeding her enough, and I agreed. In the week she had been there her face had started to look gaunt.

Since we were going to start solo courting, one of us may even stay the night, if that's what Sage wanted. We went together, Ma and two of my dads, Harold and Nolan, drove in their car and my pack bundled into an SUV.

The Haven was quiet when we got there which made me happy. Maybe they were finally respecting nighttime hours so Sage could sleep. God knew she needed it. We walked through the building up to the door of Sage's viewing room. A guard stood outside.

"Sorry, no alphas at the moment."

"No problem, we are just delivering a pizza." Bellamy's

smile was tight, holding up the box. "Plus, we're the pack solo courting Sage. We're allowed in at all times."

"No alphas," the guard repeated. "Omega's request."

"Fine, I'll go and take it, I'm an omega and you can't stop me," Ma announced with a frown. "Surely no alphas didn't apply to them? "Bellamy, give me the pizza." She took the pizza and waltzed off into the back. Nolan following her, even though he could only go so far before being stopped. They didn't even think of stopping Claudia though, my mother demanded respect.

"It's sad you won't get to see her again tonight." My dad, Harold, patted my shoulder in a comforting gesture.

"At least she's got food, proper food not the health crap they keep feeding her here," I said.

"Are you sure you're ready for this? It'll be the best thing that ever happened to you, but probably the most stressful. I was always on edge those first few months thinking Claudia was uncomfortable or unhappy—it physically pained me," my dad warned us, looking between me and my packmates.

"She's worth it," Bellamy said.

"Harold! Nolan! Help! Quick!" Ma came running round the corner, a panicked look on her face, no pizza in hand. She didn't say anything, only ran back from where she came, waving her hand in a desperate gesture for us to follow. Without hesitation we passed the guard who was now looking terrified.

Keeper Claire came running out of a room, yelling, "You can't go in there!" But we ignored her.

We burst into Sage's room, and were immediately overwhelmed by the scent of fear. Not just fear, *terror*.

Sage was curled up in a corner, covering her head with her arms.

A roar from the other side of the room made her flinch, grabbing my attention. Nolan was on top of another alpha, slightly larger than himself, the pair grappled with each other, blood had been drawn, staining the room further in the coppery scent.

Harold and Callan both lurched forward to grab the pair, hauling them apart. My dads weren't fighters so I was shocked to see one of them lunge forward into action.

Sage shrank into the corner, hands over her ears. I moved to her, crouching next to her, reaching my hand out to her but thinking better of it. Everything in me was screaming to touch her, comfort her. People were shouting, it was so loud and uncomfortable she must have felt terrible. The burnt sugar smell was thick in the air. She looked at the floor where there was blood splatter, probably from that cut above her eyebrow.

"Get off me! The fucking omega was asking for it," the alpha snarled. I recognised him immediately. Lex Bove. His lip was split and he looked feral with rage. Eyes wide, spit flying out his mouth with each word.

"Let's get him out of here," Nolan growled. Bellamy and Callan helped manhandle Lex out of the room leaving me, Sage, Alaric and my mother in the room. I didn't care about that, I needed to focus on Sage. My pack were more than capable of handling one alpha asshole.

Ma gently touched Sage's arm, pulling her attention. Sage flinched away, further retreating into the corner. Ma's hands fluttered over Sage. "Are you okay dear? Oh my, your face." She gently cupped Sage's face.

"S-She let him i-in. Claire," Sage stuttered, trembling. Ma's eyes were wide and worried as she gently fussed over the sobbing omega, trying to gently brush her tangled hair from her face. "I want to leave." Sage sobbed, curling into Ma. They clutched each other tightly, Sage trying to calm her breathing.

"Is she okay?" Alaric asked, coming to stand near to where I was crouching next to Sage. His eyes were dark and thunderous, and she instinctively shrunk away from an alpha's anger whimpering and looking down.

Claudia tutted, but Alaric ignored her, crouching down, making himself smaller in an attempt to look less intimidating.

"I'm not angry at you, Sweet Girl. I'm mad they allowed this to happen to you. I promise it won't happen again." His nostrils flared. Sage's honey was muted, drowned in the acidic scent of fear and panic.

My every thought was on edge, demanding I grab Sage, pull her close, and comfort her. My instincts were the weakest out of the pack, so god knows how Alaric felt, as he was the most overprotective of us all. I hated the glassy look of terror in my omega's eyes. We had only spoken a handful of times but I was starting to think of Sage as mine. As ours.

"You have to leave. I've called the authorities," a nasally voice said from the doorway. Claire stood there, standing tall, not a hair out of place. "It's despicable that you would intrude on an omega's space like this."

"We are not fucking leaving her, not with you," I growled. "There was an *alpha* in her room. She was meant to be safe here and somehow a low life like Lex Bove had managed to get into her room and attack her?"

"She is an omega, in our sanctuary, if there was an error here, it won't happen again." Claire's voice trembled slightly.

Alaric stood up, and I placed a hand gently on Sage's ankle. She flinched lightly, and I took a closer look, noticing the deep red finger marks, already starting to bruise on her ankle.

"We have to get her out of here," I whispered to my mother, trying not to scare Sage.

"They'll throw us out within the hour. If that Keeper did this, we can't do shit until we call several meetings of the Haven boards." I was pained at Ma's words, my eyes travelling over Sage.

Alaric rounded on the piss poor excuse for a Keeper standing in the doorway, pure unadulterated rage pouring off him. She shook, but stood her ground. "You have to listen to me, otherwise you'll never be allowed back in a Haven."

"You sold access to an omega. You put her in danger. We'll have your job for this," Alaric snarled. "I'm sure you've broken several laws." He was right, we knew something wasn't right. We knew it, and we did fuck all to protect Sage. Not anymore.

"I would never sell an omega," Claire hissed. "That is a disgusting accusation!"

"Sage told you her decision, didn't she?" Ma seethed, never pulling away from Sage. "She told you she only wanted to court my son's pack and so you did this? You are fucking vile and by the time I'm done with you, you'll wish I had let these men get rid of you."

"You have no proof of that. There was a terrible accident. One that probably could have been avoided if your pack hadn't forced us to dismantle the omega's security cameras."

"How much are they paying you?" Alaric growled. "I'll triple it."

The beta paled. We had hit the nail on the head.

Sage whimpered into Ma, who gently stroked her hair away from her face. Cupping her chin she looked her in the eyes.

"Sage, dear, I know this isn't what you want," Ma whispered, so the other's couldn't hear her. Only I could because I was so close. "But you're not safe here. By the time we get you help they could do anything with you. I know my boys. They'll keep you safe."

"I want to leave," Sage cried, furiously wiping at the tears falling down her cheeks. Her voice cracked as she spoke.

"Alaric! Get Callan and Bellamy. Claire, get the hell out of here." I jerked my head at Claire who scoffed, but paled when Alaric turned on her, totally prepared to manhandle her out of the room. She scuttled away, spluttering about how proper forces would be there to remove us shortly and we would never be able to see an omega again.

Sage took a few deep breaths, closing her eyes and opening them again only when Bellamy and Callan joined us. It was just her, Ma, and my pack.

"We need an agreement," I spoke a bit louder. "She's not safe here." Looking between my pack brothers, still crouched next to her, his hand gently stroking her ankle, soothing her. "She isn't ready to be a pack omega yet. She needs to go slow. But we need to sort something!"

"Choose us, and we won't even touch you until you want it, if you ever do want it," Bellamy said. Usually agreeing to go home with a pack meant the omega was almost entirely sure they wanted to bond. Sage wasn't even really considering it yet.

"I won't let anyone touch you, even these fuckers," Alaric declared, looking between everyone in the room. We all nodded, looking between one another and back at the omega.

Before Sage could open her mouth and reply, Claire opened the door, striding in accompanied by several large guards, carrying weapons that would work even on an alpha. "The Rivers' pack is banned from these premises. Escort them out," she demanded.

The guards stepped forward, and Callan raised his hands.

"We mean no harm. The staff let in an alpha who attacked Sage. As soon as she's safe, we'll leave with no complaint," Callan reasoned, his speech was calm, clear.

"We'll secure the room now, but to do so you must leave."

"No," the voice was small, but clear. Sage. Everyone in the room turned to look at her, the acidic smell of her fear was so strong it marred the sweet honey scent. Even the beta's could smell the overpowering acidic tang.

"Ma'am?" the guard spoke, his head down, a mark of respect. That's how omegas were *meant* to be treated.

"I choose them," Sage's voice cracked. "This Haven has fucked up, I wish to go with my chosen pack today. Right now."

"Are you sure, ma'am? Your scent..."

Sage's head whipped up and she glared at the guards. "The Keepers of this Haven have broken several rules and allowed access to me when it's inappropriate, preying on my lack of knowledge on the workings of the omegas. I have made my decision, which is my right, I'll leave with the Rivers pack today."

"You can't do that. You're courting Pack Bove!" Claire squeaked, horrified.

"You heard her," Callan spoke. "She's chosen us of her own volition, whatever deal you made with Lex Bove is irrelevant."

"You can't!" Claire insisted.

"The omega has chosen, Keeper." The guard said, looking over them. "I assume this is a legitimate courting?"

"We were invited to court her, paid the fees of nearly a million dollars and she has chosen us, as you heard. We also started solo courting in the last twenty-four hours."

"A million dollars?" The guard looked at Claire. "Fees are just over half a million."

Claire paled. "G-given the unique situation, we felt higher fees were due for this particular omega as she needed more care and education."

The guard sighed. "Let me guess, if the logs are checked it will show as these packs paying the standard half a mill, won't it? Fuck." He turned to Callan. "Take her with you. I'll be filing a report with the Clearmont Haven to let them know everything I've witnessed. Someone will be checking in with you either tonight or tomorrow morning to schedule a home visit."

"Of course, we were trying to get her moved to that Haven to complete her courting time. We'll welcome their Keepers into our home." Callan nodded.

I smiled gently at Sage, sliding my hands under her and picking her up with ease from Claudia's arms. "Come on, pretty girl, let's get you home." She burrowed into my chest. I hoped that being close to an alpha would ease her stress.

"Do you need anything from here, Sage?" Bellamy asked. Sage shook her head.

"You can get her anything she needs, better stuff than here," Claudia confirmed, placing a comforting hand on Sage's arm while she was still curled into me. I wanted to shout and vibrate with anger, having the little omega in my arms soothed me, but we needed to check her over.

"Wait, My fleece, the one you got me." She pulled her head away, looking around the room.

"I'll grab it, don't worry," Claudia soothed. "Ev, I'm going to stay here and get all the emergency paperwork sorted and make sure your dad is okay. I'll ring if I need you." She turned to Sage. "My dear, if you need me, just call me and I'll come straight to the packhouse, okay?"

Sage nodded, her throat was bruised badly and she clearly didn't have the energy to answer. She buried her face in my neck as we walked out to the car. Her scent was marred by Lex's, and it made me sick to my stomach. It smelled wrong. It was worryingly easy to take her from the sanctuary. Shouldn't there have been more paperwork, or regulations, or something?

CHAPTER SEVENTEEN
Bellamy

Everett slid into the backseat of the SUV, Sage still curled into his lap, her hands clutching the fabric of his grey T-shirt. Alaric cranked up the heat. She was only wearing tiny nightclothes, and violent shivering racked her body.

"Sage, are you hurt?" Alaric asked from the front passenger seat. She didn't answer, only curling deeper into Everett.

"Talk to us, Sweet Girl," I murmured, reaching out a hand to touch her, but thought better of it.

"I think she's going into shock," Everett said as he looked down at her, his brows furrowed. "Bell's gonna check you over once we get home, okay? He's an army medic, so he'll take good care of you." My eyes travelled over her, noting several mottled bruises already forming on her bare legs and arms. Suppressing the snarl of anger, I made a mental note of each injury. Lex Bove was a dead man in my book. Anyone who could hurt someone so much smaller and weaker than them was a pathetic low life in my book.

"Bell, are you okay to check her over as soon as we get to the house?" Alaric asked me, watching us through the rear-view mirror. I nodded, my eyes never left the shaking omega. I was now entirely thankful for having been a medic many years prior. I suppose it would be best if one of us cared for her, another stranger would just cause her more distress.

"Sage, where are you hurt?" Everett asked her again, running his hand through her hair, stopping when Sage squeaked in pain. "Fuck me, she's got one hell of a bump on her head."

Me and the others were used to bumps and bruises, we were a pack after all, and often roughhoused, but no one would ever, *ever* come after the sweet omega again if we had anything to say about it.

Callan pulled up at the house and parked at the front door, not bothering with the garage. Alaric was out of the car first, hurrying around to open the door for Everett so he could gently get out with Sage in his arms as it appeared she was refusing to let go of him. I worried as the cold air made her shiver even more violently as Everett carried her to the house, she needed checking out pronto.

"Go to the sitting room. Her rooms aren't ready yet," Alaric instructed.

All the things we'd ordered wouldn't arrive for a few days yet—all the pillows and blankets were useless on the back of a delivery truck or in a warehouse.

"Shit, we have nothing for her," Everett agreed. "She'll need nest stuff, everything. Love, I'm going to put you down on the couch so we can check you out," reassuring her as she clung to him. "I'm not going anywhere, but we need to let Bell check you out."

Knowing Sage was being watched by Everett, I left the

room to grab a medical kit. I had an old one in the downstairs storage room. Re-entering the room, bag in hand, I saw Sage sitting on the couch, clutching Everett's hand, hunched in on herself. Her vacant eyes had dark circles under them.

Gently crouching down in front of her, I put some latex gloves on and grabbed some antiseptic wipes out of the bag, ripping open the sachet with my teeth. "Sage, can you tell us what happened?" I asked, keeping my voice low and soft.

Sage looked at us all surrounding her, taking a moment before speaking. "He threw me against the wall. I hit my head," she croaked. I kept my face blank, but I wanted to snarl, get back in my car, go find Lex Bove and ensure he could never get a boner again. "He grabbed my ankle and dragged me across the floor. He...he grabbed my neck. I don't know what else." She lifted her hand to her throat, hovering over the bruises for a moment before letting her hand drop back into her lap. Her voice was hollow, void of emotion.

Alaric kept his face calm, though I could tell from his scent he wasn't happy. His usual smoky vibes were smelling off. "Okay, why don't I clean up that cut on your face first? Do you know how that happened?"

Sage absentmindedly lifted her hand to her face. "He hit me. He was wearing a ring." She went to say more, but was stopped by a coughing fit racking her body.

"Okay, take it easy. I can already see the bruising on your throat." I turned to look at the others, "Can someone grab her a cold drink? It may help some of the soreness."

Callan nodded, uncrossing his arms, and made his way to the kitchen. A frown crossed his face. I assumed it was what we were all feeling—we didn't want Sage out of our sight, but he knew we had her.

I gently cleaned and bandaged up her face, ignoring the

grumpy growls from the others whenever Sage winced in pain at the antiseptic being applied. I was almost grateful for it because it was the first real reaction from her I'd seen since we'd left the Haven. "Okay, now all I recommend is keeping that cut on your face clean, resting your voice and a nice hot bath to help ease those bruises. I'll keep checking on you, but you just need a bit of time to let your body heal."

Callan returned a moment later and handed Sage a tumbler with a straw. She took a sip and looked at the cup in surprise.

"Peach iced tea.. you remembered my favourite," she said, her voice full of soft wonder. Was it so shocking that we'd listened and stocked up on her favourites?

"Can I get you anything else?" Callan asked.

"No, thank you," Sage said quietly while I carefully placed a butterfly bandage on her face.

"Now, your face should heal in a week or two just fine," I reassured her, brushing her hair away from her neck, revealing the mottled purple bruises. I reached to gingerly touch one and Sage flinched back.

"Can I take a look at your ankle?"

Sage nodded, and gently lifted her ankle up for inspection.

"It looks like some nasty bruising, but it's not broken. Stay off it for a few days and it'll be good as new."

I grabbed a compression bandage before thinking better of it. "I'll put this on after you clean up, there's no point getting this bandage wet."

"What do you want to do?" Callan asked, "Get some rest or have a bath?"

"A bath, I can't stand the smell of him on me."

I agreed. I hated the smell of that piss poor excuse of an alpha coating our omega.

"Where's Claudia?" Sage asked, only just realising Everett's mother wasn't with her. She still seemed out of it, although it was good to see she was now slowly becoming aware.

"Nolan was pretty beat up, so they took him home. She muttered something about shopping for supplies after she dealt with all the paperwork."

Sage nodded.

"If you want her here sooner, I can give her a call. She'll understand."

"No, it's okay. I don't want to bother her. I'll just go have a bath, if that's okay?"

"Of course."

Sage went to stand, forgetting about the bruised ankle, and let out a yip of pain when she put weight on it. Alaric caught her before she hit the ground and swung her up into his arms.

"No walking for you until that ankle is better," he told her, his voice leaving no room for discussion. She nodded absent-mindedly, saying nothing. Alaric carried her up a set of stairs, through a room, and into a familiar ornate bathroom with deep green tiling and gold detailing. I chuckled quietly, so Sage wouldn't hear. The fucker wanted her in his room, his bathroom. I couldn't blame him. I wanted her honey scent in my room, but I wasn't going to argue over that while she was injured.

As we walked through his room I noticed his bed, which used to be very sparse, had several pillows piled high on it, and two comforters.

Alaric sat her gently on the edge of the bathtub leaning down to put the stopper in and turn the water on. As he leaned over, his T-shirt rode up ever so slightly, giving Sage a perfect view of his muscles. I saw her noticing and smiled. Leaning over he gently cupped the back of her head, placing a chaste kiss to her forehead. The normally harsh Alaric was softening up around Sage, one could almost call him a softie, not that I would say that to his face. The fucker would destroy my favourite espresso machine if I did.

"Do you want me to stay?" he asked, hand still cupping the back of her head. He waited until she gently shook her head before leaving. Callan, Everett and myself were all standing in his room, waiting.

"Your bathroom, Alaric?" Everett asked with a smile.

"It's best that she stays here tonight," Alaric confirmed.

"Yeah, I noticed that," Everett said, nodding his head over to the bed. "When did that happen?"

"When we started researching bringing an omega into the pack I got more. It's nowhere near enough for a proper nest, but it's better than the empty bed frame in her room currently."

"We should have thought of that, my bed has literally one blanket and one pillow," Everett said, scratching the back of his head sheepishly.

"None of us expected this. We should have had weeks to prepare. Though, who knows if she'll even want to be in our beds. She didn't exactly choose us willingly," Callan said.

I nodded. "No, she didn't. We were simply the safest option, but now that she's here we really can court her, can't we? Show her what sort of pack we are and convince her to join us fully."

"We'll have to go slow," Callan cautioned. "Remember she's not like every other omega. Three weeks ago she was a beta living a normal life. All these changes have got to be wreaking havoc on her emotionally."

"For now we'll just focus on ensuring she's settled and comfortable. I bet she could use a few days lounging in bed, watching TV, and eating junk food."

"One of us needs to be here at all times with her. She's not fully attuned to her omega instincts yet, but Claudia said Sage will be craving human interaction," Alaric pointed out. "It's another reason that room they had her in was so fucked. You idiots should read a damn book. For some reason us merry band of morons have an omega in our home. The least we can do is ensure she's safe and her basic needs are met."

"Uhhh can I borrow one of your books?" Everett asked sheepishly. "I thought I knew more, but apparently I'm an idiot." Everyone laughed lightly.

"We're all idiots, it seems," Callan agreed. "I'm going to make a few calls, we need to make a plan for tomorrow. We need to sort her room out, file official Haven paperwork and put a complaint in regarding that Keeper. I'm assuming they will have reached out to the police about Lex, but I think we better double check."

"I'll have someone look into her," Alaric informed him. "She was clearly doing something illegal. Do you think the Lex pack will try to retaliate for us taking her?"

"I think they'll be pretty pissed. Maybe two of us should stay with her at all times for now, until she's settled. It's not like she'll be able to leave the grounds much while she's not bonded." Just the mention of marking had me thinking about Sage moaning as I sink my teeth into her neck, filling her with my knot. Fuck, I wanted her. Inside and out, I wanted her bite, wanted her to smell like me, and be in my bed.

"Two at a time is doable, and we'll beef up security," I confirmed. My packmates' knowing smiles let me know they knew exactly what I had been thinking about.

CHAPTER EIGHTEEN
Sage

I was doing my best to scrub off the smell of my attacker. It helped that the large claw foot tub was filled with floral-scented salts. Why did a pack of alphas have floral bath salts? I hadn't wanted to cry in front of the others, but now that I was alone and the severity of my situation was starting to sink in. I was attacked by an alpha who wanted to do god knows what to me. For the foreseeable future I was stuck with this pack I really didn't know much about. Yes, they were by far the best option given the alphas I'd met, but that didn't mean they weren't secretly hiding a mean streak. Though, part of me found that hard to believe, even Alaric, the grumpiest of the pack, had treated me with surprising kindness and a gentle touch.

Once I was sure that Lex's scent was completely removed from my body, I got out of the tub, keeping my weight on my good foot, and grabbing one of the fluffy dark grey towels to bundle myself up in. Looking at the discarded pyjamas I realised I didn't have anything clean to change into, and I refused to put on the clothes that had Lex all over them.

"Umm, is anyone there?" I called out at the closed door I had hopped towards.

"Everything okay?" a voice asked.

"Callan?" I guessed.

"That's right, Honey." I'm surprised I could recognise him by only his voice already.

"I-I don't have any clothes. The ones I was wearing smell… like him," I mumbled.

"I'll go grab you something, stay put."

Callan returned a few moments later. "Hey, I got you some things, can I pass them in?"

I opened the door a crack and reached my hand out so he couldn't see me as he handed me the bundle of fabric.

"Sorry, it's all we've got for now, tomorrow we'll sort out getting you a wardrobe and bedroom put together."

I hurried to change, and couldn't help but giggle at the sight of myself in the mirror. The T-shirt was so long it fell to my mid thighs, and the hoodie on top of it went all the way to my knees.

"Something funny about my clothes?" Callan asked, clearly amused.

"Not at all, I just look like I'm being drowned in fabric."

"It's not my fault you're pint sized!" Callan laughed.

"It's not my fault you guys are all super sized!" I said as I opened the door. I yawned, rubbing my eye with the sleeve of the hoodie.

"You look dead on your feet, let's get you to bed." Callan scooped me up.

"You guys pick me up like I'm nothing, a girl can get used

to this." I gave him a small smile, and let my head rest on his shoulder.

"Didn't we just discuss how miniature you are?" Callan asked, eyebrow raised. He plopped me gently onto a bed.

"Whose bed is this? It's not a guest room."

"Alaric's. He had the most blankets and pillows. He's going to sleep on the couch downstairs tonight. We have rooms for you, but there's only a bed frame so far. We'll get a mattress and you can pick out new bedding tomorrow though."

"This was all a bit sudden, wasn't it?" I asked, burying myself down into the blankets. "This smells like the T-shirt Claudia got me."

"That sneaky woman somehow added one of Alaric's gym shirts into the clothing she got you. I think she was trying to play matchmaker while being subtle."

"She certainly wasn't subtle about you guys," I laughed, another yawn taking over.

"Sleep, it's late. We'll get everything sorted in the morning."

I stayed quiet, too exhausted to respond and already dozing off, wrapped up in the familiar scent.

Rest didn't last long, maybe less than five minutes, but I kept myself wrapped tightly in the blanket. Now that I was alone, I could take in the details of the room. Every surface was saturated with that smoky scent I had loved at the haven. I had kept that T-shirt on for as long as possible. My cheeks started to heat as I realised that Alaric must have noticed I was wearing one of his shirts. Now I was wrapped up in his bedding, and as much as I wanted to be embarrassed, I liked it.

The door opened gently, and Callan poked his head in. Upon seeing I was decent, he ambled over to me, a plate in hand. Whatever was on the plate smelled divine.

"I thought you might be hungry," he explained. "It's not much, just some leftover pasta and garlic bread Bellamy made yesterday, but it's better than nothing." Placing the plate on the bedside table he took a seat on the edge of the bed, and I watched his arms flex as he did so. I had never really been up close and personal with alphas. I was starting to see that they were large... much larger than I expected. Did that also mean they were large in other ways?

I banished the thought, sitting up so my back was against the headboard. I took the plate and dove in, the white garlic sauce paired perfectly with the garlic bread. "Thank you," I managed around a forkful of food.

"There's no need to thank us, it's the least we can do."

I took a moment to swallow before asking. "You're...not in any trouble, right? I mean you're the head of the pack...aren't you? Am I in trouble, as well?"

His face broke out in a wide grin, lighting up his face and making him look five years younger. "I am. As for you...we may get into a little trouble, but we should get everything cleared up in no time. You're not in any trouble at all, Honey."

The door opened again and Alaric and Bellamy wandered in. Both of them took seats around the room. "Is the food okay?" Bellamy asked.

"Really good," I complimented. Bellamy's face lit up and his entire demeanour perked up.

"I wondered where you all were!" Everett stood in the doorway, an easy smile on his face. He must have showered because his blonde curls were still slightly damp. "Coming in!" he declared, throwing himself at the end of the bed like a golden retriever taking their spot for the night. Despite the gravity of the situation, I found myself letting out a small giggle.

"I bring you something of great value." Everett lounged at the end of the bed with a childish grin and pulled out a bag of candy from his pocket. "This is the good stuff, from my private stash. If I kept this in the kitchen it would be stolen. For you, Pretty Girl, you could use a sugar fix." He handed me the candy. It was brightly coloured, artificial and looked amazing.

"Thank you," I croaked.

"Make sure you eat the pasta before that stuff, that'll rot your stomach. Make sure you at least have something semi balanced first." Callan frowned.

"I will." It was sweet that he was concerned and wanted me to eat more and healthily. That was a definite improvement on Claire, and it was comforting to know he cared.

"So, is there anything you want to know about us?" Everett asked after a quiet moment of me eating. "We didn't exactly get much time to get to know one another before…this."

"Ev. She's exhausted. She doesn't need an inquisition," Alaric scolded.

"Uh, actually, I don't mind. It'll distract me a bit," I admitted, looking at Alaric shyly, scared I would upset him.

"In that case, ask away." He nodded his head gracefully with an easy smile, despite the events of the day and what I've gathered so far as a rather stoic nature.

"How did you all meet?"

"Ric and I have been friends from childhood. We reconnected a few years ago when he needed help with a few things and we knew within a week or two that we were pack," Callan admitted.

"Is it instant, figuring out you want to be pack?"

"Not always," Everett spoke this time. "Callan and Bell were friends for years before they realised they wanted to be pack."

I continued to eat as I looked at Bellamy and Callan, "And how did you two meet?"

"Pure dumb luck," Bellamy said. His voice was softer than the rest. Alaric's was powerful, Everett's was loud and playful. Callan's was a controlled ease.

"I got into a bar fight one night with several guys larger than myself. Bell saved my ass and we've been together ever since." Callan sounded proud of his packmate, which I liked.

"You were pathetic, I had to jump in and help you," Bellamy said, giving Callan a small glare with no real heat in it.

"That's why you're the one who checked me over?" I asked.

"That's right."

"Thank you."

"And Everett joined the family because he was a stray and we felt bad for him," Alaric smirked.

"Hey!" Everett laughed, lifting his head to look thoughtfully at Alaric. "I mean, it's true, but that's mean." They all smiled.

"You've got all the time you need to get to know us now," Callan reassured. "We're open books, so you can ask whatever you want, whenever you want."

I put my bowl down and tucked my hair behind my ears, silently cursing that I didn't have a hair tie.

Callan frowned. "What's wrong?"

"Oh! Nothing, I just don't have any hair ties on me."

"Here." Callan pulled a tie off his wrist and handed it over. "I've got plenty."

"I didn't realise," I said.

"Callan's like a shaggy dog with all that hair, if he didn't tie it back occasionally he would look feral." Everett laughed from the end of the bed. "Once, he forgot a hair tie and was in a foul mood all day, complaining about tangles."

"Just because you've never seen a brush," Callan growled.

Everett looked up at his leader, a look of horror on his face. "Callan Rivers, you do not get curls as stunning as mine by brushing them. Heathen!"

Callan turned to face me. "No one here appreciates the struggle. Claudia is constantly telling me I should have a trim."

"I like your hair," I admitted shyly, but Callan seemed to bathe in the compliment.

"Thank you, Honey. I like it, despite what these degenerates think." He shoved Everett's leg playfully so he almost fell off the bed. "Do you need anything else? I think Claudia is planning to drop a few items off."

"No this is perfect," I reassured him, loosely redoing my braids to keep them out of my face.

CHAPTER NINETEEN
Callan

When Sage lifted her arms, a waft of the sweet honey filled the room, I stiffened at the smell. I wanted to be close, to be on the bed like Everett, but I wasn't as warm and approachable as him.

Callan's phone buzzed, and he pulled it out of his pocket, checking the message. "It's the Clearmont Keepers scheduling the home visit for tomorrow."

"We have a lot to get ready before they get here," I reminded everyone. "And we need to be prepared for a load of political bullshit."

"I'm sorry," Sage said.

"Don't you dare apologise. It's worth it, one hundred percent. I'm just terrible at dealing with people, especially people in the wrong. Those idiots mistreated you at every turn, but we'll have to play nice tomorrow because there's no way in hell you're leaving this pack house, at least not unless it's your choice."

"Here, here!" Everett declared playfully. "Our fearless leader shall protect us!"

"I feel like he causes the majority of your stress," Sage stage whispered to Callan, her nose scrunched up playfully.

"I can hear you, Pretty Girl, and yes! I *am* the cause of our fair leader's grey hairs, and rather proud of it to be honest."

"I don't have greys." Callan frowned.

Bellamy snickered, but said nothing.

"Maybe one or two," I confirmed with a shrug.

"Don't listen to them," Sage said. "They're just jealous of your hair."

Callan grinned at his packmates. "You hear that, you fuckers are just jealous!" He shoved Everett hard enough that he actually fell off the bed this time. Sage watched as his head popped up over the bed, his curls bouncing with the movement.

"Abuse!" he declared. "You saw that, didn't you, Pretty Girl?"

Sage hummed thoughtfully. "I saw nothing," she said, putting on a cute little thinking face, her nose scrunching.

"I saw nothing," I confirmed with a dark grin, that didn't seem to scare Sage, in fact it looked like it intrigued her.

"You must be imagining this, Ev." Bellamy couldn't contain his laugh.

"Yeah yeah, side with the beautiful omega." Everett pouted.

"Naturally." Bellamy shrugged.

Sage looked happy and comfortable as she nestled down deeper into the blankets, clutching one of the pillows. My chest tightened at the sight of her holding one of *my* pillows, burying her face in it and gently inhaling. She clearly liked my scent. She'd chosen my T-shirt to wear and seemed perfectly at home in my bed.

Sage yawned loudly, covering her mouth and blinking rapidly like she was fighting sleep.

"We can leave, Honey, you must be exhausted," Callan told her.

"No...it's kind of nice," she admitted with a small smile. "I'm not used to having people around." She was probably feeling attention deprived after Claire's bullshit, even if she didn't realise it.

"You never told us about your family," I enquired.

"Nothing really to say. We aren't close, and I haven't spoken to them in years." She shrugged. "They'll have no idea I'm an omega."

"Do you have any omegas in your family?"

"No, betas through and through. I do have an alpha uncle somewhere, but I never met him."

"That could be why you're an omega."

"How does that even work?" Everett asked.

"Omegas are usually born to alphas. It can be different, but if there's some alpha in her family that makes her omega status more likely."

"We were from alpha families, my ma's an omega, and none of us have close relatives that are betas, do we?"

"I do, but that's a weird case," Bellamy spoke.

Sage's eyes drifted closed and she hummed gently, listening to us talk between ourselves.

"Sage, did you have any other alpha or omega family?" Callan asked, turning to look at her but her face was smushed into my pillow and she was snoring lightly.

"She's down for the count," Bellamy observed.

"She's had a long day," Callan said, gently leaning forward to brush a stray strand of hair out of her face.

I shifted in my seat. "I want to slit that asshole's throat. We need to increase security."

"I agree. We never really had strong security here because we've never had anything to protect," Callan admitted.

"Now we've got something precious to protect," Bellamy said, his tone wistful.

"We sure do," Callan agreed. "I'll call Winton and get him to up the protection. He and Harrison aren't going to cut it anymore." Harrison was nearing his fifties and Winton wasn't far behind him. We liked them, and they did a good enough job keeping an eye on things when it was just us but now an omega was involved, we needed more.

"She needs a better nest," I said, looking at my bedding. An omega needed more, they needed throw pillows, multiple blankets and so much more. There were whole warehouse stores dedicated to omega nesting materials.

"Don't you like her being in your bed?" Bellamy asked with a grin.

"Of course I do, fucker. She deserves a better nest though, her own space. The Keepers will want her to have one too before allowing her to stay."

"Bell, Everett, tomorrow I need you both to go shopping to outfit Sage's nest before the Keepers arrive."

"Fuck yeah, what's the budget?"

"No budget," I interjected. "Just get as much as you can and if she doesn't use it, she doesn't use it. Take my card if you want." I was the most rigid with money, and likely had the most savings. We were all well off, and most of our money was combined, but I saved religiously just in case there was an emergency. I wanted to provide for the omega, I wanted to be the one to purchase her soft and pretty things.

Everett raised his eyebrows. "Mr Budget is happy to splurge

on the pretty girl," he chuckled, keeping his voice low so he didn't wake Sage.

"Yes," I answered simply.

"We should sleep, tomorrow we'll work on getting her more comfortable. I'm not looking forward to how much money I'll have to throw at this whole situation to get it sorted out with the Keepers," Callan sighed.

"I'll liquidate some property portfolio tomorrow in case we have to re-pay our fees to the Clearmont Haven," I said.

No one answered and we sat in silence, listening to Sage's soft snores.

"I don't want to leave, do you?" Everett asked us, in a whisper.

"No, she does draw you in," Callan admitted. "But we shouldn't crowd her, come on." He got up, stretching. "She needs her space and we need to let her heal."

"Then we need to woo her." Everett grinned.

"We will," I stated, "but in the meantime I'd better go get some blankets for the couch."

"How is it we have this giant fuck-you sized house and no guest bedrooms?" Everett asked with a frown.

"We agreed we didn't want guests in our space…so none of the guest rooms actually have beds, remember?" Bellamy laughed.

"Oh, we should probably correct that." Everett chuckled.

"You think?!" Bellamy asked, exasperated.

CHAPTER TWENTY
Bellamy

Our home first thing in the morning was amazing, tranquil, calm. Most of my packmates didn't start waking up until eight at the earliest, so I loved getting a workout in beforehand. I had been working out more frequently, a certain omega was probably to blame for my restless energy.

Sage's scent was infiltrating every corner of the house and my cock had definitely taken notice. Every night I would take matters into my own hand in the shower, usually more than once, and still the moment I got into bed I would think about a particular blonde joining me and would instantly be hard again. Now she was just down the hall from me, not locked away in a Haven.

That's how I found myself getting up at four in the morning, deciding that a workout would help take the edge off some of my frustrations. I lost myself in the familiar routine of weights, moving until my muscles ached and ending with a quick treadmill run. By the time I was finished, a thick sheen of sweat coated me and I was panting like an alpha in a room full of omegas.

Stepping off the treadmill I could smell Sage, she was near. Taking my headphones off so my ears weren't full of angry, pounding bass, I could hear the soft footfalls of Sage making her way down the main corridor. I glanced at the clock. *What is she up to at five in the morning?* Curiosity urged me forwards. *Should she even be walking with her injured ankle?*

She was padding through the hall, heading in the direction of the kitchen with a slight limp. Wearing my oversized T-shirt and boxers, she took slow, steady steps. I should have left her, let her enjoy the calm of our home early in the morning, but I needed to be near her.

"Sage?" I softly spoke from behind her, making her jump and spin around sharply.

"Bellamy!" Sage gasped, her hand over her heart in fright. "You scared the crap out of me!" her voice was hoarse from the bruises and I winced at the sound. That shit had to hurt.

She looked sleepy and dishevelled, her hair sticking up. It was adorable, and if I didn't know better I would think she looked thoroughly fucked. *If only.*

"Sorry, is everything okay?" I asked gently. She took a few deep breaths taking in my appearance.

"I, uh, sorry. I shouldn't be wandering around alone, should I?" She fidgeted, keeping her gaze to the floor.

"You can go wherever you want here. It's your home as long as you want it to be, Sage."

"What are you doing up at this time?" she asked.

I quirked an eyebrow. "I could say the same thing to you."

"I was thirsty, and possibly planning to raid the kitchen for some snacks," Sage admitted. "You?"

"Working out. I couldn't sleep and I like to get a head start on the day. Come on." I walked up to Sage, nodding down the hall for her to follow me. "I'll get us some breakfast...or a midnight snack in your case."

The shy omega avoided looking me in the eye as she nodded. Her nostrils flared as I swept past. I had just run three miles and my scent would have been pretty potent.

I had opted to walk in front of Sage so she wouldn't see the effect her sweet honey scent and rumpled, sleepy look had on my body

"What do you want to eat?" I asked as we entered the kitchen.

"What would you usually make?"

"Eggs," I admitted.

"Eggs it is then! You need my help?" Sage asked.

"Sure, I could always use a hand, especially one as pretty as yours."

She rolled her eyes at me.

"I'll grab drinks first, what would you like?" she asked, already heading to the fridge to check out what we had.

"Just a protein shake, please."

She grabbed a strawberry-flavoured shake and a bottle of water for herself, walking them both over to me. I kissed the top of her head on instinct with a muttered thanks, instantly freezing when I realised what I'd done, but Sage didn't seem to mind. She leaned into me for a brief moment before she shook her head slightly, stepping away.

"Could you please grab me the frying pan from the cupboard behind you?" It was near enough she didn't have to walk, and she had asked to help, so I wanted easy tasks for her.

"What do you do when you wake up so early?" she asked,

watching me set the pan on the burner and fetch a carton of eggs from the fridge.

"Usually I just enjoy the peace and quiet," I admitted, cracking a few eggs into a bowl.

"Oh..."

"I can see those cogs turning in your brain, Sage," my tone was soft, but stern. "You don't count. You're not interrupting me at all. The others can get..."

"Loud?" she suggested. "Boisterous? Obnoxious?"

I laughed, throwing my head back. When I looked back, Sage's eyes were wide, staring at my neck. Was she turned on by my scent?

"I love them, really do, but sometimes it's nice to get up early and enjoy the quiet."

"It's so calm. At my apartment it was never quiet. Even in the middle of the night, I could hear cars and sirens." Sage leaned her weight on the counter, tracing the pattern with her fingertip. "How did you go from the military to owning cafes?"

"After years of being a medic and seeing that level of damage, I just wanted out, and I love coffee, *actual* coffee, not the sugary crap most people drink." She opened her mouth to complain, but I continued before she could. "Just because you enjoy it, doesn't mean it's true coffee! I'll stand by that, but I'll still make you sugary coffee if that's what you want, Sweetheart."

"Now?" she asked, her face lighting up.

"No." I pointed at her. "You need a decent breakfast before we caffeinate you. When's the last time you drank water?"

She held up her bottle of water she had just retrieved from the fridge.

"That's unopened, it doesn't count. Before then?"

Sage pouted. "A while ago."

"Drink that, then I'll make you your iced white mocha. I ordered hazelnut syrup and vanilla sweet cream so we'd have it on hand for you. Deal?"

"Deal!"

I'd stock an entire fridge full of ridiculous coffee flavourings if it meant it would get her to smile at me like that again.

"I'll need that sugary coffee to deal with whatever today brings." She opened the bottle and took several long sips. I also cracked open my protein shake, chugging half of it in three gulps.

"Do you think I could visit one of your cafes? I miss being out and about."

"Sage," I hated that I had to destroy that hopeful look on her face, "maybe in the future, but right now you're an unbonded omega."

"Ahh yeah, I'm a *menace to society*." She adorably added air quotes.

"Hardly!" I laughed. The only thing she was a menace to was my self-control. I was going to develop friction burns from jacking off to the thought of her.

"Yeah…" Sage trailed off, absentmindedly picking at her nails, a hint of distress sneaking into her scent.

"What's wrong?" I asked gently.

"I just can't switch my brain off." Sage raked a frustrated hand through her hair, tangling in the remains of her braid. "I feel uprooted."

"It'll take time to settle. It's pretty normal to miss your own space, especially when you worked so hard for it. I don't presume to know you entirely already, but I do know you're an independent woman. I can't imagine that suddenly finding yourself dependent on alphas has been easy." I walked over to the fridge, pulling out some bell peppers and cheese.

"You're right," Sage admitted. "I'm not exactly used to being taken care of. I'm grateful, don't get me wrong. It's just…"

"Really fucking weird?" That got the laugh out of her I'd been hoping for. "Do you want to chop peppers or grate cheese?"

"Cheese, please."

I passed her a brick of cheese and a box grater before getting myself a cutting board and chef's knife to chop the bell peppers. "I know I would feel uncomfortable in your position. If you think of anything that we can do to make this transition easier, tell us. This isn't a dictatorship."

Sage worked on the cheese, chewing her lip thoughtfully. "Well, I've read several contradicting things. How can an omega be soft and submissive, but also dominate and rule the pack like the books say?"

I smiled, indulgently. "I think omegas adapt to what their pack needs, and alphas adapt for them. We all have things to figure out and adjust to during this process. Plus, you're stuck with us for a while, so there's time."

"I know that, and I don't hate it here, it's just…"

"Not yours."

Sage nodded, setting the cheese aside as tears formed along her lashes. "I'm usually so collected, and now I feel off kilter. I'm turning into a damn faucet." She wiped at her face as tears slid down her cheeks, cursing quietly, trying to gain control.

I set the knife down and gathered her into my arms. The simple action was enough to open the floodgates.

"It's normal to feel out of sorts. I would be shocked if you were okay. You've been so resilient until now, I'm surprised. We want you to feel safe here, you do what feels good for you." I passed her bottle of water to her with a silent command to drink, she wasn't drinking enough already, add crying to that and she could easily become dehydrated. "Your safety here isn't contingent on anything. I'm guessing no one has explicitly told you that?"

"What do you mean?" She wiped her eyes, pulling back to look at me.

"You worry this is temporary—because you may not choose us—and if that's the case you have to leave and you don't know where you'll go from there. I'm guessing you feel like you have no true anchors right now."

She looked at me intently for a moment, and I could practically see her mind buzzing behind her hazel eyes. "I think you hit the nail on the head," she admitted after a moment, surprised at her own revelation.

"We should have ensured you understood this before you even entered this house, so let me make something clear: we expect nothing from you—you'll always have a place here. If you don't choose us then the omega rooms will still be yours, once we actually set them up. You can stay, or go to a Haven. Whatever you think is best for you is what we'll support and encourage because we're pack."

"But I'm not really pack, not until I bond with you."

"Bullshit! You became pack the moment you chose to come with us and we chose you. You *are* pack, even if you aren't our omega. Pack takes care of each other. Sage, if you decide to never pursue a relationship with us we will still be here for you in whatever capacity you need…just maybe at a slight physical distance because you do smell really good." I gave her a lopsided smile, cupping her face gently before returning to the eggs, and tossing them in the pan alongside the peppers.

"That sounds nice, but if this doesn't work out between us, what happens when you find a new omega? They wouldn't like me hanging around."

"We wouldn't be looking for another omega. My pack and I wanted to do this because of *you*: the woman who teased us over our pizza choices and gave Alaric a nickname, and who is realistically smarter than all of us. We aren't ashamed to admit that. Do we want to protect you because of our alpha nature? Fuck yes, but that doesn't change the fact that our instincts are that much stronger because it's *you*."

Placing the egg scramble in front of her, I added some of the cheese she'd grated so it could melt before reaching over, wiping a tear from her cheek with my thumb before gesturing to eat.

Her appreciative hum at the first bite of food pleased me. Sage's focus was on her food, so she didn't notice my hungry gaze as I sat next to her, digging into my own plate of eggs.

"This is nice."

"I know I can be more reserved than the others, but I want my feeling to be clear, I like you Sage, a lot."

"Thank you, I like you guys as well," Sage admitted shyly.

The sun was starting to rise outside the kitchen window.

"Do you think Lex'll get into trouble for this?" Sage asked after a moment.

I swallowed before speaking, I had already eaten the majority of my food, whereas Sage was just picking at hers.

"It was an outright threat to an omega, they take that seriously."

"Am I safe from him here?"

"Yes, we've got cameras all over the place, and security guards outside"

"Security guards?" Sage asked, "I haven't seen anything... have you always had them?"

"They stay out of sight, they never enter the house, we've always had one or two but we've increased it recently," I said as I got up, putting both our dishes in the sink frowning at the food she had left, she really needed to eat more. Sage stretched, yawning adorably. "You finally getting tired?"

"Maybe, we've been down here a while."

"We needed to talk," I said. "If you want I can take you around the grounds to meet all the guards one day? They'll never enter the house, but it may be good to know their names and faces."

"I would appreciate that. I'm happy we talked. What are you doing today?"

I grinned. "I may have to nip into work to deal with a food delivery, but someone will be here with you at all times."

"Okay." Sage replied. I went to pass her, but she stopped me. Her hand reaching out and gently touching my forearm.

"Bellamy?" Her voice was soft. She looked up at me, her expression open, her pupils dilated.

"Yeah, Sweetheart?"

Sage frowned, obviously conflicted about what she wanted to ask. "Can I, uh... You know what, never mind." She shook her head and turned away.

"Now I'm going to die of curiosity. You have to tell me."

"It's nothing, I was being silly. I wanted to try—" she sighed, shifting away ever so slightly. I looked down, confused and concerned.

"Can I..." she trailed off her question. She was close, the hungry look in her eyes held so much need.

My eyes widened in surprise. My voice caught in my throat, so instead of verbally answering, I nodded.

Soft hands grabbed my neck, pulling my head down. Reaching up on tiptoe, Sage gently pressed her lips to mine. Just a brief touch, but I wanted *more*.

My arm instinctively slid around her waist, bringing us together, feeling every curve of her against me. The sensation of her so close was heady, intoxicating. I was shocked, but wasn't going to question Sage's actions. Head tilted down I returned the kiss, my lips bruising hers with far more force than her light, nervous touch. I deepened the kiss, elated when I was rewarded with a sweet little moan and her fingers tightening round my neck.

Caged between the counter and myself, she melted into my embrace. One of my arms rested on the counter behind her while the other stayed wrapped firmly around her waist anchoring her to me.

Pulling apart, I rested my head against her forehead, panting. Sage stroked her fingers over my jaw gently. "Uh, wow." Sage giggled, removing her hand away from my jaw. "Uh, sorry, I kind of attacked you there, didn't I?"

"You can attack me anytime," a voice from the doorway chuckled. Sage let out a little squeak at the sight of the others all looking at us and buried her head in my chest, doing her best to hide. I laughed, wrapping my arms around Sage and keeping her close.

"Jealous?" I asked the others as they filtered into the kitchen, a shit-eating grin affixed to my face as I rested my chin on the top of Sage's head.

"Of course we are," Callan smiled, striding over to the fridge and grabbing water for himself.

"Sorry, I—" Sage pulled away from me, her face pinched with worry.

"Don't you dare fucking apologise," I growled, kissing the top of her head, and keeping her caged in my arms. "They're just grumpy and jealous."

Everett grinned, leaning against the door frame. "I'm not even mad, that was kind of hot to watch, I didn't think I was a watcher. What's the word for that? Voyeur! Heck yeah, I'm a voyeur."

"Stop embarrassing her," Alaric growled at him, but Everett just grinned wider.

"I think I'm going to go grab my phone," Sage mumbled, trying to turn away from me. I was unhappy at the loss of her up against me. I pulled her a little tighter, resting my chin on the top of her head.

"You idiots are ruining my moment," I groused at my brothers who just laughed. I lowered my voice so only she could hear me, "If you're really uncomfortable you can go, but don't let these morons chase you away, they'll cope."

She thought for a second before nodding and whispering back, "I'm okay."

Callan walked over to us. "Leave us alone," I sighed dramatically, playfully dragging Sage away from the approaching Callan while she giggled.

Curling deeper into my chest she yawned deeply.

"Honey, how long have you been awake? Did you get enough sleep?" Callan cooed softly.

"Maybe an hour? I couldn't sleep."

"I think you need to get back to bed."

I let Callan gently guide her from my arms and tug her toward the staircase.

The moment she was out of the room, Everett turned on

me. "Looks like you were having a good time." He waggled his eyebrows.

"We got to know each other a little better. She's sweet but still shook up from what happened yesterday. We have to be gentle with her."

"That didn't look gentle to me." Everett laughed.

"She instigated it, I wasn't going to say no."

"It's okay if she instigates it, but we can't do so. Not yet," Alaric said, looking over at Everett. "You're with her this morning. Don't push, not even a dirty joke."

"Yes, daddy." Everett grinned.

"And stop letting her walk on that fucking ankle."

CHAPTER TWENTY-ONE
Everett

> Hey Pretty Girl,
>
> I checked in around midday but you were dead to the world. Drop me a message once you wake up and I'll come see you. We have a meeting this afternoon with the Keepers. I left some water and Tylenol on your bedside table. Thought it best I add you to a group chat with all these idiots.
>
> - From your favourite

I didn't sign my name, but I was sure she would know who had written that message. I distracted myself with some emails while I waited for her answer. Her morning snuggle with Bellamy had clearly exhausted her, not that I was complaining. Seeing her kissing Bellamy had stirred all my hopes up that maybe this could work. Her reply didn't come until early afternoon.

SAGE

Hello Everett, bold assumption on your part.

I was right, instead of replying I went through to see her. I knocked and poked my head round the door, being immediately hit with a wave of her honey scent. She was still nestled down on the bed, cuddled into the blankets. Her eyes met mine and she gave me a sleepy smile.

"Well, good morning," I said as I entered. "Clearly you're feeling a bit better if you're already calling me out in the group chat."

"You're the only one who calls me Pretty Girl," she replied, her voice hoarse.

"True, I'll need to get more creative." I sat on the end of the bed. "Are you hungry?"

"A little, but my throat is killing me. I'm not sure I can eat." She gently ran her hand over her neck, wincing at the pain. The bruises had darkened impressively overnight, and the sight made my blood boil.

"We'll get you some tea and something easy to eat. Are you comfy?"

"Yeah, I slept like the dead didn't I?"

"I came in this morning and you had your face smashed into the pillow, snoring. It was absolutely adorable."

Sage groaned, "Oh lord. I can't believe you saw that."

"It was cute! So today you can stay up here, Alaric has a remote to that giant TV somewhere, so how does doing fuck all, eating snacks and watching TV sound?"

"Sounds pretty nice, but surely Alaric wants his room back, where is he? Where is everyone?"

"Callan and Bellamy are shopping for omega supplies so it

looks like we've got our act together when the Keepers get here. Alaric is in his office trying to make sure everything's in order for our side of the paperwork to keep you with us." I reached over to a shelf on the bedside table, pulling out the TV remote and passing it to Sage. "Pick something to watch while I go grab food." Sage sat up on the mound of pillows, wincing in pain.

***

Sage was flicking through the TV when I returned with a plate of food in one hand, a tumbler of iced tea in another. "Burrito or Fajitas? I brought both. Bellamy made it for us after you went to bed so it's still nice and fresh. I'll have whatever you don't have."

"Fajitas please! I'll have some iced tea for my throat first, though." She reached for the tumbler and I passed it over, separating out the fajita ingredients onto a separate plate for her.

"Nice choice," I said, motioning to the TV and plopping down on the bed next to her. I was careful not to interrupt the specific way she had arranged the blankets. Despite sleeping, she looked tired and sore. Maybe some trashy reality TV would distract her for a bit.

"So who's dating who?"

"I dunno yet. I thought this was a regular reality TV show, but these people basically talk to each other through a wall, unable to see each other, and then decide if they want to get married! It's insane."

"At least we got to see each other first," I said as I took a bite of my burrito.

"Oh god, this is too similar to us, isn't it? *Date an Omega*. It sounds so trashy," Sage gasped, realisation dawning on her face as she took a bite of the fajitas, wincing when she swallowed.

"Let's just judge people's choices. Take that guy for example, he's *clearly* a giant douche." I tried to lighten the mood.

"Really? I was thinking he reminded me of you." Sage grinned up at me, her eyes dancing with mischief.

"Cheeky!" I exclaimed but Sage just grinned. "Eat your food." I laughed.

At one point she dozed off again, and I took the chance to get a good look at her. Hugging a pillow she looked so peaceful and serene. Her hair was fanned out and she was curled up into a ball. Even with the bruising she was stunning, button nose, large eyes and pillow lips.

Picking up my phone from the bedside I noticed several messages in the pack group chat, a chat that Sage wasn't part of—yet. We didn't want to worry her with details of the current situation, she needed to rest, to heal. We had added her to a new group chat with all five of us that morning.

> CALLAN:
>
> God Damn Haven is going to make this hard for us, they're claiming we put Sage in danger by making them disable the cameras.
>
> BELLAMY:
>
> That's bullshit!
>
> CALLAN:
>
> I know, but Claudia says they will probably need a statement from Sage soon regarding the situation. We also need to pay fees again because apparently the shitty Keepers who had Sage pocketed our fees.

EVERETT:

> They're not going to look into Claire stealing from packs?

CALLAN:

They will, but that'll take time. If we want Sage we have to hand over money to the new Haven while they investigate.

ALARIC:

She's not leaving the Manor.

BELLAMY:

I agree. Pay whatever we need to.

CALLAN:

Clearmont is sending Keeper Ethel Hanover today. Apparently she's been there decades, was a Keeper when Claudia herself was in the facility and they're good friends.

BELLAMY:

That's good, it means we can trust her.

CALLAN:

Hopefully. How's Sage doing?

I snapped a quick picture of the dozing omega next to me and sent it.

EVERETT:

> Fast asleep, she ate, watched some TV and dropped off again. She seems okay, if a bit sore. I gave her Tylenol like Bellamy suggested.

CALLAN:

You're a lucky git you know that Everett? We all are. Fucking hell, she's sweet.

ALARIC:

He has the Kleinson job this afternoon and will have to miss the meeting, so he's not THAT lucky.

ALARIC:

Bell and Callan will be home soon with everything they've bought. Everett make sure Sage is ready for the Keepers while I finish up this paperwork

EVERETT:

Do I have to? She's so cosy!

CALLAN:

I get the feeling this pack is somehow going to get even more chaotic.

I threw my phone down and looked over at the omega who was now stretching, wiping the sleep from her eyes.

"I fell asleep? How much did I miss?" She looked at the TV.

"I paused it as soon as you drifted off, so you've missed nothing."

"Thank you, you didn't have to stay."

"I've kept myself busy reading some emails."

Sage bit her fingernail absentmindedly, looking at the window where daylight was filtering in. "Hey, Everett? Do you think we could go soak up some sunshine for a bit? I kinda missed fresh air while I was locked up."

"Of course, Pretty Girl." I hopped off the bed, my scent clinging to the sheets. "Alaric won't care about having your scent all over the sheets, but he'll be grumpy at me. Luckily, it's fun poking the bear."

"Surely we can wash all the scent off for him." Sage scrunched her nose. "There's got to be a washing machine around here, I don't mind!"

I scooped her up into my arms. "I would bet my left nut sack that any of my pack members would happily have your scent left all over their bedding."

"Only the *left* nut sack?" Sage asked, her arms winding round my neck. "You know I can walk right? My ankle is just a little sore."

"It's my favourite." I ignored her comment about being able to walk. She was being stubborn and Alaric would murder me if I let her walk unaided.

"You'll probably be in here for a few days until we get your room ready. They're buying supplies today, but it'll all need to be washed first, and the furniture is still en route."

"I hate kicking Alaric out of his room for so long." Sage frowned.

"He volunteered, happily. In fact, he kind of insisted."

"It is pretty comfy," she agreed as I carried her down the stairs. "This place is giant," she mused, taking in her surroundings.

"I'll show you around later, carry you through the whole place and give you the grand tour. Callan bought this house years ago when it was run down and falling to bits, but he did some major remodelling and now it's a stunner. He did most of the remodel himself, we helped a little toward the end, but he deserves most of the credit."

"Impressive, he did a lovely job. Where are we going now?"

"Kitchen, there's a patio that has some nice garden furniture, even one of those porch swings on an old oak tree. You probably didn't see it this morning as it was dark and you were distracted." Heat rose in her face, but she didn't address it. "That sounds lovely."

"I thought you would like that."

Footsteps alerted me to someone else's presence behind us. Bellamy.

"Where are you off to?" he asked me. "And how are you feeling?" he asked Sage.

"Good," Sage replied.

"I'm taking her out onto the patio, she's been cooped up for a while."

"Excellent, I'll join you guys." Bellamy grinned. "I've got nothing better to do." He walked alongside us, subtly checking over Sage.

Our gardens were stunning. There was lush green grass, plenty of flowers and even a pond. None of us had a green thumb, but Callan hired someone to take care of it. There was a porch swing hanging from the giant oak tree and several garden chairs sat around a fire pit, a picnic bench and a barbecue.

"Wow." Sage looked around in awe.

"I'm going to guess you want to sit on the swing?" I asked.

She nodded her agreement but said, "I can walk, you know. I walked down to the kitchen this morning."

"I think Alaric may actually kill him if he lets you walk on that ankle." Bellamy chuckled. Sage just rolled her eyes as I placed her on the swing. Bellamy ducked back inside, only to come back a moment later holding a blanket to go on her lap.

"I don't need to be wrapped in bubble wrap," Sage protested weakly.

"Indulge us, at least until you heal up a bit. You'll need all the rest you can get. My mother is going to be here soon so she can act as witness for the Keeper interrogation."

"I think she's already here, Ev." Bellamy pointed to the patio doors, where we could just see into the kitchen where Callan and Claudia were having a conversation. Callan was holding a mug of coffee wearing a faded pair of jeans and a grey T-shirt. His hair was a wild mess almost reaching his shoulders.

"Oh, are your dads here as well?" Sage asked, interrupting my thoughts.

"I doubt it, it's likely just Ma, I bet she wouldn't even let them around you right now. She wants you to have space to relax with as few alphas breathing down your neck as possible."

"I've got four crowding me already." Sage chuckled lightly.

"We're not crowding you too much, are we?" Bellamy asked, crestfallen.

Shit. Were we coming on too strong?

"Oh, no! You're not, it's a lot to get used to, but you guys have been amazing. Too nice if anything!" Sage rushed to say, her brows furrowed.

She needed to speak her mind, not worry what we would say.

"Sage! How are you feeling?" Ma made a beeline for Sage, enveloping her in a hug. "I'm doing well, These men won't stop feeding me, and I'm going to burst." Sage chuckled.

"They probably need reminding that you can't eat anywhere near as much as these bottomless pits."

"Do you think they would listen?"

"Nope," Ma said, at the same time I snorted, "No."

Ma rolled her eyes at my answer and sat down on the porch swing next to Sage. "Why don't you go make yourself useful and get your mother a drink?"

"I'll get you one, Claudia." Bellamy gave her his most charming smile and my mother fell for it, hook, line and sinker.

"Thank you, Bellamy, it's nice to know some of Pack Rivers have manners."

"If I have no manners, what does that mean about the woman who raised me?"

"That they're a saint for putting up with you!"

"My mother, so loving!" I put my hand over my heart and pouted. She simply rolled her eyes again and turned to Sage who was watching our exchange happily.

"I bought you some goodies, some decent blankets and pillows. I know your rooms are bare, where did they even put you last night?" Ma told her, her attention now on Sage fully.

"Alaric's room, apparently he has the most bedding out of all of them, I feel bad he slept on the couch, though."

"He can handle a few nights on the couch." Ma waved her concern away. "More importantly, how did *you* sleep?"

"Really well actually, the scent was familiar so it wasn't hard to fall asleep at all. It was almost like I was used to that particular smell...." She raised her eyebrows.

"To be fair, I gave you many options, only one or two of them were scented like the pack. You just happened to gravitate to Alaric's scent."

"It smells really good!" she giggled.

"I'm not disagreeing, when I first got a sniff of Nolan I was obsessed."

"Nolan was the one who..." she trailed off.

"Was at the Haven yesterday? Yes, he was."

"I never got to thank him. Is he okay?"

"Don't worry dear. He's doing fine and enjoying an excuse to take things easy for a few days. Now, let's go back to chatting about you. I know you must be feeling a little claustrophobic.

In my pack's early days being able to retreat to my rooms was a huge relief. Is there anything else you want?"

"Everyone has been so nice, I can't ask for anything more."

"I'm glad to see you shopping for your own clothes so you're not stuck wearing a wardrobe that belongs to the boys."

"Hey, she looks stunning in our clothes!" I interjected.

"Everett, sweetie, I love you, but shut up. Sage, we should make a proper list of other things you need. I know the boys went shopping today, but they're not omegas so I'm sure there's plenty they missed."

Ma turned towards Sage, declaring, "I was blessed with alpha boys, but I always wanted a daughter, and I've decided that regardless of your choices with my often ill-advised son, you're now mine!"

Tears welled in Sage's eyes, and she clutched Ma's hand. "Thank you," she whispered. I wanted to reach out, to reassure her, but it felt wrong to intrude on the moment.

"You don't need to thank family. Now, I brought my laptop with me, and I think some internet shopping is in order!"

CHAPTER TWENTY-TWO
Sage

Sitting on the patio, we ate a delicious cheese and meat board Bellamy had prepared while we scrolled through websites, picking out clothes. Everett interjected every now and again, playfully suggesting wildly inappropriate clothing like a ski suit.

I frowned at the screen as the basket slowly filled. "Are you sure it's not too much?"

"Not at all, you need clothes, just don't pay attention to the prices!" Claudia said.

That felt like a physical impossibility. Still, I was restrained with my purchases and stuck to the basics. Wearing the guys clothes wasn't a long term solution.

Leaning back, I basked in the sunshine. It had been too long since I had been in the fresh air and natural light. The Haven had smelled almost sterile, and every day I was becoming more and more sensitive to various smells, the faint aroma of coffee that clung to Bellamy after he had been to work. The pine in Callan's shampoo.

We had just finished filling the shopping basket when Callan came outside from the kitchen.

"Ladies, the Keepers are here."

I froze, panic setting in. Were they going to take me back, or force me to spend time with Pack Bove?

"None of that dear," Claudia soothed, seeing my breathing hasten. "I know these people, they're good. We'll be with you the entire time, okay?"

I nodded, taking a deep breath. Three Keepers had turned up. I settled on the couch in the main living room between Claudia and Bellamy with a blanket on my lap. Callan escorted the Keepers into the sitting room, gesturing for them to all sit on the couch or armchairs.

"Thank you." One Keeper nodded as they took their seat.

The oldest, a sweet lady in her fifties with slightly greying hair pulled into a neat bun at the nape of her neck, spoke to me as she sat down, "Hi, you must be Sage. I'm Keeper Hanover. With me I have Keeper Gregory from Clearmont and the Haven's security specialist, Brandon. He liaises with the police when appropriate."

Keeper Gregory was a middle-aged man, wearing a smart suit, his dark hair slicked back. Brandon was significantly younger, he couldn't be older than twenty-two. He had messy hair that he had combed back and wore plain black cargo pants and a grey T-shirt.

"Hello," I said weakly, my voice cracking. Keeper Hanover frowned at the sound, her eyes roamed over the bruises on my neck, clearly visible over the shirt I was wearing.

"We're here to get an idea of what exactly happened at the Mencaster Haven, and figure out the best steps going forward. I'll have to ask that we talk to Sage alone as well first." She looked pointedly at the members of the Pack Rivers.

"We'll happily leave you to chat, but then we need to talk about what's being done to protect Sage and punish those who have exploited her." Callan's voice was firm.

"I'll be staying," Claudia informed their guests, her tone leaving no room for disagreement. "I am the only omega Sage has met since she presented and she needs a familiar face, an advocate."

"But you are the mother of a member of Pack Rivers, correct?" Keeper Gregory asked with a frown, adjusting the sleeve of his suit. He seemed uncomfortable, shifting in his seat. Maybe he wasn't used to wearing suits.

"She is," I confirmed. "But I trust her. She has never coerced me to choose her family. In fact, she's been the only person, Keepers included, to give me fair and honest advice in this entire process. She stays with me or I won't feel comfortable speaking with you."

"We will have to insist, just for the first two minutes or so we can talk with Sage, but then you're welcome to join Mrs Thorn." Keeper Hanover reassured Claudia.

"Okay, but I am just a shout away, Sage," Claudia assured me. At least she would be near if I needed her.

Bellamy placed a glass of iced tea in front of me on the small coffee table. "Just shout if you need me." He smiled easily at me before exiting the room, leaving just me and our guests. My chest ached in their absence. I mentally shook myself, I had known them for such a short time how could I be physically feeling their absence.

"Now we are alone, the first thing we have to ask is, are you okay, Sage? Are you safe here? We are so sorry this happened, even though we don't really know what *this* is yet. We hope to get to the bottom of that today."

"I'm safe here, if that's what you're asking. The guys have been taking great care of me. I feel safe here, a lot safer than where I used to be."

"You were attacked by an alpha?"

"In my own room," I confirmed. "But Pack Rivers have never intimidated me, pushed me, or treated me badly. I wouldn't be able to live with myself if they faced repercussions for taking me when they were just keeping me safe."

"I can assure you if they were acting in your best interest, they wouldn't be in any trouble." Keeper Hanover smiled at me, warm and motherly. "Can you tell us everything that happened in your own words, Sage?"

"Of course, but now I've assured you I'm safe, can Claudia come back in?" I asked.

Keeper Hanover nodded, though Keeper Gregory looked like he was going to complain, but was cut off with a sharp look from his colleague.

Grabbing my phone I shot Claudia a text. She didn't reply, but entered the room with a plate in hand and sat next to me.

"I brought some pastries with me, in case you're hungry." She sat next to me, placing the plate in front of me. My stomach was in knots and the last thing I wanted to do was eat, but I wanted it to be obvious that Pack Rivers was looking after me, so I grabbed a raspberry pastry and nibbled.

The familiar cinnamon scent of Claudia was comforting as she sat next to me. I wanted to lean into her, embrace her warmth.

"Now, back to explaining what happened," Keeper Gregory said, derailing my train of thought.

I ran them through the last few weeks, from the odd set up of my room and the pack meetings.

"Despite my repeated requests to Keeper Claire, they didn't allow me privacy or more food. They kept me on a very strict diet of chicken and salmon with vegetables, nothing else."

"They should have given you whatever food you requested." Keeper Gregory frowned. "And most viewing rooms are separate from the omega's bedrooms. The meeting rooms are never used long term, they're for short meetings of an hour or two. They gave you privacy to bathe, use the facilities, right?"

"No." I shook my head, taking a sip of the iced tea to collect my thoughts before speaking again. "The door to the viewing room was always unlocked and packs were coming through at all hours. If I wanted to bathe, I would have to do it in front of a pack, or at least risk a pack entering at any moment."

"That's a blatant security risk," Brandon muttered with a shake of his head.

I snorted, *I'll give them security risks*. "They also gave Pack Bove access to the cameras in my room. I discovered right before I left they had been watching me for several days."

Keeper Hanover paled, and Brandon cursed.

"I can't believe that..." Keeper Hanover sounded shocked, which was a relief that it at least wasn't common practice.

"And the pack meetings?" Keeper Gregory pressed on.

"Frankly, they were horrible. Several packs said derogatory things, brought me lingerie and got angry when I didn't try it on in front of them."

Keeper Gregory's lip curled in disgust at that, but Keeper Hanover looked *pissed*, despite her small stature given the look of fury marring her features I bet she would have easily been able to take an alpha.

"There were some decent packs, like Pack Rivers. I got along well with them," I continued.

"And the situation escalated?"

"Yes, Claire was pressuring me to go with the Pack Bove. I didn't even want them to visit me. She told me they were the only pack to register interest in me officially and that given my age, I wouldn't find a better situation."

"Pack Rivers registered interest after their first meeting, and Sage was never informed," Claudia told them.

"You weren't?" Keeper Hanover frowned.

"No. I didn't learn that until Pack Rivers came to my aid. They realised the extent of what was happening, and they contacted Claudia," I gestured to Claudia next to me, "who came to the Haven and ensured I could shower in private and advised me of my rights. Over the next few days we discussed my options, trying to move me to another Haven, etc. Claudia advised me on solo courting. That evening, once Claudia left, I informed Keeper Claire that I would like to solo court Pack Rivers. She tried to force me into choosing Pack Bove again. Not an hour after I refused and insisted on Pack Rivers again, Lex was in my room. He's the one that put these bruises on me. When Pack Rivers saved me, I made the decision that I wasn't safe at the Haven and wanted to go with them."

"Sage, I am so sorry this happened to you. You'll be safe and protected at the Clearmont facility," Keeper Gregory said. "It's the biggest and best equipped in a three hundred mile radius."

"I wanted to discuss my options. I intended to go there before this happened. The last thing I want to do is to impose on Pack Rivers."

Claudia snorted softly, but didn't say anything.

Keeper Gregory cleared his throat. "Well, we are more than

happy to welcome you into Clearmont, after you've finished your ninety days here."

I stilled, frowning at Keeper Gregory. "Ninety days?"

"Yes, when you came here with Pack Rivers, you agreed to the ninety-day courtship period. After which you're free to come to Clearmont, or any facility of your choosing," Keeper Gregory explained.

"I had only briefly mentioned courtship times at a pack house," Claudia admitted. "Sage seemed to be a long way from that, so I didn't give her all the details about the next steps after solo courting."

"So I can't leave, even if I wanted to?" I asked, scratching the back of my neck, my mind racing a mile a minute. I was trapped? I didn't *feel* trapped.

Keeper Gregory shook his head. "No, not unless Pack Rivers are mistreating you in any way—we can remove you today if so."

There were much worse places they could trap me, and with far worse company, but the idea didn't sit right with me—and now they were asking if they were abusing me, when Pack Rivers had *removed* me from the abuse they had failed to protect me from?

Claudia made an indignant huffing sound as I spoke. "No —not at all. They've been total gentlemen. I was already getting attached to Pack Rivers, so this jump, while sudden, feels a safe option for me."

"And you don't feel coerced into this at all? This is a... unique situation and we will bend the rules if it's best for *you*, no matter what Pack Rivers want. All we want is whatever is best for you." Keeper Hanover affirmed.

"I honestly believe that being here, while not ideal, is safest for me at the moment. You'll be in regular contact with myself and Callan in case anything changes?" They nodded. "Then, I guess there's not much else we can do," I sighed.

I had only been awake a few hours but I wanted to go back to Alaric's bed and nestle down into the delicious smelling sheets. *Or you could just cosy up to the nice smelling alpha yourself...*

"In that case," said Keeper Hanover, "we shall bring the rest of Pack Rivers into this discussion to decide where we go from here."

Claudia whipped out her phone, no doubt texting the guys. The door opened and they filtered in, they must have been waiting in the next room. Everett and Bellamy took seats, Callan perched on the arm of my chair close to me, while Alaric remained in the doorway, leaning against the frame, arms crossed.

"Now, it's clear you've been treating Sage well and with complete respect, but you have to understand there was a reason we never approved you to court a pack, despite your past applications. That being said, we are here now, and we are going to be keeping a *very* close eye on you, far more so than we do with other packs."

"That's fair, you're welcome to visit whenever you want," Callan added.

"Wait, why weren't they approved?" I asked with a frown.

Keeper Gregory swallowed hard, looking around at everyone. "I would be remiss if I didn't mention that Alaric Beckett has negative family connections and—"

"You must be kidding me!" Claudia snarled, sitting up straighter, glaring at Keeper Gregory. "You're holding the actions of his uncle against him? Alaric is nothing like that vile cretin!"

"Um...can someone explain?" I asked. Keeper Gregory

neatly folded his hands and focused on me, his gaze darting to the alphas around me. "Oliver Beckett was convicted of trafficking an omega several years ago."

"Trafficking an omega?" A sinking feeling settled in my stomach.

Claudia growled, "That man was a disgusting, loathsome toad and Alaric has had nothing to do with him since that came to light."

Gregory cleared this throat, tilting his head to the side as he tried to find the right words to explain the situation to me. "Oliver kidnapped an omega, and, how do I say this politely..."

"Raped them," Alaric filled in the blank, not bothering to beat around the bush. "My uncle was a monster, let's not mince words here."

"Ah...yes." Keeper Gregory cleared his throat. "So you can understand why we never approved Pack Rivers to be near an omega."

"Alaric isn't the pack leader." Callan's voice was tight, a muscle in his jaw twitching as he obviously tried to hold back the depths of his anger. "And he has never been personally involved with or convicted of trafficking. It's unfair to punish him for his uncle's crimes."

"Yes, but—"

"Do... do you think Alaric is going to just hand me to his uncle? Is he still under investigation? Why are you concerned about him if he's actually done nothing wrong?" I asked, my brow furrowed, looking between the Keepers and Claudia. I *felt* safe with Pack Rivers, but my feelings were all over the place. I didn't know if I could trust them.

Keeper Hanover sighed, "There's nothing to indicate you're in any direct danger staying with Pack Rivers. While we did not approve them to court an omega, they also were never deemed dangerous to one."

"In that case, I think that business isn't relevant here—Alaric has been firm in ensuring I'm safe." I nodded at him, because he had been. Since day one he had been strict in ensuring I knew when to stand up for myself, and was the angriest when I was mistreated. My heart hurt for the omega his uncle harmed, but that wasn't Alaric's fault.

"Okay, we can file the paperwork and make your stay here official. Callan Rivers filed the petition this morning." Keeper Hanover gave me a small smile. "There is a small issue, there is no record of fees ever being paid, now I know this is a unique situation but not having any official fees on record could damage Pack Rivers validity to care for an omega."

"We paid $750,000. I can get the necessary paperwork to prove that," Callan said.

$750,000? That's insanity, there is no way I'm worth that much!

"That will take time, and if the funds were misplaced...well it'll look like you never paid in the first place. I know, it's unfair, but I want to be honest with you."

"It's no worry to us," Alaric said from the doorway. "I have the cash ready to re-pay today—and before you ask I liquidated some of our property portfolio in case this issue arose. Claire was clearly not trustworthy and we weren't going to take a risk when it came to Sage's safety. What I want to know is what is being done to prosecute Lex Bove and his pack, and deal with the Keeper who exploited Sage."

"Keeper Claire is currently missing, we are working hard on locating her. We thought she could clear up some of these issues, but her absence is telling," Brandon said, shaking his head. "She clearly isn't on the up-and-up."

"And Lex?" I asked.

Ethel frowned, looking nervous. "Technically because the events of last night took place in the walls of the Haven it is our jurisdiction to decide how we want to go forward. Usually this would be dealt with in house—"

Callan let out a snarl. "How would you possibly be able to deal with this in house? He fucking assaulted an omega, tried to rape her!"

Brandon looked calmly at Callan. "I agree, which is why we are handing everything we know over to the police regarding Lex Bove. They already suspect him of several crimes and this will be added to the growing list. The Haven is focused on finding Claire as she is still very much our problem. The best we can do in the meantime is ensure you are safe, Sage. Have you received medical attention?"

"Uh, yes. Bellamy was a medic in the army, he checked me over."

"She has a bruised throat, sprained ankle, a potential concussion and a nasty cut. It's fucking atrocious but she will recover physically over the next few days," Bellamy said.

"Regarding what happened with the Haven, we are deeply sorry. This never should have happened. We will cease all operations at that Haven immediately and launch a thorough investigation into how this happened in the first place. You were the only omega within the facility and we need to find out how and why you were isolated," Keeper Hanover said.

"Bellamy will also be checking on her healing regularly and getting her more help if needed," Claudia confirmed. "And I'll be here every few days in case Sage needs any advice or information from a fellow omega."

"Good. I also brought these." Keeper Hanover pulled out a blister packet of some sort of medication. "Heat suppressant tablets. They don't work all the time, but it should help dull your scent. An omega at full scent would be rather uncomfortable for the pack. They can have some side effects though, a little nausea, some headaches, so keep an eye on how you're feeling."

I took the packet with a thankful nod. I hadn't thought about suppressing my scent. If it would make things easier on Pack Rivers, I was willing to try it.

"Thank you," I said, popping two pills out and taking them with a gulp of iced tea.

"Are you being given financial support as well?" Keeper Hanover asked. "Usually we would entrust that to your pack, but this situation is...unique. We haven't recovered your purse yet, otherwise we would hand over your own cards and such."

"There's no need," Alaric assured, reaching into the back pocket of his slacks, opening his wallet and taking out a card, handing it over to me. I frowned at it. "I ordered a card under Sage's name the moment we discussed solo courting." It was a black card. Even I knew what that meant... serious money.

"In that case, I think we've discussed everything, and I feel confident we can leave you in the hands of Pack Rivers, but if you have any questions or concerns, just give us a call. We will probably come by every few days until you're truly settled."

"Call us, Sage, if Pack Rivers mistreat you in any way," Keeper Gregory reiterated with a critical look. "Remember, we have the best facilities at Clearmont Haven." Every member of Pack Rivers frowned at that, clearly not happy with the idea of me leaving, and Alaric looked silently murderous at his words.

"Goodbye, Keeper Gregory," I kept my reply simple.

—--

After the meeting Claudia had to leave. Her own pack was

waiting on her and I was exhausted despite how little I had done.

Alaric came over, handing me two pills and a small glass of water. "For the pain," he explained. "Your last dose will be wearing off."

"Thanks." I took the pills, gratefully. My throat was starting to throb again.

"All that talking must have hurt," Alaric observed. I merely nodded in response before a deep yawn took over. Alaric looked at me indulgently. "Come on, let's go to the den, the others are all congregating there after being kicked out. I think Everett is wearing a hole in the carpet with his pacing." He gently scooped me up before I could protest, not that I even had the energy to protest. Resting my head on his chest I inhaled deeply, letting the smell of smoky dark cherry fill my senses, lulling me to peace.

Bellamy and Everett were both already settled on a large corner couch when we entered the dark, cosy den. I hadn't seen this room before, but den was definitely the right word. The walls were a dark navy, with two large corner couches made from buttery looking brown leather.

Alaric placed me between Everett and Bellamy. Bellamy grabbed a throw off the end of the couch, tossing it over my legs. Were these men just hoarding blankets? Again, not complaining. I love a good blanket, but they didn't seem to be the fluffy blanket sort of men.

"How did it go when it was just you guys?" Bellamy asked.

"Okay," I said. "Keeper Gregory seemed to really want me at his Haven. They're going to let me stay here, but check on me regularly for the next few weeks as you heard."

"That's not too bad," Everett agreed.

"Yeah, I'm sorry they'll be coming here pretty often, I'm sure you could do without that."

"It'll be worth it," Callan spoke from the doorway, a bowl of popcorn in hand. "We were in that meeting quite a while, so shall we just order some dinner?"

"I'll order some Thai," Bellamy said, pulling his phone out. That sounded amazing.

"Alaric picked out some horror film." Everett smiled.

"We can change the film, Sweet Girl," Alaric said, looking over at me, concerned. He had removed his suit jacket and rolled up his shirt sleeves.

"I can handle it," I told him.

"You smell different?" Everett frowned.

"Oh, I'm sorry, I probably need a shower." I blushed, I was probably stinking the place up.

"You don't smell bad, Honey. Just muted," Callan said. "But it's rude to comment on it," he admonished, glaring at Everett.

"It's just the suppressants working, trust me you smell fine. Let's watch the movie." He turned back to the screen and I settled into the couch, nibbling from the bowl of popcorn in Callan's lap.

Without conscious thought, I found myself drifting towards Bellamy, lured in by that chocolate scent I wanted to bathe in. He didn't skip a beat when I leaned into him, he just threw an arm around me and let me cuddle into his chest.

I didn't even make it ten minutes before I passed out, the day's events exhausted me and curled up with Bellamy, I felt safe.

CHAPTER TWENTY-THREE
Sage

ALARIC:

I've got your laptop in the office, it's all set up. Grab it whenever you want.

I had been curled up in Alaric's bed for most of the morning, trying to forget about my kiss with Bellamy the previous morning. I had even resorted to touching myself in the shower, but it just didn't have the impact I wanted. My body was wanting alphas. Knots. And I wasn't ready to give it that. I thought the suppressants were meant to help, but they didn't wholly eradicate the desires and gave me some killer headaches.

I didn't want to leave the bed, but the new laptop meant I could start working on the spreadsheets, and my mind was craving the familiar task of managing numbers. Putting my e-reader under my pillow, I rolled out of bed. Decision made.

Alaric was the only one in the office today. He wore his

usual suit, but the jacket was removed and the sleeves rolled up. He was drinking a coffee and frowning at his computer.

"Glaring at the computer won't make it behave for you."

"Hey." Alaric turned to me and gave me a tight smile. "If only glaring at emails with idiots would make them go away," he sighed.

"I can leave you to it."

"Nonsense, come in. I've got your laptop here." He reached into a drawer and pulled out the sleek, compact laptop. I could tell, even from a distance, that it was more expensive than any other device I had owned.

"Thank you," I said, entering the room, Alaric stood up and handed me the laptop.

"All the programs you should need are on there, but if you need me to sort anything else out, let me know."

"I will. You look tired, Alaric, have you even slept?"

"We've got a lot of work to do at the moment. I'll deal with that later."

"I've noticed you take care of most of the pack business."

"I do," Alaric admitted.

"Callan is so relaxed, you're the one always rushing around to various meetings. It's like you have the weight of the world on your shoulders."

"I don't mind." Alaric smiled, but it didn't reach his eyes.

"Can I ask a question? It may be a little intrusive."

"Ask, I'm an open book."

"You run the business, you seem more…in charge. Why aren't you the head of the pack?"

"I'm more business minded," Alaric admitted. "But I used to have a temper, I'm not ashamed of it. Callan is, as you said, far more relaxed. He can lead with more rational decisions than I can."

"You seem scarily calm to me at times." I observed. "I can't picture you getting angry, you're always so composed, well other than with Claire, but there was a wall between you and her..." I trailed off, hugging my new laptop to my chest. Alaric took a step closer to me, until we were inches away. His hand cupped the back of my head in a gesture that made me quickly inhale. His dark eyes bored into mine.

"I can get angry, easily, Sweet Girl, but only at those who deserve it. When we found out what Lex had done, I would have happily killed him with my bare hands. Fuck the consequences."

I let out a small whimper, the thick scent of my perfume filling the air, and heat flooding my body. Apparently Alaric talking violently made my omega instinct sing with joy. "But you didn't," I whispered, breathless. My hands rested lightly on his chest.

"Because Callan pulled me back. He keeps me sane. I have control, but if the wrong buttons are pushed, I will snap and when I do it's brutal."

"Should I be scared?"

"No." He smirked at me, the smile was predatory, but I wasn't afraid. "I would kill for you, little omega. You're a part of this pack now, and I protect my pack." He gently kissed the top of my head, his hand loosening on the back of my neck. "You should probably go, your scent is soaking the room." His was also filling the room, and I wanted to drown in it.

"What if I don't want to go?" I ask with a clear voice despite the nerves running rampant.

"You're not ready for all of me, Sweet Girl." I pouted and Alaric's answering grin warmed me. Leaning in gently so our lips touched, his were warm and surprisingly soft. My hands flew to his sides, fisting the fabric of his shirt and attempting to pull him closer.

The dark smoky smell made me think of campfires, of smores—did he taste like this everywhere?

Slick trickled down my inner thigh. Alaric groaned and closed his eyes for a moment pulling away and resting his forehead on mine. When he opened them his pupils were blown. "It seems you like hearing about the things I would do for you, Sweet Girl," he smirked. "Maybe another time." He let me go, striding out of the room without another word, leaving me staring at the door in shock, and panting with need.

After acquainting myself with my new laptop down in the kitchen where I could enjoy the sunlight, I was interrupted by Bellamy coming in to prepare lunch for everyone.

"Can you do me a favour and go let Callan know lunch will be ready soon? I already let Ev and Alaric know on my way, but I think Callan was in the middle of a call when I walked by."

"Yeah, of course," I replied, closing the laptop to head upstairs and pausing in front of the door that I was pretty sure hid Callan's office. "Uh...hello?" I knocked on the door. "Callan? I'm hoping this is your office and I'm not knocking on a random door."

I waited a moment, thankful when I heard movement on the other side. The door swung open and Callan stood in the doorway, looking down at me with a smile. "Hey, this is my office, you got it right. Are you okay? Why are you on your own?"

"Lunch is almost ready." I took the opportunity to look

past him and check out his space. "So this is your daytime lair? I've never seen it in the light."

Callan stood back, letting me get a better look. "Feel free to explore."

"What's the other desk for?"

"It seemed practical for the times we're both needed for the same projects to have me and Alaric in the same space. Easier to work together if it's already set up for it." He smiled.

"That's nice, you like being close."

"We're pack." Callan shrugged.

"I never really understood what that meant."

"Pack is more unbreakable than family. There is no one else I would rather spend time with, and I would trust every one of them with my life."

I hummed. "That sounds…really nice."

"It is, and it'll be yours one day. Even if you don't choose us, you'll end up with a pack. You're an omega." Callan ushered me over to the currently empty desk. "We need to set up some sort of office space for you, somewhere to work on your numbers. I can set up the next room if you want…or in here."

I perked up at the idea. I may not be ready to admit it out loud, but I was getting attached, and being able to sit alongside Callan while I worked was appealing.

"You know what?" Callan nodded decisively. "A desk in here may be best. The room is massive, and I'm sure Alaric would be more than happy with that."

I gave him a small grin and a nod. "That would be nice, thank you."

"I'll text Alaric to let him know." He gently grabbed my hips from behind, guiding me towards the door, leaning so his mouth next to my ear. "Now, let's go get some food, shall we? I'm craving something with honey…"

I wasn't thinking about food anymore. My midsection cramped and my hands grew damp with sweat.

"Not fair," I mumbled, making Callan laugh in my ear, a delicious deep sound that made me perfume.

Although Callan was a gentleman and didn't mention it.

—

"How's the spreadsheet reports going? Have you had a chance to take a look yet?" Bellamy asked over dinner later that day. Pasta carbonara.

"Well, it's just a case of organising and sorting at the moment before I can start really analysing the transactions. Give me another day or two and I'll have it done, I'm just being lazy."

Alaric placed another roll by my plate, encouraging me to eat more. I took it with a smile, ripping some off and dipping it in the pasta sauce. "You're *not* being lazy," he said.

"I would usually get it done in half the time, but I can't stop napping."

"You've been through a lot, your body is changing, that's understandable. You need to rest."

"I suppose." I frowned, picking at the bread.

"Keeper Gregory will be visiting again in three days," Callan informed me between bites. "He called me today."

"I'm being goddamned spoiled here. I hope he gets over his idea that I'm being mistreated." I snorted.

"By omega standards this is pretty basic," Callan admitted, grabbing a roll. "Some omegas get an entire wing devoted to them with custom decor."

"That seems so excessive. What more could I possibly need?"

"Your room is too basic, we need to order more, and there weren't really any courting gifts."

"You got me the hoodie, and the books!"

"That doesn't really count. Usually omegas get jewels, cars, property."

"I don't need any of that, anyway any property would technically be yours, because I can't own any." I snorted. "What would I do with jewels? Wear a crown while working on financial reports? That seems a bit over the top!" They all laughed.

"I noticed you haven't used the card," Callan mentioned.

"I haven't needed anything." I shrugged. "I'm fed, have a bed – though Alaric should really get his back, and internet access. Claudia bought me an entire freaking wardrobe."

"You mentioned a white board for the office," Everett said.

"Yeah, but that was just an idea. I haven't decided," I rushed to say. I didn't want Everett getting any ideas and going out to buy the most expensive white board he could find for me. A series of laughs broke out.

"You're so easy to read." Bellamy chuckled, leaning over and gently grabbing the back of my neck to kiss the top of my head affectionately while I blushed.

"But would you mind buying some things?" Callan asked. "It'll show the Haven that we are happy to provide."

"They won't believe that an omega wouldn't want to use our accounts to buy themselves things," Callan said.

I frowned. I did need a few things, but I didn't want them to get into trouble or be looked at negatively because my behaviour wasn't exactly the norm. After a moment I had an idea.

"Okay, I'll use the card to get a few little bits."

There were no rules saying I had to only buy things for myself.

That evening I snuggled down in my nest, my new laptop resting on a pillow in my lap as I played around with some of the fancier features. It was way nicer than my old decrepit laptop that sounded like it was going to take flight whenever I turned it on. It was naturally the latest model with all the bells and whistles. Rolling my eyes, I laughed to myself. It was Alaric, of course he got the nicest one he could find.

The first thing I did was boot up an internet search on omegas. I had never bothered to look before, and I hadn't really had time or the privacy to do so. The first things that came up were some cheesy romance books about sappy alpha and omega matches and some articles. It seemed the tabloids liked to follow the 'it' girls of the omega world. They were high society women, impeccably dressed, and hosting lunches for other elites. I shuddered. That would never be me.

Taking a swig of my peach tea I typed in omega and alpha relationships. The Havens were built for omega protection, I knew that. How do alpha and omegas bond? Do alpha and omegas bond for life?

Curiosity gnawed at me. I was already feeling comfortable with these alphas, and I wanted to find out more about what to expect. The internet rabbit hole didn't tell me much about the rules of the Haven or my specific situation, other than I was in a trial period with Pack Rivers. But if a pack officially bonded- which was when they bite during sex, they would be fully official, more official than marriage, no take backsies.

CHAPTER TWENTY-FOUR
Sage

I was *finally* going to get to go back to my apartment. I hadn't seen my little home for weeks and I was eager to collect things that were *mine* and not things I'd had to borrow or that the pack had bought for me.

"How did you even get a key to my place?" I asked with a frown as I buckled my seatbelt. "My handover was somewhat rushed…"

"It was amongst the paperwork when we officially took charge of you. The Haven had it from your purse I think."

"Creepy, at least all my things have been kept safe."

"Yeah, a team will have gone in and ensured there wasn't any food or such left out and then locked the place up tight."

Callan looked around the street as he pulled up, his mouth pulled into a frown. I knew it wasn't the best of neighbourhoods, but hadn't considered how the pack would react to my old neighbourhood. "You *lived* here?"

"The inside is nicer than the outside, plus the rent is

cheap!" I bounced in my seat, eager to get inside. "I know you're used to fancier accommodations, Mr Mansion, but for me, this is good!"

"Not anymore," Callan muttered.

"You don't think I could convince you to live here?" I pointed out the window, my face scrunched up in a smile. He tried to school his features, but he was clearly uncomfortable.

"We would live in a shoebox with you, you know that," Bellamy grumbled.

"Ahh, this is the omega power everyone's been talking about!" I giggled, the excitement of being able to get my own clothes, my favourite pillow and more was exhilarating. "Let's go!" I hopped out of the SUV, the men following shortly behind.

I was halfway up the stairwell when I was overcome with an odd sensation in my stomach. My muscles stiffened and my breath became shallow. Callan put his hand round my waist and pulled me back slightly so I was behind him. I spluttered in shock, ignoring how nice the large hand felt around my waist.

"Do you smell that?" Callan asked the others. Alaric nodded.

"Yes."

"What is it?" I asked, pulling myself from Callan's grip before he could stop me, pushing the door open despite one or two of the alphas protesting as I did it.

I caught a glimpse of wreckage. Fabric was everywhere, and it smelled wrong. What on earth had happened to my home? I usually kept it so neat and organised.

Strong hands grasped me and pulled me away from the door, gentle, but very firm.

"Everett, take Sage back to the car," Callan's voice was stern, angry even.

"Wait, what—" I started to splutter as I was passed into Everett's arms and yanked out to the stairwell.

"What the hell, Everett?" I batted at his arms, but his grip didn't loosen. "You can't just drag me away! What's going on? Why is my place a mess? I swear if the Keepers messed up my things…"

"Sorry, Pretty Girl, something doesn't smell right up there and there's no way in hell you're going up there until we know."

"But, Ev—"

"*No*. No way in hell." He threw me unceremoniously into the passenger seat before getting into the driver's side as I struggled to find the right words.

As he closed his door I settled on, "You're an ass!"

"You're damn right," he growled out. "When it comes to your safety I'll be an ass if I need to."

I sat back, crossing my arms and pouting like a petulant child. I didn't know what to make of Everett being so firm with me when he was usually so gentle. He was the soft one, the playful one. I didn't like this version.

The car was full of the acidic scent of my fear.

"Do you want a milkshake?" Everett asked, buckling his seat belt.

"You just want an excuse to take me away from my own apartment," I grumbled, knowing exactly what he was up to. The bastard was trying to distract me from the fact that several alphas I had known for hardly any time were going through my home, without me.

"Yep." Everett wasn't at all ashamed, shrugging as he turned out of the street. "Until the guys give us the all clear we're going to go get something to eat or a milkshake. It's up to you what we get, but we're not hanging around here. Now put your seatbelt on."

"But it's *my* place!" I growled. My attempt at assertiveness was met with a smile that told me Everett thought it was cute, and not aggressive as I'd intended.

"And we'll come back later, when it's safe." He threw the car into drive and pulled out, ignoring my complaints. "Sage. Something was obviously wrong in your apartment, and we couldn't in good conscience let you go in. We don't even know if the building is safe. You're an unclaimed omega."

"I fucking hate this," I exclaimed, running my hand through my hair. "This whole situation is so fucked up!" Tears welled in my eyes, but I did my best to stop them falling. "I want to go back to my life, where I was invisible and safe!"

Everett laced his fingers with mine, which didn't at all help stop my tears. I stared out the window, trying to focus on being back among familiar buildings instead of the fact that I'd been barred yet again from my apartment.

"Coffee," I finally grumbled.

"Coffee?" Everett asked.

"You said I could choose where to go, well I want one of those stupid iced coffees that have enough caffeine in them to kill a linebacker. I don't care if it's bad for you, I want caffeine."

"Okay, coffee it is." Everett knew better than to question my decision now I was kind of accepting the situation. "Do me a favour, text the group chat and let them know where we're going so they don't freak out."

"I forgot my phone."

"Use mine." Everett passed me his phone, his eyes never leaving the road. "It's unlocked."

Flicking open the phone I went to the messages. I saw our group chat, and then another group chat right under it. I shouldn't be snooping, but I couldn't help myself. I clicked into it, reading only the messages that fit on the screen, realising what it was. "You guys have a group chat *without* me?" I scrolled a little further, unable to stop myself as my stomach dropped and a cold feeling spread through my body. "Oh, a group chat *about* me it seems."

"Ah, shit." Everett took his phone back, keeping his eyes on the road. "You weren't meant to see that."

"I thought you guys added me to the group chat so I could be in the loop about everything?" I asked, unable to mask the hurt in my voice.

"We did! That chat is just where we've been talking about some of the finer points of the Haven and such."

"And me." The last message was about picking up my suppressants. Why didn't they just discuss that with me?

"We didn't want to embarrass you."

"Okay." My voice was quiet, and Everett knew he had fucked up.

"Sage—"

"No, it's okay. It's not like I've been struggling with misinformation and things being hidden from me for weeks." I wrapped my arms around myself, trying to keep steady and not explode at him. "I'm not entitled to know most of that shit anyway, right? It's above my station or some bullshit. Just leave it." They were talking about me behind my back, what on earth could they be saying? Complaining that I wasn't adjusting well enough? That they were getting sick of waiting for me? What was bad enough that they wouldn't say it to my face? The idea made me sick to my stomach. It didn't matter how well I'd been settling in, how much I felt they'd been opening up to me, because in reality I didn't know these men at all.

"Pretty Girl, it's not like that," Everett spoke softly.

I stared out the window. Refusing to look at him. "I said leave it."

—

I had hardly touched my giant iced coffee by the time we pulled back up outside my apartment. Everett had remained silent the rest of the drive except to confirm my drink order, which was probably in his best interest because I wasn't feeling very friendly.

I despised that despite how mad I was, I still wanted to be near Everett. I used to be so damn independent, and now I was getting used to having people around. I was letting myself become weak.

Callan was waiting on the pavement for us, his face stoic.

"What was it?" Everett asked.

"It seems Lex and his pack have been here." He looked at me, sympathy etched into every frown line. I climbed out of the vehicle and Callan looped his arm around me, and I let him, my anger temporarily forgotten to deal with whatever was coming. "I'm sorry, the place is pretty trashed."

"Trashed?" I squeaked. "I was told it was locked and safe while I was in the Haven, what do you mean it's trashed?"

"They went on a rampage in there, and the whole place stinks of them. I wanted to warn you before you saw it. I knew you would want to go in, so we contacted Haven officials and they already sent someone over to take pictures and grab a few pieces of evidence. We contacted a cleaning company as well to come in after we see if we can salvage anything of sentimental value, but most of the stuff is ruined honestly."

We paused outside of my door, and the deep breath I'd taken to calm myself only made the pit in my stomach grow. Lex saturated the air. "Why would they do this?"

"Anger, I'm guessing, over how we removed you from the Haven," Callan sighed and opened my door for me, Everett at our heels. "Come on, let's get this over with and go home." My home was ruined. Looking around at the carnage I couldn't believe it. Every surface was destroyed, my couch was torn up, as was my bed, the TV smashed, my bookcase torn apart. An acidic stench filled the air and made my eyes water.

"What on earth is that smell?" I asked, holding a hand over my mouth and nose.

"Urine," Bellamy confirmed with a grimace. "They peed everywhere like mutts trying to claim their territory."

"Oh god." I moved down the hall toward my bedroom, finding the mattress bare and torn to shreds. "Where's my bedding?"

"We got rid of it after a sample was sorted out for the authorities, it smelt particularly bad and was torn up." Bellamy didn't look me in the eye as he spoke. I shook my head in disbelief, this place had been my sanctuary for so long. It was my first major purchase several years ago and I had taken my time painstakingly making every room my own.

"Is there anything you really need?" Bellamy asked.

My anonymity and security, I thought ruefully. "I've got some jewellery that's sentimental, but I think everything else isn't savable, like my books and clothes."

"We can get you new ones, where is the jewellery?" he asked.

"Box under the bed," I told him, and he ducked under to look for it. All the guys were sifting through the area, dismayed at every destroyed item they came across. It looked like I had done well with the space provided, were it not for the current state they could easily imagine me there.

They made quick work of finding the one or two items I

wanted while I stood in the middle of the living room, looking around blankly at the mess. "I'm sorry about this." Bellamy gently placed his hand on my back, wanting to comfort me, but I just shrank away, a gesture not missed by his brothers who all watched intently.

"Is Lex going to come after me?" I asked.

"We won't let him." Callan stood in front of me, but I shrugged him off as well, unable to accept their comfort.

CHAPTER TWENTY-FIVE
Callan

We picked up pizza on the way home, all of us too exhausted from the day's events to consider cooking. Sage insisted she wasn't hungry and just wanted to rest, leaving for her room the moment they were back at the mansion. I could tell when I told her that we would keep her safe she didn't believe it. Her eyes had been dull, and she seemed deflated.

"Should we leave her alone?" Bellamy asked.

"She's got every right to be upset." I sighed. "I'll ring the Haven after we eat, deal with the bullshit paperwork this is going to cause. They should have ensured her home was secured, and Pack Bove should have never been told her address. He got to her at the Haven and found her home. It feels like it's only a matter of time before he tries to find her here." I sighed, rubbing my hand over my face. "She really doesn't look good, does she?"

She'd been so pale on the drive home, staring blankly out the window, and only giving us quiet, one word answers.

"It's not just the apartment she's upset about. I may have also dropped us in it," Everett confessed. We all looked at him for an explanation. "We went to get coffee when you told me to get her out of there, and I asked her to text you, let you know where we were so you didn't freak out. She didn't have her phone, so I told her to use mine. She clicked on the wrong group chat and now knows some of the things we've been saying about her."

"Fuck," Bellamy groaned, resting his head on the table. "She probably thinks we're a bunch of knotheads."

"We're making a mess of this, aren't we?" I grimaced.

"She thought we were trusting her by adding her to a chat with all of us, only to find out we had a separate chat discussing her, of course that stung," Bellamy said.

"I'll correct it," I said.

--

Later that evening, Sage wandered downstairs to grab a snack, passing my office.

"Sage," I called her name and got up from my desk, keeping my voice low and gentle. "Come here please."

She padded into the room wearing a pair of sleep shorts and a T-shirt that smelled like it belonged to Bellamy.

"Clearmont Haven is probably going to increase its visits after today, because of your apartment."

"Why? They're not going to make me go back, are they?" she asked, her head whipping round to meet my eyes.

"No, not at all! They just want to check in like they have been and see how you're handling everything. They just want to ensure that you're safe because they didn't fully approve of us. We are making a strong case to bring charges against Lex's pack and ensure they or the packs they associate with are never allowed near a Haven again."

"That's good though, it means they can't do this to any other omegas?"

"Exactly. To be fair, the only reason they were able to get near you to begin with was because of Claire breaking all of the safety protocols."

"I hope they find her and can protect other omegas from her. I'm going to go, I've still got loads of sorting to do." She gave me a small smile, but refused to meet my gaze.

"Sage, wait." I leaned against the desk, "I know you're upset about the group chat."

She wilted, curling in on herself. "I'm not…it's not my place to say what you guys can and can't do."

"Actually it is," I told her. "You're pack."

"I'm not mad about it, Callan. I get it, this whole situation is weird, it makes sense you guys will want to vent about how irritating I a—"

I burst into laughter, and her ears went red as she blushed.

"There's no need to laugh at me," Sage whispered angrily, holding even tighter onto herself.

I took two steps toward her until we were within arm's reach, offering her a bright grin. "You think *that's* what we were talking about?"

"Well… yeah. I'm not exactly the omega you planned to have in your life."

"Sage," I chucked, pulling out my phone and handing it to the frowning omega, "take a look. Better yet, I'll add you to the chat because the only thing we've been discussing is how our dicks are probably going to drop off from blue balls over your scent, but we want to make sure you're comfortable."

She opened and closed her mouth a few times, eventually

taking the phone I held out, already open on the group chat. Flicking through a blush rose in her cheeks. "Oh."

"We didn't want to embarrass you with copious talk about our dicks."

"Wait, I thought the suppressants helped?" she asked, cocking her head to the side ever so slightly.

"They're the only thing stopping us from going full on horny teenager but that doesn't mean you don't still smell fucking amazing to us." I smiled. She glanced over a message from Bellamy discussing how many times he had to masturbate the first night in the shower because of her.

"Umm, sorry? I guess?"

"Don't apologise. You can't help how you smell."

"How do I smell? I'm curious. I was told my scent would have changed dramatically when I presented, I knew I smelt sort of sweet before."

"Honey. Even with the suppressant you still smell sweet." I tilted my head, a small smile gracing my lips.

She continued to scroll through the group chat, as I leant lightly on the end of my desk. Her eyes widened and she choked a little, I stood up straighter. "That bastard Lex jacked off in my sheets?!" she screeched looking pale and slightly sick, I didn't blame her that sort of violation would shake even a stoic alpha up.

"Ah, yeah. The Police had to take some samples for evidence, but they've assured us they will be incinerated," I reassured her.

"Good, oh god, that's so gross. I feel dirty."

"We don't want to keep anything from you, and I definitely don't want you thinking we are talking badly about you behind your back."

"These are surprisingly complimentary. I guess I'm not used to it." She blushed at some of the cruder messages.

"You're so much more than just an omega, Sage, surely you see that?"

"I was invisible before this." She shrugged. "I liked it, no one tore up my home or tried to kidnap or buy me. Sure it was boring, but it was safe."

"You're safe now, I'll make sure of it." My words were full of promise. "I know you're not used to relying on others, and asking you to trust us is a big ask, but let us show you." I took the phone off her and tapped a few buttons. Her phone pinged. Letting her know she had been added to the group chat.

> CALLAN:
> Sage is now part of this chat, try not to embarrass yourselves too much.

"Thank you," she sighed. "I mean, I probably won't read it much unless it's about the Haven business. I don't want to be feeling bad for Bellamy losing his dick from overuse." She giggled.

"I think we're all going to be suffering for a while, and don't you dare feel guilty about that." I smiled. "The puppies will cope."

"Puppy is a good description for Everett, he's like a German Shepherd puppy that's not fully grown into his paws yet." I barked a laugh.

Standing up she gave me a blinding smile before stepping forward, wrapping her arms around me and burying her head in my chest. "Thank you, for being so kind," she mumbled.

My heart rate stuttered as I wrapped my arms around her, drawing her into me and resting my chin on the top of her head. I remembered reading that omegas crave touch, and she had been rather starved of it lately. Sage burrowed into my chest, maybe not even aware of her own actions, but I relished it. The top of her head hardly reached my chin, and she fit against me perfectly, consuming me with an overwhelming sensation of how *right* it was to have her in my arms.

"Sorry, I didn't think about my scent." She started to push away, apologising but I was having none of it, pulling her closer.

"Hush, I'm a big boy, I can cope just fine. I happen to quite like having you here." My voice held a smile. I ran my hand up and down her back gently and she eased into my arms, boneless and relaxed. A soft rumble rattled my chest, and the sound only further relaxed her.

"Okay, why does that sound you're making make my body just melt?" she grumbled with a slight laugh.

I beamed. "Alpha's purr. It relaxes omegas." I had purred a few times, but it had felt forced. Purring for her felt... effortless.

"I'll say, I feel so sleepy now. I think I need a nap."

"Sorry, I may have been a bit strong." I looked down at her hooded eyes and the small blissful smile on her face.

"Not at all, I know who to come to next time I can't sleep." Her face was so relaxed, I couldn't help but wonder if she would look like this in a post orgasmic state. The thought was enough to make my pants tighten, which Sage didn't miss as she was pressed up against me. She grinned, a blush rising in her cheeks. "I should probably go, shouldn't I?"

"Probably, I've got good restraint, but fuck me you're tempting," I groaned.

"I'll uh...see you at dinner," she said, before turning on her heel and fleeing.

CHAPTER TWENTY-SIX
Sage

"Are we going out?" I had just settled down to watch a movie marathon with Bellamy when Callan had dragged us out to the car. Bellamy had gone along easily with a knowing grin. Neither said anything until I was belted into the front seat. "I thought I wasn't allowed to go out until, well, you know, my smell?" I avoided mentioning the whole biting and bonding thing, it felt too awkward to say out loud.

Callan kept his eyes on the road as he spoke, the corner of his mouth tipped up in a small smile. He had put his hair up into a loose bun and strands were already starting to fall out. I resisted the urge to tuck the strands back into place.

"That's kind of true unfortunately, but we've made some arrangements for a quick trip. It'll be completely safe, I promise. Everett and Alaric are meeting us there in their own cars."

"Where are we going?" I asked.

"You'll see," Callan smirked.

Looking out the window I tried to guess but I was totally

clueless. I wasn't used to these parts of the city. All the streets were in perfect condition, with well kept, large beautiful homes, the neighbourhood far richer than I was used to.

It wasn't until we pulled up outside of the giant department store I recognised where we were.

"Pillowpoint? Why are we here? This place is going to be packed." Pillowpoint was a luxury homeware store that specialises in bedding—or nesting materials I suppose. The store was open to anyone, and I had ordered my sheets from their online store a few years ago. I had been too intimidated to go in. Even one of their cheapest items had been a luxury for me.

"Usually it would be busy, but because this place caters mainly to packs with an omega I paid to have the store cleared out and they were more than happy to. The place is totally empty for us to do some shopping." Callan turned to me as we pulled into a parking space.

"Wait, you paid to empty the place out, that's too much! I can't repay you for that!" I started running through the mental calculations of how much something like this would cost. Surely it was easily more than my yearly wage, my savings weren't going to be able to cover this at all.

"Sage, remember money is no issue, you don't need to pay us back," Bellamy said from the back seat. "Come on, don't you want to go and explore a bit?" He got out of the car, not giving me time to reply, and Callan followed suit.

The parking lot was so empty, it was unsettling. I kept glancing around. I felt open, exposed, like Lex could be lurking around any corner.

Everett and Alaric were already waiting for us at the entrance, both smiling. "Ready for this, Pretty Girl?" Everett was vibrating with excitement.

"I uh, I guess?" I tried to sound enthusiastic, but it felt wrong. I didn't like the idea that they had spent so much for me to pick out some sheets I could have easily ordered online.

Sensing my discomfort, Bellamy pushed me gently through the door. "This stuff is important, you need it."

The store was gigantic, and smelt amazing: like clean cotton and comfort. The walls were stacked with so many fabrics and textures, and I wanted to reach out and touch them all.

"Where do I even start?" I asked quietly.

"Let's start with bedding, you need to pick the sheets out then we can go from there," Callan suggested sensibly, placing a hand on my back to gently guide me towards the relevant section.

My eye was immediately drawn to a familiar brand, the same as my old sheets. They had new colours.

I wanted them.

I *needed* them.

The sight of so many sheets excited me, more than it ever had before. Maybe my omega instincts were kicking in? My hand instinctively reached out to touch the sample sheet, humming happily at the softness.

"You like?" Callan asked from behind me.

"Yeah, but it's like three hundred dollars for one sheet, that's ridiculous. I can't justify that." I pulled my hand away, trying to hide my sadness.

Callan hummed, and before I could turn to walk to another section he grabbed me by my hips, spinning me around to face him. My hands shot out, grabbing his forearms to steady myself. His earthy, woodland smell washed over me. Instinctively leaning in ever so slightly as he pinned me with a stare. Uh oh. He was frowning. Why was he frowning?

"How about this? You're not willing to spend money on yourself, but what if for every item you buy—items you actually want and enjoy—we'll buy the same item to donate to the local shelter. So every nice and pretty thing you get, can also go to someone in need. We can afford it. Everett only spent sixty grand on a quad bike, the other day, it doesn't even run and he never intends to fix the damn thing."

"—It was pretty!" Everett interjected with a laugh. "You know I like pretty things!"

Callan rolled his eyes, then pinned me with a glare again. "What do you say, Honey?"

"I, uh—" How could I say no to that? Would they really do that? It was manipulation, but dang it I was falling for it hook, line, and sinker. "Ugh! Fine." I grabbed the sage green sheets and threw them in the cart that had appeared courtesy of Bellamy. "But make it *two* items to every one I buy," I bargained.

"Sold!" Callan grabbed some sheets and placed them in a second cart. He caved far too easily, like he was expecting my reply. Maybe it wouldn't be so bad. If I got some basic comfort items then there would probably be twenty items donated. I could cope with that.

"We're going to go sort out a good mattress, what kind do you like?" Alaric asked.

"Uhh, the softer the better," I admitted. Were they also going to buy mattresses for the shelter?

Alaric nodded. "Good, I'll go sort that out and a few extras to donate." He grabbed Everett by the scruff of his neck and dragged him away, muttering that he couldn't move a mattress alone.

"Okay Sweet Girl, pillows." Bellamy gestured me along, with him and Callan following. I spent a good twenty minutes dithering over pillows. How many did I need? My heart was saying all of them, but my head was saying one or two would suffice.

"Just think," Bellamy said with a shit eating grin, "every pillow you buy is *two* for the mothers and kids at the local shelter. Surely you want them all to have good pillows?" He pouted, looking at me, attempting to look all nice and innocent.

"Fine!" I growled, throwing a pillow at Bellamy. "I'm going to get so much god damn stuff you'll be able to open a whole new shelter!"

"That's the spirit!" Bellamy cawed.

"We would happily open a shelter in your name if you wanted a project, Honey," Callan told me, looking thoughtful as he pushed the cart. "Actually that would be a good idea."

My only reply was to throw a pillow at him. I could not let them buy a whole freaking building for me... but then again it was for a good cause.

Taking a deep breath, I decided to just follow my heart, and grab anything and everything I wanted. They were so certain they could afford it, and I wasn't going to stop them. Deep down I wanted all the squishy soft things. I wanted to be comfortable, and logic clearly wasn't going to work with these alphas.

They remained quiet as I threw multiple pillows in the cart. Alaric and Everett returned, I assume having dealt with the mattress, and they took one look at the carts and went to go take a load to the car.

"Don't they need to check out?" I asked as I watched them waltz right out the front door to the carpark.

"Nah, we've been keeping track of our tab," Bellamy said. "Oh! Look at this throw pillow, it's fluffy!" he declared, grabbing the pale lavender pillow off a shelf and holding it out for me to inspect. My hand buried in the soft fibres, humming in happiness.

"Get it."

It was like the floodgates had opened. Once I decided to just get whatever I wanted, I ended up grabbing all manner of soft things. Bolster pillows, fluffy blankets, memory foam pillows. Every item I grabbed thrilled me, satisfying a deep craving I didn't know I had. I *needed* these things.

Once I had acquired what felt like one of every pillow in the store I moved on to bath products. I spent a few moments dithering between bath products until Everett came up behind me with an overly dramatic sigh.

"Just think, if you get both, that's *four* sets of fancy bath things for the women at the shelter. They deserve nice things, don't you think?"

"I agree, but can it, Everett, or I *will* throw one of these at your head."

"I can take it," he laughed from behind me.

"I don't know man, those bath salts are heavy. Even your thick skull might suffer," Bellamy snickered.

I ignored them and continued going through the dizzying display of products. Taking my time to sniff every one, sticking to mainly sweet smells. I cringed at the smell of a tropical body scrub, and Everett was taking it out of my hands and putting it back before I could say anything. "That made a frown. We don't want that. We want things that make happy smiles or those cute as fuck squeaks of excitement."

I mean, he wasn't wrong.

. . .

I had thought that the three SUVs full of nesting materials were for both me and the shelter. Turned out that three entire car fulls were just *my* purchases. My alphas had put all the donations to one side and were going to get a truck, yes a damn *truck* to transport it all. How had I not noticed how much I was gathering?

My omega brain was an unashamed whore for soft fluffy things. Despite the part of my brain demanding we return the bedding, that it was too much and I could never pay Pack Rivers back, the larger, instinct driven part of me was jumping with glee at the sight of all the nesting materials being taken up to my rooms for me to sort.

"We'll assemble the furniture. Is there anything else we can do to help?" Bellamy asked.

"No, thank you." I wanted to set the bed up myself. There was a palpable excitement in my gut at the prospect of rearranging all those materials, and while I liked the alphas, I didn't want their scent on my nest...yet.

"Okay, we'll get to work and let you do your thing." He kissed the top of my head lightly as he passed me, and I couldn't help but lean into him for a brief moment before grabbing my sheets, ignoring the pulsing cramp that made me crave a hot water bottle.

I was damn happy with my nest. Every time I added something my excitement and contentment grew. I did remove some throw pillows, opting to add them to the small couch on the other side of the room. They just didn't feel right in my nest. There was no logic behind my decision making when it came to what was placed where. It was purely instinct driven, my mind was a flurry of fabric, and by the time I stepped away to admire my handiwork all my other furniture was built. Callan had even managed to put up my curtains and the fairy light wall I had found that gave off a soft yellow light.

The pillows were arranged in a semicircle, creating a wonderful sunken area to sleep in, and I was desperate to get in there.

"It's a fine nest, Sweet Girl," Bellamy said as I crawled in, grinning as I clutched a pillow to my chest.

"It's a perfect nest," I replied. I never wanted to leave.

CHAPTER TWENTY-SEVEN
Sage

That night sleep evaded me. I had stomach cramps again and couldn't get comfortable. Maybe my suppressant dose wasn't high enough. I should probably contact the Haven about it. The cramps had gotten a little worse each night, and now that I was two weeks into my stay with Pack Rivers they'd reached the point of keeping me awake at night. Between the stomach cramps caused by being constantly turned on and the stomach aches caused by the suppressant pills, I wasn't particularly happy. I had rearranged my bedding time and time again in an attempt to get comfortable. I was tired, moody, and most of all *horny*. My situation really wasn't helped by the fact I was surrounded by handsome as sin men.

Rolling out of bed, I decided a snack was needed. It was just before two in the morning and the house was quiet. There was leftover taco meat Bellamy had made the night before so I quickly threw together a quesadilla and grabbed myself an iced tea, sipping on it while I fried my food, ignoring the steady stream of cramps ripping through my midsection.

"Sage?" A sleepy voice from behind me spoke, Everett.

"Heya, just wanted a snack." I turned to look at him over my shoulder. He was standing in the middle of the kitchen staring at me with wide eyes, his pupils were almost entirely dilated. "Hey, you okay?" I asked when he didn't answer.

He shook his head gently, giving me a hazy smile before walking over. Warm vanilla washed over me, delicious and inviting. "Sage, you smell…" He leaned in closer, taking a deep breath.

"Yeah, so do you…" I trailed off. I needed to be closer. I desperately needed his scent on me, on my skin. Covering me. A ripple tore through my abdomen, but I didn't even flinch.

Alpha.

His hands roughly grabbed my hips drawing me closer, closer to that smell that I wanted to drown in. Before I could form another coherent thought we leaned in, our lips crashing together, tongues tangling. I let out a moan of pleasure upon realising that he tasted just like his scent. Sweet vanilla, almost like a cupcake. I wanted to fucking *devour* him.

Gripping his neck, I pulled him closer. There was too much fabric between us. I needed skin. Craved it. I was going to burst into flames if I didn't feel it soon. Trailing my hands down, I snaked them under his shirt. Everett's responding growl of pleasure only made me even more amped up. I could feel my slick, more than before. My body was screaming that it needed an alpha. A knot.

Thankfully a moment later we were stopped from doing something I would regret when Everett was pulled off by a grumpy faced Callan. Grabbing him by the neck he hauled him away from me, his own eyes dilated from the thick scent clouding the room.

I whined at the loss of Everett, reaching out to grab him but Callan stood in the way. I didn't mind, he could satisfy this *need* as well.

"Sage. Your suppressants seem to be failing, I think it's best you go up to your room," Callan's voice was controlled, but there was a dangerous undertone. He grabbed me with his other hand in a surprisingly gentle grip and pushed me towards the door. I pouted but clarity sank in and I scampered up to my room, practically slamming the door behind me.

Another, far more powerful cramp overtook me, and I had to bend over from the force of it. Cursing, I crawled back into bed, tired, hungry, and in pain. Grabbing the blister packet off my bedside table I swallowed two pills dry, praying they would kick in. Hopefully, the guys would be able to get hold of some stronger suppressants soon.

—

Twenty minutes later, I was still tossing in my nest when there was a knock on the door.

"It's me," Alaric told me through the door. "I've got food. Can I come in?"

I sat up, running my hand through my hair. "Yeah."

Alaric sat on the edge of the nest, passing me a fresh quesadilla. I thanked him, and took a bite.

"What happened?" I grimaced, rubbing my stomach as another cramp hit.

Alaric looked pained for a brief moment but schooled his features. "The suppressants are certainly failing. You smell almost like you're in heat. The only reason I'm the one here is because I have the best control, and Everett has the worst. He feels terrible, by the way."

"It's okay, I know it's just instinct. Callan was there to stop us. I don't know what to do now though, my stomach is cramping just like when I was at Norden, right before I was taken to the Haven. I took some more tablets, they should have kicked in already."

"Are you in pain?"

"A bit, I can't really sleep or get comfortable. I know what my body wants, I just don't think I'm ready for all that yet. Four guys, knotting, all that stuff," I groaned out, as I bent over, resting my head on my knees as I let another cramp pass.

"You need a release."

"Don't you think I've tried that? I've given myself so many releases at this point it's a shock I'm not unconscious. It doesn't work."

Alaric raised his eyebrows at me.

"You can't do it to yourself. You may not like it, but you need an alpha. You can only be on suppressants so long before they'll start to hurt you or become ineffective."

"I know! But I *can't*."

"I'm not talking about sex." He leaned over, getting closer. "I'm talking about getting you off, easing that pain, and helping you sleep." He gently cupped the back of my head, our faces inches apart. "What do you say?"

I didn't speak. I wanted it, wanted to see what he could do, but I was too nervous to say so.

"I need you to say yes or no, Sweet Girl."

"Just... hand stuff?" I asked, voice wobbling.

"Absolutely" he confirmed. I sighed, closing my eyes for a second and taking a deep breath, wincing when a cramp hit.

"Okay," I whispered breathily. That was all the confirmation Alaric needed. With surprising strength and ease he slid his arms around me, hauling me into his lap, straddling him.

The feel of him pressing against my tiny sleep shorts almost did me in right there and then. My hands flew to his shoulders, and he cupped the back of my head, fisting lightly in my hair, dragging me into a bruising kiss that left me breathless and needy. Heat radiated through his T-shirt and I hated that it was between us. I whimpered pathetically, unable to get close enough to him.

"Don't worry Sweet Girl. I've got you. I'll make you feel better," he murmured, his lips travelling down my neck in a delicious way that made my legs weak. The hand that wasn't fisted in my hair slid into my shorts, going straight for the wetness between my legs.

"Alaric," I whimpered.

"Fuck me you're soaking." He groaned into my neck, fingers brushing gently over my clit, making me grind down even harder on him.

"More," I begged.

"Tell me what you want," he commanded, nipping lightly at my throat, making me moan again.

"I need to feel full." My voice was breathless and needy. Giving me what I needed Alaric gently slid two fingers into me. Soaking hot walls clamped down on his fingers, if two fingers was a tight fit then how fucking amazing would it feel having my walls clench down on his knot? "Yes," I moaned, low and long, throwing my head back.

He started rubbing that special spot inside me that made me see stars, and his thumb brushed gently over my clit repeatedly while he continued to nip at my throat. Every time he nipped, more wetness coated his fingers. I *wanted* to be bitten. I felt like I was going to combust. Every touch set my body even more alight. I wasn't going to survive this, it was too strong, too intense.

"That's it, you ride my fingers, make yourself feel good," he murmured sinfully in my ear.

"Oh fuck, I'm close."

His fingers sped up, and I leaned forward resting my head in the crook of his neck, letting his smoky, cherry-tinted scent fill my senses.

"What I wouldn't do to get my tongue between these legs, to taste you. I can feel you clenching so damn tight. Are you going to come for me, Sweet Girl?"

I nodded into his neck making another keening whimper. I never wanted this to stop, Alaric could ruin me, and I would let him. The hand that had been in my hair slid down to my chest, plucking at my nipple which was already hard as stone.

"Come for me," he growled, animistic and rough. My body convulsed on command, wave after wave of pleasure crashing over me as I writhed on Alaric's lap. Biting down on his shoulder, Alaric let out a roaring groan. "Good girl, that's it, milk my fingers," he cooed, his breathing ragged as I came down from my high, slumped against him.

I lay collapsed against him for a moment before giggling lightly. "You're lethal." I sat up slightly, looking him in the face.

"How do you feel?"

"Good... tired." I grinned lazily at him. He gave me a wicked grin as he painstakingly took his time easing his fingers from me, letting me feel every raw nerve ending. I moaned at the delicious sensation. "Would it be weird to thank you?" I asked, yawning.

"No need to thank me, I'll happily do it again." He smiled at me. My eyes were already drooping and I could feel the sleep taking over. "Let's get you in your nest," he told me, gently manoeuvring me into the pile of comforters. My eyes were closed and I drifted into oblivion.

The next morning I rolled out of bed, oddly refreshed. Who knew a good orgasm was all it took? The cramps were gone and I felt loads better, I didn't even feel that guilty about what happened between me and Alaric the night before. I didn't want to risk venturing out of my room though, in case I was still particularly potent. Instead I stayed in bed, reading on my e-reader, the huge bay windows open and letting the cool fall air breeze in.

It was around midday when a knock on my door pulled my attention away from reading. "Who is it?" I asked nervously.

"Alaric," a familiar voice called out.

"Oh, come in." I didn't have to worry about him. He had shown a scary level of control the previous night.

He came in, a plate in my hand. "Thought you were hiding up here. You don't really smell that strong anymore, so it's safe to come out."

"Is it? I couldn't tell, I didn't want to risk it."

"You fell asleep pretty quickly yesterday, I didn't have time to tell you." He handed me the plate piled high with sandwiches and potato chips.

Warmth crept up my neck. "I was tired," I mumbled.

"*I* tired you out." He grinned. "But it did the trick, right? How did you sleep, any pain?"

"None at all. I feel quite good this morning."

"Good, I've got to go on a job, but Bellamy and Everett are here. Don't hide away all day."

"I'm not hiding per say, I did sleep in quite late. As we've already established, someone tired me out." I grinned.

Alaric leaned back slightly and groaned. "You can't talk like that, it's one thing when I do. It's another when you do."

"How come?" I asked around a mouthful of chips.

"Because when you talk like that, it makes me want to do all sorts of things to you."

"All in good time, I suppose," I said, unable to fully meet his eyes.

"I should go. I'll see you for dinner. Chinese food?" I nodded. Leaning forward he quickly crushed our lips together, leaving me breathless and smiling as he walked out the door. Flopping back I sighed. I couldn't let myself get sexually frustrated again, even though that seemed inevitable with all the testosterone around.

At least I could distract myself with my new work.

When I looked up from my work, I had managed to get over a year's finances for one account in such pristine order that the issue was glaringly obvious. Several large, unauthorised withdrawals had been taken from the account, and it wasn't any of the guys. I had shot a text to Alaric, asking him for all the paperwork for each of the Pack accounts. I had expected him to resist, or ask why, but instead I had received an email immediately with the many, many spreadsheets. It would take me days, but I loved the prospect of being useful.

I was so absorbed in the work I didn't notice the door had opened until a bashful Everett cleared his throat.

"Hey, Pretty Girl. Sorry to bother you, I knocked but you never answered. You want a snack?" he asked, his voice lacking his usual enthusiasm.

I sat up straight, stretching, and groaning as my spine popped. Working in bed wasn't the best for my posture. "I could eat, what are you thinking?"

"There's some lasagna."

"Good." I put my laptop to the side and patted the space next to me. "Come here, Ev."

"I shouldn't."

"Yesterday was a mistake and I'm over it. We're all learning right now. Alaric said I don't smell as strongly anymore, so come here." I waved him over. "Don't make me rugby tackle you, I'm small but sheer stubbornness accounts for plenty."

Everett cracked a smile. "I don't doubt you. Are you sure you want me in your space?" he spoke as he approached the nest.

"It's a new day. Was it slightly alarming, yes. Sometimes I forget that you're all so... alpha. Yes, I want you here—get in."

Everett crawled next to me, taking a seat, his legs outstretched. I didn't mind having him in my nest, in fact I *liked* it. Usually the idea of someone else in my space disgusted me.

"Do you need any more pillows?" he asked with a laugh, moving one of the many, many pillows so he could sit comfortably.

"I think I could use a few more. Callan gave me his credit card, so maybe some shopping is in order." I chuckled, leaning into Everett and snuggling into his side. Despite our actions yesterday he still felt like safety, warmth and comfort.

"That fucker gave you his credit card? You know that thing has no limit? They gave me one with a smaller limit than their own, heartless bastards," he lamented ruefully, throwing his arm around me for a quick hug.

"Wait, didn't you just spend sixty thousand on a bike?" I asked, eyebrows raised.

"Yeah, but I needed their approval. Dear old daddy Alaric likes to ensure I don't misbehave *too* much."

I snorted. "Understandable."

"Now as happy as I am to be in your nest, I can't stay much longer because it'll test my resolve-so let's go get you some food!" He vaulted off the bed with a smile, holding his hand out to help me as I detangled myself from the blankets.

"So, why do I feel like there is a reason you've got a limit on your card?" I asked as he gently pushed me out the door.

"There may have been a small incident with some collectables and a little old lady in Missouri, but I signed an NDA and can say no more!" Everett declared as I laughed. Now he knew I wasn't mad at him, his entire demeanour had perked up.

"Okay, I won't ask. I'll just enjoy my limitless card while you're restrained."

Everett grunted, "Don't talk about restraints."

"Oops. Sorry. Shall we talk about how I'm going to kick your ass at a certain video game today instead?"

"Game on, Blondie!"

CHAPTER TWENTY-EIGHT
Sage

I thumped my pillow, turning over with a grumble. In the near darkness of the room, I could make out the time. Three in the morning. I had been tossing and turning for hours. Every time I started to settle a sinking feeling would start deep in my stomach and a sensation that something just wasn't *right* settled over me. It had started while we had been eating dinner, the entire pack gathered around the TV, Bellamy and Alaric debating something to do with cars I hadn't paid much attention to while we ate pizza. It had been a nice evening.

Groaning, I sat up and ran my hands through my hair. The late autumn heat was stifling. Throwing off the comforter and swinging my legs over the edge I pulled myself out of bed, intent on grabbing a drink, and maybe a snack. Bellamy had made some chocolate brownies that evening and there were still leftovers, the smell of them cooking earlier had enhanced his own alluring scent of lightly spiced cocoa.

Rubbing my hands idly over my upper arms did nothing to

alleviate the sensation of my skin crawling. Padding down the hallway I paused outside a bedroom door, my bare feet sinking into the plush carpet. Instead of the chocolate I was seeking, a clean scent with salty and woodsy tones assaulted my senses and I found myself absentmindedly gravitating towards it. I knew I shouldn't be bothering any of the alphas this late, but something in me was pulling me towards the door, the scent calling to me. Lifting a hand to knock on the door, I paused. *Callan is probably sleeping*. He had been working constantly recently and I had been enough of a distraction. Letting my hand fall to my side I started pacing in front of the door, battling internally. I couldn't rationalise it, or explain it, but something deep in my gut felt wrong, almost longing and my instincts were telling me that the alpha could cure it.

As I decided I was being stupid and turned to leave, the door opened. My hair was dishevelled, and my scent was ever so slightly burnt. Distress. Callan must have been able to tell. My eyes widened at his appearance, trying not to look at his naked, defined chest. Given the late hour Callan was wearing nothing but a pair of grey sweatpants.

"Oh! Callan, I'm sorry. I must have woken you," I rushed my words. "I-I'll go, sorry! I don't even know why I'm here." I turned to flee, but Callan gently grasped my wrist, pulling me back to face him. Raking his eyes over my face he took in the dark circles under my eyes and generally rumpled appearance.

"Hey, don't worry. I wasn't asleep, what's wrong?"

"Nothing's wrong," I blurted. "I have anything I could possibly want. Why would something be wrong?" My words spilled out.

"Your scent doesn't lie," Callan reminded me gently, pulling me to stand squarely in front of him. Looking down at the floor I avoided his gaze. "Talk to me." He kept his voice soft, gentle.

My eyes watered, but I refused to let tears fall. "Something just doesn't feel right. I can't explain it. Something in my gut just doesn't feel okay. I can't rest, it won't *let* me." I raked my hands through my hair roughly. Callan gently gripped my wrists to stop me repeating the motion.

I liked having his hands on me. They were large, calloused and stronger than my own, but still surprisingly tender.

"I bet this is something omega related. Do you have any idea what you need? What are your instincts telling you?"

"My instincts are phoney. I was going to get a drink and then my nose brought me here, practically dragged me here like an alpha sniffing whore."

Callan chuckled, thinking. I kept trying to wrap my arms around myself but he refused to let my wrists go. "Talk to me."

"I... uh. It's embarrassing."

"Nothing is embarrassing. We're here to help you. Would you rather I get one of the others?"

"No, I...I just..." With a sigh of defeat I took a step forward, pressing right into Callan's very naked chest. Instinctively he dropped his hands from my wrists and slid an arm around my waist, pulling me closer while I tucked my head under his chin. I burrowed into his chest, and he brought his other hand to cup the back of my head. The burnt smell vanished within seconds, and I heard Callan hum happily.

"I think I know what's up," he muttered into my hair. I looked up at him with a bleary look, trusting him. "When's the last time you had any prolonged human contact?"

"I don't know." I frowned, my nose wrinkling. "Why?" I tried to pull away from his arms but he simply held me tighter.

There was no rush of panic as I expected, instead I felt relaxed, accepting.

"Omega's thrive off human contact, they're very touchy. They can physically suffer without it."

"Oh, yeah, I think I read that. I'm sorry, I'll get over it. I probably just need a few hours of sleep and then I'll be back to normal." I started to pull away, but Callan's arms remained firm. A deep rumbling sound emanated from his chest, low and strong. It hit me with such force I practically melted into Callan's arms, all resistance gone. A sensation of warmth washed over me, and I was calm, at peace.

"C'mon sweetheart," Callan soothed as he slowly picked up my limp noodle of a body, carrying me over and laying me down in bed with him. I burrowed into his chest with a contented sigh as he wrapped a blanket around us, my warm honey scented hair falling over his chest. Deep down I knew I should probably be more concerned. I was in an alpha's bed when everyone else was asleep. It was hardly proper, and I didn't want to give Callan the wrong idea, but something about the warm vibrations eased all my worries. The last thing I wanted to do was leave the protective arms I was cocooned in.

"I guess I can stay a bit," I mumbled, sleep already tugging at the corners of my mind. Callan grinned, kissing the top of my hair, taking in a deep lungful of the sweet honey scent that clung to me, making sure he never stopped purring.

"This is nice."

"It is," Callan agreed. "This is the most comfortable I've been in months." Running his fingers gently over the exposed skin of my upper arm in a back and forth motion he slowly drew in deep breaths. I sighed contentedly and snuggled deeper into Callan's chest, my nose pressing up against his pecs.

"I should be more embarrassed, shouldn't I?" I mumbled,

my face was so close to his skin my lips touched his skin as I spoke.

"Nah, no shame in craving human touch," he assured me.

"I'm sorry."

"Don't you dare apologise, I happen to quite like having you here."

"Really? You usually seem so... collected." The humming was making it difficult for me to form sentences.

"I just thought Everett and Bellamy have been doing far better at making you feel comfortable, they're more... approachable."

"They are less... big and growly."

"Big and growly?" Callan chuckled.

"You are rather large."

"I'll take that as a compliment. I thought you found my size intimidating." He smirked.

"Oh... I totally did."

"The purr is probably making you more talkative, Sage—"

"I was intimidated, but I don't think you'll hurt me. You kept me safe. You're also pretty cuddly." I smiled against him.

"I'm glad you feel safe with us," Callan said as I drifted off to sleep, pressed up against him.

CHAPTER TWENTY-NINE
Sage

The next morning I stirred awake, stretching with a low moan. My entire body was stiff, the kind of stiff you would feel after a long night's sleep. Stretching my arms out, I opened my eyes when I hit a hard wall of muscle. Callan was on his side, his arms wrapped around me as he slept. Looking up at his peaceful face I grinned. In sleep he was so much more relaxed. When awake his face more often sported a frown or a tense jaw from the stress of caring for his pack. Long strands of hair flopped in front of his eyes, concealing them from me.

A rational part of me knew I should feel embarrassed at waking up cuddled with an alpha, but my omega instincts were singing with happiness at being held and bathed in his scent. With a contented sigh I went to pull away, to let him sleep a bit longer but when I shifted, the arms tightened around me, and a low grumble emanated from his chest.

"Stay." His voice was thick and heavy with sleep.

"I didn't want to disturb you," I whispered with a small smile.

"No disturbing. Comfy," he ground out sleepily, clutching me tighter to him, burying his nose in my hair and inhaling deeply. "Omega smell nice." His voice was slurring with sleep.

I chuckled lightly, running my hand up and down his bicep gently, enjoying his hum of happiness at the sensation. "I guess I'll stay for a bit then," I acquiesced. It took only a brief moment before Callan was snoring lightly. Nuzzling into his chest I sighed, it felt so right. I was wide awake, but comfortable just laying there drinking in his scent.

After a while I heard a door open, but Callan didn't budge, and I couldn't see as my face was still buried in a pectoral muscle, but judging by the light snores he had fallen back asleep. Twisting my neck I caught a glimpse of Alaric standing by the bed dressed in gym shorts and a T-shirt.

"Uh... hi," I said, suddenly shy.

"Hi, I was wondering why Callan didn't show up for our usual morning work out." He smiled. "I think I have my answer."

"What time is it?"

"It's already ten."

"Drat, I need to get up. It's already so late!" I whispered with a sigh. "I'm kind of stuck, every time I try to move he just holds on tighter."

"How long have you been awake?"

"An hour or so. I didn't want to disturb him."

"You're too good to him." Alaric grinned. "But I'm gonna have to wake him, he's meant to be on a phone meeting in ten minutes." I frowned, and turned back to my captor.

"Uhh, Callan, we need to get up." I shook him slightly but

he didn't flinch, his arms constricting tighter around me. "Not funny!" I declared, poking him in the rib.

Next thing I knew, his arms tightened, and I was under him, his mouth on mine. I didn't even feel shock, my body reacted instantly, melting into the sensation of Callan's lips, my hands flying to his hair.

Slick gathered in my underwear, the smell filling the room, making Callan groan a deep, guttural groan that made everything in me want to beg for release.

I was just about to let my hands wander south, to feel the ridges of his chest and lower, when a pillow hit Callan over the head.

"What the fuck?" he grumbled.

"Get off Sage, you've got work," Alaric said pointedly. Callan looked down at me with an apologetic grin.

"Sorry."

"Any time." I laughed.

"Alaric, why are you bothering me? I'm comfy," he growled, his grip never easing on me.

"The Anderson phone call is in ten minutes. I would offer to take it for you, but you know I can't."

Callan groaned and opened his eyes, glaring at his packmate before smiling down at me. "Sorry, Honey, I've got to take this." He loosened his arms, running a hand through his hair lazily as he sat up.

"Now I've got the prince up, like his loyal butler, I'd better get on with my own work before this smell fogs my mind up." Alaric smirked and turned to leave, shooting a seductive grin at me.

"Ric, wait." Callan clambered out of bed with a grace I could only dream of. The moment he separated from me I felt a pang deep in my stomach. "Stay with Sage."

Alaric raised an eyebrow. "Okay."

"I'm okay, honestly."

"She's struggling with the lack of human contact, I think her omega side is freaking out a bit," Callan explained.

"That explains the cuddles." He smiled at me. "I'll keep her close. Coffee?" he asked. I nodded absentmindedly. Holding out a hand he helped me out of bed while Callan dove into his closet to find something to wear, the outline of his erection prominent. The sight of it made me blush and perfume again. Alaric groaned, "Let's get you out of here."

Leading me out of the room he didn't let go of my hand, keeping me next to him. I appreciated the connection more than he knew.

"Sorry to be a pain," I mumbled, looking down at my feet as we entered the kitchen. Following him to the fridge where he grabbed the milk and passed it to me to hold while we walked over to the coffee machine.

"It's no pain." He stood me in front of the coffee machine and from behind me worked on making our drinks, his arms caging me against the counter—keeping me close but still able to complete his task.

"Don't you have work?" I asked with a frown.

"I do," he hummed in agreement. "But nothing that needs to be done right now, I can stay with you until Bellamy or the puppy get home."

"Ugh, I hate this!" I growled. "I don't need a babysitter, I'm used to being on my own."

Placing the mug he was working on filling down, Alaric's hands gently grasped my hip, turning me to look at him. "Sage, we are not babysitting you, this is normal for omegas. Frankly I was surprised you weren't more touch starved when you first came here. Most havens are full of omegas constantly touching or snuggling with one another. It's just part of your instincts." He grinned down at me, one hand resting on the side of my neck, keeping me close. I resisted the urge to snuggle into his palm. "It's one of the reasons omegas work so well with packs, because there's usually someone around for physical contact. You're also like a walking relaxant for us. I don't recall the last time I saw Callan sleep past seven in the morning, that man has a ridiculously rigid internal alarm clock. Trust me, none of the pack members will be upset at having to spend time with you close. In fact, I bet Callan has already texted everyone." He pulled his phone out of his back pocket and passed it to me. "Passcode is 2483."

Taking the phone gently I tapped in the passcode, shocked it worked. Alaric worked with security, and he just gave me the passcode to his phone? Sure enough there were several new messages on the pack chat.

> CALLAN
>
> Heads up guys, Sage is struggling with needing human contact at the moment, make sure at least one of you dumbasses are home. Someone needs to be around at all times in case she needs us.
>
> EVERETT:
>
> Snuggles? Fuck yeah, you okay with that Pretty Girl?
>
> You're home with Callan and Alaric now aren't you? I can guarantee I'm a better snuggler than them. I don't think they even know what a hug is.

I snorted at that, turning the phone round to show the

messages to Alaric who grinned, taking the phone back and typing one handed so I could see him answer.

ALARIC:

Well, I found Callan in bed at 10am, dead asleep refusing to let her go. He was a total cuddle monster.

EVERETT:

No fair! I'll be home in two hours.

BELLAMY:

I'll be home in thirty minutes, so suck a dick Ev.

EVERETT:

No way, you are not absconding with her!

CALLAN:

In my defence she smells so damn good and is so relaxing.

I smiled. "They don't seem too put out."

Alaric chuckled, "Put out? Those fuckers are excited and planning how to get the most time with you now."

"This isn't a permanent thing, is it?"

"No, it'll ease in time. Like Callan said if you're with one of us all the time over the next few weeks it should help. You've been irritable and you've gotten thin the last two weeks." The phone in Alaric's hand pinged.

EVERETT:

Wait, at all times? I call dibs on night time snuggles, if that's okay with Pretty Girl.

CALLAN:

Nope.

> **ALARIC:**
> Hey guys, it's Sage here, I left my phone upstairs. If Callan thinks I'll be okay at night, then I'll leave you all in peace.

> **CALLAN:**
> Not. What. I. Said.

> **ALARIC:**
> ??

I frowned. "Did I upset him?"

"I think the opposite." Alaric smiled as we watched the screen, the coffee machine chugging away dispensing our espresso shots.

> **CALLAN:**
> Sage is with me at night.

My eyebrows raised. The next message came through only seconds later.

> **EVERETT:**
> No way, you can't be greedy.

> **CALLAN:**
> I'm head of the pack, I'm pulling rank. I have never slept so damn well in my life and I will fight you fuckers, don't try me.

I frowned. Alaric noticed. "If you don't want to share a bed with him again, you don't have to. You know that right?"

"It's not that, I was pretty comfy last night. It's silly."

"Nothing you say is silly, talk to me." He passed me a bottle of vanilla syrup to pour into my mug.

"His bed doesn't have enough pillows in it," I whispered.

Looking away. "I sound like a spoiled brat. I'm sorry, it just wasn't quite right."

"Stop apologising for being the omega you are." He kissed my forehead and took the phone.

> ALARIC:
> Callan, she's sad your bed doesn't have enough pillows and comfort items. She didn't want to say anything though. She's being stubborn.

> EVERETT:
> My bed has the most pillows now! I bought loads!

> CALLAN:
> Everett, shut up. Honey Girl, move whatever you want into my room, or I can come to yours whatever makes you happiest. It's not a bother at all.

I sighed, "He's just saying that to be polite."

Alaric growled. "He isn't. It's going to take time for you to realise we want to do these things for you." He shook his head, pulling me into a hug. "Come on, let's go drink our coffee and watch some TV."

We were three episodes deep into a police drama show when Bellamy came home, Everett hot on his heels apparently having skipped whatever he was doing in an attempt to get home first. They had managed to pull up at the house at exactly the same time.

I was snuggled into Alaric's side, watching TV while he absentmindedly played with my hair, scratching my scalp lightly creating the most euphoric feeling. I had been stiff when

Alaric had first pulled me into his arms as we sat down, but I relaxed within moments.

"Well this looks nice." Ev grinned, walking over to the couch and sitting down next to me. "Has Grumpy been treating you okay?"

"Wonderfully." I smiled lazily. "I am a happy, comfy pile of mush."

Bellamy laughed. "Head scratches?" he guessed, and I nodded.

"I swear it's like crack."

"I can tell. The whole bottom floor of the house smells like your contentment."

After Bellamy made dinner we were all exhausted. Alaric gave me a kiss on the head and went off to his office while Bellamy and Callan started cleaning. Looking around I decided to slip off, head up to my own room for the night, not wanting to disturb anyone and ignoring the deep gnawing sensation in my gut at being away from them.

Nesting down into my small mountain of blankets I hugged myself tightly. Refusing to give into the urge to go crawling back downstairs and beg for attention from any of the alphas.

I was just starting to feel the uneasy pull of sleep when someone entered my room without knocking. Lifting my head out of the blankets, my eyes wide with trepidation I saw Callan standing in my doorway with a frown.

"I told you to let me know when you wanted to sleep, Honey Girl."

"I didn't think you were serious, you don't need to do that. I saw how much work you have to do," I said, sitting up.

Striding over to the edge of my nest, Callan pinned me with a stern look. "I was dead serious about that, now do you want to pick pillows to take with us or do you want me to stay here? I won't sleep in your nest until you say it's okay. Omegas can be territorial about their space."

I opened my mouth to speak, but Callan cut me off. "You're about to give me a bunch of excuses, but I'm not giving you a choice whether or not you sleep alone tonight, 'cause I know you want the company. What I am giving you a choice in is if you want to sleep here, or take a fuck ton of pillows back with us to my bed. What will it be?" he asked, eyebrow raised.

Gaping at him, I tried to formulate an answer and failed, saying nothing for a moment.

"In that case, come on." He grabbed me in a surprisingly gentle hold as he hauled me out of the nest, despite my weak protests. Throwing me over his shoulder as he strode out of the room. Giving me an impressive view of his ass. Lifting my head up I saw Alaric grinning in the hallway.

"You being stubborn?" he asked.

"Grab the pillows in the cupboard, not the nest ones, for me," Callan called out behind him as he made his way to his room. Throwing me on the bed, smiling at the glare I gave him.

Alaric entered the room a moment later, arms full of pillows which he threw playfully at me whilst I glared at him. Alaric simply shrugged. "If you need anything else Cal, just drop me a text. Night!" He walked out of the room, but not before pinning me with a smouldering look that made me clench my thighs.

"I need to grab a shower, sort the bedding however you

want it," Callan told me, leaning over so his face was right by mine. "You better be here when I get back, because if not I will come get you and spank your ass for misbehaving." He laughed, leaning forward and planting a quick, bruising kiss on my lips before turning away to shower, leaving me dazed.

Dazed and wet.

After taking a moment to compose myself I got to work. The act of adding my pillows to the bed that already smelt like me and Callan from the night before was satisfying on a primal level, not that I would admit that to him. Once I was happy with the arrangement I sat in the middle, observing my handiwork.

"A beautiful nest," Callan muttered behind me, wrapping his arm around my waist, pulling me back against his chest. His chin easily rested atop my head given my short stature.

"Thanks."

"C'mon, you're exhausted." He nudged me towards the nest but I craned my neck to look up at him.

"I don't want to disturb you, I can go back to my own bed."

The arm around my waist tightened. "I'm not even going to dignify that with an answer." His deep growl reverberated me to my core, slick rushing between my legs. Callan could smell my arousal, but his only reaction was to chuckle lightly at my clear mortification.

"Don't be embarrassed," he soothed. He pressed his lower half a little tighter against me, and I could feel the outline of his erection on my back. I must look like a tomato now. "I'm constantly in this state with you around. It's totally natural. But for now we both need sleep." He pushed me towards the bed and we got in, Callan keeping his arm on me the entire time. Once we were both situated, he dragged me closer so we were spooning.

I didn't have the energy to listen to the nagging voice in the back of my head telling me I shouldn't be snuggling. Instead I burrowed deeper into the embrace letting sleep overtake me.

CHAPTER THIRTY
Everett

"Come on, Pretty Girl, time for lunch," I spoke next to her ear, pulling her from her slumber. She had wandered off for a nap a few hours ago and Bellamy had sent me to wake her up for a late lunch.

"Hello, Everett." She smiled, craning her head to look at me. I was grinning, and leaned over to plant a kiss on her cheek before sitting up. She followed suit.

"Dream of anything good?" I asked.

Her face lit up in an adorable blush and she hid her face in the pillow. I smirked.

"Did our sweet pretty girl have a dirty dream?" I asked, leaning back over, my face an inch from hers. She swatted me away, grabbing the comforter and throwing it over her face in a poor attempt to hide. Having none of it, I pulled the comforter from her arms, climbing over her so she was essentially pinned under me.

"Everett!" She laughed, attempting to roll over to get away, but she was caged in my arms. I took her wrists in my hands and pinned them next to her head.

"I'm not above pinning you down to stop you running away," I informed her. Her body reacted to our new position instinctively, the smell of her perfume filling the air.

"Uh, sorry." She cringed.

"If you want me to stop, pretty girl, just say the word."

"No!" Sage rushed to say, shaking her head.

With a grin, I leaned in, taking a deep inhale of her neck. "You smell fucking glorious." I groaned, my tongue reaching out to give her neck a gentle lick. The sensation made her jump, and ooze slick. "Fuckkk," I moaned, looking her in the eye. "I should really get off you now, shouldn't I?"

"You could..." she said breathlessly.

My eyebrows rose. "Tell me what you want, Pretty Girl. I'm doing nothing without your permission. Can I kiss you?" I was so close I could feel her breath on my face. Her small nod was all the encouragement I needed before I leaned in, taking my lips to hers. I did my best to treat her gently, she was so much smaller than myself. Even the hands pinning her down were gentle. We explored each other's mouths. Letting go of her wrists, one hand trailed down to her hips, whilst the other snook up to cup her breast, and I was rewarded with a deep moan which I swallowed.

"Ev..." she panted.

"Tell me what you want," I demand, my voice was just as needy as hers.

"I want this." She pulled back slightly. "Sure, my instincts are riding me hard but I *want* this. Not because I'm an omega who needs orgasms like a plant needs water, but because it's *you*, the sweet, kind man who thinks pizza solves the world's problems and that racoons are secretly vigilantes."

"It's the built-in masks," I chuckled, feeling ten feet tall. She wanted *me*. This beautiful, smart omega wanted me!

"Touch me," she whined, as my lips went to her neck, gently scraping over the column of her neck.

"Where?" I asked, causing a growl from her.

"You know where," she snarled, need making her aggressive.

I laughed at the omega growling in my arms, how did I get so fucking lucky? The hand that wasn't gently thumbing her nipple through her thin sleep shirt trailed down, slipping into her sleep shorts. I groaned in pleasure as I reached her wetness.

"You're soaked."

"Need you," she panted.

"Don't worry, Pretty Girl, I'll make you feel good," I promised, lightly biting into her neck as I trailed a finger over her clit. She fisted my hair, trying to pull me impossibly closer.

"Please, please, please," she babbled with need. She didn't have to wait long before I sank two fingers into her, marvelling at the tight warmth. How I would fit, I had no idea. She was so small, so tight. I didn't hesitate, sinking deep, finding that sweet spot inside that made her see stars.

"I want you to soak my hand, Pretty Girl." I smirked, looking her in the eye as I slowly dragged my fingers out from her heat, making her whimper at the loss. I didn't wait long to fill her again, sinking back in a firmer motion than before. She was gone, mindless with need, her hips gyrating, chasing her release.

"Ev…" she panted. "I'm close," she whined. I leaned back, withdrawing my fingers. "Wha—"

She looked at me, confused as I pulled away.

"I need to fucking taste you." I gave her a quick bruising kiss. "Can I?" I asked, voice rough with desire. "Can I fucking lap at your sweet cream? I want to feel you come on my tongue." I took a deep breath. "Say no, Pretty Girl, and I'll stop."

"Yes," she panted.

I didn't need to be told twice. The simple word spurred me into action, trailing down her body, I grabbed her sleep shorts, ripping them off her body with such force they tore. She didn't look scared; she looked excited. Her scent didn't smell anxious or fearful either.

Inhaling deeply, my fingers returned to her core, and I relished in the sweet strangled moan that fell from her lips. I felt feral, like I would go into a rut, but I wasn't going to allow that, she was trusting me, and I wasn't going to let her down. She smelled otherworldly, I wanted to find out if she tasted like the sweetest honey as well.

Lavishing attention on her clit, I could feel her squirm. Her hand flew to my hair, holding me there between her legs. I groaned at the action, loving it. I wanted her wild with need and desperation. Flicking my tongue faster, I massaged that sweet spot inside her quicker.

"Shit. Ev. Please!" she whimpered.

I used my free hand to pin her hips down under me. Her whimpers were increasing, but I didn't let up for a moment. Growling as I enjoyed the taste of her. She hardly managed to strangle out a warning. I smiled against her sweet lips.

"Come for me, Pretty Girl."

A second later she was convulsing with waves of pleasure, her nails digging so hard into my scalp they might've drawn blood. The thought gave me satisfaction, I wanted to be marked by the little omega.

She lay panting, trying to string together a coherent thought. I grinned up at her from my spot between her legs.

"You are fucking delicious," I praised. "I'm going to want to do that a lot more."

"You can do that anytime," she said in a breathless whisper.

"Don't say that," I chuckled, climbing her body so we were eye to eye again, "because I won't be able to stop." I placed a gentle peck on her lips.

"That was one hell of a way to wake up," she declared. "Uh, don't you need..." she gestured vaguely towards my cock, an adorable blush on her face.

"I can wait."

"It looks uncomfortable."

"Oh it is, but all good things will come in time. Now I came to wake you because Bellamy made food. He's waiting."

"Oh crap!" She sat up, searching her room for some of her discarded clothing. "We must be so late!"

She didn't even look at me as she made herself decent, throwing her hair into a messy bun. "Let's go, I don't want to be rude."

"You sure?" I asked, one eyebrow raised.

"Yes!" She rushed out of the room.

--

Bellamy had made burritos. Sage was usually the first one in line to eat, but we had been distracted when I went to wake her. Callan and Alaric had already taken seats at the breakfast bar, Sage's usual seat between them empty.

The thick, sweet scent hit them before they even heard Sage coming and I struggled to keep the grin off my face. It was stronger than usual, and everyone in the room stared at the doorway in surprise, their own pants tightening as Sage entered the room.

"Sorry! I didn't keep you waiting, did I?" She paused a few

paces into the room when she noticed all three alphas were staring at her. "What?" she asked, brows furrowing.

I appeared behind her, a shit eating grin on my face.

"They can smell what just happened, Pretty Girl." I placed a kiss on the top of her head before striding into the kitchen and taking a seat. The smell was overpowering, and the scent of her slick and cum coated me.

"Wait! You..." Sage looked between the men, her face turning a beautiful shade of red. "I..." She took a step back, preparing to retreat to her own room and hide.

Alaric got out of his seat, gently grabbing the panicked omega and guiding her to the bench. "You have nothing to be embarrassed about," Alaric told her.

"No, she doesn't," I piped up from my seat, breakfast burrito in hand, grinning from ear to ear. "She's goddamned delicious!" I smirked, Sage groaned, burying her head in her hands.

"You're a bloody idiot, you know that?" Callan said to me as Alaric plated some food up for Sage. "You know if you show off, that shit probably won't happen again."

My grin remained. "Judging by how happy Pretty Girl was, I will be blessed with repeats."

Sage scowled at me, taking a bite of her burrito. "A heads up would have been nice, butthead."

"I tried, but you rushed out of the room so quickly." I gave her my best puppy dog eyes. "I'm sorry. I can prove how sorry I am by making you feel good."

Sage snorted, but it was Bellamy who spoke next. Walking over to his seat he passed Sage, leaning down to give her a quick bruising kiss that was over so fast she was left looking slightly dazed. "Our girl has plenty of options if you don't behave."

My face fell. "No! Pretty Girl!" I looked playfully outraged.

Sage, still blushing, opted to focus on her burrito.

Callan leaned over and spoke quietly to her. "You may want to grab a shower before Claudia comes, she'll be able to smell you a mile away." Sage's face somehow went redder. He gently tucked a stray hair behind her ear and she gave him a soft smile.

"Thank you."

CHAPTER THIRTY-ONE
Callan

Her honey aroma was driving me insane. All morning we'd been sitting at our desks with Sage happily typing away, lost in the numbers. Occasionally she would tut or frown. That didn't bode well for our finances. Her perfume soaked the air.

Alaric's swivel desk chair had mysteriously been swapped out for Sage's. The seat was large enough that she could tuck her legs under herself while she worked. I suspected it wasn't her who had changed the chairs around, but my second.

Gently biting the end of her pen, Sage jotted down a few notes. I shifted in my seat, glad my desk hid the uncomfortable bulge in my pants. Ever since Everett had strutted into the kitchen, drenched in her sweet scent, I could think of little else. I wanted to taste her, to make her lose control. Every time I was near her she would perfume slightly, the air around us growing sickly sweet with thick honey.

Sage wiggled in place, as if she was struggling to focus, her shoulders held tightly up to her ears. She slammed the pen down with a huff and my head snapped up from my work at the sound. I hopped off my chair, padding over to her desk.

Standing, I towered over her. "Everything okay?"

"I think so. I'm just really fucking horny," she admitted with a laugh. "Think we can remedy that? I really need to focus on work."

I watched her, completely still. Did she know what she was asking for? "Honey...are you saying?"

"I want to try a knot, with one of you guys, of course, not some random alpha... It doesn't mean we're y'know...bonded or whatever, does it?" she asked with a tilt of her head.

"It doesn't."

"Perfect." Sage smiled brightly at me, her gaze dropping to my mouth. That was all the encouragement I required. Standing I took three large strides to where she sat. Bending down, I demanded entry past her lips. Her hands flew to my forearms, her nails digging in as she pulled me closer still. It was a small pain that only intensified the sensations as I pulled her out of the chair.

The thick scent of her arousal was all consuming. I wanted to drown in it, to taste it, to live in it. Grabbing her under the backs of her thighs, I lifted her with ease, her legs wrapping around my waist, her core sliding delightfully up against my erection. Restraining myself, I took my time, rubbing circles with my thumbs as I gently walked her back so she was flush up against me and the wall. The action made her press deliciously against me and she let out a sweet, needy whimper. Her perfume exploded around me, and I had to know if she tasted exactly just like her scent.

Her skin was burning. I needed her now, nothing else mattered, I wanted to use her, own her, fill her.

"Please," she begged, pulling her mouth from mine as she ground against me.

"I'll take care of you Honey," I soothed. "There's no rush."

She shook her head. "There *is* a rush. If you don't do something soon I'm gonna combust and I won't survive."

I grunted, her hand raking down my chest, trying to find purchase in the fabric of my shirt. Her other arm stayed wrapped around my neck, trying to draw me closer. I took my time though, grinding against her at a leisurely pace, revelling in the warm wetness I could feel through her leggings.

"Are you sure?" I asked, one hand snaking around to caress her nipple.

I never imagined I would be so lucky, I knew the moment I learned of Alaric's uncle... of *my* uncle that we would never be approved to court an omega, yet here I was.

"Yes! Please, or I'll get one of the others." She looked at me defiantly, the challenge clear in her eyes. She was desperate for release, and if I wouldn't give it to her, another Rivers male would.

A grin spread on my face. "As you wish." I smiled, before hauling her off the wall. She buried her head in the crook of my neck, gently nipping while I moved us. I carried her through the hallway, and up the stairs until we entered my room where she could be surrounded by my scent. Tossing her down on the bed, she bounced in place while I crawled over her pulling my shirt off.

"I don't think it's fair if I'm the only one shirtless, is it?" I asked.

She shook her head and traced the lines of my chest with her tongue.

"Allow me." I grinned, reaching for the bottom of her hoodie, peeling it off her to reveal a simple T-shirt bra. She looked down at the garment, cheeks flushing as if she was embarrassed by it. I poured all of my desire for her into my gaze, hoping that would ease any worries. I wasted no time in reaching down, my tongue running over her cleavage, nipping a path along the way. Each nip made her mewl in pleasure and writhe under me, much to my glee. Her skin tasted like sunshine. I would have happily feasted on her for the rest of my days and never gone hungry.

I needed this woman like I needed air.

Impatient, she reached behind herself and unclipped her bra, allowing it to slide off. I wasted no time lapping at her nipple, the sweetest torture. She moaned with desire. "I need to be full," she whimpered. She had never been knotted, but she seemed to instinctively know what she needed.

She tried reaching down to grab me, but I tutted, taking her hands and pinning them next to her head.

"Mmm, such a needy little omega," I crooned, nuzzling her neck. My words were thick and rough. "All in good time, I plan to take my time with you. I want you nice and ready for me."

"I already am." Sage's voice was husky. "See for yourself."

She lifted her hips up, driving her point home. I wasted no time, moving her hands so they were both pinned in one of mine, the other trailing slowly down her torso, leaving goose-bumps in its wake until it slipped into her panties, dipping into her core.

"Fuck me, you're soaked," I groaned out, my fingers finding her clit and giving it a few gentle rubs, making her keen in delight.

She whimpered when I pulled my hand out of her panties, looking her in the eye as I lifted them to my mouth and sucked every drop of her juices off them, closing my eyes in pleasure at the sweet taste. I knew she had to taste amazing, but having her flavour in my mouth, the room thick with her saccharine honey scent was almost enough to send me into a rutting frenzy.

"You taste fucking amazing, Honey," I snarled, fingers returning to her clit for a moment before dipping into her pussy, filling her. I wanted her prepared for me. Her body was literally designed to take me, take my knot, but she had never experienced that before and I wanted it to go as smoothly as possible for her. I wanted her to love it, to want more, because I would happily oblige her anytime she needed filling up.

My fingers stretched her so deliciously and she writhed under me, begging for release. She hadn't even noticed I had let go of her hands until I was inches away from her sweet cunt, pulling down her panties and inhaling deeply. Growling before taking a long, hard lick of her sweet honey. She almost vaulted off the bed.

I was in heaven, and I was hard enough to break steel but I wanted her to come first. I needed her to. I wanted to hear her whimpers and cries as she flooded my mouth with her cream. I wasn't gentle. I devoured her like a starving man, lapping at her clit, sucking on it occasionally while I slowly sunk my fingers in and out of her. With every thrust she tightened slightly, she was getting close. Using my free hand to pin her in place I kept her my prisoner.

In future adventures, one of my packmates would be able to help me keep her still, hold her in place for me as she writhed, or maybe we could employ the use of some ropes or cuffs. I knew Alaric liked them and possibly Bellamy as well—I was sure the perverts had some I could use. I focused on my task, upping the tempo until she was clenching down painfully on my fingers, her sweet cries becoming unintelligible. With one harsh, keening cry her muscles started contracting repeatedly on me as she convulsed, whimpering sweetly as she came.

The circulation in my fingers was being cut off from the sheer intensity and I knew it would feel fucking glorious around my cock. I was going to pull orgasm after orgasm from her body until she couldn't take it anymore. Giving her slit a few more licks as she came down from the high I grinned up at her as she stared at the ceiling taking deep breaths. The surprised look on her face made me feel like a god.

Grabbing her hips, I laid down, pulling her onto my lap as I sat up so we were face to face. "You set the pace. Use me however you want." I grinned.

"I... Are you sure?" she asked quietly.

"Positive. Now ride my cock, Baby Girl. Take what you need," I instructed her, my voice held a hint of that alpha command. I needed her to take control, for both our sakes.

Angling herself above me I easily slid against her wetness, brushing her clit slowly. As if we were made for each other she guided my cock to her entrance with ease and slowly sank down.

I saw white. The heat and intense pressure of her warmth was almost too much. No pussy had ever felt like this, the iron grip was mind blowing. Omega muscles were something else.

She whimpered at being stretched around me.

"Fucking hell, Honey," I groaned. Her hair was mussed and her pupils blown, she looked incredible.

"I know," she whispered, sinking even lower until she was fully seated on me, impossibly full. "I need more" she moaned, sliding back up with agonising slowness, mewling at the feeling. "So stretched, I—I can't..." she started to stammer.

"Yes, you can," I growled. Snaking a hand up to the nape of her neck, I pressed our foreheads together. "You're going to ride my cock, use it to make yourself feel good, every inch of it filling you. I want to feel you come apart around me, milking my cock with your heat." I smirked at the rush of wetness that accompanied my words. Our girl liked it when I was talkative.

Giving me a hazy and hungry look she sunk down once again, faster this time. And again. And again. The sensation took my voice until all I could focus on was her. Leaning forward I took a nipple into my mouth and was rewarded with a sweet, low moan. Her movements became jerky as she clenched around me. I held her hips, pulling her down on me with more force than she had been using, swallowing her whimper as she clenched impossibly tight around me.

"You're getting close, aren't you? Just imagine how good my knot will feel stretching you nice and full—I want you to clench down on my knot as I fill you," I rumbled into her ear before thrusting up, hitting a spot deep inside. The movement pulled her over the edge and she let out a keening cry. I threw my head back, letting out a string of curses. She was squeezing me so tightly I swore my cock would drop off from the pressure. The telltale swelling at the base of my cock started and she let out several gasps and whimpers as it stretched her further. The feel of her walls fluttering around my knot finished me, and with a groan I released deep inside my omega, marvelling at just how right that was.

"That's it, take my knot. Good girl. Feels good doesn't it?" I soothed as she rode out the waves of her orgasm around me.

Every time she started to come down she would clench around my knot. Eventually she slumped over, her forehead resting on my pec while I gently trailed my hand up and down her spine as we both gasped for breath.

"Fuck, are orgasms meant to last this long?" she asked breathlessly after a few minutes.

Once her breathing slowed she looked up, her gaze meeting mine with a shy smile. We were still locked together, so there was no escaping me, no matter how embarrassed she was. I grinned lazily at her, running my hand through her hair gently. She was fucking stunning, and I couldn't believe she was mine. There was no way in hell I was letting her go now. I leaned forward to give her a soft kiss "How do you feel?"

"Good." She yawned. "The cramps have gone. Just tired now." She smiled lethargically at me.

"Then rest. I'm not going anywhere anytime soon." Indicating my knot that was still buried inside her.

"Okay." She snuggled in and allowed herself to drift off in moments.

CHAPTER THIRTY-TWO
Sage

I was getting used to waking up with Callan's warmth around me, but as light trickled into the room I was starting to think of as ours, I realised that I felt even closer to him, because we were both still naked. His arm was thrown loosely around my hip, enough so that I was able to turn and look at his sleeping face. Callan had become a lazy bones since I had started sharing a room with him.

Grinning to myself I looked at the sleepy alpha. The previous night had been amazing, I knew that knots were in theory really good but nothing could have prepared me for the electric sensation. My old vibrator could never hold up. I could easily see myself becoming addicted to knots, and luckily for me I had four alphas on hand, eager to give me them.

As if he could feel my eyes on him, he stirred awake, gently pulling me closer. "Morning," he grumbled, his voice was gruff, heavy with sleep.

"Good morning." I bit my lip. I was naked next to a

sleeping alpha who looked sinfully gorgeous. His hair was wild around his face, and combined with the facial hair he was looking like a wild jungle man, and I wasn't complaining.

"How do you feel? Are you sore at all?"

I stretched, taking stock of my body. "No, in fact I feel good, relaxed. Maybe we'll have to do that again." I giggled. Callan's eyes were hungry, the single, heated look was enough to make me start to slick for him.

"Fuck, if you start perfuming, Honey, we won't be leaving this bedroom today." Callan growled. I just laughed, rolling away. That didn't sound like a terrible idea.

"I need a shower!" I declared, padding over to Callan's bathroom, which now had several of my products in, intending to shower. I made it halfway across the room before I was lifted into the air in a fireman's lift by Callan who strode into the bathroom without breaking a sweat as he turned on the shower with one hand before softly putting me down. "And what are you doing?" I asked with a laugh.

"I'm being a good alpha, and making sure my omega is clean." He grinned, opening the shower door and dragging me under the water. It was glorious on my muscles. They weren't overly sore, but the slight burning sensation let me know that they had certainly been used. The two of us fit easily into the shower stall, with Callan pressed up against my back. His skin covered every inch of mine, the friction and heat giving me a heady feeling.

He was a caretaker through and through. Maybe not as overtly as Bellamy but I could see it in his actions. He had treated me with such care, and I wanted to return the favour. I could easily see myself falling in love with him, fuck it, I was already halfway there.

Turning to face him, I ran my hand down his chest,

watching as Callan's head fell backwards at the feeling of my hand going lower. Gently, I brushed my hand over his length. He was smooth, and there was already a slight swelling at the base. *His knot.* The same one I had felt stretching me the previous night.

"Can I?" I asked in a breathless voice.

"Fuck yes." Callan groaned as my hand clasped around him, stroking him up and down, watching his face contort in pleasure at the simple touch. The confined shower stall only elevated our scents. The sweet honey and fresh woodland smells blended together.

Leaning into him, I trailed my lips across his chest, to his shoulder, where I bit down lightly. Callan's reaction to the small nip was instant, his whole body jerked, and he got impossibly hard in my hand. Growling, his own hands lashed out, grabbing my hips in a bruising grip.

I wasn't scared, I was turned on. I wanted Callan feral for me. After the night we had shared I was so sure he wouldn't hurt me. "Does that feel good?" I asked, coyly.

"Amazing." Callan looked down at me. "I don't think I'll last long, and I don't want to come in your hand like a teenage boy. Unless, are you still sore?"

I hummed, my hand still working his length. "No, I'm not sore, but I'm having fun here." I grinned at Callan, maintaining eye contact with him as I slowly sank to my knees, curious. His eyes widened when he realised what I was about to do.

"Sage, you don't—ughh—" His words were cut off as his cock was enveloped in the warm heat of my mouth. My jaw strained under the pressure, he was far bigger than any cock I had played with before, but the mechanics were mostly the same...other than the knot swelling at the base. Slick pooled between my legs as I slowly took him down my throat, never breaking eye contact.

"Fuck, I won't last," Callan declared, his hand coming to rest in my hair, assisting my movements.

The feel of him controlling my head, even though I knew I really had all the control, was intoxicating. I wanted to bring this man to his knees. Swallowing around him, I listened to the strangled moan with pleasure.

"Sage, I'm going to come, let me..." he warned me, thinking I would back off, instead I doubled down, increasing the suction, making his legs shake. "Fuck! Sage! I'm gonna come."

I let one hand drift up to his knot, gently massaging it as it grew. My other hand trailed down to my clit, playing with it. With a deep groan, his hand tightened on the back of my head as ropes of sweet, salty cum filled my mouth. I took every drop happily, never looking away from his eyes, even though his vision blurred with the intensity of the orgasm. "Fuck," he moaned, as I swallowed around him, milking him for every last drop.

Once I was satisfied he was completely drained, I pulled back, letting his semi hard cock pop from my mouth.

Callan was leaning back against the tile, his hand still tangled in my hair.

"How was that?" I asked, with a small grin.

Callan looked down at me, and with a growl hoisted me up by the upper arms, until I was standing in front of him. Pressing my back against the tile he devoured my mouth, not giving the slightest fuck that my mouth tasted like him.

"You are fucking perfect," Callan said. Resting his forehead against mine. "Let me catch my breath, then I'm returning the favour..."

CHAPTER THIRTY-THREE
Sage

Setting up my desk for the day with a cute mouse pad, I laid out everything the way I liked it. The chair was comfortable. In next to no time I was deep into the spreadsheets, working on isolating particular transactions.

I had been hyper-aware of Callan and Alaric at their desks, typing away, but when I got lost in my work the scent of us in the room was almost comforting. I got so absorbed in my work I hadn't noticed that Callan had moved until he was next to me, placing a glass of peach tea with ice and a straw on the desk before giving the top of my head a kiss, then leaving without a word, returning to his desk to continue with his own work.

The simple gesture of getting my favourite drink while I was working made me feel warm inside. I gave him a shy grin, and he smiled warmly back. Proximity with him felt easy now, I had been sleeping in the same bed as him for several nights now, and found myself looking forward to it. Alaric gave me a knowing grin. Our scents made it pretty obvious what Callan and I had been up to recently.

And ever since I had taken the leap and slept with Callan the pack had become more...hands on. They took any opportunity to touch me, even if it was just a quick peck on the cheek, or a hand to my lower back. My body was taking note, every touch made me happy and my thoughts often drifted into dirty territory. Now that I knew just how amazing it felt to be knotted, I wanted more. No wonder most omegas didn't work when they could be doing *that* all day.

Callan's phone rang, distracting me from my laptop screen. Callan frowned, looking at the caller ID.

"It's the Haven. I'll put it on speaker. Hello?" His voice was clipped and controlled, never taking my eyes off me.

"Callan Rivers? It's Keeper Gregory. Is all well?" the familiar voice asked.

"Hey, Keeper Gregory, you're on speaker, Sage and Alaric are in the room." He sat down at his desk, gesturing for them both to come closer.

"Oh, perfect. Hello all. Sage, how is everything going?"

"Very well," I said, as I came to stand next to where Callan was sitting. Alaric stood on the other side of the desk, so they were within speaking range of my phone. His arm snaked around my waist, pulling me near. I didn't resist, opting to lean into his warmth.

"I just wanted to give you a quick call and check in, I got the reports about what happened to your home, Sage. I am sorry. I'm assuming Pack Rivers have increased security?"

"We have," Callan confirmed. "One of us is with her at all times. None of her belongings were salvageable, I assume the

Havens will be compensating her for that since it was their failing."

"I'll bring it up with my superiors, she more than deserves compensation."

"What's being done on your end regarding Pack Bove?" Alaric asked quickly, before Gregory could continue.

"We are working with the police to track them down, we've given them anything they could need from Mencaster Haven."

Callan nodded, eyes on me. "Thank you. I assume you'll call us if there is any news?"

"I will. Is Sage being guarded at night? I know she's separate from you at night."

I bit my lip, heat rising in my cheeks "Uh, actually I'm with Callan at night now," I admitted. "I was struggling with lack of human contact."

The line was silent for a moment. "That makes sense, and are you comfortable with this Sage? We'll speak privately soon if you want."

"Oh, there's no need for that," I rushed to say. "I'm happy with how things are, I have Claudia a call away if I have any questions."

"If you want more security for Sage she is welcome here."

I shook my head, even though Keeper Gregory wouldn't see it. "I'm comfortable at the moment, I don't want to go to a Haven."

"Okay, if you're sure. The offer is always there, Sage."

"I'm sure," I reiterated.

CHAPTER THIRTY-FOUR
Sage

Despite being tired out, I couldn't get to sleep. Something felt off, and it was stopping me from settling. Next to me Callan snored lightly, his arm draped over me as I snuggled into his chest.

Slipping out of the alpha's hold I shimmied down, out of the bed, ignoring Callan's small growl of annoyance at the loss of me. I smiled. He would fall asleep again soon. I nipped to the bathroom, cursing when I caught my toe on the vanity. I did my business before returning to the dark room. Padding over to the window I sat on the ledge, looking out over the darkened gardens below. The forest and gardens were beautiful in the moonlight, from my spot I could even see the little vegetable garden I had decided to plant the other day. Callan had insisted I plant the garden there. Was it because he could see me out of the office and bedroom windows? Grabbing the e-reader I had left there earlier I settled in, deciding to pick up another romance book, because I had recently found myself even more enamoured with the genre.

I easily got lost in the familiar story. The heroine was just about to declare her feelings for the dark and twisted villain, when out of the corner of my eye something moved in the garden. Flicking my eyes back up, looking over the grass. Convincing myself it must have been a badger, I looked for a moment more until something, no...someone caught my eye ducking behind a tree. A tall black figure, I couldn't make anything else out. Staring so hard my eyes stung I waited for more movement, but none came.

My stomach felt heavy and panic slowly rose. Glancing over to my sleeping man, I dithered for a moment before getting up, walking over to an asleep Callan and shaking his shoulder.

"Callan?" I whispered gently.

"Hmmm?" he replied, sleepily, reaching out and rubbing my leg gently. "You okay, Honey?"

"I'm probably being silly, but I think I just saw someone outside," I whispered, voice strained.

Callan stilled, his eyes opening, suddenly more alert. He swiftly sat up, making me jump back. Now he was fully awake his nostrils flared as he took in the slightly burnt scent of my anxiety and fear.

"Repeat that," he asked, in a normal speaking voice.

"I couldn't sleep, so I went to read, but I saw something move. I thought it was a badger or something, but it moved again, and it was far bigger than any wild animal. I'm probably being silly. I didn't want to worry you...it's probably just a rabbit." As I spoke, Callan slid out of the bed silently, making his way over to the window, standing to the side of it, glancing out.

"Honey, will you just pass me my phone?" Callan asked, his eyes never leaving the window. I scrambled over the bed, grabbing his phone off the bedside table, and handing it over, all while his gaze never moved. He pressed the speed dial without even looking, raising the phone to his ear.

"Ric, can you come to my room? Possible security issue," he said simply before hanging up.

"What's going on?" I asked, worry making my scent sour. The bedroom door opened and Alaric walked in, his eyes assessing me as he walked over to Callan.

"What is it?" he asked.

"Sage thought she saw something," Callan explained.

"Probably a rabbit!" I exclaimed in a tired whisper. "You didn't need to wake Alaric for that."

Callan turned back to me now that Alaric was looking out of the window.

"Yes I did. Better safe than sorry." Callan shrugged, walking over to me and pulling me into his arms. I melted into his embrace.

"Callan, get her to the safe room. Something just moved and there's no way in hell that's a rabbit," Alaric's voice was low and gravelly.

Callan stilled for a second as Alaric spoke, but quickly sprang into action, the two of them pulling me with him as we strode out the room. I had to jog to keep up.

"Wait, what did you see?" I asked.

"Drop her off, I'll alert the security team, grab the others and meet you in the foyer," Alaric told Callan, ignoring my question. Callan made a grunt of agreement and dragged me down another hallway, separating us. His arm was a steel band across my midsection guiding me.

"Callan! What are you doing?" I asked. "You're freaking me out."

"Someone else is here, other alphas."

"It could have been a fox?" I asked, not really believing my own words.

"I'd rather be careful, I'm taking you to the safe room then we shall check it out."

"You have a safe room?"

"Our office. It's secure, the doors are reinforced and electronic in case of emergency." That was new information to me, in all the days I had worked in that room I hadn't been told that. We rounded another corner into Callan's office and he pushed me gently towards the armchair. "I'm going to lock you in," he told me.

"Lock me in?! Wha—" I spluttered.

"I'm sorry, we don't have time to explain, you're safer here." He gave me a quick kiss on the forehead before closing me in the room, the lock making a clicking sound as it engaged. I hadn't even realised the lock was there. Flabbergasted I ran up to the door, attempting to pull it open but it didn't budge, it was solid. Anger rose in me as I beat my hand against the door.

"Callan! Don't you dare leave me in here!" I yelled, though he was already gone. I scratched at the door praying it would open. I couldn't get out, I was trapped. Once again I was locked in, unable to leave.

While I loved this room it now felt claustrophobic despite its large size. I hated being trapped, like I was in that sterile room at the Haven, and I was about to be attacked. Was Lex here, on the grounds? Had he come for me? I couldn't run, just like the last time. Taking deep breaths, the air felt thin and my head swam lightly. *Panic attack*, I'd had a minor few before, but this one was strong. The window wouldn't open either. I couldn't get any fresh air, and the room was stifling. Sinking into a corner of the office I curled up, hugging my knees, praying for this feeling to pass.

CHAPTER THIRTY-FIVE
Callan

I was fuming. Someone had been on our fucking property, and we hadn't even realised. It was only when Sage, of all people, saw something through my window we were alerted to it.

After a better look through the grounds we summarised that someone had been there, but was now long gone, they must have had a vehicle nearby to make a speedy getaway, but none of the cameras picked it up. There were traces of an unidentifiable scent. Our security had combed through the grounds repeatedly, and were checking all CCTV. Whoever it was, they were good to make it so close to the house unnoticed. Once the all clear was given, I went to retrieve Sage, wanting her close, and needing to remind myself she was indeed safe. Everett followed me while the others stayed speaking with security.

I tapped the code into the console to open the office door, expecting Sage to be happy to see me. I didn't expect to be on the receiving end of a hardback book hurtling through the air, clipping me on the side of my head.

"What the fuck?" I growled, looking around the room to find the assailant only to see an extremely pissed off looking omega. Her eyes were red and puffy, she had been crying, but now her features were distorted in anger.

"I've been locked in here for over an hour!" she yelled. "How much of an ass can you be, Callan?!" She was vibrating with rage.

"We put you here to protect you," I grumbled. "It was for your own good, I'm sorry if we worried you."

Sage laughed, but it wasn't a happy sound. "You think I'm mad because I didn't hear from you for an hour and was *worried*? Callan, you fucking confined me, like a pet that needs putting in their crate. Never mind that you know I hate being trapped after the Haven—but no, lock up the omega because you don't want to lose your favourite screw! Don't you fucking touch me!"

I dropped the hand I had reached out instinctively to comfort her. "Sage, I'm sorry. I wasn't thinking; are you okay?"

"If you consider a panic attack okay, then I'm just peachy! You goddamn dumb dumb," she growled.

Panic attack? She had a *panic attack* and we weren't there to help her. *Fuck*.

"Someone was here, you needed to be safe." Everett attempted to soothe Sage, but she was having none of it.

"I get that, but there's a thing called a *conversation*, a discussion, not locking someone up against their will," she snapped. "Are we safe?" She glared at me, her face blotchy and red. Her hair was wild and messy, were it not for the situation I would assume she had freshly fucked hair.

"Yes, there's no one on the property anymore, security has combed through every inch of the grounds," I confirmed.

"Good. Then I'm going to bed, and all of you better stay the fuck out of my room!" she hissed, passing me and Everett to storm off into her room, slamming the door angrily.

She was crying. I fucking hated it when she cried.

"What the fuck did you do!?" Bellamy asked, alarmed, as he and Alaric joined us.

"Locked her in the panic room to keep her safe. Turns out that's really pissed her off." I grimaced.

"Did you at least give her the code to get out if she needed to?" Bellamy asked.

"No, I wasn't thinking straight, I just wanted her safe while we dealt with the threat. We need to up security, by the way," I groaned exasperatedly.

"You're an idiot for not giving her the code, Callan," Alaric called me out. "I'll make the call first thing. We'll double the guards, at least. I'm also going to reach out to a few other packs, give them a heads up on what's going on. If these assholes are bold enough to come onto our land, then maybe they'll go into other pack lands. I assume Sage is their target, but she might not be the *only* target they're looking for."

"I've been messaging with an old military friend, and Gage asked if we needed any extra help. He's also mentioned that rumours are starting to spread about the Haven selling an omega," Bellamy added. "How long do you think it will be until she comes around to the idea of fully bonding with us?"

"Well considering she threw a book at Callan's head, I think we'll be waiting a while," Alaric said dryly.

"Wait, she threw something at you?" Bellamy laughed as I nodded. "Damn, I wish I had seen that, I've yet to see her truly pissed off. Bet she looked good." He grinned, then frowned. "Although I don't like that she's upset."

I shook my head. Yes, she had been beautiful, even when spitting mad at me, but I would much rather have her happy.

"Are you going to laugh or are you going to go see if you can make her stop crying? One of us needs to be with her at all times, even if she's unhappy with us," I growled belligerently.

"I'll give it a go." Everett smiled, bounding off down the hall.

"She's going to destroy him," Alaric commented, watching our packmate run off to his death.

"Either she's cheered up, or he gets his ass handed to him. I'm happy with either result."

Chapter 36

Sage

CHAPTER THIRTY-SIX
Sage

I curled up in my nest, clutching my knees to my chest. I felt sick to my stomach. Every fibre of my being wanted me to go and throw myself into the arms of one of my alphas, but I was *livid*. "Sage," a voice called from the doorway.

"I mean this in the nicest way, Everett, but fuck off," I ground out, still crying.

"I don't like you being upset."

"Well you guys shouldn't be asses then!" I sat up, glaring at Everett, who was standing at the edge of the bed, hands up in a surrendering gesture.

"I won't deny Callan was a bit heavy handed, but he was worried about you, Pretty Girl."

"I feel trapped here," I snapped. "The lot of you are everywhere! I can't leave." I ran my hands through my hair, scratching my scalp in the process.

"Sage..." Everett frowned, he opened his mouth to speak, but couldn't find the words.

"Please. I just need some space, Everett." I sobbed.

"No can do, Pretty Girl." He shrugged. "Someone was here, one of us has to be with you at all times. I volunteered." He walked over to the armchair near my bed, sitting down with a sigh, slapping his hands on his knees and tilting his head in my direction.

I buried my head under a blanket, not wanting to look at his frankly adorable face right now. It was hard to stay angry at the human equivalent of a German Shepherd puppy.

"I can smell how pissed off you are."

"Good," I huffed out. The entire nest was saturated with the burnt aroma of my anger and fear.

"I'm sorry," he said softly.

"I know." I hiccuped. "Callan can go suck a dick right now, though."

Everett laughed. "I'm not going to disagree with you, Pretty Girl. Should I tell him to stay away? He'll be wondering why you haven't gone back to bed."

"I am not getting back into bed with that ass," I growled.

"He just wants to keep you safe." Everett hesitated. "Want me to join you?" he asked.

"No!" Was I being mean? Probably, but Everett took it all in stride.

"Okay, get some sleep, Pretty Girl. I'll be here." He settled into the armchair, kicking his feet up.

Everett fell asleep easily, sitting up in the armchair. I glared at him over my pillows, if only it was so easy for me. My midsection burned with angry cramps. I knew what my body needed, but I didn't want to give in. My traitorous body wanted Callan. We had a routine, every night we slept together in Callan's room and that satiated my need for physical touch and relaxed my body. Without it the pre-heat cramps got worse.

But he was an ass, and I didn't want to be near him. Rolling over I tossed a few pillows across my nest, rearranging them in hopes it would help me sleep better.

I considered waking Everett, but I was pissed he insisted on staying in my room, trying to talk to me about Callan, plus he didn't have the greatest control. Everett couldn't a hundred percent be trusted while sleepy. He could easily revert to baser instincts.

Looking over at him again, his head was thrown back while he lightly snored. He was dead asleep, his vanilla and pastry scent slightly burnt from the stress of the night. What else could I do?

With a new idea in mind, I slowly rolled out of the nest, careful to avoid making any noise. Everett didn't stir. Gently padding across the room I slipped out of the door, throwing a look his way before slowly going down the hallway to the familiar bedroom.

The dark, smoky scent greeted me the moment I opened

the familiar door. Without a word I walked up to the bed on the far side of the room, lifting the cover's and getting in.

Alaric's eyes were open, and he gave me a questioning look.

"Just... don't say anything. My stupid omega instincts mean I can't be alone, but I don't want to discuss it and I don't want to be near Callan right now, okay?"

His arm snaked around my waist, pulling me into him.

"Go to sleep then."

Prying my eyes open, I could feel warmth radiating under me. I was used to waking up with Callan, so the sensation wasn't foreign, but the smell was different. Alaric's smoky scent coated every surface and I knew I was also covered in it. Callan and I tended to spoon, but with Alaric I was sprawled over his chest. His *naked* chest. His hand gently ran over my lower back as his chest rose and fell under me.

"Good morning," he rumbled, voice thick with sleep.

"Morning." I grinned up at him. The room was still dark, the sun only just starting to rise.

"Are you feeling okay?"

"Yeah, I am, actually," I said. The empty feeling I got when isolated wasn't there anymore. Physically I had been a mess after being left alone in the office, but that pain was gone. One night sleeping on an alpha and I was fine. If I hadn't been so distressed I could have stayed in my own god damned nest.

"I'm surprised Callan hasn't tracked me down and dragged me back to his bed," I remarked.

"I think the paperback projectile gave him pause." Alaric smiled ruefully.

"Yeah, I wasn't the nicest."

"It was understandable, you were stressed. The whole house smelt like burnt honey."

"If he had just taken a moment to *explain*."

"He should have found a moment, but Sage, everything we do is to keep you *safe*. Can my pack be boneheads? Of course, but do you doubt that they would protect you?"

"No... It was more than the being trapped. I felt like Lex was around the corner coming for me again."

"We won't let that happen. Callan probably wasn't thinking straight last night. A few years ago he learned how bad it could be for omegas who are stolen from their homes and trafficked. My guess is he thought of you in that situation and freaked out."

"I suppose."

"Sage." He placed a finger under my chin, tilting my face to look him directly in the eye. "You've heard about my family. My uncle was part of something disgusting. I've seen the photos and I will *never* allow that shit to happen to you, even if I have to lock you in a damn closet to keep you safe."

My mouth opened and closed a few times before I found words. "I know why Callan did it, but just..."

"Talking. We should have spoken about this stuff long ago. You know my uncle?"

"The one who was arrested?"

"Yes, he was part of a ring that kidnapped omegas for their own perverted fun. I've seen the photos, and it's sickening. My uncle had a whole collection of them. I would go feral before allowing anyone like that near you. Callan and I... we are more similar than we like to admit. You know we are actually brothers?"

"Wait, like his bio parents?"

Alaric nodded. "I met Callan when he took a DNA test. We share a parent, we weren't sure how as he's adopted, raised by betas—but it's how we found each other. The DNA test made it clear that Callan's mother was an omega, yet my mother is a beta. Given how close my father and uncle were… there's every possibility that Callan is the child of a trafficked omega who was abused by my own fucking father. We decided it was best to avoid diving into my family's past and digging up any more skeletons. Callan was raised right by Fred and Ann Rivers, and he would get nothing but heartache from my family, so no one but us and the pack knows."

"Oh, Alaric." I reached forward, gently running a hand through his hair.

"My father has never been convicted, he is still seen as a good man, which is bullshit. I know he's a bastard, I just never realised how much of one he was while I was growing up."

"I'm sorry you had to go through that."

"I'm not. Callan finding me led to us forming pack Rivers, which ultimately led us to you. I wish we could have stopped so many omega's suffering—"

"You were a child, Alaric. Don't you dare blame yourself for the actions of a monster. That's like me blaming myself for Lex finding me attractive." A growl escaped Alaric and I raised an eyebrow. "Exactly."

—

"What's with the frown?" Alaric asked. His hair was messy, he usually kept it so neat and formal. I liked it.

"I was kind of a brat to Everett, I left him fast asleep last night, he has no idea I left." I cringed.

Alaric chuckled lightly, his head falling back onto his pillow. "You were probably being ruled by instinct. I bet you can find a way to make it up to him."

"Actually…" I trailed off with a grin.

"Yes?"

"I have a favour to ask."

After discussing my plans to a highly amused Alaric, I slipped out of his room, slowly making my way back to my own rooms. I hated that my rooms were so far from the guys, but they had done that to give me space. *Maybe I'll just get one or two of them to sleep in my nest.*

CHAPTER THIRTY-SEVEN
Everett

"You left?" I asked, voice dejected. "Callan?"

She snorted. "No. Alaric."

I gave her a rueful smile. "Poor Callan." I sat up straight, running my hand through my mess of blonde curls. "I'm sorry I couldn't be what you needed." I tried to keep my voice playful, but she could tell I was upset.

"Well, about that…" She held up a silk bag.

"What's that?" I asked. Instead of answering, she walked over to me slowly, a playful grin on her face. Once she was only a few feet away she pulled the item out of the bag. Handcuffs. Strong ones. Confused, I looked up at her, whose grin was almost predatory in nature. "Pretty Girl?"

"So, you wouldn't let me play with you because you were scared of losing control, correct? Well, these are reinforced steel, courtesy of Alaric. If your hands are cuffed behind your back I could have my fun, and you wouldn't be able to do anything permanent if you lost control."

I sat, stunned. The idea already had me making a tent in my gym shorts.

"We don't have to!" she quickly said, taking my silence as a bad thing. She took a step back, already shrinking in on herself. "It was just an—"

"Get them fucking on me!" I grinned wide, jumping up, suddenly very awake. The enthusiasm made her giggle.

"Are you sure?"

"A hundred percent, Pretty Girl. If it means you can get your hands on me, then hurry up!" I turned my back to her, my hands behind my back, out and ready to be cuffed. "Do it!" I bounced on the balls of my feet.

"So eager."

"Fuck yeah." I laughed as she undid the cuffs, placing them on my wrists. The telltale clink of them closing just made me even more aroused. "Anything for your hands on me," I said again, turning around to face her. "Where do you want me?"

"Well, who said it was going to be my hands?" she asked with a wicked grin, eyes never leaving mine as she sank to her knees right there in the middle of her room.

Fuck fuck fuck.

"Pretty Girl..." I moaned. She was eye-level with my erection, smiling up at me. How the fuck did I get so lucky?

"Hush, let me have my fun." She tugged at the waistband of my shorts, my cock springing free. Wrapping her hand around it, she gently stroked it a few times, her eyes never leaving mine.

I groaned, throwing my head back at the sensation. How was her hand so hot?

She took advantage of my lack of eye contact as my head was thrown back to softly lick down my length. I jumped at the sensation of her wet tongue trailing slowly from base to tip, she was licking me like a lollipop, teasing me.

"Pretty Girl..." I growled.

She laughed. "What are you going to do about it, Everett? I appear to have all the power here."

And I fucking loved it, despite the deep ache in me. Before I could formulate an answer, I was put out of my misery. Hot, wet softness enveloped my cock as she took me in her mouth, and I twitched with pleasure. "Fuck!" I cursed, pulling at my restraints—they held up shockingly well. I would have to thank Alaric later.

Slowly, she eased me to the back of her throat. My cock was just as big as Callan's so her jaw strained under the pressure, but it only made her slick flow more.

The only noise I was capable of making was unintelligible mumbles of pleasure as she reached the base of my cock, gently swallowing around me.

"Fuck, god, fuck," I moaned, tugging on the cuffs. Slowly increasing her speed she started to retreat, until my tip was barely brushing her lips, then sank back down, repeating the motion and slowly increasing her pace.

"I'm not going to last," I choked out with a moan. "Fuck me, that mouth. Fucking swallow me, Pretty Girl. I can smell your slick—fuck!" I broke off with a curse as she started to hum softly. "You're going to have to back up, I'm gonna cum," I panted.

I was trying to warn her, but she doubled down her efforts, increasing the suction and going faster. Moments later she was rewarded when I let out a low, elongated moan. My cock twitched in her mouth.

Swallowing repeatedly she made sure she didn't miss a

drop, while I swayed slightly on my feet, shudders running through my body.

Once I was thoroughly clean, she released me with a pop and grinned up at me. I gave her a lazy grin.

"Why the fuck didn't we think of that sooner?"

CHAPTER THIRTY-EIGHT
Sage

I had spent the whole day resting after the stress of the night before. Everett had even curled up with me in my nest for a quick nap midmorning before plying me with snacks. He was wiped after our little experiment. When I first built my nest I had worried I would never want anyone in it, same as my bed back at my apartment, but I actually liked having him in there. Vanilla coated the pillows and I revelled in it.

That night I crawled into bed with Alaric again. I hadn't seen Callan all day—apparently he was working. I wasn't truly mad at him anymore, but I wasn't actively seeking him out yet, either.

The following day I decided to be productive. Moping around the house wasn't going to help the situation, Callan had tried to speak with me about what happened but I had been belligerent. Still he had added a few blankets and pillows to the office in case it ever happened again. Alaric was in the kitchen chopping fruit so I made both of us a coffee and joined him. He held out a piece of watermelon and fed it to me, his eyes darkening at my acceptance. His pleasure over it seemed to be an alpha trait, like the guys got off on looking after me. A girl could easily get used to it.

"So what's your plans after breakfast?" he asked as I chewed.

"Spreadsheets, so many spreadsheets." I grabbed another piece of watermelon, and Alaric's hand shot out, gently but firmly holding my wrist, plucking the offending fruit out of my fingers before tutting and lifting the fruit to my lips himself, still holding my wrist in a vise-like grip. His eyes burned into me as he watched me take a bite, looking him dead in the eye.

"That's my job," he murmured, low and rumbling.

I couldn't help my body's reaction, the rush of slick scenting the air.

"Does someone like feeding me?" I asked as my lips tipped up into a smirk.

"You're playing with fire, Sweet Girl."

"Sorry." I grinned. Pulling away, I took a step back, only to yelp in surprise when a strong hand gripped my waist, hauling me up onto the counter. Alaric drew me close until our faces were inches apart, my legs on either side of his hips. I was painfully aware how close his cock was to my core through my thin sundress.

"That fucking scent suggests you're anything but sorry," he rumbled.

I giggled and shrugged. "What can I say? You're pretty attractive when you're all growly."

Over the last few days a switch had flipped, and I wanted to discover all the amazing ways these men could make me feel.

Alaric grinned wickedly, leaning forward to run his tongue up my neck, gently nipping at my pulse point. The sensation set my body on fire, and I shifted, trying to rub against something to ease the sudden pressure.

"You like playing with fire, don't you?" he asked.

Raking my hands through his hair, I gripped it, holding his eyes. "I know you'll never hurt me."

Sliding a hand up to my neck he pulled me forward into a bruising kiss, swallowing my little moans of pleasure.

"Alaric," I whimpered as more slick dampened between my legs.

"Mmm, someone's feeling a little needy today aren't they?" His eyes darkened as they took me in, his free hand slowly running up the inside of my leg to the seam of my panties. "I bet if I slip my fingers in you'll be soaked."

"Drenched," I panted, unable to look away from him. Our lips met in a heated rush. I wanted to devour him. I tried to reach forward to grab him, but his hands shot out to mine, pinning them to the counter, leaving me open and to his mercy.

"Well this looks fun," a voice from the doorway declared happily. Alaric loosened his grip on the nape of my neck enough for me to turn and see Bellamy standing in the kitchen doorway.

"Someone is being stubborn." Alaric leaned down to kiss behind my ear, making me shiver at the sensation.

"How so?"

"Not letting me feed her," Alaric mumbled as he nuzzled my neck.

"I don't think she's complaining. I can smell her slick from the gym," Bellamy said.

"Want to give me a hand here?" Alaric asked, raising an

eyebrow. My brain stuttered at the thought of having them both in the room while Alaric was making me writhe with need, but it only lasted a second before my body reacted, slick flooding my panties, soaking through. Both men groaned at the scent filling the room.

"I think our girl likes that idea." Bellamy strode up to the island, his own spiced chocolate scent setting me even more on edge, another cramp ripping through my abdomen. "Do you want both of us?" he asked as Alaric continued his assault on my neck.

I whimpered and nodded.

Alaric pulled back, removing his hands from the counter where they were pinning mine, grabbing me roughly by the chin, forcing me to look him in the eyes. "Use your words Sweet Girl. I want to hear it."

The deep tone of his voice turned me to mush.

"I—I want to play with both of you." I bit my lip, trying to stop my nerves showing, but failing miserably.

"Good girl," Alaric praised, and I preened. "We're going to go slow, and just say if you want us to stop, am I clear?"

I nodded.

"Words, Sweet Girl," he reminded me.

"Yes." I looked him dead in the eye, desire making me bold.

"Bell, hold her hands down, I need a taste…and I want to see how much she can handle." He grinned as Bellamy came up behind me, pinning my hands behind my back, thrusting my chest out to Alaric who hummed appreciatively before sinking down to his knees, hands snaking underneath my sundress to deftly remove my panties. The cool air on my clit sent shivers down my spine, making me moan and writhe and push against Bellamy's grasp as he leaned down to suck on my pulse point.

Alaric's strong arms pulled my legs apart, as I was helpless in their arms, my sundress skirt hoisted up exposing me to them both. "I've wanted to taste you since the moment I sunk my fingers in this sweet, eager pussy." He leaned forward to take a long lick that made me leap off the counter, only to be locked in place by Bellamy's strong arms. Prying my legs open even further he dove in, lapping at me like a man starving.

"Fuck," he murmured against my core. "I could eat this every day for the rest of my life and die a happy man."

Alaric circled my clit, alternating between teasing and forceful strokes.

I couldn't think straight. Between Alaric's tongue and Bellamy sucking on my pulse point I felt like I was going to implode. Bellamy grazed his teeth over the freshly formed bruises.

"You love having your alpha on his knees for you, don't you Omega?" Bellamy rumbled into my ear, one hand snaking around to slide into the top of my sundress, plucking at my nipple.

The overstimulation was too much for me. My vision became unfocused, and all I could think was how I ached for more.

"Now you're going to be a good girl for us and cum on his tongue, aren't you?" Bellamy asked in a seductively commanding voice. "I want to see you come undone, using his mouth for your pleasure. Give it to us."

Alaric's hands tightened on my thighs as I detonated, throwing my head back with a cry, muttering unintelligibly. He didn't let up until he was sure every wave of my pleasure had passed and I slumped in Bellamy's arms as he cooed compliments into my ear. Alaric grinned up at me, his gaze almost predatory, "Do you think I'm stopping yet?"

I looked at him questioningly but instead of answering he

dove back in, lapping at my now very sensitive clit. My back arched as I babbled, another climax fast approaching. It didn't take long to push me over the edge again.

"Bed?" Alaric growled, looking up at Bellamy, who nodded in agreement. I was still trying to catch my breath as I was hauled into Alaric's arms, my ankles instantly locking behind his back, my head on his shoulder. Bellamy followed him as he strode out of the kitchen.

"The counter is covered in her slick. Ev is going to be so jealous when he gets home."

"Let the pup be jealous," Alaric laughed as we climbed the stairs. Opening a door with one hand, he deposited me on his bed. Before I could look around too much Bellamy crawled onto the bed, leaning down to capture my mouth.

"I want your nectar all over my sheets, Sweet Girl," Alaric told me, watching as Bellamy made his way down my neck, lavishing it in kisses while he trailed a path to my chest, lightly nipping at my chest.

"Please," I whimpered, trying to sit up, only to find my hands pinned next to my head by Bellamy.

"All in good time," he cooed, mouth going back to my neck. "You look fucking good with my marks on your throat, you know that?"

"Hmmm, she does," Alaric agreed. "But I'll have to add my own into the mix."

The idea of being marked by another alpha had even more slick leaking down my thighs.

"I think she likes that thought." Bellamy sat up and let me go, leaning with his back to the headboard, and pulling his shirt off, just as Alaric had.

Sitting up, I faced Alaric who was staring at me with a

hunger that only fed my need further. Palming his cock through his jeans, his eyes raked over my body.

"I think that dress has to go, Sweet Girl. Take it off," he instructed.

I reached for the hem of my dress, sitting up on my knees to yank it off with shaking hands. Alaric gazed appreciatively at my bare body.

In a moment of boldness, I leaned forward, grabbing the buckle of Alaric's jeans.

"You want to play with my cock?" he asked with a grin.

I nodded.

"Words," he growled.

"Yes, Alpha, I want to play with your cock," I whispered, watching Alaric's eyes close as he relished the words.

"Go on then," he commanded, looking down at his unbuckled belt. I made quick work of it, and pulled his cock out, gently stroking up and down the length, biting my lip. I could already feel his base getting slightly more swollen, preparing to knot.

"Fuck," Alaric groaned, throwing his head back.

While he wasn't looking I leaned forward, running my tongue along his length, humming at the musky taste setting my nerves on fire.

"Shit," Alaric cursed, his hand flying to the back of my head, fisting in my hair. Looking down at me, he growled low and dangerously as I smirked up at him. Without a word I opened my mouth, taking the entirety of his length while he rumbled and clutched at my hair. Alaric continued to moan as I worked his length, enjoying the taste of him and the sounds my actions elicited.

"Fuck, if you keep doing that Sweet Girl, I'm not going to last," he moaned.

Hands slipped round my waist, sliding through my folds and gently stroking my clit. "You like having Alaric in your mouth, don't you? You like sucking alpha cock, like a good little omega," Bellamy purred as he strummed that little bundle of nerves. My every instinct wanted to deny it, to say I didn't love sucking Alaric's alpha cock, or that I didn't want to submit like a good little omega, but that would be a lie. Every bone in my body was screaming for release and all I wanted to do was beg my alphas to fill me and knot me one after another.

Bellamy removed his fingers and I whined at the loss. "Fuck, she's dripping, Alaric."

"She's fucking magnificent, isn't she?" Alaric smiled down at me as I was still working him over. "So wet and desperate, just for us. Do you want to come, Omega?"

I hummed in agreement. I most definitely wanted to come. Pulling his cock out of my mouth, he reached down to my chin, tilting my face to look him in the eye. "Bellamy's going to fuck you now Sweet Girl, is that what you want? Use your words."

"Yes, Alpha," I panted. My own voice was unrecognisable to me, so whiny and full of need. Pleased with my answer, Alaric leaned down, claiming my mouth, his hand sliding from my chin to gently grip my throat. The feel of his hands there sent sparks down my spine, and even more slick flowed.

Bellamy didn't make me wait long, he lined himself up with my entrance, edging in agonisingly slow while Alaric kissed me, his hand pressing against my windpipe, not enough to stop my breathing, but enough to exert a level of control that once would have scared me, but I now found intoxicating. Since I had jumped off the proverbial ledge and let Callan knot me I had been excited to feel the others. Bellamy had been so sweet my first night and now I desperately wanted to feel his knot.

"Please," I whimpered, trying to back up on Bellamy, to make him take me deeper but he held my hips in a vise-like grip. A sharp sting on my buttocks startled me. Yet the impact only added to my heightened lust.

"Behave, Omega," Alaric growled out, undeniably alpha, his voice full of power. "Bellamy's taking his time with you."

I whined, but Bellamy didn't speed up. If anything he sank in even slower. The sensation of being stretched millimetre by millimetre was mind numbingly good. I had taken Callan just a few days prior, but Bellamy stretched just as much, the burning sensation of being split open made me beg for more.

"Good girl," Alaric cooed. "You're taking him so well." He peppered my neck with kisses around his fingers.

Eventually, painstakingly slow Bellamy was fully seated, and instead of moving, he stilled inside me.

"How does our omega feel?" Alaric asked Bellamy with a grin.

"Fucking fantastic. Perfectly warm and wet. I could fucking live here."

I whined in agreement.

"Good girl, do you want to be fucked?" Alaric whispered into my ear.

"*Please.*"

"Beg Bellamy to fuck you."

"Please, fuck, alpha. I need your knot, please fuck me," I whimpered. What little restraint Bellamy was holding onto broke and he pulled out almost entirely, and before I could even recognise the sensation he slammed in to the hilt, cursing. I saw stars, unable to make words. I moaned in pleasure as Bellamy set a punishing pace. Holding me in a bruising grip, he pulled me closer to him with each thrust reaching parts of me so deep I knew I would be feeling him the next day.

"Mmm you look so good like this, Omega." Alaric gently ran his hand through my hair, watching my face contort in pleasure, my eyes blurry and unseeing. Heat crept up my neck, rising in my cheeks. I blindly grabbed for Alaric, wanting more. My arousal was answered a moment later when Alaric pressed his cock against my lips, his scent filling my senses. Opening my mouth, I swallowed deeply around him, desperate to please him, to make him come apart, to taste his cum. I needed his cum more than air. My entire worldview tunnelled, only able to focus on the two cocks pistoning in and out of me.

"I think our sweet little omega is getting close," Bellamy said.

"Mmm," Alaric looked me in the eye, his hand gripping the back of my hair, guiding me as I sank down on his length. "Are you close, Omega? Do you want to come?"

I hummed in agreement.

He pulled his cock out of my mouth, ignoring my whine, and batting my hand away when I reached for him. "No. I'm going to watch you cum first. I want to see your face as Bellamy knots you."

"You're fucking amazing, Sage," Bellamy said breathlessly. "So much fucking sweet honey. Now I've had a taste of you I'm not going to be able to stop, I'm going to want to sink into this sweet warmth every fucking day. I want you to come. Milk my knot. Right. Fucking. Now!" With his last three thrusts his knot slipped in and I exploded, screaming as my walls stretched around his knot, his cock twitching and filling me in the best way.

Bellamy slumped over, resting on his elbows to keep himself from crushing me. Softly kissing my spine, he praised me, telling me how fucking perfect I was. I couldn't make words just yet, and instead lay there panting, trying to regain feeling in my limbs.

"You're not done yet, Omega." Bellamy kissed my neck. "Look at Alaric."

I turned to see Alaric sitting back, relaxed and slowly stroking himself. Despite the earth shattering orgasm, even more slick leaked out of me. "Our girl likes that sight, Alaric, she just fucking clenched all over my knot."

"Really?" Alaric leaned down to kiss me. "Well as soon as Bellamy is no longer knotted into you, I'm going to have my turn, and I'm not going to be gentle."

I whined.

"You like the sound of that Sweet Girl?" He chuckled

"Yes," I moaned. "Fuck. I can't believe I already want to go again, fuck," I panted.

"That's the omega in you," Bellamy murmured. "I bet I could make you cum again with my knot buried deep in you." His hand slid down my stomach to my clit, making me jerk in shock, then moan at the sensation of Bellamy's knot pulling at my insides and burning in the most delicious way.

"Oh fuck," I groaned, writhing under Bellamy, and grinding myself down onto the mattress. I needed a release again, already. I didn't know how but I was climbing to that peak again.

"Come on your alpha's knot, Sage," Bellamy crooned. His words pushed me over the edge and I came, screaming into the covers.

We lay like that for a while as we came down from our respective highs, Alaric watching from across the bed, his gaze calm but hungry. I looked up at him, gently stroking his cock he watched me wriggle, trying to get away from Bellamy. My heavy honey perfume was so thick in the air we could choke on it. I looked back at Bellamy, still knotted in me, and I buried my face back into the covers.

"Don't go shy on us now," Alaric ordered.

"I'm not."

Bellamy pulled out, his knot now deflated enough to do so, and I couldn't help but moan at the emptiness.

"Don't pout." Bellamy leaned down and kissed my cheek. "Something tells me you're going to be nice and full in just a moment."

Alaric grabbed me by the waist and flipped me over. Gasping at the sudden movement, I went to grab Alaric's shoulders, but my hands were pinned by his large ones above my head.

"I'm not going to let you distract me, little omega." He positioned himself at my entrance. "Keep your hands up here or I'll have Bellamy tie them up."

At the threat, the scent of slick filled the air. "Hmmm... that's good to know for the future. But for now..." He gently reached under both my legs, leaving my hands up when he sank himself into me in one hard, almost violent thrust, holding my thighs as leverage. Holy fuck it felt divine.

"I am going to knot you and keep you right here in my bed."

"Fucking wonderful, isn't she?" Bellamy softly ran his hand through my hair while I threw my head back and surrendered to Alaric's punishing pace. I didn't think it was possible to come any more, but Alaric kept hitting that delicious spot inside me, every growl of his triggering yet more juices. Bellamy tweaked my nipple gently, only adding to the overloading sensations. I couldn't survive another orgasm.

"I'm not going to last, your pussy is clamping down on me

too well, Omega." He sped up, every thrust making our pelvic bones crash together, him hitting my clit and making me want to scream. "I'm not going to knot you until you cum on my cock."

"I need your knot," I begged.

"And you'll get his knot. Good girls who take knots come for their alphas," Bellamy whispered in my ear. "Maybe next time we'll tie you down, or even blindfold you. Get you close, and then take it away. We're going to have so much fun. We're going to keep that beautiful pussy constantly full of knots and cum. You'll always feel one of your alpha's in you. Do you like that idea?"

His filthy words threw me over the edge and I spasmed, screaming with the sheer force of my orgasm, writhing in the restraint of their hands. The fluttering of my walls was too much and Alaric bellowed, his knot swelling, sending me over the edge again.

CHAPTER THIRTY-NINE
Sage

I sat at my desk in the empty office staring blankly at the computer screen. Callan had popped into the office a few times to check on me between calls, taking a moment to give me a quick kiss before rushing off again. I had taken some time to cool off and had forgiven him for locking me in the office, but I wasn't going to forget anytime soon. I understood he was worried for me, but he needed to learn to use his big boy words in the future, and not be a giant dumb dumb. Callan had a soft, pleased expression every time he came in, adding his scent to Alaric and Bellamy's on my skin. I had woken up sandwiched between Alaric and Bellamy, their combined scent made me crave chocolate cherries. Maybe I would use the card the pack gave me and order some.

They had been reluctant to let me get up to work for the day, insisting that anything for them could wait. Alaric had dragged me back into the nest every time I tried to clamber out and refused to let me leave until my legs were shaking from multiple orgasms. The entire pack had become cuddle monsters, not that I was complaining. Every time I wrapped myself up in them I felt inexplicably calm, their embrace like a sedative. The issues of the world melting away in their arms.

The spreadsheets in front of me were starting to make sense. I had been chasing an odd looking account that had withdrawn an eye watering amount of cash over the last two years, all in small increments so they went unnoticed. I was just chasing up all leads in case it was a legit account, but I hadn't linked it to any of the pack or anyone who should have account access. There were several accounts taking money, but those were for things like fuel expenses, lawyer fees, and other legitimate costs. I had been chasing this particular account for several days.

With a sigh of frustration I closed my laptop and picked up my phone, searching to find the contact I wanted to call.

"Sage, dear! How are you?" Claudia's voice was as warm as her cinnamon scent.

"I'm not disturbing you am I?" I asked.

"Never! What are you up to?" she asked pleasantly. "I just saw some darling curtains, I need to send you the link."

"Just working. The guys aren't around so I took the chance to try and sort more of their books."

"It makes me so happy that your career meshes with theirs!" I nodded even though she couldn't see my reaction. It was working out rather well, the guys let me work in peace when I needed and never questioned or spoke down to me when I brought up issues or queries.

I was silent for a moment, trying to formulate words. "I had sex with Bellamy and Alaric at the same time," I blurted, my face heating when my words caught up with my brain. I chewed on my thumbnail absentmindedly.

"That's amazing! How was it?" Claudia sounded ecstatic, her voice high pitched and fast.

"It was overwhelming when I started playing with more than one of my guys at a time, but in the best way! It was really good. It's gone from zero to a hundred very fast though, but I like it," I admitted.

"Are they listening to you, respecting your desires?"

"Completely." I took a deep breath before asking what was on my mind. "Claudia, how did you know you were ready to bond with your pack? How did you come to that decision?"

She was silent for a moment. "I just couldn't imagine my life without them. I thought about what I would be leaving and I couldn't even think of it. They were mine."

I tried to do as she suggested, thinking about never making breakfast with Bellamy again, of never working side by side with Callan or Alaric, never having Everett turn my bad mood into laughter. My throat felt thick, tears forming instantly. I didn't want that. Going to the Haven…trying to find another pack…the idea alone made me feel sick to my stomach.

"I don't want to leave *them*. It's such a strong feeling, and it's scary."

"Oh, Sage," Claudia gushed, "that's normal. My emotions were so intense and all over the place, and I was in a normal Haven and had a much easier time getting to know my guys, I can imagine you're all over the place, too."

"I think I want to bond with them," I admitted in a rush. "But I'm scared."

Claudia made a little cry of excitement and I smiled at her enthusiasm. "That is *amazing*, it truly is. You know this will legally make you my daughter?"

"It will?" I grinned. I had never been close to my family,

but the idea of being tied to Claudia wasn't daunting, in fact it was all the more reason to hurry up and bond with the guys.

"You'll be stuck with me," Claudia giggled.

"I'm nervous about the whole biting thing… Do you think you could talk me through it?" I asked.

"Of course! Buckle up, I'm going to be graphic, and feel free to take notes." She laughed. "You will be experiencing some of the best orgasms of your life!"

The call lasted almost an hour, and I was thankful none of the guys came to check on me in that time. I would have died of embarrassment if they had walked in on Claudia talking me through the finer points of bonding. By the time I hung up my mind had been made.

Pack Rivers were it for me. I was going to bond with them, and have a damn good time doing it. Now I just needed to figure out when.

CHAPTER FORTY
Sage

Humming quietly to myself I made scrambled eggs. I had woken up to an empty nest. Bellamy had fallen asleep with me the night before and I vaguely recalled him kissing me at some ungodly hour and mentioning something about the gym. When I had poked my head into the gym he wasn't in sight so I decided to quickly eat before hunting him down because I was hungry.

I had yet to find a good time to discuss with them about bonding. I wanted to get them all together in one place, and tell them all at the same time.

Alaric had told me that everyone would be home for dinner that night as he kissed me goodbye before he had to rush off for a meeting. So with any luck, tonight was the night.

A knock on the kitchen door pulled me away from my staring contest with the eggs I was scrambling. Winton, the security guard Bellamy had briefly introduced me to in the garden last week, was standing in the doorway. They usually didn't enter the house, but Callan had assured me that they would occasionally to ensure it was safe given the recent break in attempt. Although they were all supposed to keep their distance from me.

"Morning Winton, is everything okay?" I asked, turning to look at him while still stirring my eggs.

"Everything is good, Miss Sage. Just doing a house check—Mr Bellamy had to rush into one of his cafes. Some sort of emergency with the business so I've been instructed to keep an eye on things."

"Oh, I hope everyone is okay." I plated up my eggs and grabbed my usual iced tea from the fridge before sitting down at the table and digging in.

"No one was harmed, to my knowledge." Winton stayed in the doorway, watching me intently.

Pulling out my phone I shot a quick text to Bellamy, and when I got no response, messaged Callan.

SAGE:

> Have you heard from Bellamy? Winton said there was an emergency at the cafe and I haven't seen him.

I picked up my fork and took a bite of eggs while I waited for a response, lamenting that they were nowhere near as good as Bellamy's. That man had some impressive kitchen skills. My phone pinged as I took a sip of my tea.

CALLAN:

> Winton? There's no emergency. Honey, where's Bellamy?

SAGE:

> Bellamy's at work. Winton popped in while I'm eating breakfast saying Bellamy had to rush off for some work emergency.

CALLAN:

No. Listen to me, make an excuse ASAP to go up to my office and lock the door, okay? I need to locate Bellamy. There's been no emergency serious enough to justify him leaving the manor, and his phone is still there.

I resisted the urge to react, knowing it could put me in more danger than whatever I was in now, lazily continuing to eat my eggs while I tapped away on my phone with one hand. Winton probably assumed I was playing a game, or reading.

SAGE:

> What's going on?

CALLAN:

Staff have strict rules to not enter any rooms you're in. You haven't seen Bellamy at all?

SAGE:

> No, I got up half an hour ago. Was just making eggs in the kitchen when Winton told me he left for an emergency.

CALLAN:

I'm watching you now on the CCTV. Honey, just finish your food calmly and go upstairs, like normal, okay? Go to my office and lock the door.

"Is everything okay Miss Sage? You look worried," Winton asked, voice emotionless.

"Yeah, just a little worried about Bellamy. He's not answering texts. I've also got a spreadsheet kicking my butt." I smiled, hoping it was believable. I was starting to feel queasy and a little lightheaded. "You know what? I'm actually not feeling great, I may go lie down." It was no lie, my head was starting to spin and my stomach felt heavy. "Can you tell Bellamy to give me a call as soon as you hear from him? I worry."

I stood up, and Winton took a step toward me, arm outstretched to help.

"No, it's okay. Omega, remember? Don't want to piss off the guys by getting another man's scent on me." I laughed lightly. Was I getting physically sick from worry? That wasn't even possible, was it?

"You're going to need a hand, Miss Sage, your tea was quite strong today."

I looked slowly between him and the iced tea on the table, my head swimming. His words held a hint of something more sinister.

"Wait, did you?" I asked weakly. My hand flew to the table to keep me up as I stumbled. Winton appeared next to me, his arm steadying me.

"Oh, Miss Sage, you're unwell," his voice screamed of fake niceness. "I'd better get you to the doctor. We can't have an ill omega, the pack would have my head." Grabbing his walkie talkie, he spoke into it while I tried to regain my footing. "The omega has taken sick, prepare an SUV. We're going to immediately transfer her to a hospital—Callan and Alaric are meeting us en route. Omega is unconscious." He smirked, taking his hand off the communication device and muttering the last part only for me to hear, "Or at least you will be in a moment."

"Let go of me." I tried pulling my hand away groggily. I knew I was drugged. I knew I needed to get out of there, only I didn't know how. Where was Bellamy? Was he okay? My breathing became heavy and laboured as black spots appeared in my vision.

"It's okay Miss Sage, we'll get you to a doctor," he soothed in that painfully sweet, fake caring voice. It was the last thing I heard before I slid into the darkness.

CHAPTER FORTY-ONE
Callan

I was a failure. A failure as an alpha and a failure as a man. I paced the foyer barking orders at the security team, Harrison was nowhere to be seen. I assumed he was searching the grounds after I sent the alert out. Claudia and her mates were also here, having rushed to our side the moment they heard the news of how my omega had been taken from her own home against her will.

"Winton fucking drugged her, I checked the CCTV and he slipped something into the iced tea only she drinks," I growled while pacing back and forth. "I saw him take her away! That shithead nearly killed Bellamy to get to her. He's going to pay when we find him."

"Callan, none of us saw this coming." Everett attempted to soothe me, whilst also tearing his hair out himself. All of us had lost a part of ourselves and it was shredding us up from the inside out.

Alaric had found Bellamy in a closet when he got home, out cold and bleeding from the back of his head. We had bundled him into an ambulance and sent him off with Harold while we focused on a plan to find Sage, knowing that Bellamy would get the care he needed. Unless he took a turn, all our attention had to be on getting Sage home. There was no way in hell we could let what happened to the other kidnapped omegas happen to her.

"Why do we think Winton took her? He's been loyal to us for so long," Everett asked.

"Money most likely. It always comes down to money. He has no use for an omega."

"Do you think he sold her to Lex? Those fuckers have money, but it would have taken a lot to turn two members of our security team." We had already called the police, family and anyone we could think of. "There's got to be something more. We pay Winton and his team almost ten times what is standard. Why would he risk doing this?"

"He probably thought he could get away with it. He didn't know about the CCTV inside the house, did he? We never told any of the security we had cameras in here."

"Why not?" Nolan asked.

"Would you want people seeing what you got up to in most rooms of your home the first few months of Claudia joining the family?" Alaric asked, eyebrows raised.

Nolan's face lit up in recognition. "Ah, yeah. Understandable."

"Do we have any way to track her?"

"No, my guess is follow the money," I rubbed the back of my head.

"I know it feels like the world is dropping out from under

you," Nolan soothed in a gruff voice. "But all three of you need to keep your heads on straight, no griping at each other. You're already an alpha down, and you can't afford to be squabbling amongst yourselves."

"We need to interview every member of our security team to find out exactly how this happened, and then fire every single one of the fuckers," I growled testily.

"She'll be safer once she's claimed. I don't know why you didn't just get on with it." Claudia wrung her hands. "She loves you guys, you know that."

"We were waiting on her, you know that Ma," Everett said.

"Sage came to her decision a couple of days ago, she rang me and we spoke about it. Hadn't she told you yet?"

"No!" I turned to Claudia. "What did she say?"

"That she was ready to go ahead with the claiming, she asked me loads of questions about it and didn't even seem daunted at the prospect."

"Why didn't she tell us immediately?" Everett whined, low and painful, like a wounded animal.

"This isn't the time to be talking about this. I thought you knew," Claudia's hands flitted as she spoke.

"We've been busy with work," Alaric's voice was steady, almost emotionless. "You know what she's like. I'd put money on her not wanting to distract us."

I knew Alaric was likely right. She was so thoughtful and selfless, and it drove me mad. I had fallen in love with the tiny blonde and now I felt as though my heart was being ripped from my chest with every breath.

"That's exactly what she would do, knowing claiming would kick off a heat she wouldn't want to pull us away from fucking work for several days. She's never understood she's more important than that shit," I growled.

"Well let's get her back and then we can make this right," Alaric told me, the corner of his lips turning up ever so slightly. "She picked us, so we better go get her. I'm not fucking waiting around."

CHAPTER FORTY-TWO
Sage

Everything hurt. My head was pounding like it was going to explode and my eyes were heavy, refusing to open. My body ached. I was lying on something hard and cold. Rolling over, I moaned in pain when my muscles and joints all complained.

"Looks like the little bitch is finally waking up," a voice spoke a short distance away, but I couldn't see where it came from, my eyelids were so heavy. Why was I here? I wasn't in my nest, nothing in my nest was *this* uncomfortable.

The kitchen. The security guard. The drugs. Eyes flying open, I winced at the dim light making my head spike in pain.

I was in a cell. A goddamned jail cell, on the floor, looking at large metal bars keeping me in. The place smelt vile, like burnt plastic and human waste. In the corner of the room sat a familiar face.

Mitch. From Pack Bove. The reality of the situation sunk in, and I sat up, letting out a small whimper of pain when my body protested. Mitch grinned at the sound. This fucker enjoyed my pain.

"Hello again, omega." He smiled, his eyes filled with something sinister.

"Where am I?" I asked, my voice hoarse. "I belong to Pack Rivers."

"Well actually, you don't. No bite marks equals no bonding." He smirked, gesturing to his neck. "Not that something like that would have stopped us. You insulted us, accusing Lex of acting inappropriately with you, causing quite a bit of fuss."

"He tried to rape me, I would hardly call that appropriate!" I snarled, dragging myself backwards so my back was against the cell wall, as far away from Mitch as I could get.

"He was just going to show you who you belonged to. We paid that Keeper Bitch a lot of money for you."

"Every alpha pays fees, that doesn't make you special."

"Oh, we paid more than the fees. We paid that bitch *directly* for you. You were up for purchase, Claire made that known, and we paid the most for you. Then we had to fucking pay off that shit security of Pack Rivers to get you here. Now Lex wants to ensure we get our money's worth."

I tried to school my breathing, praying silently that my pack had raised the alarm and someone was looking for me. I was an omega after all, they wouldn't just leave me in a situation like this, would they?

"You're going to be fun, once you've had a few days to understand your place. I'll enjoy taking my turn with you. After Lex, of course. He's the head of the pack, so he gets to have first crack at you."

"Fuck off," I hissed. It wasn't the smartest move, but I was backed up into a corner and didn't know what else to do.

Mitch's only response was to laugh. "You're going to be

fun to break, even watching Lex break you in will be a sight to behold. He's got other...business to take care of first, so you get a few days to relax. Maybe a few days without food or water will mellow you out."

With a chuckle he stood up, leaving the room with a parting, menacing grin.

The door banged, signalling he had left. My cell was in the corner of what looked like a warehouse, and was empty other than a small threadbare blanket in the corner—not enough to provide any warmth or comfort. The floor was so cold I could feel it in my bones.

Turning my head, I winced as a shooting pain shot up my neck, and my view spun. The drugs were still in my system making everything fuzzy and focusing seemed impossible. I knew I was in a very dangerous situation, but stringing two thoughts together seemed like a monumental task.

Shivering, I grabbed the ratty blanket, intending to throw it over myself to try and stay warm when the scent hit my nose. Lex. I recognised that smell from the night Claire let him into my room at the Haven, that rancid smell was imprinted on my mind. With a grunt of disgust I weakly threw the blanket into the corner of the room before curling up into a ball and pleading mentally for the sickening blurring of my vision to end.

I didn't know how much time had passed. Occasionally I woke to the same brick wall, the same numb pain infiltrating my body. Each time my mind felt slightly clearer, but I had no idea how long I had before Lex came for me. I needed to escape.

. . .

A sharp pain in my side jolted me awake again. The force of the blow was so hard I instinctively rolled over. Looking up blearily, I saw the fuzzy form of Mitch standing over me, laughing, having just kicked me at full force in the side to wake me up.

"Bitch is still outta it. Fucker gave her way too much. It's taking its sweet time to get out of her system. Oh well." He grinned, aiming another kick in my back, the blow making me yelp out in pain. "Are you thirsty? It's been a few days," he taunted, holding something up. A bottle of water. I was *so* thirsty. My throat burned with desperation.

"Please," I croaked.

"Hmmm, maybe if you suck my cock."

I didn't answer. I couldn't even sit up.

"Suck my cock," Mitch commanded. The alpha bark clear in his voice. Omegas could be compelled by alphas—we couldn't resist. Only, I was so dehydrated and exhausted that I couldn't have complied even if I wanted to, and I really, *really* didn't want to.

Mitch laughed. "Oh well," he said. Ice cold water hit me in the face as he upturned the bottle of water over me. "What a waste. Lex will be home tomorrow. I'm excited to see what he has planned for you."

Coughing as the water invaded my nose, choking on it with my lungs burning, as I dreaded the thought of what was to come.

The next day I was more lucid, or at least I thought it was the next day. Time was wobbly. There were no windows so I had no way of knowing whether it was day or night. I could hear people moving in and out of the room. I had started shivering violently in the night. The cold water and the frigid room was making me feel worse. I whined thinking about my nest, my home. I wanted nothing more than to be curled up with my alphas, basking in their warmth and comfort.

"Better wake up, Omega Bitch, Lex is on his way." Mitch was in my cell, crouching over me. When I didn't look at him he roughly grabbed my hair, lifting my head to look at him. All I could see on his face was pure evil.

"We get to see you be broken in today," he declared happily. "And when Lex is done with you, I'll get my turn. You know what's going to happen after that? After my pack has all had their fun with you? We've been trying to decide. We could breed you, but then we'd need to hire a beta to raise the brat until they're a teenager, or we could use you to grow our business. Can you imagine how many deals we can make if we add a night with an omega into the mix? You'll make us a lot of money. Fuck it, we may even make back what we paid for you."

My stomach turned at the thought.

The next time I jolted awake was when the door to my cell was thrown open, the noise loud enough to pull me from my hazy slumber. I didn't need to look to know that Lex was in the room. His scent was assaulting my senses. I tried groggily to open my eyes, get a clear picture of where he was in the room, but it was fruitless. My vision was nothing but a grey haze. Despite the frigid temperature of the room I was boiling, my skin felt like it was on fire but I couldn't stop shivering.

"If it isn't the little bitch, at our feet, where she belongs," Lex's slimy voice spoke. The sound of it sent chills down my spine. "How long will it take for her to come out of it? I want her to know what I'm doing to her," Lex asked someone, presumably Mitch because his scent was still strong.

"She's been pretty out of it. Didn't need her putting up a

fight... until we wanted it. Seems like the initial drugs took a long time to wear off."

"It won't be any fun if she doesn't fight, not that she'll be able to fight for long," Lex laughed. "When that bitch contacted us and took our money to keep her at her shitty Haven I thought we would get her a lot sooner."

My stomach rolled, Claire had clearly been underhanded and now I was going to pay for it. It didn't take a genius to know the sort of plans these monsters had for me.

"Let's grab some food, maybe she'll be more awake in a few hours," Lex spoke as his steps got quieter, leaving the room. Mitch followed, actually leaving me alone in the cell. *I need to pay attention!* They're gone, now is my chance. I willed myself to open my eyes, to move... anything. My body wasn't listening, I couldn't even move a finger. The familiar sensation of oblivion tugged at the edges of my thoughts, and unwillingly I fell into it.

The next time I woke I felt more lucid, my eyes cracking open almost immediately. The acidic stench of Lex filled the room. My eyes opened to reveal the alpha crouching in front of me, staring at me like a predator, like I was something they wanted to destroy, consume.

"Welcome back. How are you feeling today?" he asked with an almost manic grin.

I sat up, shuffling back until my spine rested against the concrete wall. The movement made Lex grin wider. "I see you're a little more alert than before... good."

"Rivers..." I started to gasp.

"You really think Pack Rivers can do fuck all to help you?" Lex laughed, crazily. "Those fuckers don't know the first thing about security. They have no idea where you are, and they won't be able to find you either." He spoke with such confidence, my belly turned to lead. I needed to steel myself for what was going to happen here. I had been captive for days, and hadn't heard anything or seen any signs that someone was looking for me. It was unlikely that someone would come for me anytime soon, which meant that Lex would likely get his way.

He had a gun tucked into his waistband and a knife in a holder on his side.

"Why?" I spat.

"We don't like being told no, and when that bitch Claire agreed to sell you to us and didn't deliver...well, we weren't happy. She felt the brunt of our wrath. She was fun to destroy, but you'll be a lot more fun..." he chuckled.

I was going to be sick, what on earth did they do to Claire? I hated the woman, but I doubt I would wish whatever these monsters did on her.

"We've been trying to get an omega to play with for a while, we're even going to keep you for a bit. Do you like that idea? Claire...well she was only a few hours of fun. But you? You'll be weeks of fun. We're going to keep you until your body gives out," he stated caustically, enjoying the fear in my eyes.

Feeling for the ground, I pulled myself up, wanting to be further away. Every bone in my body hurt, and my vision swam. What did they mean they *destroyed* Claire? What was going to happen to me?

"Our security?"

Lex stood up in one fluid movement. "That was easy. You pretty much did that to yourself. As soon as security realised you were looking into Rivers' financials, they were desperate to get rid of you. You know how they found out? One of Pack Rivers decided to *brag* about the smart little omega in their home." He chortled hysterically, tilting his head. "You had no idea, did you? Pack Rivers' own security was embezzling from them, and they thought *you* were getting close to figuring it out. The idiots didn't even ask for much money to sell you out... you really just have a way of making people hate you, don't you, Omega?" He inhaled deeply, his pupils widening. "I don't know why people say the smell of an omega's fear is disgusting. Me? I love it, you smell so fucking good." He took several long strides towards me, until he was right in front of me, leaning in, and taking a deep breath. Lex groaned at the smell, the sound making my stomach turn in revulsion.

Lex grinned as I turned away from him, but he grabbed my arm, keeping me against him. Crouching down I tried to shrink away from him, but he was too close, in my face.

"There is one... slight problem though... Do you know what it is?" He laughed lightly. When I didn't answer he continued. "You need a mark. Once you're marked, legally, you're *mine*." He grinned. "Oh, the things we're going to do to you..."

My heartbeat stuttered. Fuck. He was going to force a bond, the thought filled my dazed mind with dread. He couldn't. My pack was meant to mark me. With all my strength I pulled away, diving to the side, but I hardly made it an inch before Lex had an iron grip on my upper arms, slamming me into the wall. My shoulder protested in pain. I was so dazed I didn't even feel the blow to my face until after it happened, Lex had backhanded me hard enough to make my neck pop painfully.

"Behave! Bitch..." he snarled. "You'll learn... It'll be so much fun breaking you." His lips retracted.

Shit. This is it, he's going to fucking bite me. Bonding via just a bite was rare though, usually an omega had to be actively exchanging bodily fluids while receiving the bite to make it effective, even better if they were in heat.

Lex reared his head back to bite me. With a surprising strength I yanked one arm up. Lex's teeth clamped down on my forearm. The feeling of my skin tearing under his teeth made me scream in pain. My other hand reached for his trousers, finding purchase on the knife Lex kept there.

If I died here, I needed to at least die *fighting*. I refused to go down easy. Using Lex's momentary distraction I grabbed the knife, pulling it out and giving in one quick, short stab, right above his hip. It sank in easily, despite my weakened state.

"Fuck!" Lex snarled, taking a step back. His mouth was coated with blood. A quick glance down let me know that my arm was fucked up. Lex's teeth had ripped the skin. A wave of nausea at the sight of my blood pulsing out made my head spin. Lex stumbled, falling to one knee. "You fucking bitch!" he screamed.

I glanced around the cell, my head swimming. The door was open. Knife still in hand I staggered out of the cell, slamming the door behind me. The telltale click let me know it had locked, trapping Lex inside as he groaned and got to his feet, realising the situation he was in.

I didn't wait for his reaction. I ran... or stumbled is likely a better term, limping toward the door, holding my arm at a weird angle as it dripped blood.

"Let me out! You fucking whore! Your death is going to be so fucking slow," Lex snarled from behind me. I didn't turn back. The outside door was a few metres away, and when I pulled on the handle I was surprised at how easily it opened. Where was Mitch? He couldn't be far.

The sun was blinding, I squinted, raising a hand above my eyes. I had run out into a parking lot, looking through the cars until, what seemed like hours later, I spotted an old truck, with the keys in the ignition. *Thank fuck*. I wanted to cry in relief at the sight.

Yanking the door open, I let out a sob, launching myself into the seat. Behind me the warehouse door opened with a crash. Sparing a quick glance, I saw Mitch standing in the doorway, eyes wide with shock at seeing me in the truck. Before he could take even a step out of the doorway I threw the truck into drive, peeling out of the parking lot before he could come after me.

Once onto the main road I just drove. Within minutes I had a rough idea of where I was. Only…I had no idea where the mansion actually was. They had taken me there after I had been attacked and Callan had never actually told me the address, or even the neighbourhood! *I'm an idiot*. I cursed at myself. I was an injured omega, and I had no idea where my pack was. I needed to go somewhere safe.

And as much as I despised it, there was only one place I could think of.

CHAPTER FORTY-THREE
Sage

I pulled up on the side of the road, utterly exhausted and waning from the prolonged lack of substance, looking at the giant grey building in front of me. A pale blue sign at the front of the building clearly read *Clearmont Omega Haven*. I knew this location because all the correspondence from the Haven included their address, and I recalled seeing it. Just an hour outside of the city, secluded near woodland and an old industrial estate, there were a series of gates and guards. It wasn't an ideal place, but it was temporary safety. Sighing, my decision made, I threw the truck into drive and pulled up to the first gate where a guard dressed in swat gear greeted me.

"What business do you have here?" he asked, before looking up and taking in the sight of me. His hand flew to his gun at this side while he looked around, checking if anyone else was around. "Omega?" he asked, as if he couldn't believe it, his nostrils flaring at the scent of me.

"Hi there, my name is Sage, I've had a pretty bad few days.

I was hoping to speak to Keeper Gregory. Is he around?" I asked calmly, my injured arm laid limply in my lap. I wanted to scream, to shout but I was so goddamn tired. Opening the car door I slid out, despite the guard's protests for me to stay put.

As soon as my feet hit the floor the world tilted and I toppled over, my body weak and limp. The last thing I heard was the guard shouting into his radio desperately.

"Sage! What on earth happened? We've been looking for you for days!" I opened my eyes to see Keeper Gregory crouched beside me and the security guard, his eyes taking in the plethora of cuts and bruises that now marred my body. He didn't hesitate to get close to me, checking me over, ensuring none of my wounds were urgent.

"I was kidnapped by a security guard, who then sold me to Pack Bove. I escaped a few hours ago, but I don't actually know where my pack lives, and I don't have a phone, so I just drove here. I'm sorry for disturbing you," I stuttered.

"Do not apologise young lady! Come on, we need to check you over."

"Apologies, but you know, I'm a little distrustful of Havens, I think I'd rather wait." I shrugged apologetically. "You'll immediately call Callan to come get me?"

"Yes, but you will be around other omegas inside, and won't be isolated. I'll call Callan if that's what you want. If you still want him, then his, and his pack's claim to you still stands. Otherwise you could join this facility, that offer is still open."

"I don't want to be part of a Haven, it's scary enough coming here now. I just need help getting back to my pack."

"In that case, come in. I don't like the look of that cut on your arm and after that episode I'd like medical to look you over properly." He gestured to my sleeve, now soaked red and dripping onto the seat.

"Oh yeah, I can't really feel that anymore. That's not a good sign is it?" I asked, weakly. Gregory grimaced, confirming that it wasn't. "Okay, lead the way." I slowly dragged myself to standing despite the pain and hovering guard; but the moment I was upright my knees buckled, and darkness overtook my vision. The last thing I remembered was Keeper Gregory's pine scent as he rushed towards me.

When I came to, I was laying on a gurney, inside a medical room. It felt familiar, and I didn't like it. Sitting up I noticed two people in the room.

A tall willowy blonde doctor in a white coat grabbed my wrist, checking my pulse. "Hi Sage, I'm Dr Morrigan. You passed out at the gate, twice, you've clearly been through an ordeal, I just want to check you're healthy, is that okay?"

Keeper Gregory stood on the other side of my bed. "You've been missing for days."

"Now, you were kidnapped?" she asked, eyes raking over me, taking in my dishevelled appearance.

"She was drugged and kidnapped from her home six days ago now," Gregory confirmed.

"Well I need to get an IV started first, you look dehydrated, I'll struggle to get a vein I think. Sage? Are you okay with me doing that?" I nodded. "Good, I've been a doctor here for years, and I've been told I make needles painless." She gathered all the supplies and brought the small tray over to me.

The needle took a few attempts but she found a good vein and quickly started an IV.

"That arm needs seeing to. Gregory, step out for a moment?" The doctor gave him a pointed look.

"Ah, yes. I'll try and get Mr Rivers on the phone while you work." He nodded, leaving us in the room.

"Would you be willing to take this top off, Sage? I'm going

to clean and stitch the arm." I nodded wearily. I had a small cami on underneath the jumper I wore. The doctor helped me gently pull it off, tutting over the bruising. "This is disgusting, they better string up the pack who did this. How someone who was cleared to enter a Haven did this is beyond me."

"They weren't really cleared. The Haven I was at sold access to me. I, uh, never knew what the procedure should be. I've only been an omega for a few months."

"But selling access? That's preposterous. That shit would never fly here. I want to give you a full check up while you're here as well, because I doubt you were given a proper one at your last Haven and presenting as an omega can create havoc on your body in the best of situations." She turned over my arm, gently prodding it with gloved hands. "I'm going to have to stitch this up, I would numb it but I don't know what you've been recently drugged with until we do a blood test. Is that okay?"

"I can handle a few stitches. When will my pack get here? I don't think I'll settle until they're here."

"Tell me about your pack while I work. That'll help distract you a bit. Gregory said you were unclaimed?"

"Technically, I decided on a sole courtship to get out of the Haven I was in before, but right before this mess happened I made the decision that I wanted to stay with them forever. I never got a chance to tell them before all this."

"Well congratulations!" She picked up her tools and started stitching up my arm. I took it well, only wincing and hissing a few times. "I must ask though, did anything... happen in the last six days?" I knew what the doctor was hinting at.

"Uh, no, at least I don't think so. I was drugged for a good few days, took a beating or two. When the leader decided it was time to claim me whether I liked it or not, I kind of... stabbed him," I spoke the last part in a rush. "I'm gonna be in trouble for stabbing an alpha aren't I? Oh dear god." My breathing quickened and I could feel the panic rising. Betas had been punished for offences a lot less severe than stabbing an alpha.

Doctor Morrigan smiled kindly. "You are in no trouble whatsoever, and good on you! I'm proud of you, the bastard deserved to be stabbed." She frowned, trying to place a few stitches. "How did this happen? The skin is mangled, are these *teeth* marks?"

"He tried to bond me, I managed to move so he didn't get my neck but he got my arm. I should be more panicked shouldn't I? It's weird, I'm feeling quite calm about my injuries."

"You're exhausted, I bet now that you're safe the events of the last few days are catching up to you, that's why you crashed and are probably feeling numb now. I'm going to sort antibiotics out as well, because I don't know where that alpha's teeth have been."

Gregory chose that moment to come back into the room, mobile phone in hand. "I've got Callan on the phone, he's insisting on talking with you." I held out the hand that wasn't being stitched up for the phone.

"Sage?!" Callan's voice was hoarse.

"Hey Dumb Dumb," I grinned, happy to hear his voice.

"Are you okay? What happened? We are coming to get you," Callan spoke quickly.

"We're already in the car!" Everett shouted from somewhere in the background.

"I'm okay, a little beaten up, but okay."

"Why did you go to the Haven?" Callan asked in a rush. "Gregory said you weren't rejecting us?"

"Well, a particular dumb dumb never showed me their

phone number, or even the house address. This was the one place I could think of that would be safe for someone like me, especially near my heat. That's not important though—Winton and Harrison, they're your embezzlers!"

"You would be safe with us! I'll make you memorise our numbers and addresses now, not that it will matter. You are never leaving our sight again. Wait, what?" Callan asked, confused.

"They've been embezzling from you for years. I'm assuming they found information in your office and used that to set up secret accounts. I was so close to figuring out they were the embezzlers—one of their names was linked to a sketchy account I found, that's why they kidnapped me and planned to sell me to Lex."

"Winton and Harrison? Are you sure?"

"Positive."

"Fuck. Harrison is at the house, he's been helping us hunt for Winton! That fucker is dead," Callan growled.

"I'm with the doctor, I'm safe if you need to go deal with that first."

"No way in hell," he insisted, and a chorus of similar sentiments rang over the line, making me smile.

"I'm safe guys. Don't worry about me. Make sure our home is safe before you come get me."

"Of course we're going to fucking worry about you, Sage. You were taken from our *home*, we were worried sick. We'll take care of Harrison and be with you as soon as possible, are you sure you're safe?"

"I am. I've been seen by a doctor, and I'm gonna grab some food and rest. Please. Get the bastard."

"We will, but we'll be calling constantly."

"I'm counting on it, Dumb Dumb. I uh, I'm not sure

they'll let you in the Haven, I'm around other omegas," I looked around. There was truth to my words, other omegas milled around the rooms, chatting with one another. It was very relaxed, nothing like the Haven I had been part of before. "It's actually kind of nice."

"We'll wait in the waiting rooms, they won't let us through, but we want to be there."

"I'll see you soon, thank you."

"Don't thank us, you saved yourself sweet girl. I'm so fucking proud of you. Can you hand me back to Gregory? I want to make sure I have clearance to enter when I get there." I handed over the phone, sad at the loss of my alpha's voice. Callan was my alpha, it felt right admitting it. The knowledge warmed me.

Gregory spoke to Callan for a moment, confirming I would be safe and that he would be allowed to enter the building to collect me before hanging up and looking at me.

"I'm sorry I've caused all this fuss," I said.

"Nonsense, protecting omegas is why we're here. Once you're done here, let's see about getting you a hot shower and some food. Your pack will be here within a day or two once they've dealt with the threat at home and ensured their pack house is safe for you to return. No doubt they'll break every traffic law to get here."

I smiled. "Thank you, I hope they don't disturb the peace here too much."

"We're used to it, well maybe not to *this* situation but having over excited alphas to deal with. Imagine a pack of bright eyed eighteen-year-old alphas all excited to be meeting their first omega. It's a challenge getting them calm enough to even tell them the omega's name before they meet them."

The medical exam was quick and after laying down for twenty minutes and letting the IV do its magic, Doctor Morrigan quickly bandaged me up in waterproof bandages so I could go shower and clean the grime off of myself. She had escorted me to a small but luxurious bathroom a few doors down and a kind nurse had dropped off clean towels and some fresh clothing. A buttery soft slip dress and a cardigan made of some beautifully soft fibre was also waiting for me. Stepping into the shower I threw my dirty, blood stained clothes into the corner, happy to have the disgusting fabric off me.

Putting the water on as hot as possible I picked the first body wash I found, a coffee coconut scrub and went to town erasing every offending scent off my body. Once my skin was pink and slightly raw and I felt better, I wrapped myself up in a towel andquickly dried off, throwing on the clothes provided, happy to find them void of scent other than a very faint apple smell from the detergent.

CHAPTER FORTY-FOUR
Sage

Stepping out of the shower room and looking down the corridor I noticed a tiny brunette wearing jeans and a large jumper standing into the hallway. At the sound of the door opening her head lifted to meet my eye.

"Sage! Hi, my name is Lavender. Keeper Gregory asked me to keep you company and take you to get some food." She practically skipped over to me, sliding her arm into mine without an invitation. Her bright floral scent was soothing. Omega. "Hold on to me, you look a little weak on your feet."

"O-oh, thank you," I stuttered. "Do you live here?" Probably a dumb question.

"I do, Keeper Gregory mentioned you weren't at a suitable Haven and don't really know how things work here. I've personally been here for three years now, this is a facility for older omegas looking for a pack, before that I was at an omega dormitory. My schedule isn't that full, so I have plenty of time to help you out." She pulled me towards a corridor with surprising strength for one so small, she was the only thing stopping me from keeling over in exhaustion.

"Three years? Is that long?"

"It's on the longer side for pack meetings, but none of them have felt particularly right—if you know what I mean."

"And the Haven is okay with that?"

"Totally! There's been girls courting for almost a decade before they decided to switch from actively looking for a pack of their own to dedicating their lives to helping other omegas within these facilities. We are in the adult part of the Haven where we can meet packs and such. Before I was here I was at omega dormitories, similar to this but we have lessons, focus on getting our education and such. I'm only a few weeks away from graduating."

"From high school?"

"University. I'm doing a STEM degree. Did you undertake any education? I know most omegas choose not to, but I couldn't resist personally. Plus my family is so backwards they think an omega getting an education is unnatural, so I did it just to prove a point."

"That's really impressive. I did my Bachelors and Masters in accounting before this, but I didn't do it at a facility. I went to a normal beta university."

Lavender's eyes widened. "How did you do that? That's wonderful! I would *love* to do that, it must have been an amazing experience."

"I was a late presenter. Only learned I was an omega a few weeks ago. I never presented or perfumed until one day at work everything went haywire."

"Oh dear! I'm glad it's all turned out okay. You're safe here, I promise. The staff here are like family. I know all the guards by name. Christopher is the guy following us right now. He's got two babies at home and a wife who is so sweet. She's constantly making baked goods for him to bring in for us." Lavender turned back and grinned at Christoper. "Those chocolate chip cookies were the best."

"I'll let Lacey know." The guard nodded affectionately. Lavender turned back to me.

"The doctors have cleared you, haven't they? Keeper Gregory mentioned you'll be hungry so we'll stop by the canteen then if you want we can hang out in one of the nest rooms? There's a spare nest in my dorm room right now, it'll give you some space to rest."

"You share nests?"

"No, omegas love their nests far too much—we have dorms with like one big central room and four smaller, warm, cosy nests branching off. Though we often end up in each other's nests, we like having our own as well. We just crave contact so much—it seems so natural to us. I'm sure you get it, even if you've only been an omega for a short time?"

"I think I do. Before I lived alone, I wasn't really close to anyone but after I presented I found I craved human touch. When I went with my pack despite being terrified I still found myself wanting to be around them, to be near them."

"Why did you go with a pack if you were scared?" Lavender asked, eyes wide and curious. She stopped walking, turning to face me with a serious look. "If you need protection from them just say. They said your pack was coming back for you, but they don't have to! The Keeper's won't allow them within a mile of this place if you say the word," she spoke quickly, reassuringly.

"No, not at all." I shook my head, giving the fellow omega a small smile as we continued slowly walking towards food. Why was this place so big? I was exhausted. "My Haven wasn't the best. I didn't know because I didn't know what it meant to be an omega. I was on my own in a room meeting packs that weren't appropriate. There weren't any other omegas there to guide me. My pack protected me from a lot of that—I really like them. I think I'm going to bond with them once we get home after all this."

"They left you with zero human interaction? That's downright cruel." She looked horrified, stopping to look at me once again before pulling me into a crushing hug. I stiffened for a moment before relaxing into the hug, letting her lavender scent wash over me. "This place is nothing like that. You won't be left alone or have to meet with anyone unsuitable. Do you understand?" I nodded. "Good, now let's go feed you and then you can tell me more about this pack of yours."

After some of the best pasta and salad I had ever tasted, I slowly followed the bouncy omega to the dorms. I was even more lethargic after eating as much as I could. When we finally made it to the dorms I marvelled at their nests. Each one was dark and warm, inviting and stuffed to the max with blankets, bedding and pillows. Lavender had shown me her own nest which had been covered in bohemian tapestries and fairy lights to give it a lovely inviting feel. The common room was still comfortable, but nowhere near as impressive as the nests. Several soft sofas surrounded a TV and a coffee table with books stacked on it.

"My roommates must be either out or in their nests. Here, I'll show you the empty nest. Oh! And I'll bring my tablet and show you a few things." She rushed over to the coffee table, grabbing a large tablet computer with a bright and colourful cover. I thought I would feel overwhelmed, but I just felt comfortable around this small spark of life.

The empty nest wasn't quite as colourful as Lavender's but it was still inviting. Mountains of pale blue and green bedding filled the alcove, the entire floor of the nest was a mattress and the room itself was small enough to help me feel secure and warm. There was very little scent to the bedding, just the faintest hint of apple from the same detergent I assumed they had washed my clothes in.

"This is lovely," I said, crawling into the nest, Lavender following and sitting next to me.

"They are pretty awesome, we tend to spend a lot of time in our nests either with other omegas or on our tablets chatting to the packs."

"You can talk to packs on there?" I asked, snuggling down into the blankets. The stress of the last few days had caught up with me, especially now I was in a nice comfy nest and felt... safe? Lavender's presence was relaxing and I was comfortable with her only inches from me.

"Sure we can! Often we chat to packs on here first, see who we get along with before we start meeting them. There's just so many packs it helps stop too many unnecessary meetings. I'm currently chatting with a few alphas, getting to know them better before I decide to have a meeting with them. They seem decent, a little cheeky, but I like that." She smiled. "Here, these are the profiles we get." She lifted up the tablet so I could see, scrolling through several pages of alpha profiles, photos and lines of information like their interests, jobs, etc. It was fascinating. This sort of thing would have been really useful for me.

"I wish I had been taken here," I admitted, cuddling one of the pillows. "It's so much nicer."

"I wish you had been here as well, I bet we would have got on like a house on fire. Eaten all the pineapple pizza together. Maybe once I'm bonded and out of here our packs can meet up?" Lavender lay down next to me in the blankets, snuggling close. I embraced it, happy to have another omega near. It had been days since I had felt so comfortable and relaxed, and without even meaning to I burrowed deeper into the nest, drifting off to the peaceful sound of Lavender humming and tapping away on her tablet.

"Sage, dear." A small hand gently shook my shoulder and I groaned, stretching lazily and lethargically. I didn't feel like I had slept for long, but I had slept well.

"Lavender?" I asked sleepily at the omega bending over me. She had changed into a pale blue T-shirt and short sleep set.

"You've been asleep for a few hours. The Keepers wanted to wake you to get you to eat again, but I told them I would do it. I've got some food for you to eat, then you can rest again."

Sitting up, I wiped the sleep from my eyes and noticed the plate next to Lavender: a sandwich and a bottle of water. "Thank you," I croaked. Now my adrenaline had well and truly worn off I felt like a bus had hit me. Leaning forward to grab the bottle of water I winced in pain, and Lavender grimaced.

"The doc said you would be in pain. Here." She handed me a pill bottle. "This should help a lot with that, but you need to eat first." She picked up the sandwich and handed it over to me. Grabbing it and taking a bite of what ended up being a very good BLT.

"Any news on when my pack will get here?" I asked between bites.

"Should only be a few more hours, but don't worry, rest some more and we'll wake you when they get here—or if you want to stay awake you can help me scroll through these alpha profiles, they're getting on my nerves tonight." She grinned playfully.

"You're being so nice to me," I said groggily. "Thank you."

"No need to thank me. You're one of us, Sage, and we take care of our own." She kept a careful eye on me, ensuring I finished my sandwich.

"May I ask an odd question?" Lavender asked me hesitantly.

"After everything you've done? You can ask me any odd or intrusive question you want." I laughed lightly.

"What do your alphas smell like? We get all this information on alphas we can potentially date but we never actually get to smell them until we're deep in the getting to know them phase, then they gift us articles of used clothing... I've never got that far. Is it as potent as they say?"

I thought for a moment. "It's pretty damn strong, I won't lie. Sometimes being within sniffing distance of them sets my whole body on fire. At the same time their scents are so damn comforting, I could lay on top of them for days and never feel uncomfortable. Callan—he's the head alpha—smells like the woods to me, like clean crisp air. It's so relaxing. Bellamy cooks a lot, and he smells just like dark chocolate and usually cookies, he's been baking them loads since I moved in with them. Everett is the youngest, he's all vanilla, bright and crisp like pastries. Alaric... he's got a darker smell, smoky, with a hint of dark cherry. I didn't think I would miss their scents so much, but I really do. I don't know when it happened, but I got addicted to the smell of them and nothing feels quite right without it."

Lavender sighed wistfully. "It sounds lovely, I wish I could find a pack like that. They got any friends looking for an omega to complete their pack?"

I laughed. "They weren't even looking for an omega when I stumbled into their lives. Alaric was there when I presented for the first time. He protected me and later I met him properly at the Haven." I ran my hand through my hair gently untangling it.

"That's so sweet." Lavender smiled. "Here, sit up and I'll brush your hair out, it's a mess." She pulled out a brush and got to work detangling my waves. The fancy conditioner I had found in the shower worked wonders and it didn't take much.

"Have you found any packs you'd like to meet?" I asked.

"Not really. I've been chatting to a member of a pack on my tablet for a while, I'll see where that goes. I'm hoping I'll find someone eventually, I just haven't clicked with anyone yet."

There was a knock on the nest door and Keeper Gregory poked his head in, smiling at the sight of us sitting crossed legged, chatting away happily. "Sage, your pack is here. If you want longer to rest though I'll happily make them wait."

"Not at all!" I squeaked, attempting to get up and tangling my legs in the blankets in my excitement, making me fall backwards into the nest of pillows. Lavender laughed while Gregory looked concerned, hovering in the doorway.

"Take your time, hon, we want you to make it back to your alphas in one piece." She got up gracefully, helping me as I thanked her. We made our way out of the nest and into the common room. Lavender turned to me with a smile. "I guess this is where we say goodbye, I won't be able to go out into the meeting rooms. Would... would you mind if we kept in touch?"

"I would love that, you've got my number right?" I asked.

"The Keepers will give it to me," Lavender beamed. Throwing her arms around me she hugged me tightly. "Good luck with your alphas! Hopefully I'll be joining you out in the real world eventually."

"We could meet for lunch, like normal people!" I laughed, hugging her back.

"How mediocre—I love it!" Lavender declared pulling away with a final smile and a goodbye. I felt a twinge of sadness. I didn't really want to leave this omega—she had been so kind and open to me.

"Thank you, Lavender. For everything." I turned and went over the doorway, ignoring the pang of sadness, because soon I would be in the arms of my men once again.

CHAPTER FORTY-FIVE
Bellamy

It had been a long fucking day but *finally* we were getting our omega and bringing her home. None of us had slept more than an hour or two since Sage was taken, and it showed on our faces. The hospital had let me come home after the first two days, and while I was mostly cleared, my head still ached from the attack. Alaric had taken care of Harrison rather violently, and now Harrison and Winton were looking forward to a very long stay in a correctional facility, minus a few teeth.

We were all dishevelled, I hadn't bothered to change my shirt since I had woken up to Everett pulling me out of the closet with a splitting headache. Claudia had tried to convince me to stay at home and rest, but quickly realised I wasn't going to listen.

We had piled into the SUV, each of us too tense to talk. We felt the loss of our omega keenly, and without a word, we set off. Callan had only given us a brief description of everything Sage had endured.

Halfway there Alaric broke the silence. "Tell me again, what *exactly* are her injuries." His entire body was tense, he wouldn't relax until Sage was home.

"Bite mark on her arm with some tearing of the skin, they gave her stitches. Bruises across her ribs and back, exhaustion and dehydration," Callan recited.

"I shouldn't have handed Harrison to the police. I should have ended him myself," Alaric snarled.

"We should have, but we want Sage to be safe and with us," Callan reminded them.

I spoke up, "And Lex? Why haven't the police found that bastard yet?"

"It's only a matter of time. The police and the Haven are throwing all their resources into tracking the bastard down," Callan said.

"Maybe we should move house. A fortress? That could protect her," Everett butted in.

"We aren't leaving her alone ever again. I don't care if she wants to be alone. We aren't losing her again," Alaric stated aggressively.

Keeper Gregory met us at the door. His hair was slightly dishevelled, like he had been running his hands through it.

"Mr Rivers, hello. Sage is making her way to a meeting room at the moment. Come sit down. We need to talk about how she turned up here."

"How bad were her injuries?" Callan asked as we walked through the corridor.

"She's had an IV for extreme dehydration. I don't think she ate or drank the entire time she was gone. Her arm required stitches, and our doctor has given her some antibiotics in case of infection. She's exhausted, she fell asleep right away after a clean shower and food."

"And we can take her straight home?"

"Yes, but only because that is her express request. Is your home suitable for an omega? You allowed this to happen."

"*Allowed*?" Alaric's voice was stony. "Keeper Gregory, I think you'll find that this started because the Haven allowed it to happen. You put Sage on Lex Bove's radar. You allowed one of your facilities to manipulate the situation and mistreat an omega. We have kept quiet about this, but you will not interfere when it comes to us taking our omega home, are we clear?"

"I'm sure the press would be very interested in Sage's story," I mused out loud.

Gregory blanched. "I admit, things went wrong. Horribly wrong, but Clearmont doesn't deserve that reputation. The facility Sage was at has been permanently shut down, the investigation lasted less than five hours before we realised how bad it was. Claire was abusing her position, securing Sage, for her own profit."

"What's to stop her from doing it again?" Alaric questioned.

"Claire Readford is dead. Her body was pulled out of a river two days ago. Her body was so destroyed it was hard to get a match even through dental records," Keeper Gregory said with a grimace.

"Damn. Bove?" Callan asked.

"Yes, so we are going to take Sage home and she's not going to be left alone until they are found. We are hiring even more security, ones we've triple checked and are willing to allow us to check their financials regularly."

"Okay, we will be happy to help pay for your security," Keeper Gregory said, running his hand through his hair. "If I'm honest I don't want to let her go with you. You failed to protect her but she's adamant. I also can't deny that a Haven played a part in this... so let's take you to your omega."

Callan was the first through the door. Rushing straight to the bundled up Sage sitting on the couch. She had clearly been through a lot. Her skin was pale, and there was a bruise under her left eye. Her arm was wrapped up in bandages which she cradled in her lap.

"Thank fuck," he muttered, taking her in. The scent of honey filled our noses and I wanted to cry with happiness. Our omega was with us, everything was right again. She didn't smell like us anymore, but me and the pack would see to that quickly enough. I wanted to rub my scent over her.

"Hi." Sage grinned. "I'm so happy you're here." She beamed up at Callan, clutching his shirt in her hands.

"I'm never letting you out of my sight again," he vowed, gently stroking her cheeks with his thumbs, memorising every inch of her face, taking in every mark, every bruise, every bandage.

"Good. Can we go home?" she asked quietly. "I want to sleep in my nest with my pack." She nuzzled into his chest, covering herself in his familiar scent. I felt a rush of joy at her calling the pack house *home*.

"Of course we can, Honey." He beamed. Looking up from Callan's arms she held her hand out to me. I pulled her gently into my arms, resting my chin on top of her head.

"It's so fucking good to see you, Sage," I murmured into her hair. Everett was next to me, already reaching out for her, but I didn't want to let her go. After a moment Sage pulled away, turning to Everett while I lamented her loss. Everett didn't hesitate to bundle her into his arms, swinging her around happily.

"Hey Pretty Girl, don't you dare scare us like that again!" He guffawed as they span.

"Everett, she's injured!" Alaric barked.

"Oops, sorry." He gently put her down, checking her over. Sage just beamed up at him happily. Alaric took the chance to embrace Sage, cupping her neck and tilting her head so he could look her in the eye.

"Heya." Her face softened as she looked at him.

"Let's get you home."

"Please. Is it safe to go home? Did you deal with…"

"Harrison is gone. I saw to that. It's safe to come home," he reassured her.

"Then let's get out of here." She turned to hug him tightly, smiling up at him.

Alaric didn't say anything, just gently but firmly held her around the waist, refusing to let her go. She sat on his lap in the car, curled up into him, her face pressed into his neck, inhaling the familiar delicious smell as he gently ran his hands through her hair.

SIX MONTHS LATER
Sage

I sat in my nest, staring at the pill bottle in my hands. Alaric was fast asleep next to me, sprawled out on his stomach. We had slept in late, sunlight was already streaming in. I had been home for weeks. Weeks of my pack coddling me, refusing to let me go anywhere alone, hovering over me like deranged mother hens, ensuring I ate, slept, and rested. So. Much. Rest.

They hadn't touched me otherwise. I was horny. So fucking horny. If I leaned in to kiss one of my men they would just give me a gentle peck, then divert my attention to something else. I wanted to throw something, shout at them, scream and be a brat. How could I, though? They were looking after my every need, their concern was obvious. Getting so close to losing me had clearly upset them greatly. None of them had left the pack house much at all, and even then it was usually one at a time.

My bruises had healed. The ripped skin on my arm was starting to scar—I didn't even need to cover it when I showered anymore. Physically I was totally healthy... just a needy little omega. With a sigh I twisted the bottle open. Doctor Morrigan had told me that they would hit me quickly, and I knew the guys would be pissed, if only for a minute or two... but I didn't care anymore. Grabbing two pills I swallowed them, leaning over Alaric to get my bottle of water off the bedside. My heat had been fighting with the suppressants for weeks anyway. It was time to wave the white flag and let my hormones run riot.

"Sage?" he grumbled sleepily, "I can grab that." His face was smashed into his pillow, muffling his voice.

"I am perfectly okay, Alaric," I said, smiling despite the mild pre-heat cramp already rippling through my torso.

"We've covered this, sweetheart. You need rest," he spoke into his pillow.

I hummed, neither agreeing or disagreeing. Settling back into my blankets I smiled to herself. "Well, I won't be resting much for the next few days." I giggled.

Alaric lifted his head to look at me. "Why?" he asked, his eyes narrowing in suspicion.

"I was sick of how the blockers were making me feel... so I just took a reverser." I shrugged, acting nonchalant despite my erratic heart rate.

Alaric sat up, eyes wide. "Wait, what?"

"Yeah... so let me say this before you freak out. I chose this, I am lucid and I consent. Any questions?"

"Sage! You're not well enough to go through a heat," he scolded. His arms flexed as he crossed them.

Yummy. I licked my lips in a not so subtle gesture.

"Sage!" Alaric growled.

Ooo growls. Yes please.

"The doc said I'm healthy enough to go through a heat,

and frankly she said I needed to go through one sooner or later."

"You should talk to us about this!"

"Why? None of you have touched me since everything!"

"We touch you loads!"

"Cuddles, forehead kisses, yes all lovely—but I want to *fuck*. Now you guys can see me through this heat, or I swear to fucking god I'll go find another pack!" I growled. Alaric's features stilled. I had hit a nerve. Grabbing my waist, he flipped us so he was on top of me, staring down at me.

"I'll fucking kill anyone who lays a hand on you that isn't pack!" he thundered.

"Well then, you'd better get to it yourselves hadn't you!" I snarled back, it took all my strength because every fibre of my being was insisting I submit to my alpha. My perfume was starting to fill the room and the cramps were increasing.

With a snarl, Alaric got off me, leaving me momentarily stunned until I saw him grabbing his cell phone off the bedside table, angrily pushing a few buttons before tossing the phone gently onto the armchair, his attention back on me. The soft vibration from my own phone let me know he had probably texted the group chat.

"Summoning backup?" I asked with a giggle.

"Fucking brat," Alaric grumbled. His large hand wrapped around my ankle, and without warning he pulled, dragging me to the edge of the bed so my ass was just on the edge. Burying his nose in my crotch he growled. Pretty soon I would be in full heat. Mindlessly in need of knots.

"It looks like being a brat gets me what I want." I laughed, before groaning at the sensation of Alaric slipping his fingers into my pyjama shorts, not even brushing my clit, but sliding straight into me, massaging that sweet spot inside that made me writhe in pleasure.

"What was that message about? We agreed she wasn't—" Callan broke off when he took the sight of me at the end of the bed, writhing in need. The room was thick with honey, and he was instantly hard. "What?" he asked, dazed.

"This one decided that she was sick of our hands off policy and took matters into her own hands. She took suppressant reversing pills, and now she's going into her first heat." He punctuated his words with each thrust of his fingers.

"Shit!" Bellamy was behind Callan, a grin on his face.

"She can't fucking consent if she's in full heat," Callan frowned.

I snarled, sitting up, Alaric still in me. "Callan, I *chose* to bring on my heat, I swear to fucking god if you morons don't fuck and claim me I will find another pack who will! I want to fuck and I want to bond with you idiots because I love you!" I was sick of waiting, sick of needing. I wanted to be bonded to my pack. Glaring at Callan I couldn't help the tears that sprang in my eyes. Pulling away from Alaric I shuffled back, resting my back against the headboard. "Unless you don't want me? I mean... you haven't touched me in weeks." My voice was quiet, meek. My hormones were starting to make a perfect storm, the back of my neck was coated in sweat, dripping down between my breasts.

"Fuck that," Alaric growled, hauling me towards him, his hand tangling in the hair at the nape of my neck.

"*Alpha*," I whimpered as his dark, smoky scent clouded around me. I gripped his forearms so hard I was certain I was going to leave marks. I wasn't going to complain, I liked the idea of marking him as mine.

The bed dipped behind me and I felt Callan's hand dance

across my waist, slipping into my thin sleep shirt and gently plucking at my nipple. The electric sensations made me squirm in Alaric's grip.

"Fuck me, you smell delicious," he murmured in my ear, trailing kisses along my neck. "You ready for us honey girl?"

"*Yes,*" I nodded frantically, opening my eyes. Over Alaric's head I could see Bellamy lounging with this back against the headboard, stroking himself, staring intently on Alaric's fingers as they filled me. He grinned when he noticed me looking at him.

"You're already getting impossibly tight," Alaric grunted. "Are you going to come for us?"

Callan chuckled against my neck. "Oh, she's going to come many, many times over the next few days. I don't think our omega is ready for that."

I was ready. I was *more* than ready. I wanted to drown in knots and orgasms until I passed out, which from what I had heard from Claudia and my own research, was a very real possibility.

"She can handle it, can't you, Sage?" Bellamy asked. I merely nodded in response.

Alaric thrust his fingers faster, and all the words I had been formulating died as a long moan escaped me. He smirked up at me as I shattered around him. Leaning back against Callan, I slowly came down, twitching as Alaric slowed, wringing every last pulse from my core.

"Good girl." Callan placed a kiss on my shoulder.

"Do you want to rest?" Alaric asked.

As he spoke a cramp fluttered across my core, not as strong as the previous ones, but still unpleasant. "No." I shook my head. "I need more, I need knots. *Please.*"

"Ric, give her to me," Callan ordered.

I whimpered as Alaric slid his fingers from me, despising how empty I felt without them. I didn't have to wait long. Callan's hand made quick work of slipping my shorts off, flipping me around so I was facing him, my legs spread open. Without hesitation he dove in, tongue lapping at me. I gripped his hair as he circled my clit, the sensations already so strong. *How am I so horny so quickly again?*

Alaric's hand gently danced across my throat, making me clench. "Once you come for Callan he's going to knot that sweet little pussy of yours. Only this time while he's buried in your tightness he's going to sink his teeth into you and make you his. Then as soon as he's done, it's *my* turn." His voice was low and full of promise.

"Please!" I whimpered.

Alaric tutted, "All in good time, Sage."

Callan nipped at my clit, and I convulsed at the sensation, looking down at him with a pout. He was looking up at me, his facial hair damp with my juices. "Patience, I happen to enjoy tasting you." He flashed me a grin, returning to his work with gusto. One of his hands gripped my inner thigh, holding it open with a punishing grip that was going to leave a bruise. His other hand gently circled my entrance, teasing me as his tongue did the same with my clit, never really touching it. It was maddening, I wanted to scream.

Babbling, I tried pulling his head closer, praying he would get the message. He showed me some mercy, simultaneously sinking his fingers deep and rubbing my g-spot in short, sharp thrusts and sucking on my clit, gently rolling it between his teeth. I saw stars, bucking as I screamed through my release.

"Fuck, sweet girl, you fucking drenched Callan with your cum. Well done," Alaric praised.

I didn't have more than a moment to recover before strong

hands grabbed my hips, flipping me so I laid splayed out on my stomach, lifting my hips so they lined up perfectly with his cock.

"Such a good omega, so fucking wet and ready."

Alaric pulled his cock out his pants and settled against the headboard next to Bellamy to watch the show. Turns out, I love being watched. Alaric and Bellamy's eyes on me with their hands on their cocks made me feel powerful, and desired. Glancing around I found Everett sitting on the armchair, cock also out. I licked my lips in anticipation.

Warmth settled over my backside and Callan lined himself up with my slick entrance, giving me a few shallow thrusts.

"Goddamnit Callan, *fuck me*," my voice was strangled. I desperately fisted the sheets, trying to find purchase and ground myself.

"So impatient," he tutted, making me wait a moment more before thrusting in entirely, making me scream with pleasure and the delicious stretching sensation. He didn't give me a moment to adjust, picking up his pace with a groan of his own.

"Fuck, you feel fucking perfect," he said, never faltering in his movements. I just clung to the sheets and enjoyed the ride. His hands gripped by hips so hard they would likely bruise, but I didn't care, it only added to the burning desperation that was consuming me.

"*Knot!*" I demanded with a whine. His movements were so fucking good but my stomach hurt, cramping and demanding more. More stretching, more orgasms, more knots.

"Ask nicely." Alaric smirked from his spot in front of me. "Ask nicely for your alpha to knot you, and maybe he'll reward you."

"*Please!*" I cried. "I need you to knot me, and bite me.

Please, oh fuck. Please bite me!" I sobbed. It was too much, my body was demanding it.

Callan's arm snaked around my waist, lifting me up so my back was pressed against his chest as he continued thrusting.

Teeth scraped at my neck and I melted internally. "Please," I begged.

"Once I do this Honey Girl, you're *our* omega forever, there won't be a day when we aren't with you. Is that what you want?"

"Yes! Please," I cried out. My muscles tightened as I approached the edge, so close, I needed to come. My walls started to stretch as his knot grew, making me impossibly full in the best way.

The sting of Callan's bite was deliriously good. Red hot fire burned through my veins the moment the skin broke and my head swam, pushing me over the edge. That, and the burn of his knot stretching me was almost too much. I convulsed with the sheer strength of my orgasm, babbling incoherently as he held me in place with both his grip and his teeth.

I don't know how long I came for, it seemed like every time I started to come down the waves intensified again. Deep in my chest was a strange sensation, like contentment, but not my own. It was Callan's. It was overwhelming and amazing at the same time.

"I can feel you," I said in awe. He gently released my neck from his teeth, lapping at the wound with his tongue. Every touch made me shiver in pleasure as my walls fluttered around his knot. "My turn?" I asked, turning back to look at him. His gaze was so warm and caring, and love radiated through the bond.

A hand appeared in front of my face, Callan bearing his wrist to me with one arm while the other remained on my waist, gently grinding me on his knot. I was already starting to feel the rising tension as his knot tugged inside me.

My teeth bit easily into his wrist, and he groaned at the sensation, his knot twitching inside me.

"Fuck me, you're amazing," Callan panted once his knot deflated somewhat. Pulling me gently off his knot he turned me to face him, so I was straddling his lap. He gently brushed my hair out of my face, gently placing a kiss on my forehead. "I can sense you, it's so good. I love you."

"I love you." I grinned lazily up at him, basking in his warmth and happiness. A pang of need hit me, and my shoulders hunched as I groaned in pain.

A dark voice spoke behind me, Alaric. "She's already getting needy, aren't you?"

I nodded, and Callan gently pulled me off his cock, and I moaned at the sensation. I was overly sensitive. "I know, but you're going to be taken good care of. Why don't you go to them?" He nodded over to his packmates.

My thighs were coated in slick, and I was already desperate for more.

"Do you think you could handle one of us in your ass? Both me and Everett at once?" Bellamy asked with a grin, fisting his cock as I watched, biting my lip. I had only ever played with toys, no man had actually ever done *that* with me but with my alphas, I was more than happy to try. I nodded, hungrily watching his movements.

"Then hop on, Pretty Girl," a voice spoke as the bed dipped behind me, Everett taking Callan's place, already naked.

Not needing to be asked twice, I crawled over to him. Straddling his legs I sank down with no resistance, still sensitive.

"Holy fuck, Pretty Girl, you're gripping me like vise. Fuck, so warm and wet. Jesus fuck," he babbled, throwing his head back. It made me feel powerful, and I set a fast pace, revelling in the sensations and the sweet vanilla scent as I chased my own release.

Hands gently gripping my hips from behind stilled me. The familiar chocolatey smell let me know it was Bellamy.

"Lean forward," he ordered softly, and I complied. Gently cupping Everett's neck I kissed him, swallowing his moans. Bellamy's hands ground me down on Everett, giving my clit friction that made me see stars.

I was so lost in the kiss, of being so full, that I jumped when Bellamy ran his fingers through the slick gathering around my entrance where Everett was buried, and slowly dragged it back to my ass.

I instinctively went to sit up at the sensation but Everett's hand gripped my neck, keeping me to him. "Nuh uh, Pretty Girl, let Bellamy have his fun."

There was no resistance as he slipped a finger in, keeping his movements slow and meticulous as I ground down on Everett's cock.

"Fuck, Bellamy, she just got even tighter."

"Imagine how tight she'll be when I'm buried in her ass and you're knotting her pussy," Bellamy chuckled. "We are lucky fuckers."

"Literally," I moaned.

I was so full, but it still wasn't enough. Between Bellamy's fingers and Everett's cock, I was swiftly slipping into oblivion again.

The guys silently communicated somehow, and I was lifted off Everett's cock just enough that Bellamy's could slip in. He gave a few thrusts, coating his cock in my slick before pulling out and sinking me back on Everett once again.

I felt the cock at my back entrance, slick and ready. I tensed in anticipation, and Everett directed his attention to my breasts, pulling at the nipples gently, twisting them so they burned maddeningly.

Slowly Bellamy inched forward, and despite the burn there was little resistance. I gasped at the intrusion, I was impossibly full, like I would explode.

"Good girl," he cooed as his hips sat flush with my ass, and my body flushed with the praise.

"I'm close."

"Good," Bellamy growled. Grasping at my hips, lifting me off both their cocks, and slamming me down, making me scream in both pleasure and pain. The soreness only heightened the sensations, and I could feel myself quickly reaching another climax.

Unable to form words, I babbled incoherently. Everything was hazy, and all I could think about was more, more cock, more orgasms, more *them*. Why had I been worried about this? It felt glorious.

"So fucking tight, I think she's going to strangle my dick," Everett grunted, thrusting up, the angle hitting my g-spot perfectly.

"Shit!" I cursed, nails digging into Everett's pecs. There was a warmth in my chest which I instinctively knew was Callan, he was enjoying watching what they were doing to me, he was excited.

I'm going to fuck these men until I drop.

"I'm not going to last long, darling, your ass is fucking wonderful, and right now it's *mine*," Bellamy murmured.

I don't know how many times I came on both of them, it could have been several times or one stupidly long, mind blowing orgasm.

Everett sat up, sandwiching me between him and Bellamy. "You ready?" I nodded.

Their bites didn't hurt, there was no sting as their teeth broke the skin on either of my shoulders. There was only sweet, glorious oblivion as they held me between them and I came again. Just like with Callan, I could feel both of them in my chest and I was overwhelmed with the sensation. Everett stuttered a series of curses as he swelled and knotted me, making me keen in pleasure. Bellamy kept his knot just outside of me and when I realised I whined.

"No, not yet Sweetheart, you need to work up to two knots at once."

"I fucking love you, Pretty Girl." Everett gently kissed me while Bellamy placed a soft kiss on his bite mark.

"As do I," Bellamy agreed.

"I love you too, both of you," I said breathlessly. I felt like I had run a marathon. I was wet, sticky, and exhausted. My eyelids drooped, tired despite the desire to keep going.

"Sleep. You need it," Bellamy said, his hands rubbing soothing circles on my hips. Both he and Everett were still inside me, filling me completely. Bellamy was the first to move and I despised the loss of him. I stayed splayed on Everett longer as he was knotted in me so we were stuck together until he deflated.

Fingers ran through my hair and I blearily opened my eyes, my cheek stuck to Everett's damp chest. Alaric was watching me, a smile on his face as he brushed strands of hair from my face. His shirt was gone and his zipper was undone. Despite the copious orgasms, just looking at him made a pang of neediness assault me.

"Do you want a shower while the others clean the nest?" he asked.

"No, need you," I responded simply.

"Are you sure, Sweet Girl? I can wait."

"No. Gimme." I made a half-tired grabby gesture at him with one hand, my cheek still on Everett's chest. Alaric and Everett both laughed, making my head jiggle.

"I think I'm down enough, Pretty Girl, go play with Alaric." Everett kissed the top of my head, gently lifting me off him. I whined at the emptiness, even though I knew I would be full shortly.

They passed me between them easily, which I was thankful for because my legs were like jelly and I doubted my ability to move unaided.

I laid back in the nest pillows, Alaric hovering over me. "You're a brat for bringing on your heat without talking to us, you know that?"

I shrugged. "No regrets here."

"Once your heat is over we'll have a chat about that," he warned. Was I going to be punished? I didn't really mind that prospect.

"Bring it." I grinned, he just smirked and leaned down to kiss me.

Alaric was the thickest of all of them, and despite my poor pussy having been knotted twice already when Alaric lined himself up with me and slowly pushed in I keened with the stretching sensation. My hands flew to his neck, keeping him close to me. He gave a few shallow thrusts, he was holding back.

"Alaric, *fuck me*," I begged. I trailed a hand down to his nipple and tweaked it, while simultaneously taking my mouth to his neck and biting down—hard enough to break the skin. I hadn't bitten the others in my delirious, cum-drunk state, but I was going to.

The bite set something off. Alaric's hips crashed down violently, quickly taking up a punishing pace, chasing his own pleasure. His eyes were wide, pupils blown and wild. It didn't scare me, it excited me.

"Mine," Alaric snarled.

"Yours," I agreed. "Knot your omega," I demanded through my gasps. His pace was so hard I could hardly breathe, but it was so good. One of his hands was on the bed next to my head but at my words the other snaked up to my throat, gripping firmly.

"I'm going to keep you knotted and in this nest for days, until you can't take it any more." His voice was rough, he sounded almost feral. "I can see how desperate you are for it, such a good little omega, aren't you?"

"Then get knotting, please!" I begged. The waves of pleasure were becoming too much. "I can't, I need a knot!"

My pleas were answered a moment later when he slammed down one last time so hard I knew I would feel it the next day, filling me as his knot swelled, throwing me over the edge. Just like with the others, the bite hardly stung, instead it was pleasurable as Alaric went for high up on my neck, only an inch or so below my ear.

It was all too much, Alaric twitched as he knotted and filled me. I came down, drifting off. Normally I would have been worried, but I could sense all of them, all their care and concern. I knew I was safe with them.

"Sleep, Sweet Girl," Alaric rumbled.

I didn't need to be told twice.

Four days later I emerged from my nest with every muscle sore, but thoroughly satisfied. The time was hazy, but I could recall occasionally showering, being fed, and many, many knots. Now that we had officially bonded, including my bites on all four of my alphas, the guys knew my wants before I even realised it sometimes. It was uncanny, but I had never felt more cared for.

"You sure you want to come down for breakfast?" Everett asked as I threw on some loose shorts and one of their shirts. "We could always stay in the nest and play."

"I'm sure, we can do *that* later." I grinned.

Bellamy was cooking enough food to feed an army, every surface on the kitchen hosted plates of eggs, bacon, hash browns, three kinds of sausage, pancakes, waffles and more.

"I didn't know exactly what you wanted, I could tell you're hungry..." Bellamy said with a shrug as I took in the chaos.

"I'm so hungry I could eat it all," I admitted.

"In that case, sit and get eating." He pointed a spatula to the stool next to where Alaric sat drinking coffee. I leaned in as I sat, giving him a short kiss. Everett sat next to me, his hand on my lower back. I tucked into the first plate Bellamy gave me, eggs, as I looked around. Callan wasn't there, but I could tell by the low humming in my bond that he was near.

I was so content. I couldn't believe I resisted this for so long. Feeling every one of my packmates was a lovely thing.

"My ma has been blowing up my phone," Everett laughed, grabbing a bagel. "We'll have to call her later."

I nodded. "Of course."

Callan entered the room in nothing but a pair of sweatpants, and my poor abused pussy twitched at the sight. I physically couldn't handle more sex, but my body had other ideas. Callan was frowning, stopping my perverted thoughts in their tracks.

"Hey Honey." He came over to us, giving me a kiss on the top of my head. "Have you got your phone?"

"No, I haven't seen it since before my heat, why?" I asked.

It was probably shoved between the couch cushions somewhere.

"Keeper Gregory has been trying to get in touch with you," he said.

"Why? I'm a bonded woman now, I'm not going anywhere!" I giggled. Callan grimaced and took a sigh before speaking.

"Lavender has been kidnapped."

Also by Melissa Huxley

Havenverse Series

Knot Their Burden

Knot For Keeps

Knot That Delicate (Coming 2024)

Pucking Alphas Duet

Packed in the Penalty Box

Pack Power Play

Pucking Pregnant

Pack Plus Three (Coming 2024)

Printed in Great Britain
by Amazon